W9-BMB-345

IT IS 1892.

A WOMAN VANISHES.

A CORPSE IS FOUND.

GUNSHOTS ECHO IN THE PARIS STREETS . . .

BLOOD FLOWS TO THE PANAMA CANAL . . .

"Brilliant . . . not since Umberto Eco's *The Name of the Rose* has there been a detective novel of ideas as scintillating as *Panama*."

ACCLAIM FOR ERIC ZENCEY AND
PANAMA

"A full-fledged murder mystery with huge fortunes made and lost, bribery—and it seems—half the French government and the entanglement of a distinguished nineteenth-century American historian . . . Zencey creates a delicious tension between an educated sensibility and a world where real bullets fly and real blood flows. The result is masterful."
—*SAN FRANCISCO CHRONICLE*

"Compelling . . . affecting . . . vivid . . . Zencey's Adams is certifiably human, a rounded character capable of being brave and ridiculous, passionate and grief-stricken, terrified and resourceful."
—*NEW YORK* MAGAZINE

"He deftly conveys a sense of atmosphere—the clatter of horses and carriages, the eerie glow of gaslight—as he craftily escalates the drama . . . Zencey has created a compelling picture of technology's corrosive effect on morality; his search for the truth nearly a century ago is relevant today."
—*PEOPLE*

"An extremely rare find . . . That Zencey can create a headlong read, with a piercing climax and a poignant final note, out of such esoteric material, is almost miraculous. A wonderful debut."
—*PUBLISHERS WEEKLY*

"A tour de force . . . Zencey has never been to Paris, but his Paris is real. His *gendarmes* have panache, the Frenchness you expect of them. You keep turning the pages, you cannot get enough. And in the end, you have been royally entertained."
—*MEN'S JOURNAL*

"A full cast of ruthlessly greedy businessmen, ruthlessly ambitious politicians, beautiful women of honor, beautiful women of ill repute, honest detectives and corrupt policemen and a plot that involves murder, dismemberment, bribery, abduction, seduction and mistaken identities guarantees that *Panama* amply fulfills the requirements of suspense."
—*LOS ANGELES TIMES BOOK REVIEW*

continued on next page...

"Mr. Zencey conveys the atmosphere of menace very well, conjuring up a Paris as murderous as the Panamanian swamps. This is a brilliant debut." —*DALLAS MORNING NEWS*

"Elegant and sure-handed . . . This is a book dense with information—from why frost forms geometric patterns on Paris streets to a disquisition on the quality of blue light in the stained glass of Chartres—yet all this weighty, big-thinking freight hardly impedes *Panama* from plunging ahead speedily . . . Zencey gives this bookish material the crackle and spark of fresh reportage." —*NEWSDAY*

"Intelligent and fresh . . . Eric Zencey does a bang-up job of describing one of the great minds of history as it both solves a crime and explains the contemporary world to itself." —*THE CHRISTIAN SCIENCE MONITOR*

"In *Panama* Zencey explores the hubris of men, the greed of men, the racism and duplicity of men, the secrets of men. By the by, he also looks at French culture at the end of the century, the rise of forensic police work, crowded cities, changing morals, mass production and Adams's off-quoted oxymoron 'mass democracy.'" —*MIAMI SENTINEL*

"*Panama* delivers a fast-paced plot and an indictment of a society losing its moral center." —*THE ADVOCATE*

"Zencey has brought a brilliant man out of the dusty shadows of our history and made him human." —*THE SUNDAY OREGONIAN*

"Zencey has gone the detective analogy one better by making his story a historical thriller . . . Zencey pays tribute to the contemporary novelists who best wrote about Americans in Paris. Take Edith Wharton's poignant Parisian ending to *The Age of Innocence,* or Henry James's excruciatingly proper Lambert Strether of *The Ambassadors.*" —*THE NATION*

PANAMA

ERIC ZENCEY

BERKLEY BOOKS, NEW YORK

PANAMA

A Berkley Book / published by arrangement with
Farrar, Straus, & Giroux Inc.

PRINTING HISTORY
Farrar Straus Giroux edition published 1995
Berkley edition / January 1997

The Putnam Berkley World Wide Web site address is
http://www.berkley.com/berkley

ISBN: 0-425-15602-8

BERKLEY®
Berkley Books are published by The Berkley Publishing Group,
200 Madison Avenue, New York, New York 10016.
BERKLEY and the "B" design
are trademarks belonging to Berkley Publishing Corporation.

PRINTED IN THE UNITED STATES OF AMERICA

10 9 8 7 6 5 4 3 2 1

for
KATHRYN

The author wishes to acknowledge the generous assistance of the Vermont Council on the Arts during the preparation of portions of this manuscript. Thanks also go to Alexandra Altman, Paul Garstki, Louise Glück, Barry Goldensohn, Kate Greenspan, Wilfrid Hamlin, Coleen Kearon, Deborah Schupack, and Elaine Segal for their perceptive readings and critical encouragement. To Brigid Clark, Kathryn Davis, Carrie Grabo, Christopher Noël, and William Vander Clute I owe the largest measure of thanks: they read the manuscript at many of its various stages and helped me make it what it wanted to become. Without them, no book.

PANAMA

SEPTEMBER 5, 1892

Ancon, Panama

8:45 P.M.

NIGHT FALLS SUDDENLY in the tropics. The sun dives straight for the horizon, with none of the oblique angling of temperate climates. In the brief tropical twilight, darkness seems to materialize out of the very air, as if it leaked from the transparent nothingness between things; as if, Henry Adams thought, it were a colorless, coagulant fluid, undetectable by any sense but sight, kept at bay somehow by the oppressive force of the sun.

In the darkness he could no longer see much of anything. He had lingered too long at the window, watching the shadows lengthen by visible degrees, watching the cobbled relief of the jungle canopy below grow deeper and deeper and then disappear completely. No stars; no moon.

He turned from the window and walked carefully to his right, advancing tentatively, hands extended to catch the wall. He hurried, thinking one of Hay's stewards would be along soon to light the lamps. When he found the wall he floated his hands on its smooth, even surface: native mahogany, he had judged it that afternoon. The photograph he wanted had been at eye level for a man of normal height. Adams reached up, running his hands across the wall in slow, wide arcs.

When he located the wooden frame he lifted it quickly off its hook. Even when he brought the picture close to his face he could make out nothing. He should have thought to bring a lamp, should have planned ahead. But no: to have done so would have been to premeditate theft, and he found it easier to tell himself he acted on impulse. Besides, the night shielded him from discovery.

Slowly, taking small steps in the darkness, Adams made his way toward the door. Out of sight beneath his coat he held the photograph of Jules Dingler, Chief Engineer of the French Interoceanic Canal Company.

Adams had arrived in Colombia two weeks before. From the deck of the steamer that had brought him to the port of Colón, the province of Panama seemed all space and primary color. Far above the bay cumulus glided in long trains, a trail extruded from each of the highest peaks in the distance; they unfurled downwind like badly blotted script. White clouds; blue sky; green land; and everywhere the blazing orange of abandoned French machinery. His steamer passed a huge rusting dredge contraption that poked its pilothouse and a canted derrick of chain-ganged buckets out of the harbor. On the docks commerce threaded between piles of rusting railroad trucks and the twisted latticework of a derelict crane. Here and there in the village, buildings had been patched, or maybe decorated, with salvage: identical flat sheets of iron. The brightness of color, the jarring size of the decrepit French machinery, and most of all the heat, the intimate, stealthy heat that pressed on every inch of him, made Panama seem an absolute extremity of the earth, a place where temperature and color and feeling were somehow more elemental, more penetrating, capable perhaps (who could say for certain?) of reaching through the organs of sense to leave their direct and permanent impress on the soul.

On the train ride from Colón to Ancon Station, where Hay was to meet him, he'd caught glimpses of tangled clearings that opened from the rail bed like niches in the wall of a cathedral. They held not statues of saints but broken, rusted machines, each a brilliant flash of orange in the enfolding green. In Tahiti he had seen how rust feeds on tropical heat and devours its host—oxidizes it, really—with a florid appetite. By that slow fire nature was absorbing these machines, pulling them back to the soil from which men had wooed them, as if the jungle itself were jealous of the achievement they represented, as if it sought to demonstrate that what it abhors is not a vacuum, not just a vacuum but something more general: distinction, any distinction at all. Adams, sitting uncomfortably erect on the slatted wooden seats of the train, tipping his toes down to rest them on the floor so his legs wouldn't sway annoyingly, had smiled to think that nature might approve of him, grandson of one President and great-grandson of another, for failing to achieve the place in politics that seemed an Adams birthright.

At Ancon Station the train pulled past the French railway building, sagging but not yet fallen down. In size it clearly exceeded any current purpose. Adams wondered whether the Panamanians of Ancon had a sense of being overshadowed by their past, whether they had an Egyptian or Roman or Athenian sense that daily life was pressed into mundane sameness by the weight of the monuments that stood above them. And what if one's fall from glory were measured not by something as permanent as stone but by wood, mere impermanent wood? Wouldn't this emphasize the suddenness of the fall? Then, on the platform, he saw John Hay, bearded, gone tropical in government-issue khaki damp with sweat at the arms and neck. Hay was scanning the windows of the train as it slowed, looking for him.

Adams rose and moved away from the window. He would catch Hay unawares. With his leather necessaries bag in one hand and his boater in the other, he made his way down the aisle, taking pleasure in the inertial charge of acceleration as the train stopped beneath him.

Panama, at least at Ancon Station, was a furnace. Beneath his clothing Adams was moist all over his body. From the step of the car he watched Hay for a moment before calling to him. Smooth of skin, tanned, dark-eyed, his friend struck him as being in some essential quality similar to an aquatic mammal—looking this way and that, pausing with head held high, as if to sniff the air. An otter. A mink. Minkish. Like an old, white-muzzled mink. Hay was graying at chin and temple, and had gone fully white in his long mustaches; these he kept long, while the dark hair on his cheek and jaw was trimmed close to the skin.

Hay had been in Panama for a month, on a mission for the State Department about which he had been uncharacteristically vague. To Adams this hardly signified: it didn't take special cleverness to deduce that Hay's purpose involved the French canal concession, soon to expire, and the work and works the French had abandoned there years before. Likewise, one needn't be clairvoyant to see that the United States must be the nation most interested in advancing the French project by fresh means; a glance at any world map showed that America's future as a continental power depended on it. Secret or not, Hay's mission was transparent.

Adams called to Hay and soon the two were embracing on the platform. They were built to the same scale; Adams was the shorter of the two, but Hay also knew the daily experience of looking up to the people with whom he conversed. At the new house in Washington, on Lafayette Square, across from the White House, Adams had directed that all the chair legs be shortened, so that his feet might rest comfortably on the floor. Hay, whose home was next to Adams's, had not yet duplicated the gesture, but meant to. In each other's company they could be reassured that it was the rest of the world that was out of proportion.

"Are you hot? Hungry?" Hay asked.

"Yes to both."

"Can't do a thing about the heat. I'll feed you when we get you settled in. You don't want to eat here." The sweep of his gaze took in the abandoned stationhouse and the shacks of the village beyond. Adams smelled the acrid scent of sewage. Whatever the French had gotten with their famous expenditures, it hadn't been housing or sanitation—not here, at least.

Hay took his arm to steer him to the baggage office. Walking brought new perspiration into Adams's beard, and he could feel it rolling from under his hat and gathering toward his chin; the boater protected his bald head from the sun but seemed to work as a species of oven. At the railway freight office they discovered that the portage was not up to domestic standards—and if walking was work, then lifting his own trunks, even with Hay's help, was an unimaginable effort. He was annoyed and then too drained to be annoyed.

On the badly sprung seat of Hay's native wagon they jounced behind a small, swaybacked horse. Adams tried to hold himself exertionless in the heat as he listened to Hay explain the arrangements, but the movement of the wagon defeated him. The French administrator was being very helpful, was even allowing them to stay in *la folie Dingler*, the house built atop Ancon Hill for Jules Dingler. Hay proposed Dingler as an interesting case: for a time he had been the chief engineer of the effort in Panama, a man whose faith in the power of moral rectitude against disease had not been enough to save his family from malaria. His wife and daughter succumbed within a year of joining him. He was remembered for that tragedy, and for the hubris with which he had once announced, from his pre-Panamanian safety in Paris, that the climate was not deadly for those who lived pure lives. It would have been unkind to castigate him for his pride; wifeless, childless, every day he must have been reminded of the error of his faith. And yet his responsibility for their deaths could not go unremarked. And so his house, opulent by local standards but not out of character for the architect of what was to have been the eighth wonder of the world, was known, through an act of transference, as *la folie Dingler*.

As Hay spoke, the wagon lurched on a rutted road out of town and into an enveloping fogbank of flora, its shapes strange and seemingly animate, each leaf-like thing an alien hand or blade or tendril, outstretched, gesturing, ready to grasp, to press upon, to engulf. Adams shrank from contact with it. "How old was Dingler?" he asked.

Hay glanced sideways. "I don't know. Why?"

"No reason." Adams was willing to bet that Dingler had been young—in his thirties, maybe. Young enough to belong to that generation to whom steam was not a novelty; young enough to have known no other world, to have accepted the power of coal and steel as a given, as part of the necessary furnishing of life. Young enough to have believed that all there was to know about the corrosive effect of power on the self could be read in the mirror of its smooth, well-oiled surface. Well, maybe the flamboyant rust of the tropics had taught him differently.

Adams was about to speak, to offer a jest in a familiar theme—they were old and virtually useless in this world, Hay's continued employment at the State Department notwithstanding—but Hay spoke first. "Any word from Lizzie? How is she?"

"Fine, so far as I know," Adams answered evenly.

"She'll be coming to Paris?"

"So she says." For a moment Adams imagined not telling Hay what else he knew. "Le Havre, too. She'll meet us. Then on to Pontorson." He'd have a week in Normandy with her. "She says her only thought in going to Europe was to see me the sooner."

Hay was silent for a moment. "That sounds . . . comforting."

"Mmmm." Was comfort what he wanted? What *did* he want?

"She's very good for you. Anyone can see that."

"Friends are important," Adams allowed.

"That's not what I meant."

Adams knew that wasn't what he meant, but said nothing.

"She isn't happy," Hay continued. Then, more pointedly: "She certainly isn't appreciated."

Adams looked at his shoe, thinking for the first time that the smooth black leather and seams and stitching bore no resemblance to the foot within. He rotated his foot to see it from different angles. "This is my posthumous existence, Hay," he said finally. "I have grown comfortable in it."

"Too comfortable," Hay muttered, but when Adams looked at him, expecting an explanation, Hay merely widened his eyes, returning the query.

Adams smiled and shook his head, and for a time they rode in friendly silence.

In Adams's judgment Dingler's Folly, achieved after a horse-lathering climb up Ancon Hill, did not live up to its name; plain in design, square, a two-story box with a mansard roof, it was neither lavish nor large nor obviously foolish. Its one striking feature was the encircling veranda, from which was flung, north and south into the jungle, a mirror-image pair of covered walkways: scouts, architecturally speaking, symbolizing the French mission in Panama—

to carry order and civilization into the jungle—while serving the practical purpose of connecting two mansard-roofed pavilions to the house.

Hay gave him a quick tour while a pair of Navy ensigns hauled his baggage up to a bedroom. "Dingler didn't stay in Panama long, just a few years," Hay explained, leading Adams out of the parlor. "Long enough to lose his family. A month after his wife died he was sent back. He built this house for her, but she never lived in it." A glance told him that Hay's thought was his own: *Like the house on Lafayette Square.* Hay showed him the study, where Adams lingered in the doorway as Hay moved on toward the kitchen, talking brightly about food and some menu mix-up of the day before. Adams followed but hardly listened: his thoughts were in the paneled room with its wooden desk, oak chair, bank of dark file cabinets, and view of the jungle below. To one side of the room had been a wardrobe-sized cabinet with a regimented grid of pigeonholes, each with a roll of paper— plat maps of the canal route, he guessed, ready to be rolled out on the desk and studied. Incredibly the room still held the Chief Engineer's personal belongings—his inkstand, blotter, hand blotter, pens, framed photographs on the wall, a handful of leather-bound books on one corner of the desk.

The tour ended outside, in a pavilion, with a view of the Caribbean far to the north. Hay picked out the larger peaks to the south for him, and as he spoke about the total cube of the French excavation, the difficulties Dingler faced, the chronic undercapitalization, the unending need for money, the rains and the deaths and the disease that crippled the work, Adams tried to imagine how the view would have looked to the man who had once figured to behold it regularly. Far off to the southeast the horizon would have carried smudges of smoke from the shovels at Culebra, there in the notch between Gold and Contractor's Hills. According to Hay the Culebra Cut was the most difficult work on the canal; of course the Chief Engineer would have stood in this exact spot, contemplating it, measuring his fate from this distance; like a tribal chieftain reading blood omens, he would have searched the wisps that rose from the shallow cut, finding in these vapors from the entrails of the planet some intimation of the future, some clue to what was to be. Here, at home, Dingler would have been well beyond hearing the gang bosses who, paid by the cubic yard, sometimes worked their men to death from exhaustion or killed them with a too hasty ignition of dynamite. He would not have heard the screech of metal on rock as the shovels ground into the flaky schist beneath rain-softened clay; he would not have seen men weak from yellow fever collapse in the thigh-deep muck that oozed from the hills during the rainy season, wouldn't have had to face the irony that Hay spoke of, how the particular slope of bedrock and a deep, rain-lubricated layer of clay meant that here, in the Cut, every shovel of earth extracted caused two shovels of earth to slump into the hole. He would have known all this, Adams thought, but would have been expected to persevere despite the difficulty, to transcend the cloying burden of detail. Perhaps from the vantage of this pavilion he'd been able to consider the Culebra as a clean and lifeless abstraction, a mathematical equation whose only corporeal effect was the heat generated by large ideas rubbing against each other: cubic yards moved versus time to move them, work to do versus money to spend. Or perhaps it was no more than a distant panorama— an epic struggle orchestrated by his will, a product of his authority, the greatest challenge he would ever face, all of these, yes, but above all an arena he could enter and leave as he chose: not a world he ever thought would intrude upon his own, stealing into his home and seizing from him his family, his happiness.

A man could be judged by the tasks that defeat him, Adams thought. Dingler's defeat was spread out in this jungle for all to see. His own had been less obvious, less a matter of public record. It was his own failure, no mistake, but packed around its root were Dingler and those like him: engineers, lacking breadth and vision, with no clear idea of whom they served or what moved them, even as they moved and served. The industrial age had made man over in its own image; new men required a new sort of leader. And here, in Dingler, they had found one. Within his class he was, in all particulars, indistinguishable from any of the others; a product of the coal and steel and steam that made him, he bore

its impress and was on that account as indifferently inter-
changeable as any of the machine-stamped revolver parts
with which Colonel Colt had revolutionized manufactures.
And what of individuals, the ones who didn't fit? What of
those who saw politics being transformed from moral state-
craft to a mere resolution of forces, and who understood that
in such transformation lay a loss, a profound loss?

The new world didn't offer paid employment as moral
witness. No, he was irrelevant, displaced by Dingler, by the
optimism of coal and steam.

And here, Adams thought, looking at the grand sweep of
the jungle below, here that optimism had met a force larger
than itself. Here, in Panama, coal and steam had been defeated.

Had Hay seen it, he might have mistaken Adams's smile
for contentment.

Immediately after dinner he excused himself, pleading tired-
ness, but on his way upstairs took a detour into Dingler's
study. He sat at the man's desk for a moment before his eye
was caught by a pair of framed photographs on the wall to
his right, which he got up to examine more closely. In the
first, a dozen men stood on a wide set of steps, ten in front
and two in back. Across the bottom of the photo, in a steady,
backward-slanting hand, a caption had been lettered in white
ink: *Directorate, 25 Janvier 1883, Paris.* Behind the two
men he could just make out a legend painted on a glass door:
COMPAGN curved upward and disappeared behind a gray-
suited shoulder, while CANAL INT was printed below, straight
across, ending abruptly at the same man's elbow. Compagnie
something de Canal Inter, Inter, Inter-océanique. That was it.
Compagnie Universelle. Yes. That had been the name of the
company that went bankrupt, what, five, six years ago.

He was surprised that he could remember; he hadn't exactly been paying attention to events in the world back then.

Hay was at his elbow. "This one," he said, tapping the
white-haired figure in the back, who stood at attention, ut-
terly solemn, "is Ferdinand de Lesseps. The consummate
entrepreneur. He built the canal at Suez, hadn't a lick of
training, not an engineer, just an organizer. *Le Grand Fran-*

çais, they called him. Lucky in Suez, unlucky here. Well, call it bad luck—or criminal stupidity. He's the one I told you about—the one who just put his finger on the map and said, 'There, dig it there.' No route surveys for him! Next to him is his son, Charles.''

The son was balding where the father had a loose mane; he looked to be trying and not quite succeeding to match his father in dignity and gravitas. Not dignity but wary vigilance seemed to be the mark of the man. ''He was a director of the company. The others I don't know.''

''That one must be Dingler.''

Adams pointed to another balding man, short with a round face and a long, downswept mustache, who stood in the middle in front, shaking hands with the man immediately to his left. Something about his corner-lidded eyes made him seem sad, despite the smile on his face. ''He's in the other picture, here.'' The same man squinted at the camera from atop a horse, which stood before the gate of an unfinished house, a two-story structure whose spindly ribs poked up into a broad, cloudless sky. Though the shape of the house was barely outlined in wood, it was instantly recognizable: the frame for the surrounding veranda was in place, anchored at each end by the distinctive skeleton of a mansard-capped pavilion. Next to the man and also mounted were a woman and two children, a boy and a girl, aged about eighteen or nineteen, each looking very comfortable on their fine, strong horses. The woman and girl rode sidesaddle: old-fashioned. Behind the woman he could see a wicker hamper, such as one might take on a picnic. Jules Dingler and his family in happier days.

''So he is,'' Hay murmured.

Adams drew closer to look at Dingler, to see if he could find in the man's face any clue to his future. He glanced back and forth from one picture to the other, comparing the thumbnail-sized faces. He imagined that in the first photograph, in front of the company offices, Dingler looked younger, less careworn, but Adams knew he might be generating difference where he expected to find it. Did he read history through its result to find, even in the earlier picture, a sad wisdom in Dingler's eyes, a clear dissent from the brightness on the faces of the men flanking him? In the sec-

ond photograph he saw the same intelligence on the man's
face. His right hand, free from the reins, reached toward his
daughter, seeking to hold her hand, a gesture that made him
seem dynamic in some way that subverted the formal rigidity
with which he, like his wife and children, awaited the shut-
ter's long blink.

Having seen the image of the man, having put a face to
the title of Chief Engineer, Adams understood: he and Dingler were victims of the same thing, the same ineluctable
force. True, Dingler had served that force, and had served in
the van, where he had been crushed by its too-ambitious
expectations, by the hubris of its attempt to manufacture a
path between the seas; and he, Adams, in no sense a soldier
in this cause, had been left in a backwater, outpaced by a
world that seemed no longer to need his kind. But for all
their apparent dissimilarity they were united, two halves of
one whole, front and back, obverse and occiput, pressed to
the edges of cultural life by the swelling mass of middling
sort of men, the sort who every day came to greater prominence, the sort who were more and more becoming creatures
of force, constrained from without by a logic that was necessary and irrefutable, at least on the ground on which they
encountered it. Such a man was incapable of positive assertion, incapable of true autonomous action. Yes, he and this
poor engineer were paired; the coincidence of their losses,
and of their new, empty widower's houses, merely confirmed
it.

Hay pointed to the second picture. "These must be the
horses he shot."

"What?"

"It was the morning after he buried his wife. He was passing the stables and saw her horse, her favorite horse. Something happened to him—went into a rage, I suppose. He took
all the horses out to a ravine and shot them. Two weeks later,
he was on a boat for France."

Adams's own wife, Clover, had never had a favorite horse.

"Adams?" Hay asked. "Are you all right?"

Not rage, no, not that, but something else: call it a com-
pulsive attention to the necessary means of continuing. Negation to match negation. That's what it would have been.

He himself had burned diaries, his own and Clover's, page after page, on the hearth of the new house.

"Do you think anyone would mind if I took that picture with me? As a memento?"

Hay looked at him quizzically. "The French have been very kind, letting us stay here." He frowned. "That's no way to repay their hospitality."

SEPTEMBER 24, 1892

Mont-Saint-Michel

3:30 P.M.

FROM THE EDGE of the platform two hundred and forty feet above the shining tidal flats Adams swivelled his gaze down to the foot of the wall. The precipice fell nearly a hundred feet to the rock below. Leaning out, his forearms on the balustrade, he grew dizzy: the masonry was reorienting his sense of gravity, was massive enough to generate its own pull. Its surface became his ground, a flat pavement stretching to a rock-strewn, bushy horizon. Feeling versus habit, body versus eye: the body feels the pull of the center of the earth but the eye believes what it sees—believes, through long custom, that *down* is defined by mass, by the solidity that occupies the bottom of its range of vision. He steadied himself by looking out to the water. Then, curious, he looked down the wall again, trying to catch the precise moment of change.

"Uncle Henry! Do be careful! What are you doing?"

Amanda Cameron stood at a respectful distance, obviously worried. His niece-in-wish, he called her: the avuncular was a close match to the mix of relation, interest, and affection he felt for her. "Surveying the height," he said, scarcely turning his head. "It's quite a drop. Want to see?"

"Heavens, no. I want you to step back from there."

Her stepmother's child, he thought, charmed by her directness. Carefully he drew himself away from the balustrade. His feet had never left the pavement; he hadn't felt himself at risk at all. "Mother sent me to find you," she said when he faced her on solid ground. "She said we should have our picnic. And then she wants that tour. Or had you forgotten?" A gust billowed the folds of her bright summer dress and she shot a hand up to steady her hat, helping the ribbon under her chin. At sixteen she was more and more a woman every time he saw her, and there were times he found this change too indescribably sad for words.

"No, I hadn't. Tell her I hadn't forgotten. Tell her a proper tour begins outside, here on the platform, with the contemplation of the ocean. With 'the immense tremor of the ocean,' which is how Louis XI described it. Those are the words he had put inside the collar of the Order of Saint Michael, which he created. You have to understand the abbey in its place, as a building clinging to a precipice; every stone was shaped by the knowledge of danger, of isolation." He had thought to engage her interest, but could see he was speaking past her. "Tell her I'm waiting here, would you please? There's a good girl."

He watched Amanda cross the paving to the church door. He sighed. An indulgence: they would leave the fortress rock for lunch and return, taking the little tramway back and forth, because Elizabeth had asked. "Too closed in," she had said at their hotel breakfast that morning. "I could hardly sleep, for thinking I had no escape." He had caught a glance he was sure Amanda wasn't meant to see.

They left the tramway station and climbed a likely path on a wooded hill. Amanda scrambled gamely up a tree-root ladder but Elizabeth needed him more, needed to steady herself on his arm while using her other hand to gather her skirts off the ground. "They do get in the way, don't they? It's enough to make a woman a *sans culotte*." She smiled, and he saw for the hundredth time how perfect was the slate blue of her eyes, streaked here and there with black, framed by the black of her lashes, lashes perfect against the cream of her skin, her skin perfect against the dark, soft brown of her hair. She had pulled her long, curly hair back in a braided bun, leaving her square forehead framed with ringlets. Elizabeth, the famously beautiful: how much of the pleasure he found in her company could be ascribed to sheer appearance?

Certainly she was a pleasure to be with, certainly part of the pleasure was aesthetic. She was having trouble with her footing and he took her hand in his: small, warm, soft, white. They crested the difficult rise and with a last appreciative smile at him she let her hand slide away.

After a few minutes of uphill walk they came to an open field: a suitable picnic grounds, with a view of the fortress, rolling fields, and the waters of the bay as the tide brought them back. Out in the field they found the day had become bright and clear and sweet and warm—the sort of day, Adams thought, that seemed part of an argument for the existence of God from design.

With the blanket spread they sat, and Adams shared out the contents of their hamper—sliced meats, cheese, bread, condiments, fruit. As they ate they watched the tidal surge. Its advancing edge raced into pools and depressions, swirling this way and that, forming great muddy spirals that would remain visible until the bay returned at depth. No invisibly minute change here: the water moved quickly—"faster than a horse can gallop," as the catchphrase of the town had it. Elizabeth stopped eating, lost in contemplation of it.

"Elizabeth? Penny for your thoughts," Adams said softly to her. He was nearly reclining, leaning on an elbow, his feet pointing downhill toward the bay.

"Oh. I was just thinking—thinking of all that we might do together." Another pregnant glance, one Adams turned aside by looking to Amanda. She saw his point: it would be best to include her husband's daughter. "It's Amanda's first visit to Paris, isn't it, sweetheart? And oh, we have plans, big plans. There's the Louvre, of course. And Notre Dame. And the great markets at Les Halles—she has to see those. Her father wants to go to the opera one night, but I think she's still a little young for that. A taste you haven't acquired yet, wouldn't you say, Amanda? There is so much to do, you'll be so excited, I know."

Elizabeth went on, speaking of the shops and wonders of Paris, and the marvels that she and Amanda would experience; and before he quite knew it, her enthusiasm had extracted from him a promise: he would go with them for a day of sightseeing. It was a promise he willingly gave, and in truth he could think of few things he would like better. But her method left a small burr, a tiny imperfection, on the smooth polished face of his contentment. And just as the eye, surveying the vast tremor of the bay of Mont-Saint-Michel, would be drawn by the lone fishing boat that crossed the wide expanse of its mouth, so was he drawn to consider this disquiet, similar for being an insignificant feature on an otherwise featureless domain. She had assumed he would join them, assumed that he could do nothing else than be willingly entrained in her parade from Les Halles to the Louvre to the Opéra to the rest of cultural and historical Paris. A burr, yes. She was an enthusiast, one whose habitual attitude toward life was the open-armed embrace. What it had done for him vicariously he couldn't deny. But he felt her pulling him in some unfamiliar direction, forward, toward a future whose shape he couldn't quite discern, assuming him comfortably and by barely sensible degrees into a web of new relation. What it portended he couldn't tell. This required thought. Out on the ocean, as he watched, the small speck of fishing boat made its way across the bay.

None of them saw the woman approach: her voice, the gentle, throaty "Excuse me," the American accent, was the first they knew of her. Adams turned and looked up, into the sun, and for a moment saw only a haloed silhouette, an unreadable face in deep shadow.

"I don't believe I've had the pleasure," he said. Quickly he drew his legs beneath him to stand. "Henry Adams."

"Miriam Talbott." For a moment he heard her given name as Marian, Clover's real name, and felt a lance of expectation pierce his stomach. It passed before he was fully standing. Her face, level with his, seemed to begin and end with her eyes, which came to him like a primary datum given twice: blue. Intelligent. Their dark-sky color was echoed in the cap she wore, their roundness somehow a complement to the angle of her chin, where she had a dimple so deep it seemed to have been made by suture. A smudge of paint at her temple darkened her blond hair, and another blued a wisp that escaped from her cap. She wore boyish clothes; her dark wool pants and shapeless black jacket looked comfortable and old. Her ease of manner bespoke confidence and wit.

He realized that in her eyes the three of them must seem a family—Elizabeth, in her mid-thirties, was twenty years his junior, but he was no older than Senator Cameron, her husband—and this vicarious intimacy seemed wrong. He immediately wanted to explain, but settled for a clear enunciation of their last name as he introduced them. The woman smiled, leaning to accept first Elizabeth's, then Amanda's hand; this done, she raised the matter that troubled her. She was apologetic but firm, and he found himself being convinced that it would be easier for them to move than for her to realign the balances in her composition around the blank spot their presence would cause. An artist! How fascinating. He would like to know more; it couldn't be easy for her, making her way in this world, a woman, and at her age, too, though of course there were those, the bluestockings, who he imagined might have shifted public opinion just a hairsbreadth closer to opportunities for women; still, there weren't a good many women artists, no doubt about that . . .

God, he was prattling. He looked to Elizabeth, but was uncertain of what he saw there; she turned away rather than meet his eye. Did she find the young woman's clothing too provocatively mannish? Clearly Elizabeth wasn't sharing his interest in the conversation. He thought to invite this Miss Talbott to join them, but she seemed all business. He wondered where her easel was. "Of course we'll move," he told her, not even looking to Elizabeth for consent, thinking that art, after all, has its imperatives. He was gratified to see Miss Talbott smile.

Elizabeth stirred, and to Adams's practiced eye her judgment was plain: she gazed steadily at the fortress rock, holding her mouth tight and thin, and while technically the corners of her mouth were higher than her lips, so that she could be said to be smiling, hers was an expression that Adams well knew signified anything but pleasure. Her hostess face, he called it, for it came to her when she had made up her mind to persevere, for etiquette's sake, in the face of distasteful circumstance.

And he knew, with sudden clarity, that there had been too many times in her presence when he felt like nothing so much as a declawed cat. "Tell me," he said, addressing Miss

Talbott, "would you mind—that is, may I—may I see what you're painting?"

The woman studied him carefully. That she should take his question as an occasion for a close examination amused him, and he tried to return her gaze as best he could without smiling. No luck. She noticed the movement of his mouth. "Yes," she said finally. "I believe you could."

He counted this as an invitation. "If you will excuse me, Elizabeth?"

"Certainly." She smoothed the fabric of her dress where it covered her lap. She did not meet his eyes, but turned absently to face the bay. She was still sitting, gazing out over the water, when Adams turned after twenty paces; like Lot's wife, he couldn't resist a glimpse of the tableau created by his own departure. Amanda waved, which cheered him.

He followed Miss Miriam Talbott through the field, uphill, away from the bay. At the top of the field they passed through a dead orchard, its apple trees standing at gray and spindly muster like the pensioners in faded uniforms that one could see taking the air on the sidewalks of Paris outside Les Invalides. He walked quickly to keep up, and fell in step behind her as the branches narrowed their path. It was good to be moving.

"You're American, aren't you?"

"Yes," she replied without turning her head.

"Do you live here now?" he asked, meaning France.

"No."

"Where, then?" The question came out a bit sharper than he intended, from lack of breath.

"Paris. I'm a student there."

"Ah," he said, "*la vie de bohème*." They exited the orchard into long grass that whisper-stroked his corduroy trousers with every stride. "What took you to Paris?" He waited for her answer. Perhaps she hadn't heard him. "I've always thought," he said, trying again, "that Paris is an important part of any education. So few Americans understand, really, how the world looks when seen from another country. We ought to make a year in Paris mandatory for anyone who's going to have a position of responsibility in industry. It already is, I should think, for artists."

When she made no response, Adams began to wonder if he should have joined her. They came upon a muddy field of hay stubble and skirted it, turning sharply at its corner, the dirt there dark and soft in the strong Indian-summer sun. On the other side of the field the young woman turned up a lane between stone walls. There was room for him next to her, but he held back, enjoying the way her legs swung with each step. She walked quickly, and if he failed to press himself the distance between them grew. The lane went uphill, pasture on either side, with a view of the bay off to the left. On the right an old barn encroached upon the lane, its stone foundation a part of the wall. The mortar, having long ago resolved itself back into powdery sand and lime, had let fall a clutter of cobble into the cow muck. The barnyard smelled earthy and sun-baked, and he imagined he could sense the wake created by her passage through its air. At the top of the low hill she paused, turned to see where he was, then without waiting clambered over the wall.

He followed.

In the field he could see her easel, her stool, and a valise for paints and brushes. The field, he noticed, was a pasture: he was careful where he put his feet. In front of him some trick of perspective had the bay, the rock of Mont-Saint-Michel, and the fields around Pontorson tilting forward toward him, like the stage in a Greek amphitheater. He wasn't dizzy; perhaps this was an illusion from the height. The tide had made the bay a part of the ocean, the great, tremoring ocean, which stretched to a far horizon. They hadn't climbed that much and yet here was a better prospect than he had thought possible. Elizabeth and Amanda were small with distance, just visible above the spidery limbs of the orchard. He could scarcely tell them apart. One collected things at the blanket while the other stood nearby.

"We aren't exactly a blight on the landscape." It would be enormously difficult to move from her view, unless they hid somehow in the orchard. Miss Talbott didn't respond, but picked up her brushes and began to work. Adams moved to look at the canvas.

In the painting, the hills and the bay and the field just before them were outlined by a dark band of color, an effect

that at first brought a two-dimensional quality to the scene.
The bay floated near the top of the picture, a vast pool in
which an occasional hint of a liquid blue-orange emerged
from the overall brownish-gray she had chosen to represent
the water. A wide band of blue suggested the sky, squeezing
down on the scene. Below the bay, the hills and fields were
as plain and dead as facts, though they were given depth by
a shading of color, a slight hint of a brilliant yellow prickling
up, like stubble, which eventually suggested to the eye an
underlying geometric form: this field was a plane, angling
down to the blue of an invented river; that hill was the tip
of an immense truncated sphere. The brushstrokes there, vig-
orous and busy, communicated a sense of commotion within
the containing outline of form. She was revealing the perspective devices that any painter used to organize a work;
she refused to disguise them, refused to collaborate in their
illusion. He found this idea fascinating—and disquieting, in
its way. The water in the painting seemed calm, but there,
too, she had created a sense of distant agitation and depth
with tiny, blue-black crescents that blended, without distinct
boundaries, into the surface. In the lower third of the painting
she was at work on the branches of the dead orchard, which
arose behind a hill and reached, with difficulty, toward the
sky.

"I like it," Adams said.

The young woman turned and looked at him skeptically.
"You don't have to be polite. I don't paint for everyone."

"I do like it," he insisted. "The way you are revealing
the forms of your work, calling attention to its geometry—
it's as though you want to destroy the illusions of your craft,
want the audience both to see and to see through at once."

"You do know a thing or two, don't you?" She switched
brushes and dabbed at her palette. Adams saw a smile widen
her mouth.

"My wife and I . . ." Adams felt it necessary to explain.
"We used to, ah, collect. Paintings, mostly. Before she
died." Why am I telling her this, he wondered.

"Oh." She glanced at him, waiting for his eyes to meet
hers. "I'm sorry."

Adams gestured with a hand, a motion meant to pass the subject off without explanation.

"Well," she said, "as you can see, the human form is an anomaly in this landscape. I could paint around you, I suppose, pretend you're not there, but that would disturb the rhythm. I need to concentrate."

"Yes. Of course. We'll move," Adams reassured her. He did not want to go just yet. Maybe there was some way he could help her. La Farge would be interested in her work, might be able to introduce her around, back in New York. "May I ask, are you . . ." He stopped to clear his throat. He was presuming too much on their brief acquaintance, and had had a moment of doubt about his own motives. He decided to change the subject. "Are you going to put the abbey in?"

"I'm not sure." She glanced at him and smiled. "I'm going to call the painting *Mont-Saint-Michel.*" She reached into her valise, pulled out a paint-smeared cloth, and twisting the tip of her brush on it she continued: "If I do that, I'm not sure it needs to be shown."

That afternoon, their picnic concluded, Adams, Elizabeth, and Amanda again climbed the winding alley through the village—a path that spiralled to the right; time future, in medieval iconography, as Adams pointed out—past the stout, thirteenth-century threshold of Madame Poulard's hotel, where they had spent the night just inside the Gate of the Mount. Adams noticed that the mood of the Mount was different now. Low tide brings sea-floor wonders to the light of day; with its smells at once fetid and yet vital, and its sense of temporary revelation, of opportunity briefly gained, low tide seems aberrant and therefore somehow festive. At high tide the island returns to its essential character: somber, ominous, locked away in a watery fastness.

As they walked, Elizabeth held a parasol against the sun in one hand and with her other took his arm. At first she held on to him lightly, her gloved hand tucked between his arm and his body, her fingers barely perceptible on the inside of his elbow. But then she pulled him to her body and squeezed, tentatively but then more certainly, holding his biceps against the softness of her breast. She held him there longer than could be ascribed simply to the random contact of walking together, the unevenness of the cobbles beneath their feet, or indeed to anything like the functional purpose of a man's giving his arm to a woman. At first he thought that she, too, felt the sense of ominous isolation that the tide's return had brought; or perhaps she had some difficulty he should assist with; yet he found in her clear face and wide blue eyes not the troubled look of a woman suddenly hobbled by a stone in her shoe, or the understanding glance of someone in tune with his own thoughts, but the sly smile of a would-be conspirator. He said nothing; he smiled back and patted her hand.

She squeezed his arm to her again and again as they walked; he noticed that this embrace was likelier and longer the farther ahead Amanda wandered. Sometimes she stroked the inside of his arm lightly with her fingers, and once reached down, briefly, to hold his hand, still pressing her bosom to him. She was granting him an intimate knowledge he had not known outside his marriage. To be sure, the intimacy was fleeting; and it was offered to his arm (not the most notoriously sensitive part of the body); and it was moderated by layers of clothing, by the bodice of her dress and who-knew-what undergarments and his own shirt and suit coat; even so, from that first soft press of her breast, bound loosely by something with unyielding whalebone stays (unmistakable, even through the clothing), his heart had quickened. This was a delicate business, in front of her husband's daughter!

The thrill was as much the result of what was being signalled as it was any purely libidinal effect; at fifty-four he fancied himself well beyond sexual need or interest, but was discovering that he was not immune to the compliment her intimacy implied. So their long flirtation, begun years ago in the give-and-take of publicly contested wit at his own dinner table, and adapted by time and mutual circumstances into the less disguised but still bloodlessly safe-because-for-her-unthinkable suit that he pressed, obliquely and (most comfortably) epistolarily and (less frequently) in person, always with mock circumspection and only as it pleased him, a flirtation he kept up in part out of genuine interest but superficially in homage to her status as the most beautiful wife in Washington—that flirtation was, with her sidelong clasp of his arm to her breast, transformed. She had moved them from the practiced fields of mutual riposte to some new and unknown ground, a place where the safely unthinkable was no longer hidden beyond the pale of possibility. The cushion of a chaste, routine flirtation no longer lay between them: no, now there yawned nothing but empty space, pregnant with the possibility of practical, physical love; a space in which bodies, not words, might meet.

In return he had only smiled and patted her hand, uncertain what to do besides not withdrawing. He would accept this overture with dignity and appreciation; he would feel as much as he could in his arm while neither pulling away nor pressing for greater advantage. And so they walked in silence, he newly aware of his biceps and consummately attentive to the nuance of her carriage, of her every movement next to him.

When they caught up to Amanda again, he felt the need for conversation. He was to give them a tour of the Mount; this, after all, had been the reason they had lingered in Normandy when Donald Cameron and John Hay had gone on to Paris. Well then, why not begin now, with the most general of background information? He had been reading his Corroyer late into the night and was ready. "The Archangel Michael loved heights," he said to them both, apropos of nothing. "He stands for Church and State, and both militant. He's the conqueror of Satan, the mightiest of all created spirits, the nearest to God. His place is where danger is the greatest—which is why you find him here, on the Mount in Peril of the Sea. He faces the ocean, the wide, unknown ocean—which, very practically, is home to England, Vikings, pirates, fierce storms, and any number of dangers to the good citizenry of this country. More poetically, you might say that the Mount marks the edge of the continent, and of life itself." When he was nervous he played the pedant—a holdover from his days as professor of history at Harvard. He knew this. He couldn't stop. "To the medieval mind the western ocean symbolized time hereafter. Sunsets, endings, and very naturally also the peril of God's judgment.

The Mount is a sort of gateway between this world and the next, and Michael is its guardian. I believe it was a gateway even for the pagans, who had some sort of rude sanctuary here. Before our good churchmen drove them out.''

"And you? Is it a gateway for you?'' Elizabeth asked.

"What do you mean?''

She dipped her parasol forward, aiming it to the western horizon. "Panama is out there. You come to us from the west, from the hereafter. From this 'posthumous life' of yours, perhaps?'' She turned to face him, her lips pursed with a suppressed smile, and squeezed his arm to her bosom again. "We ought to have sent out a welcoming party for you. Reporters, too, from the papers.'' She imitated several male baritones: " 'What did you see there, Mr. Adams?' 'And the natives, sir, how would you describe them?' 'And the food?' ''

"Not a welcoming party.'' He had let himself think, for an instant, of how pleasing it was to see her lips pursed at him. "A bon voyage party. But a reverse bon voyage party. Confetti falling upwards, champagne corks sucked back in to stopper their bottles. And at the end everyone troops off the ship, backwards, down the gangplank and back to their lives.''

Elizabeth frowned. "Not very festive, I'd have to say. Hardly the sort of send-off a man needs for the second half of his life.''

"It would depend,'' he said carefully, "on whether the second half marked a departure from the first.'' Had he misread her meaning at depth? He softened his reply: "Don't you think? A man who intends his life to stay the same . . .'' He let the thought trail off.

He saw one of her long eyebrows rise in prelude to reply, saw her mouth open, but at that moment Amanda spied the particularly graphic crucifix that stands halfway up the pilgrim's path. To Adams her astonishment, expressed loudly, was a welcome distraction. "A chance to enlighten,'' he said, smiling in self-deprecation. Elizabeth hung on, matching his quickened step. At Amanda's side he heard her assessment of the icon and then allowed that a taste for the grisly seemed eternal and was in any event a taste the Church had long ago learned to indulge; there was a tradition that stretched back centuries. It made productive use not only of the Christ but of the lives of saints. The tortures visited on them were legendary. As were, for that matter, the tortures to be visited upon sinners, whose fates were also the subject of a grisly artistic tradition.

From the crucifix he led them to other subjects—the causeway and tram that brought excursionists to the Mount, a modern and controversial convenience the abbey had gone without for close on to five centuries; to the tides themselves, the threatening tides, which, until the building of the causeway, had secured the abbey in periodic isolation. Controversial but perhaps inevitable, now that the day excursion had supplanted the pilgrimage as the main reason for visiting the Mount—

"I understand the abbot's wanting it," Elizabeth muttered to herself. He found her wry smile fetching; he made himself look away. A fraction of an inch more here, a fraction less there, and a face is beautiful rather than ordinary. It shouldn't signify.

He spoke compulsively, telling them things about the abbey that they had no desire to know, but he could find no way to stop. Roman arches and Gothic arches, the development of vaulting, the Abbot Hildebart, whose vision had crafted an abbey on the Mount, and whose exaltation of God and the archangel led him not to flatten the top of the Mount but to build a masonry floor up to it, a strategy that left the church's towers too ambitious for their foundation: Adams, through Corroyer, knew all of it. When he got to the subject of stained glass, he alluded to his excursion, on the morrow, to Chartres, where the glazier's art had reached, arguably, its highest achievement.

"You're going where? With whom?"

"To Chartres. By train. With Miss Talbott." He could see Elizabeth was not pleased. "To look at twelfth-century glass. The windows are marvellous, she says. It will continue the education of my senses. My aesthetic education," he hastened to add. "Learning about painting. Art."

For the first time since they had begun the winding climb Elizabeth let his arm slip from her hand. He tried to read her expression, but she kept her parasol dipped against him. And, once inside the Merveille, that great escarpment of a wall that holds up the church, Elizabeth made her way upstairs without him, Amanda firmly in tow. She seemed furious.

SEPTEMBER 25, 1892

Chartres

11:00 A.M.

"PAY ATTENTION TO the blue," Miriam whispered. "It's the light in a window. Light has value only in opposition, so everything relates to the blue. It's the first thing anyone who works with stained glass has to learn—how to manage blue." She and Adams sat in the nave of the cathedral, craning to study the three lancet windows and the great rose above the western entrance. "To get the value they wanted, they hatched it with lines, screened it, tied it with narrow circlets of white or yellow, beaded it with tiny drops of pigment. They must have tried everything and kept only what worked."

She whispered, even though they had the church to themselves; her sibilants echoed softly from the stone surfaces. He loved her husky whispering voice, with its suggestion not of delicacy and quiet but of damped power, of energies willfully compressed. And he found her ideas about stained glass provocative. He would have to tell La Farge—his friend John La Farge, the artist, the tutor of his senses, who had been experimenting for some time now with stained glass, and who had lighted on opacity as a novel, interesting element. Miriam leaned toward him to hand him the binocle. "I count one red, two yellows, two or three purples and greens, but dozens of blues." He scanned the window, the Tree of Jesse, beginning to see it as she saw it: not as a narrative of the genealogy of Christ, the Virgin's family tree placed here in pride of place, visible from her altar, but as light and color and tones and values, the resolution of a problem in design. She spoke of its unperspectived composition; of its harmonies of line and scale, its balance between portraits and blue background. As she spoke he came to see how perfect the window was, how Jesse and the four kings above him and then the Virgin and the Christ above them were harmonized with blue, played off it, balanced by it. "It's the one true law of glass: blue is life. Without it a window is dull, dead, dirty. You can't bear to look at it. Here, let me show you." She stood and, taking his hand, led him away.

She aimed him at the north wall of the transept. "See? Very different. The lancets have a kind of beauty, but they're aggressive, very aggressive." Five of them filled the space below the rose, with the middle one captioned *Sancta Anna*: Saint Anne, the mother of Mary. To the right of her stood a surprisingly youthful Solomon, scepter in hand, blond curls depending from his crown, his head bright against a field of red; to his left, Aaron; on Anne's other flank, David and Melchisedec. Each window placed its portrait in a field of red. Miriam was dismissive: "Not as pleasing. The artist has tried to crush us with this color."

He saw what she meant. "Why the difference?"

She shrugged. "Different artist. Different patron. Look at this." She took his arm to steer him toward the center of the transept, and Adams fleetingly thought of Elizabeth, of his contact with her the day before. "Do you know the story of this window? And the one opposite? It's fascinating." As they walked he looked at her, suddenly wanting to compare, and caught her in profile for a moment before she turned to him. He saw the small bow-shaped line at the corner of her mouth, the delicate curve of flesh beneath her jaw, between her chin and the top of her neck. He let his gaze fall to her chest, wondering what it would be like to feel this young body pressing against him. For an instant he imagined it before feeling his cheeks flush with embarrassment.

"There were two very different patrons here." Miriam had stopped in the center, equidistant from the ends of the transept. "Each paid for an entire wall—the doorway, the statues, the windows. And the two of them were at war with each other. Not just a rivalry, mind you, but a full-fledged, thirteenth-century war, a civil war, fought while these windows were being built. The Rose Window of Dreux, in the south, versus the Rose Window of France, to the north: Pierre de Dreux versus Blanche de Castille.'' Blanche being the Spanish widow of Louis VIII, Pierre the second cousin of Philippe Hurepel; the two had clashed over the merits of Philippe's rights in the succession. Philippe was half brother to King Louis VIII and was next in line for the crown after his half brother's son, Louis IX; he wanted, as was the custom, guardianship of the infant King until the latter should reach majority. The Queen Mother refused. Nearly all the great lords and members of the royal family sided with Philippe, and Pierre de Dreux was their leader.

It took Adams several tries to parse the family relations. ''Blood enemies,'' he said. ''Perhaps that accounts for the red in her window.'' He wasn't sure if he was serious.

''That could well be. Perhaps the aggressiveness you feel is directed at him—'' She lifted her chin toward the Rose of Dreux. ''Amazing, though, the conflicts the Virgin could reconcile. The union of warring halves. Every thirteenth-century pilgrim who came here would have sensed the lesson.''

Adams found this empathy charming. ''How do you know so much?''

She laughed. ''I have no mind for politics, really. It's a story that stuck with me. From art history. It explains the windows.''

She showed him how the glaziers had shaped their competing windows to represent the political doctrines of their patrons. In the center of one rose sat the Queen of Heaven, enthroned and crowned, scepter in one hand and the Christ-King, for whom she clearly served as regent, on her knee; splayed around her, in medallion windows and quatrefoils, were symbols of divinity (doves, prophets, angels, thrones) and beyond them symbols of France (lilies and, lest the message be too obscure, the castles of Blanche herself). Opposite, Pierre the Rebel asserted rival rights: his rose centered on Christ the King, enthroned, surrounded by symbols of the Apocalypse, and below, in the lancets, evangelists stood astride prophets; portents of change, all. ''Blanche's wall is on Mary's right, and so she may be assumed to have the upper hand, but look—this gave Pierre's window the southern sun.'' She stood where the Rose of Dreux, in the strong light of midday, threw color onto stone. ''Did the artist intend this? One of my teachers says that an artist sees what his public will see, and that the measure of genius is how much of what is seen is intended. These artists were geniuses, true? They must have meant for this column of light to fall to the floor.'' There was something wrong in the implied syllogism, but Adams let it pass. ''Think for a moment that this, and not the window, is the art. It has no substance, but form; no weight, but dimension. It exists—you can walk through it, see it, feel it—but you can't touch it, own it, move it, possess it.''

He moved to join her in the beam of colored light, where he held his hand out and moved it, watching the tones and colors play across it. This was an element lacking in La Farge's work; she was right. Perhaps he wouldn't tell him about this, about this lesson. La Farge would likely scowl, dismiss her ideas as old-fashioned. No. He would keep this Miriam to himself. She went on: ''It's as durable as a cathedral and as changeable as the light of day. To my mind this makes stained-glass light the queen of all arts.''

And, he allowed, an art that sometimes imitates nature. The green falling from the Rose of Dreux reminded him of light he had seen falling through jungle leaves on the ride to Dingler's Folly: eerie, unsettling, as if the vegetation had the power to swallow the very space between things, giving its color to the light itself.

''The carnivorous jungle,'' she said when he told her. ''Ten thousand workers it swallowed, didn't it? Though I suppose you could just as easily say the company ate them.''

''I thought you didn't follow politics.''

She shrugged. ''I read the papers.''

They stayed in the cathedral for more than two hours, watching the light animate the windows, studying design and subject, and, on Adams's part at least, coming to feel the presence of the Virgin from sheer proximity to this beauty created in her honor. He thought to leave for other minds the difficult problems of faith: he was standing in a church built for ten thousand worshippers, here, far from any urban center, and that fact alone impressed. What could it have been like on festival days, when the immense nave was filled to overflowing with pilgrims come to honor the performer of the Miracles at Chartres? What would it have been like to have been one of them, to have been a member of a guild that subscribed a window in the clerestory: a baker, a pastry cook, a weaver, a currier? What would it have meant to read without tutelage the stories told here, to have known of Blanche and Pierre and all the characters the windows figured, to have felt the symbols of the Virgin's reign, to have known from infancy all one needed to know to understand the force of this monument?

He excused himself to jot these thoughts in the small notebook he carried. A study of force in history would have to account for this, this monument to the Virgin.

Looking up and catching sight of her across the nave, seeing her clutch the strap of her carryall with both hands and tilt her head back to bathe her face in light, he was pleased. He had begun that morning nervous, filled with trepidation: why had he said he would do this? The woman was a stranger—what if she turned out to be poor company? He had no one with whom to commiserate: Elizabeth, of course, was not about to be sympathetic. And what if, partway through the day, it turned out that he wanted to be somewhere else? By then it would be too late. Should he cancel? He couldn't; that would be too rude.

He had been as skittish as a schoolboy on his first social call.

But his fears had been eased in those first moments on the train. He confessed to her how he had misheard her name, and that led them to talk of names, and she told him of the cruel nicknames of her childhood, how other girls had called her many things, including the one that almost stuck: "Mims." Something about her way with an anecdote reminded him of Clover; nothing in her looks, certainly, for Clover and she could scarcely have been more different, but some facial gesture: the knowing peak of her eyebrow, the comradely, inviting smile.

The notebook was open on his knee. He shut it and re-joined her.

Outside, after the stone coolness of the cathedral, they were both pleased that the day had warmed. They found a small café and ate lunch outdoors, in the sun, before making their way to the train station: the vagaries of timetables meant their excursion would cost them an afternoon of hard seats and clacking rails. Really, it would have been more practical for them to wait until they both got to Paris; as it was, they would go nearly to Paris for their connection. But to Adams it didn't matter: it was Indian summer in Normandy, and he was free, in the company of an interesting woman. Some burden in his life had microscopically shifted. It wasn't that he had achieved contentment, no, but that the prospect before him now held that possibility. How different this autumn was from the ones he had known as a child! Autumn then had meant a return to city life and school, and September was absolutely the end of summer, no matter if an accident of climate should extend it. Seated on the train, listening to Miriam talk of her courses at the art school, the two of them being jostled rhythmically in place, some deep, quiet part of his mind was drawn to measure the distance he had come since then. September had always been the end of the tropical license of Quincy, where as a child he had been free to pass his days as he chose on the marshes and fields that opened out around town. Boston was school, order, control; the routines of his grandfather's household there formed just the most obvious part of a seamless urban regimen—that unspoken conspiracy of adults into which, he always seemed to know, he would in due time be inducted. Once, when he was a child, a servant suggested to him that he might grow up to be President, and he had been stunned: it had never occurred to him he might not.

No, as a child in Boston he had been certain of his place: autumn found him in a dank and Trinitarian basement, where he endured Master Tower's lessons with a dozen other boys, while above him, outdoors and beyond his sight, the autumn afternoons on the Common had grown progressively shorter, throwing the shadow of the church's steeple farther and farther into the street. He supposed he had been taught well.

Only later, years later, had he seen that the lessons of form are a current running more deeply than those of content, and that in Master Tower's unwindowed basement there had been a corollary curriculum, implicit all the while: it taught education as a form of penance, done in a dark and musty silence; it placed the demands of the intellect in a darkness at the center of life, a darkness that eclipsed, down to the thinnest corona, one's freedom to move aboveground, one's freedom to absorb the light.

And then, in adulthood, the death of Clover had taught him that the lesson of light and the tragedy of its eclipse grew no more palatable with repetition.

Next to him Miriam napped, her head coming to rest upon his shoulder. As best as he could without moving he watched her sleep; he strained his eyes to take in the sight of her young form swaying with the motion of the train. He was pleased with her unselfconscious comfort with him, too pleased to feel any drowsiness himself.

For the rest of her time in Normandy he spent some part of every day with Miriam while she painted. As she worked he wrote letters, wrote in his journal, read drowsily in the afternoon sun, or just lay in the grass, propped on one elbow, drinking in the distance and view and light. When he read, it seemed to him that the words from the page before him— words by Corroyer or Abelard or Aquinas or even Chaucer, whom he reread for background, having conceived an interest in cathedrals and their times—had a cumulative effect, drawing together as a physical presence somewhere behind his eyes, forming something like the thick rubber-gasketted goggles that velocipede riders wore as they bounced along, straddling their spindly, wheeled charges; his learning became a filter to his vision, one that gave him the world deepened and enriched and at times even corrected by its history. The cumulative weight of his studies worked to displace him. He began to know the twelfth century from the inside, to feel at home there. And it was in a moment such as that, in Normandy with Miriam as she painted, that his reading once carried him so firmly away that he was actually surprised to look up and find her standing there, her modern dress strange to him, as strange as his own clothes, and the two of them perfect and complete and alive beneath the sun, the same sun that had shone on Aquinas and Chaucer, on Pierre de Dreux and Blanche of Castille, and on those famous lovers, Abélard and Héloïse; on, for that matter, any number of good twelfth-century husbandmen and their wives, men and women who, at the end of a solid day of work, were content to sink together into a bed of clean ticking and sleep the sleep of the familiarly and mutually beloved, their bodies entwined, embracing, and their souls shaped to match in much the same way, formed into complements through long custom and close proximity. It was in moments such as these that he was most prone to imagine, as if experiencing through an eerie sort of foreknowledge, how it would be when he remembered these times as equal to the happiest in his life.

Anachronistically, in that September the gray nadir of December seemed the farthest away it could be.

Monday,
NOVEMBER 21, 1892

Paris

1:00 P.M.

ADAMS'S HANDS, CLASPED on the handle of a walking stick, swayed with the motion of the carriage. He and Hay sat shoulder to shoulder in the open cab, the midday sun warming their faces, as Adams surveyed the passing shops, watching for a pneumatique office: he would have to send a message soon, if it was to arrive in time. Tailor, hat shop, cravats, café; porcelain figurines and settings, then a tobacconist; boots—with dozens and dozens of boots on display in the window, enough to have been, just a few decades ago, a sure sign of the cobbler's dementia, but unremarkable in a world where shoes were made in advance of orders, on speculation, in standard sizes, before any need. Telegraph. Flavored ices. Half these stores couldn't have been here when he was young; the rest sold goods that bore little relation to what they might have sold twenty, fifteen, even ten years ago. "You know, Hay," he said, straining to make himself heard above the hollow clomping of hooves on the wooden planking of the street, "I think it's our specific misfortune to have arrived at a need for permanence just when the world is incapable of offering it."

"Paris has changed," Hay said, not looking up from the papers in his hand. With his mouth closed no part of his lips was visible; his neatly trimmed mustache met his neatly trimmed beard. Perhaps behind that hair he was gritting his teeth. Adams realized he would have to watch both sides of the street.

"It isn't just Paris. The world has changed." He paused while a carriage clattered past within arm's reach. "*Is* changing," he continued, when he could make himself heard. "More crowded, less tolerant, less forgiving. Less *artistic*." Hay didn't respond, but Adams hardly noticed. "I don't think it simply a function of my getting older. Maybe there's a time toward the end of a man's life when all he wants is for the world to stay the same. *He* wants to stay the same, and so, for him to accomplish this, the world must stay the same. A man in a changing world is a man made over by circumstance. Don't you think?"

Hay was ignoring him. Adams looked at him just as a flock of starlings scavenging horse droppings in the street was put to flight, and against that rising and fluid background Hay—papers in hand, head tilted to his reading—seemed to be sinking. Adams shook the image off. "Take Paris as an example, a perfect example," he said, perfectly willing to carry the conversation himself. He scanned the street and nodded, affirming the appropriateness of this city that closed around them. "It would be a great comfort to be able to see the Paris of my youth. This, too, you might say, is a result of my age; a man is curious about what he amounts to, he's drawn to the haunts of his youth, not just to re-enact the life he knew, or even just to remember it—that's poignant enough—but for other reasons. I suppose he wants . . . wants to fix, properly, the exact measure of his own youthful folly, his own misperception of the world. He wants to know what he has learned, and the practical effect of it. To do either with any accuracy, the world has to remain unchanged. This it steadfastly refuses to do." Adams frowned at the inescapable demonstratum.

"Adams. Do you mind?" Hay looked down at his papers to indicate their claim on his attention, then squinted past his friend. "Is that the rue de l'Elysée?"

"No, it's the next one." Adams fell silent; he had no further need of an audience. But the question still nagged at him as the carriage turned off the avenue and began bouncing them over cobbled pavement toward the British Embassy.

What, so far, had been the effect of his life, his education? If science taught anything, it was that change could be measured only as relation, only against a constant. Where was the constant term in this problem? Had he changed? Or had the world?

That the world no longer had room for an Adams in the White House, he thought, was one clear sign of its change. Politics now was little more than the regulation of traffic— and the virtues a President needed were no different from those displayed by the Parisian gendarmerie, who, pedestalled at every intersection in Paris, commanded the streams of carriages and carts and cabs and wagons and omnibuses.

They wheeled through a small treeless plaza, its flower beds long past bloom, and then into a cooler pocket of shaded air. The temperature and the sulphurous tang of bitumen left no doubt: December was not far away.

"Thanks." The cab had stopped outside the British Embassy. Hay inserted his papers into his case and climbed over Adams. "We'll talk later." He pulled his briefcase out after him, and Adams handed him his walking stick. "Until tonight."

Adams nodded. Watching the departing figure of his friend, he was struck by how, from the back, the formal dress of diplomacy was nearly indistinguishable from that of mourning.

The driver hawked the road's dust from his throat with a guttural *hoit* and spat into the street. Adams winced: the man sounded consumptive. He gave his destination, the boulevard des Capucines, as solicitously as he could. If they didn't see a pneu office by the time they got to the Opéra, he'd ask.

On the street they passed through alternating pools of warmth and cool, the temperatures varying without relation to the patches of shade and sun they traversed. At one corner, between the chimneys and the jumbled copper and slate planes of the street's skyline, Adams caught a glimpse of the marble-columned portico of that mock Parthenon, the Madeleine. Anyone who had seen the original knew that its harmonies were scaled to place; here, buried in the city, the copy was an aberration, a brute leviathan of a building that shouldered its neighbors aside. This was the architecture Catholicism had come to, so different from Chartres or Mont-Saint-Michel. Napoleon had had the right idea, Adams thought: the Madeleine was more suited to serve as a monument to an army than as a church. And if it had to be a church, then that Grecian colonnade, deprived of the spiritual grandeur of the Acropolis, might better accommodate some cold, sober, practical sect—Presbyterianism, say—than the emotional currents of Catholicism. In its way, the Madeleine was as disheartening a commentary on human taste as that newer monstrosity, that cast-iron Babel visible nearly everywhere in Paris, the Eiffel Tower, thankfully out of sight behind him.

Finally he spied a pneumatique office and asked the driver to pull over. He was fascinated by the pneu, by the very idea of it: tubes threading under the city, with pneumatically propelled messages whooshing here and there, arriving as quickly as telegrams but without the violation of privacy that the telegraph, with its keyman, required. He took a place in line at the counter and watched the operator work the machine, heedless of being jostled by the small army of uniformed messenger boys who darted about, picking up messages and dashing out to their bicycles to deliver them. The machine reminded Adams of a steam press, or a printing press: perhaps it was the soft hissing sound of the vacuum, or the smell of machine oil, or something less obvious, the shape of the machine, its size, the motion by which the operator rocked open and then closed the valving system to insert a new message carrier.

It seemed to Adams that the pneumatique was intrinsically more human for being mechanical. No doubt electricity was the coming thing, but it was easier to understand the pneu. You could picture it. It stood before you, softly hissing, with nothing abstract about it at all: it carried objects in motion, so that the thing sent was the thing that arrived. He found the thought of this reassuring, compared to the telegraph's change-of-state, where what arrived was not the exact physical message you wrote out but some operator's transcription of it into an ethereal agglomeration of electronic pulses. It seemed that every street in Paris now carried an overhead tangle of wires—a celestial stave for some large and confusing music, a fat chorus of thin crisp lines, dipping and rising in regular rhythm from pole to pole, strung wide on the arms of so many crucifixes, one after another, a succession proceeding out of sight, world without end, amen. He tried to imagine the crackling coded bursts of electricity these wires carried to all quarters. That these could be messages between real people, people who lived and breathed and cried, people whose lives could be changed or affected or even simply nudged in one direction or another by what came speeding down to them through these wires—the thought was impossible. Much better to think of long, polished tubes, the oiled felt casing of the message carriers, the mechanical whooshing of paper from here to there. Paper! A real thing. Paper was what moved people: it was corporeal, and so could have moment, leverage.

When his turn came, Adams quizzed the counterman on the operation of the tubes and the valving devices until the man's patience wore thin. Hastily Adams jotted his message on the proffered form—would she care to join him and the Camerons at the Opéra that evening?—folded it, and wrote Miriam Talbott's Paris address, the one she had given him weeks ago, on the back. When he presented it, the counterman took one look and shook his head. "It is impossible. Not to that address. Not today."

"Because?"

The man was annoyed to have to explain: the tube beneath the river was blocked. Men were working on it. No one could say how long it would take. No traffic was possible until further notice.

As he climbed back into his cab he let himself smile broadly. There was no other way: he'd have to go round to Miss Talbott's and pay a call.

He'd save it for last, after getting the tickets. That would be the best way to do it. It would be a kind of reward.

1:30 P.M.

ALONG THE BOULEVARD Des Capucines he sat in the middle of the seat to feel the sun on his back through the window. The prospect of seeing Miriam had him feeling generous enough that the rococo façade of the Opéra, even the winged figures and rearing horses that capped the corners of the building, seemed to him, if not beautiful, then at least not totally disharmonious. The Paris Opéra had been Napoleon III's idea of a monument to art, and at nearly three acres it held claim to the title more through sheer girth than any refinement of taste, Adams thought. It exemplified a certain regressive tendency one could discover in imperial architecture. The urge to ostentatious display was understandable—that, of course, symbolized the wealth of the country—but why was it that emperors always turned to nostalgia, nearly to the point of parody, when they set about creating cultural edifices? There was some innocent and simple belief at work behind it, a belief that could accept the signatures and referents of old forms as a kind of talismanic protection against the future. Well, he decided, opera was make-believe; perhaps it deserved a building such as this.

He purchased tickets for the Camerons and himself and one for Miriam at the box office on the rue Auber. Miriam hadn't agreed yet, so her ticket was in a manner of speaking a gamble, but it was a risk Adams thought well worth the expense. The larger risk—that of incurring Elizabeth's displeasure by inviting her—was one he didn't dwell on. Elizabeth, after all, had Cameron. Among the four of them there would be a kind of symmetry.

At the curb he gave the cabbie Miriam's address, and they headed south, toward the Latin Quarter.

In the center of the city the streets were more crowded. Despite what he had told Hay, Adams found himself stimulated by the commotion, the rush of people and vehicles. Cabriolets, omnibuses, phaetons, dog carts and gigs, broughams and barouches, wagons, even the stages just in from the provinces, affirming in their dust and crude sturdiness that Paris was a city worth achieving: from all of them rose a din of hooves and harness clank and clattering wheels loud enough to make conversation difficult. People shouted to be heard. The traffic was carried as if by an invisible and elastic fluid, each vehicle a particle connected to the others, drawn along in a stream, like the messages that coursed through the telegraph wires above them, only real; the vehicles carrying passengers with faces and hair and clothing, real people who sweated and had their wants and desires and worries, being drawn by horses that snorted or not, consumed food and excreted droppings. There was an ominous sort of exhilaration that came in the contemplation of it. And at every intersection the easy fluid evaporated into a confusing shuffle of horses and wheels and angry shouts, each vehicle abruptly disconnected from the others, each in complete and total antagonism to every other thing that moved, and one lone gendarme flailing away, managing to create a small pocket of space and order around his pedestal. The easy flow became a knotting into: it seemed to Adams that at each intersection more vehicles and horses entered than ever came out.

In the middle of one intersection Adams was surprised to see two men in strange uniform, not gendarmes, marching forward, waving traffic out of the way with yellow flags. Behind them rumbled a mechanical contraption with tall, wide iron wheels: a steam engine, he realized, but on wheels to travel without rails; a strange thing, indeed. His driver pulled aside and Adams translated the legend on the side as the machine clanked past: Bureau of Fire Control, Second Arrondissement, Paris. Two men sat high above him on an exposed perch, craning their necks around the bulk of the machine's boiler, their hands on levers. Behind them was a brass vat, narrowed at the top like a huge, squat vase, from which sloshed small freshets of water whenever the engine lurched on the uneven pavement. In a moment Adams had paid off his driver and hopped out to follow, drawn by curiosity and by what he knew to be the perverse will to dawdle, to postpone a thing desired. Others, too, were curious (or perverse: he smiled to think they all had their Miriams to visit!) and he fell in among the rambling procession.

With a grinding, metallic sound, the engine turned off the boulevard and down a side street. Its chuffing increased in pitch as one of its operators cranked a wheeled valve on the boiler. Adams upped his pace to match its speed until he was walking briskly. The people around him swerved away suddenly, a shoal of fish scattering, leaving him isolated behind the engine for an instant until he, too, saw what they had seen—a sudden downdraft of smoke and sparks—and ducked to the curb to escape it. Adams noticed behind each wheel a powdery trail, lighter in color, sparkling: the wheels ground away the cobble, revealing fresh unweathered crystal in the granite. Ahead was the engine's destination, a soot-blackened building with a ring of fire wagons blocking the street and holding back the crowd of spectators. Adams broke into a slow trot in order to pass the machine. When he arrived at the edge of the crowd, he insinuated himself forward, ducking under elbows and gently nudging people aside, until he could see.

The fire, apparently, was out. Strewn on the sidewalk he saw buckets and ladders and canvas hosing and plaster and beam-sized chunks of charred wood. Above each window the bricks were scorched. The window casings framed a view of black nothingness inside. A sign that ran the width of the building was left with just the word *photographie* still legible. Firemen in rubberized canvas coats milled about the street to no apparent purpose. But part of the crew was still at work: from inside the building he could hear the sounds of scraping and chopping.

The engine arrived, jockeying this way and that through

the wagons and the crowd. Adams was satisfied to think that the old technology, horses and wagons, had arrived first and done the job. But the men proceeded to connect leather hosing to a valve on the bottom of the large vat, running it up to a coupling near the engine, and Adams saw that he was wrong: this machine did still have some function to serve. After another hose had been attached to the engine and stretched to the building, and the crew had emerged, black-faced and joking, to descend the stone steps at the entrance; after two men had taken up their positions, grasping the brass-fitted end of the hose, and had nodded at the operators of the machine; then, as the operators manipulated their levers and valves, the machine began to chuff and the hose swelled gradually, tumescent, until a spray of water emerged and was aimed into an open window.

A movement in the doorway of the building caught Adams's eye. One last fireman had come out, cradling in the crook of his arm some brown bottles from the photographer's laboratory. The man descended a few steps, then paused and turned. Deliberately, working against the thickness of his heavy coat, he set the bottles down on a step, one by one, arranging them in a neat row.

Adams shuddered. He decided he'd been distracted enough. He had things to do.

The walk back to the boulevard, through the mingling and curious crowd pressing toward him, was slow. In the boulevard the traffic was at a near standstill. Only a narrow stream, barely wide enough for two carriages to pass, still flowed near the middle. Adams moved out to catch the eye of a cabbie and found a row of pedestrians with the same object. Near where his cab had dropped him, a buggy and a rude oxcart had gotten tangled together, their wheels interlocked somehow and the buggy's horse chewing hay from the back of the oxcart while the drivers exchanged angry words. "Provincial," a man in top hat next to Adams muttered to no one and to everyone. "They come here with those things, they don't know what they're doing. Shouldn't let them in Paris."

In a cab again he felt the warmth of the day dissipating: the streets were cooling as the line of shade cut across the

face of the buildings on his left, throwing precise shadows
of trees onto warm brick and stone and dividing the city
clearly between the warm, almost summery afternoon of the
upper stories and the unmistakably autumnal coolness in the
street. He wondered what Miriam would make of the way
the slanting yellow light carried its color. Dimension, definition, direction, color, but no substance. For a moment he
imagined that he would like the chance to try to capture it
on canvas, as she apparently intended to; but of course he
would have no idea what he was doing.

Without his quite being aware of it, the streets and boulevards of Paris had assumed a new order as he rode: they
took shape around an axis between his residence and Miriam's, an axis that rendered the city less alien and more man-
ageable. Under the warm and slanting light the streets, the
buildings, the trees—even the traffic and the people—were
all necessary and contained: each was exactly the right shape
and location and size, and he was content.

But once they crossed the Seine, the cab turned and then
turned again, and soon turned again, into the tightening
streets of the Latin Quarter, until Adams was no longer sure
of direction. The sun, his true guide and companion, had
been swallowed by a bank of darkening clouds that rose
above the city from the northwest and lost its trailing edge
in the deepening darkness of the sky. As the streets grew
narrower, these clouds were hidden by the tops of buildings,
leaving a sense of preternatural darkness gathering above the
town. The coolness of evening welled up from the pavement,
catching at the throat: on the sidewalk in front of a match
factory, just under a sign that showed a large flame bursting
from an example of the company's product, a pedestrian
clutched the collar of his coat against the growing chill.
Aware of the irony but suggestible, Adams, too, adjusted his
coat, turning up the collar and folding the lapels to protect
his chest. Idly he wondered whether Miriam was painting,
wondered what she would be wearing, wondered what her
rooms looked like.

The directness of the route he had taken across the city
was dissolving in the cabbie's meanderings. The man chose
streets in a way that made no sense, for it seemed to bring

no progress toward a consistent goal. Adams had been trying to follow the way, marking the turns, but the last few streets confused him: he'd never be able to find the address again on his own. He looked for a landmark by which to orient himself and felt an acute discomfort when he could discern none. In every direction the streets curved sharply, limiting his view. An intersection looked familiar; was the cabbie taking him in circles?

He had just managed to convince himself to have a word with the driver when they pulled up outside a narrow building. A hand-lettered sign announced monthly rates for lodgings. He paid the fare and, after asking the driver to wait, ascended the stairs to the hotel.

Inside, it took a moment for Adams to adjust to the lack of light. Someone had gone to the trouble of making a cramped hallway seem like a lobby; there were two chairs on the right-hand wall, with fresh flowers on the small table between them. Above these was a gas lamp, beside a faded metal sign in French admonishing users *Turn, Don't Blow It Out*. To the left a long counter began a few feet from the door and stretched back to the staircase, closing off the hallway so that from the entrance one could go nowhere but upstairs.

He gave the bell a sharp rap and tried to read the names below the pigeonholes that held mail and room keys.

A door behind the desk opened and an immense human being shuffled out. "May I help you?" The voice was nasal, neither high nor low, and at once Adams felt a jangling disquiet. A template on the map of his experience had been thrown off center, so that the familiar pathways of thought did not correspond to the natural contours of the world's terrain. Neither the voluminous blue embroidered robe nor the voice nor the features of a body heavy with fat offered a clue to whether the concierge was male or female. As it drew closer, he could see its chin bore a growth of stubble—sparse and light for a man, more than one would expect of a woman—and that the left side of the face was misshapen. "Ah, yes," he answered in English, trying to reorganize his thoughts to accommodate this categoryless creature, "I am looking for a young woman who resides here. Miss Talbott,

Miss Miriam Talbott.'' Adams kept his eyes centered on the concierge's.

"There is no one here by that name." The voice was wheezy, difficult. Two puffy hands lay flat, palm down on the desk, steadying the body's bulk.

"She must live here." Adams's gaze was distracted by the jaw; he forced it back. There were concavities there, in the bone line, next to lumps that seemed rooted in the flesh, as if some malevolent parasite had insinuated itself beneath the skin to excavate the bone, piling up the spoil at the bottom of the face, distorting it. "This is the address I have for her." He showed the concierge the slip of paper on which Miriam had written her address in her straightforward block hand. The concierge nodded silently: Yes, this is the address.

"You must know her. She's a student. A painter. You would have seen her coming and going with her paints, her paintings." He had spoken quickly, nervously, and it occurred to him that the concierge might not fully understand English. "She is my height," he said slowly, gesturing, "has light hair. Yellow. Blond. Pale skin, very white skin, with dark eyebrows. Dark, like this," he added, pointing to the varnished countertop. "Have you seen her?"

The concierge looked back at him vacantly, turning one fleshy palm upwards on the counter. Adams repeated the question in French, but the concierge's posture and demeanor did not change. In a moment he realized what was expected; and, fumbling with his billfold, he pulled out a ten-franc note and placed it on the counter. The concierge delicately swept it into a hand and tucked it away, out of sight below the counter, while answering in English: "Yes, a woman like that lived here. She moved out."

A voice from the open doorway called out a single word in French—a name, Adams thought, though it was spoken so sharply that he couldn't catch it—and he looked behind the concierge to see its source. Through the open door he could see the arm of a sofa in front of a marble fireplace; on the sofa was a woman whose eyes glowered back at him. From the narrow slice of her that he could see, he judged her to be a lady. She was formally dressed, in pale purple— satin, maybe—and on her coiffed brown hair sat a matching purple hat with a bit of lace suggesting a veil. She was normal, even attractive; he found he had half-consciously expected the concierge to be mediating between two worlds, the public realm of the counter and a world of grotesque, complete deformity within. He looked back at the concierge, resolutely holding his gaze to the eyes. ''When did she leave?''

''I was not on duty, monsieur, so how can I say.''

''Is there a forwarding address?'' The concierge looked troubled, and Adams repeated the question in French. He received the same shrug in response.

Adams looked beyond the concierge again, into the sitting room, and saw the woman in purple turn her head away. As he watched, the door closed, swung by some unseen hand. The concierge smiled at him and nodded slightly, as if to confirm a basically cooperative nature. Adams realized he would get no more. ''If she returns,'' Adams said, reaching into a breast pocket, ''I would appreciate it if you gave her this.'' He handed the concierge his calling card. The concierge smiled again as the card disappeared beneath a hand.

''Of course, monsieur. Happy to have been of service.'' The smile, Adams thought, might have been meant to mock him.

Out on the street, he discovered he'd been abandoned by his cab.

4:45 P.M.

WHEN HE RETURNED to his quarters, there was a letter from Hay in his mailbox, come by pneumatique that afternoon. ''Meet me at the Chamber of Deputies. Five o'clock. *Urgent.*'' For a moment a panicky wave of guilt rose in him and he had the urge to run. But no, no, if Hay had found out about Dingler's picture, he would have come to him. There'd be no reason for a scene at the Chamber of Deputies. Hay wouldn't do that. There was a fine irony, one he knew Hay would appreciate, and which he wished he could share with him: Adams hadn't even gotten the picture he wanted, the picture of Dingler and his family in front of the skeleton-mansarded house. In the darkness he had gotten the one next to it, the picture of somber, suited men on the steps of the canal company office. Someday, perhaps, he'd tell his friend.

Adams glanced at his watch: a quarter to. He wouldn't make it, but if he rushed he wouldn't be very late. He paused only to dash off a note to Elizabeth to accompany the opera tickets: *Here they are, as promised, looking forward to to-night*. At the front desk he gave the folded note with the tickets inside to the clerk, and watched to make sure he put them in the correct pigeonhole.

At the Chamber of Deputies Hay met him at the curb with money already in hand for his driver and hurried him up the steps. They were almost running, Hay bustling him along by the elbow, pulling him through the doors, then upstairs, past the murals and fluted columns and the windowed alcoves holding statuary and gilded chairs with red plush seats. "I'm glad you got here in time for this," Hay said. "History as it occurs. You'll have a firsthand view." They turned at the top of the staircase down a long corridor with large, thick-paned windows along one side.

Hands don't see, Adams thought, but let it go; there was larger game. "*Event* is what occurs," he told Hay testily. "*History* is what historians write, if you please." He pulled his elbow away but consented to match Hay's pace.

"Here," said Hay, his hand reaching for the knob of a door. "Worth it. Shhh!"

They entered the spectators' gallery of the Chamber of Deputies, the lower house of the French parliament. Hay's shushing had been gratuitous; inside the packed chamber there was general tumult. The sloping galleries were filled with spectators, each of whom was talking loudly to a neighbor or shouting at the deputies below; and there on the floor of the Chamber, where the deputies ordinarily sat on the red plush benches that rose in concentric, semicircular tiers, all the deputies were on their feet, shouting, gesturing, arguing. As Adams and Hay squeezed into the end of the back bench in the gallery, Adams searched for and found the focus of the Chamber's attention: a young deputy at the rostrum, just in front of the president's ornate desk. The man, his hair dark and sleek with oil, stood calmly waiting for the president's gavelling to restore order. His hands rested on the sides of the podium; a wiry man, he was filled with the athletic and compressed attention of the stalker. "That's Delahaye," Hay shouted into Adams's ear. "When I heard this morning that he planned to give this speech today, I sent you that note."

The Chamber gradually quieted enough for Delahaye to resume. "I would stake my honor here against yours," he boomed. "I will give no names, but tell you that the stench of corruption reaches even here."

The floor erupted again, and the spectators, too, joined in the shouting. Delahaye held up both hands to calm the Chamber, nodding in recognition of their outrage. As his gaze swept the room, Adams watched his head rotate from profile to full face. He was handsome: square forehead and jaw, no beard, but a short, stylish mustache, his eyes wide-set, dark, bulging slightly. Delahaye waited, tilting his head back as if to gauge his audience through sense of smell. He judged the moment, found it right. "Behind that corruption," he thundered, "is an evil genius. The directors duped the public, but this man, this man, this evil genius," he repeated, shouting now to be heard, "this man duped the directors!"

"Name him! Name him!" came shouts from the benches.

"If you want names, you will vote an inquiry," Delahaye answered. "In this Chamber alone three million francs were distributed; three million francs that came from the pockets of hardworking Frenchmen, three million francs they gave to see a canal built to the glory of France; three million francs that were spent instead, here, in this Chamber, to buy political favor! One hundred and fifty deputies were bought. I have seen the list!"

At once there was a violent uproar. Some spectators were applauding; but from the floor came taunts and catcalls, and out of the commotion emerged a rumbling chant, taken up by voices throughout the Chamber: "The names! The names!"

The president was on his feet behind Delahaye, pounding his gavel while glowering at Delahaye's back. "Floquet," Hay told Adams. "A former premier." He was gray-haired and beetle-browed, with long mustaches flowing from his upper lip, the tips slicing out laterally several inches from his cheeks, held in place with some unimaginable quantity of wax.

"You cannot come into this Chamber and accuse the entire body," Floquet shouted when his gavel had quieted the deputies enough for him to be heard. There were more calls from the floor for names. Delahaye, with the uncanny calm of rhetorical fever on his face, shook his head and used a knuckle to stroke, once in each direction, his mustache. He eyed his audience. "Vote the inquiry!"

Delahaye made his way back to his seat through a Chamber in general uproar. Members were clamoring at the top of their lungs for recognition, shouting to one another in consultation, shaking their fists at Delahaye, restraining the ones who shook fists, pounding on the desks in agitation, calling for order, calling for a vote, standing on their benches to see: every one of them had risen to his feet, every one was in motion, and in that maelstrom the calmest man was Delahaye, who walked up the aisle to his seat with a resolute and evident disdain.

"Loubet," Hay shouted into Adams's ear, pointing to the man who rose from the front bench and ascended the steps to the rostrum. "The premier. With this speech Delahaye has tried to force him to support an inquiry into the canal company. Let's see if it worked."

Loubet waited for order to be restored. An older man, he seemed calm, completely at ease; he might have been waiting for an omnibus. He was well dressed, his salt-and-pepper hair smoothly combed but not oiled. He kept his long chin near his chest, looking at some papers on the podium before him while he waited. As Adams watched, he drew from his pocket a pair of reading glasses, perched them just above the bulb at the end of his long nose, and tilted his head back to read through them. The president's persistent gavelling finally began to have an effect, and when the room was nearly quiet, Loubet smiled and put away his glasses. He held out his arms for silence, as if he were about to pronounce a benediction, as if all the shouting had been in his honor.

"Gentlemen," he began, smiling broadly to the Chamber. "Such irresponsible charges have but one source—the uncontrolled political passions of the few. The Boulangists"—here he was interrupted by rising catcalls but persevered—"the Boulangists would destroy the Republic." His final words were subsumed within a chorus of deep-throated rumbling. Loubet held up his hands again, quieting the Chamber. "Now now! Hear me! Surely light must be shed on so serious a matter. It is my desire to demonstrate to all the folly of these charges. *This government will hide nothing.*"

"That's it," Hay said to Adams as the Chamber broke into a general and, by recent standards, restrained conversation. "They'll take the vote, but it's been decided. With Loubet supporting it, the government deputies have to vote for the inquiry, like it or not. If they were to vote against, the government would fall, and they'd be hammered with an inquiry anyway. I don't know why he gave in. He must have counted votes and seen how it was going.''

As the Chamber settled down under persistent gavelling, Hay filled Adams in on the background to the session. ''This morning an official of the company was found dead. Reinach—Jacques de Reinach. No one seems to know anything about it yet. Poison, I hear, maybe a suicide. There was a subpoena issued in his name Friday. The police who delivered it found him slumped at his desk, dead.'' Adams scanned the galleries while Hay spoke at his shoulder. Below them the roll-call vote was under way. ''Lesseps was subpoenaed, and some other officers of the company—Henri Cottu, a man named Fontane. Eiffel, too. The man who built the tower. He did some engineering for the company. Delahaye and the rightists, especially the Boulangist press, have been pounding on this for a couple of months now, thinking they smell a scandal, but it took this suicide, really, to get them anywhere.''

Adams knew about the Boulangists. ''There's a lesson in hope for us, Hay. The last Bonapartists in France. Just think: a retrograde political agenda, their leader dead, and still they carry on. It's amazing they get so far with nothing to offer the French voter but testimonials to the country's past glory. People lap it up.'' He shook his head. ''Just as I was saying, Hay. The world changes too quickly. People dig in their heels. They want to go back. Boulanger knew it, felt it, was shrewd enough to see and use it.''

''Well, the Boulangists are going to be using this whole Panama thing. It was a Boulangist paper that first stirred this up. *La Libre Parole*, run by someone named Edouard Drumont. A good hater, that one. Wants to bring back some one or other of General Boulanger's adjutants, as the nearest thing to a Napoleon he can think of, and thinks that anyone who opposes him is a simpering toady to the English. Or the Germans. I think he figures that the Boulangists have to benefit from anything that shakes up the government, anything that stirs things up. And if he's right, that's not good.''

''Why?''

Hay dropped his voice. ''If the rightists get in, the United States has less hope of getting the canal rights. They're extremely militaristic and they're infatuated with symbols of greatness. They'd never let the canal concession go—it's too important. There's even talk that they'd go back there, start up work again. It's another two years before the concession expires. Longer, if they can get a company excavating there.''

"Are they going to win?"

"Can't say. Every deputy the scandal touches changes the equation.'' Hay shook his head and leaned back. "Socialists, radicals, Boulangists, Christian Democrats, democratic socialists, social democrats, republican socialists, royalists, Bonapartists, God knows what all—sometimes it seems that every deputy belongs to a party of one. There are just too many different alignments, really. I *think* the scandal is going to eat away at the middle—they were the ones in power—leaving just the two extremes. But you can't really know. 'Middle' isn't quite the right word for it. It's like—it's like some blob of dough that's being continually kneaded. There's a left and a right, but it's always being folded over and pressed on itself, and at any given moment you can't tell where a particular piece of it is going to end up. We'll have to wait and see which way it goes."

Adams nodded, idly scanning the galleries as the clerk of the Chamber called out the names of deputies. There, across the Chamber, in the front row of the gallery, he spied a familiar face above a patch of pale purple: the woman from Miriam's hotel, the woman who had been on the couch when the concierge became uncommunicative. She was leaning forward in her seat, peering over the rail, watching the deputies just below her. He followed her gaze to the floor of the Chamber but couldn't tell what or whom she was watching. He looked at her again: she was frowning.

"Excuse me," Adams said, half rising to bump his way past Hay. "I see someone I must talk to."

"Who?" Hay wasn't moving.

"That woman, there in the purple."

Hay followed his gaze. "Oh. Léonide LeBlanc. 'Madame LeBlanc,' as she's known to her, ah, customers.'' Hay drew aside his knees but caught Adams's sleeve as he passed. "Adams, she's not exactly your type, is she?''

Turning back from the aisle, Adams could see that his first estimation of her had been in error. The woman was dressed a bit more flashily than Paris fashion allowed; there was some hint about her, some indefinable element of her dress, that indicated her efforts to be attractive were in service of a more baldly commercial end than most ladies would admit to. "What's she doing here?" he asked Hay.

"She runs a very popular establishment. Very popular among the deputies. Some say the bribery was orchestrated in her parlor. I suppose she's here to keep an eye on anything that might affect business. Good managerial urge, that." Hay looked to see if his drollery was appreciated, but Adams was absorbed in studying the woman. As they watched, she seemed to sense their gaze and turned to look across the Chamber. She must have seen them, two bright moons of faces fully attending to her. She glared for an instant, then gathered her skirts and started up an aisle.

Adams stood and made for the door. In the hallway he turned left and walked quickly, his feet pattering against the polished stone. At the corner he turned left and hurried on. He hoped the woman hadn't gone the other way. Worried, he broke into a trot. When he cleared the second corner, he saw no sign of her in the long hallway.

"Damn!"

He stopped to listen for her footsteps but heard only Hay's, coming up behind him. He was out of breath. "What do you want her for, Adams? A woman like that?"

"She's my only way of getting in touch with a friend here in Paris."

"I wonder at the company your friends keep." Getting no response, Hay continued: "Well, we can always pay her a visit. Her place is over by the Bourse. She gets as many stockbrokers as deputies." To Adams's raised eyebrow he held up a hand: "Don't you start insinuating, now. It's part of a diplomat's job to know such things."

"Well then. Let's go."

Hay shook his head. "We can't. We haven't enough time." He pulled out his watch. "The opera, remember? It's already after six."

6:30 P.M.

AS HE REACHED for his doorknob, he was startled to see it turn and elude his grasp. His door opened from within on a well-dressed man with gray hair.

"Monsieur Henry Adams, isn't it? Yes? The American historian. So good to see you. See, I have heard of you. Yes. Do forgive me." The man holding his door open was of average height, about five inches taller than Adams, with a round face and a sharp, clear, slicing-wedge of a nose. Beneath it was a short, well-trimmed mustache. He made a slight bow and stepped aside to allow Adams to enter. "I had just decided that you weren't coming. I am Chief Inspector Charles Pettibois, of the Paris Police." His English had a London drawing-room accent, familiar to Adams from his service as his father's secretary in that city years ago. "I do hope you will forgive me this trespass." Pettibois smiled, his mustache expanding from the center to reveal a row of even teeth. "I come to you on a matter of police business. I had the concierge let me in." He shrugged apologetically, a gesture meant to indicate his embarrassment, and also to beg understanding of the difficulty one has in calling on those who live in hotels, without proper sitting rooms or the servants who would invite one to wait in them; the rules, his gesture seemed to say, must be adapted to particular cases. There were crow's feet at the corners of his eyes as he smiled. "The law permits . . . but I see you are displeased.

Perhaps what the law permits is not always a good idea, eh?''

For a moment the two of them stood at his doorway; then Pettibois stood back, doorknob still in hand, and glanced into the room. "This is awkward, isn't it?" he asked. "I feel I should invite you in, but that's absurd. This is your apartment." He gave a little laugh, but cut it short when he saw that Adams was unappreciative. "I am sorry. I should have waited for you downstairs. I see I should have, I have made a mistake. Dear me. Please, Monsieur Adams, do not hold this lapse of judgment against me." He let go of the door and walked casually into the center of the room. Adams followed, leaving the door open. "Do you forgive me, Monsieur Adams?"

"I forgive you." He felt violated at finding someone in his rooms, and there was the practical problem of needing to hurry. "What do you want? I'm late for the opera."

"Ah, the opera. An excellent pastime. Well, pastime, actually, tends to demean it. The highest form of art, don't you think? It was Wagner who said that. A German." The inspector shrugged. "An annoying people on the whole, but I think we can forgive him his nationality this once, no? Certainly opera is the culmination of the dramatic art. The sublime union of action and music, penetrating to the very soul of its audience, unified and given force by the drama of story. Pure artifice, pure artifice, and no apologies. Not a realistic pretense about it." He smiled. "I am a great fan myself, though I hardly go. It is, I think—" He stopped and pursed his lips. "But excuse me. I see I annoy. Sorry. The purpose of my visit. Yes. I am here to request that you accompany me downtown to help clear up a little matter. Strictly voluntary, of course."

Whatever it was, Adams thought, it could wait. "Yes?"

"It's a matter of identification," the inspector said, as ingratiatingly as he could. "Shouldn't take but a few minutes. One Miriam Talbott, I'm afraid, has come to an untimely end."

There is comfort in the familiar when the soul confronts death. As Adams rode through the streets of Paris in Pettibois's carriage, his thoughts had the blandness of cliché, much as weak tea poultices had soothed the sore throats of his childhood. He saw that the paving bricks were shiny from a brief shower, saw a lamplighter scowl at the heft of his ladder. He saw them in sharp detail; his eyes, mindless and unseeing, were seduced by minutiae, bits of the world as fine and tiny and inconsequential as the grains of a plaster. Pettibois had questions for him, but Adams waved them away with a hand, wanting to be left alone to concentrate: there was something familiar here, some thought, some connection in his experience. What was it? He had been just a boy when his father hired a man to move the door to his study. He remembered watching the solid wall being stripped down to bare lathing, remembered the plaster dust that hung like dry fog throughout the house, remembered his mother saying that his cough would be the death of him. He had watched the workman with the unselfconscious attentiveness of a child, seeing him mix plaster in a bucket, seeing the smooth new plaster roll off the trowel. He had been fascinated by a bag the plasterer had, a canvas bag from which he drew a handful of shiny smooth hair, long shiny hair such as his mother and sister combed out at night in a ritual he liked to witness. He had seen the plasterer dip his hand into this bag, bring out a whole headful of long brown tresses and clip some from the bottom, then stir these locks into the whiteness until they disappeared. Adams remembered wondering whose hair it had been and how she had come to let it be used for this; he remembered it had made him sad.

A question came to him: "How did she die?" He spoke into the isinglass curtain of the carriage, where he traced with his finger the path of a raindrop as it slid down the outside.

"Suicide. Drowning. She was found at a swimming concession on the river this morning."

Adams nodded. When his mother had finally asked him what the matter was, and he had explained, she'd laughed and told him that plasterers used horsehair, not women's hair. The bag was full of it. The news had failed to comfort; he thought she must be wrong, must be lying to reassure him.

Pettibois waited for him to go on. When it was clear that Adams had no more to say, Pettibois pursed his lips. "I understand how difficult this must be for you. Were you close? You were close, no?'' He leaned forward, solicitous, and Adams could see that on the crown of his head Pettibois's hair was thinner. He could see through to the scalp.

Adams sighed. ''Yes. I would say we were close.''

''You came to Paris to visit her, then? How long had you known her?''

''No, no. A month. Two.'' He saw the puzzlement in Pettibois's round face, his eyebrows floating up like soap foam on a bubble, but the man seemed too small and far away to be talked to. A word was hard labor, a coherent sentence a week's travail. ''We—'' No. ''She was—'' Just as wrong. ''I knew she was someone who—'' He stopped and made himself breathe regularly for a minute. This was hard to explain. He couldn't possibly begin to tell the complete truth of it—the comfort he took in her company, and the physical pleasure of being touched by her, of feeling her breathing body resting against his that day on the train; and if that was beyond description, how much harder to describe the deeper, purer bond he felt with her, the mutual understanding he knew was developing between them, a bond forged out of equal parts common interest, dedication to art, and mutually sympathetic natures . . . No. But he must explain. ''She was an artist, a talented young woman. I knew we were going to be friends, that there was—'' He couldn't speak. ''I'm sorry,'' he managed to say.

''Yes, yes. I understand. This appreciation of yours I understand completely. It is a shame, a very horrible shame.''

The carriage took them across the Seine and onto the Ile de la Cité, that boat-shaped island moored in the heart of Paris, circumnavigated by the barges and the taxi launches that move continuously on the river. They passed a stretch of road with the cobbles up, the dirt from its excavation piled waist-high and marked against traffic with pickets and rope knotted through with bright cloth. On this island the city had its founding; here had been constructed one of the monuments of medieval architecture, the Cathedral of Notre Dame; and here, in the very shadow of that cathedral, at the head of the island, where generations ago a rude and uncivilized tribe of Franks had hauled the bodies of their dead to be swallowed in the marshy mud, stood the morgue. It was a blank anonymous mask of a building, low to the ground, as plain and impoverished as the majority of its clients. She had stood in the light; how had she come to this?

Inside, Pettibois greeted the coroner, a rotund white-smocked man who sat behind a cluttered desk eating something from a paper sack. The coroner wiped his hands on his smock and without a word rose and shuffled his bulk through the swinging doors next to his desk. Pettibois and Adams followed him.

They entered a large room with a stone floor and high small windows turned black with night. Gas lamps spaced regularly along the walls lit the tables, about a dozen of them, of white and solid marble, in one long row. At the base of each was a tiled channel in the stone floor and a drain. Between them there were no shadows, no places into which the hesitant witness might project his thoughts, huddling them there against the brightness of the light. On some of the tables white sheets covered forms they could not disguise; other tables were bare white stone. The coroner walked to the head of one of the sheets and stood, waiting. When Pettibois and Adams stood next to him, he spoke.

"Female, Caucasian, early twenties. Now?"

Pettibois assented with a slight nod. The coroner drew back the sheet.

There is, some people say, a kind of nobility that settles upon the features of the dead. Adams had seen it more than once. When his sister Louisa finally succumbed, after ten days of body-wracking torture, to tetanus, she had become as tranquil in death as she had been on those rainy afternoons in memory, when he would find her in the library, asleep, with the pages of a book crushing themselves against her chest, rising and falling with each of her soft breaths. He went to her in Florence from England as soon as he heard of her accident, before there had been any talk of infection, when it seemed the worst she would suffer was a broken leg. Her horse had bolted, had thrown her from her carriage. He had stayed to the last, was at her bedside as the disease advanced, exercising her body with its merciless gymnastics. He knew little comfort could be offered and less received. Throughout his vigil there weighed upon him the knowledge of what was to come, the only possible resolution. He pictured her death as a moment in a stream from which two branches flowed. In one, all that would be left would be her body, lifeless and dumb, cooling in the still air of the room, until it was undifferentiated from the brute physical matter around her, the casual furniture of life, in all particulars save one: it had a different sort of history.

And the other stream, the memory of her: that would survive too, solid and unchanging. In death a person achieved a kind of fixity. Who she had been was now impervious to the assaults of life and chance, impervious to the impress of her will, her choices; she was now as fixed and unchanging as the course of a river in winter, frozen in a channel of her own making, frozen there by everyone else's need to assimilate the meaning of her life. She was the errant one, the sibling who had escaped. That is what she was, all she could ever be. If death is some obscure exchange at the border of memory and existence, those who know you and remain alive are party to the negotiation; and for Louisa even Florence had proved not far enough from Boston to silence the claims of family. In truth, she had not escaped.

Nor had Clover. And she, too, had found some composure in death, some wisdom that had come, final and true, to assemble her features into a beauty they had scarcely known in life, making them intolerable to look upon even for a man who habitually sorted his experience through the dark sieve of irony. Was this peacefulness of the dead the source of all belief, the source of all the grand faiths in a life after this one? Did the living demand of the dead that they at last know something, something important?

But as he looked at the face of the woman before him, he could see that in death the body does not always transcend temporal care; this woman had wanted and feared to the last, and death had brought her pale features no peace, no resolve. Her eyes were wide and shallow-set, almost equine in effect; mercifully, they were closed. On either side of the bridge of her nose there were darkened spots in the flesh. Maybe, he thought, life grips the muscles of the face in habitual patterns, and in death these return, the way he had seen schoolboys cling to the familiar when confronted with the unknown.

"Monsieur Adams?" Pettibois was saying.

"Eh?"

"Can you identify the body?"

"This," he began, and he felt the force of a fact he had known the moment the sheet was pulled back, a relief that his agitation had worked to obscure, "this is not Miriam Talbott."

"You are not mistaken?"

"Of course I'm not mistaken." The woman under the sheet resembled Miriam in some particulars, so that at a glance or at some distance one might have been mistaken; and in death we all move closer to resemblance in each other—the grand community of mortality reasserts itself when the breath that animates our differences escapes; but this woman's hair was several shades darker than Miriam's, without Miriam's golden light, and some quality of her features was different, otherwise proportioned. Her face was wider at the cheekbones, and her chin wasn't as long as Miriam's and wasn't dimpled, not at all. Adams felt himself grow petulant in his relief. "This is not Miriam Talbott. Definitely not." Why had he been brought here? Why had he been misled?

"And yet her papers give the name Miriam Talbott. Passport, letters on her person, engraved jewelry—these all indicate or are consistent with an identification of Miriam Talbott." Pettibois spoke gently, out of obvious puzzlement. "How do you explain that?"

"How should I know?" Adams shot back. "Perhaps this woman is a thief. Perhaps she killed herself out of remorse at what she had done, taking all of Miriam's things. How should I know?"

Pettibois did not respond, but nodded to the coroner, who replaced the sheet. "I have some papers for you to sign, Monsieur Adams. Follow me."

At the desk Pettibois waited for the coroner to produce the proper forms from his files. The fat man extracted a folder from one of the wooden cases along the wall, and with a practiced bump of his belly sent the drawer rolling shut with the precise minimum of effort required. He wheezed as he sat, then opened the folder and held a paper out to Pettibois without looking up. Pettibois took the form and, after clearing a space on the desk, began to fill it in.

"May I ask you something, Inspector?" Adams said.

"Certainly."

"How did you know to contact me? I have not . . . haven't, that is . . ." Adams was about to explain that he had not yet contacted Miriam Talbott in Paris, and that he had only met her that fall in Pontorson. But the information seemed too personal, and he held on to it. Besides, he had met Miriam Talbott; he had never met this woman. "What made you come to me?"

"She had your card," Pettibois said, not looking up from the desk. "As a matter of fact, there it is." Pettibois waved his pencil absently toward a table at the wall and returned to his writing. Adams strolled over to the table where a large leather pouch stamped PREFECTURE had spilled its contents: the woman's personal effects. A comb and brush, some centime and franc pieces, a matchbox, a damp wallet, that was all. The papers from the wallet had been separated and laid out to dry, and among them he saw his card. It must be the one he had left at Miriam's hotel. But no: that had been just this afternoon. Where had this woman gotten one of his cards? He stooped to examine it more closely. With a glance at Pettibois, who paid no attention, he lifted the card and inspected its back. There was the inked address he had written for Miriam on the train to Chartres, still legible. How had she gotten it? "This is the card I gave Miss Talbott."

"And yet it's here, among the effects of a woman you say isn't Miriam Talbott." Pettibois lowered his pencil and frowned. He sucked at the back of his teeth as he thought, making small birdcall noises emanate from his mustache. "Yes."

The two men looked at each other for a moment.

"Tell me," Pettibois said, "do you recognize anything else here? Is there anything there you saw on the other woman?"

"No."

Pettibois nodded. "Curious. Very curious. The presence of your card supports the supposition that this woman is a thief; but then, what of the other items? The wallet? The locket? She wouldn't just steal your card.''

"I know. These other things, I can't say. I never saw Miss Talbott with them, but . . .''

"It's difficult, isn't it?''

Adams put his card back on the table as Pettibois returned to his paperwork. There were other cards arrayed there to dry. A milliner. A furrier. An optometrist. One commercial card caught Adams's eye: *Jacques de Reinach*. The name was familiar. He squinted to make out the motto beneath the name: La Compagnie Universelle du Canal Interocéanique. De Reinach . . . that was the name that Hay had mentioned, the name of the man who had committed suicide rather than face justice.

"Monsieur Adams, your signature, if you please.'' Without rising Pettibois held a form out to Adams, a single page which, curved, made a trough that led down to the inspector's upturned face. Adams took it and read. As nearly as he could make out, it attested to the fact that he had viewed a body and had been unable to identify it. Pettibois had filled in a box labelled *identification provisoire* with the name of Miriam Talbott. To sign it seemed wrong. "I told you,'' he said, placing the form on the desk, "that woman is not Miriam Talbott.''

"By necessity we must give the body some name. There is circumstantial evidence suggesting that it is she. Please, Monsieur Adams, your signature.'' Pettibois turned the paper around and pushed it back across the desk to him. "This in no way binds you to her identification as Mademoiselle Talbott.''

Warily, Adams took the proffered pen and signed. "The dead woman was apparently mixed up in the Panama affair.''

"Oh?''

"She has a business card from the man who killed himself yesterday. She must know him.''

"A deduction, Monsieur Adams! Splendid!'' Pettibois beamed. "You have what I think is a necessary instinct for police work, this desire to see connection, to explore possibilities. But I would not place such a great weight on that card. There is another possibility.'' Pettibois spoke in rapid

French to the coroner, who grunted. "Ah, you see?" Pettibois said to Adams. "Our coroner, who, I may say in English, verges on the incompetent, cannot guarantee that Monsieur Reinach's effects may not have been mixed in with this unfortunate woman's. Monsieur Reinach himself," said Pettibois, tilting his head at the door into the mortuary, "is a current resident here. No doubt there has been a clerical error." He took his pen back from Adams, twisted the cap on, and pocketed it. "Rest assured we will explore every possibility. Leave the matter to us." Pettibois stood and buttoned his suit coat; Adams noticed that he was thin, thinner than the plumpness of his face would have led one to expect. Pettibois was next to him, clapping a hand to his shoulder. "I promise you I shall not write any history, if you will refrain from detecting," he said heartily. "Have we an understanding?"

"History often requires detection." The card, he thought, had been wet; it was stained and curled. "May I see Monsieur Reinach?"

"Has our historian a taste for the morbid?"

Adams debated briefly whether to invent an excuse, something about writing someday about the Panama affair and wanting to know what the principals looked like, but he thought better of it. "Yes, I suppose."

"I can't see the harm." Pettibois turned to the coroner and spoke in French. "Maurice, we're going in to look at Romeo," he said, if Adams translated it correctly.

Pettibois led the way back into the morgue. "The baron had a history of apoplexy. The man was under a great deal of strain. He had just been indicted, you know, for his part in the Panama affair. My men were delivering the summons when they found him dead." Pettibois paused at the table with the draped corpse. "Terrible things, he'd done terrible things. If you believe what you read in the papers, anyway. The doctor considers that the publicity about this Panama affair brought on a relapse of his condition. A fatal relapse." Pettibois shook his head, then drew back the cover.

To Adams's eye, Reinach's whitened face had the mark of cruelty in it. His eyes were small and deep under his brow, and there were wrinkles at the bridge of his nose from what must have been a habitual frown. He was bald to the crown of his head, and had, like nearly any Parisian man of note, a full beard. It was not a face that would have distinguished itself in a crowd, and yet it was disturbingly familiar. It came to him: Dingler's picture. This was one of the men in the photograph, one of that row of company officials. In the roundness of his features, in the blank anonymity of his face, Adams saw a capacity for cruelty that hadn't shown in the photograph. "I thought he was a suicide."

"Oh? Who told you that?"

Adams shrugged. "A friend." He saw no need to drag Hay's name into this.

"Well, people are sometimes wrong. I'm no expert in these matters. The doctor says apoplexy. Congestion of the brain. No doubt aggravated by his—his anxieties." Pettibois met Adams's gaze and smiled grimly.

"Did you call him 'Romeo'?"

"You speak French," Pettibois said, smiling. "He had a reputation as a ladies' man. Although," he added, "looking at him, you might wonder why. Perhaps it was . . . Well, now we shall never know, shall we?" Pettibois fidgeted with the sheet. "Are you quite done, Monsieur Adams? I do not wish to detain you any longer."

"Yes. Thank you."

Pettibois walked him to the curb and waited until he found a cab. "The City of Paris appreciates your assistance, and regrets any inconvenience that this unpleasant chore has caused you," he said as Adams climbed in. He buttoned the side curtains as Adams sat down and leaned close to speak through the canvas. "I think we will not bother you again."

8:30 P.M.

ADAMS FOUND HAY in a box at the opera and called to him from behind its red velvet curtain. No response. He'd have to speak louder. He called again, and again, louder each time, until Hay turned.

The old couple who sat in the box had heard, too, and the man frowned at him over his shoulder. Hay waved Adams in, pointing to the empty chair next to him.

"Blast it, no! I need to talk with you," Adams hissed. The ancient couple swivelled around in unison, frowning.

Hay excused himself and led Adams to the hallway. "This is quite unlike you, Adams," he said as he pulled the curtain shut behind him. "Actually, I should thank you," he whispered when they had moved away from the doorway. "I really have no stomach for this." Dropping his voice even further, he added, "I dislike this opera. Intensely."

"This is important, Hay. You've got to take me to Madame LeBlanc's. Now. I need to talk with her."

"Can't it wait?"

"No!" he said sharply. "There's already been a death." He added this for effect, knowing the inference Hay would draw, an inference that hadn't dawned on him until just this moment. But there it was, an eminently reasonable conclusion: Miriam was in danger.

"A death?"

"Yes, yes, a death. I was just called to the morgue to

identify the body. Only I couldn't. They thought it was Miss Talbott, but it wasn't.''

"Miss Talbott is the friend you're looking for?" Adams nodded. "How is it that Madame LeBlanc knows this woman?"

"I don't know. I don't even know that she knows her. All I know is that I saw her at the hotel when I went there to look for Miss Talbott. I think she kept the concierge from telling me anything. I've got to find her. Take me to her place—or tell me where it is.''

"I could do that, but it wouldn't do you any good.''

Adams thought to argue but stopped himself: Hay had something in mind. "What? What is it?"

"She's here. I saw her across the house, in a box on the other side.''

Adams started to go, but Hay caught him by the arm. "You can't just barge in on her. Wait until the intermission. Come sit with me." Hay led him along. "There's room. You can keep an eye on her.''

Walking behind Hay in the curving hall, Adams smelled the baked-fish scent of hot iron and wondered if it came from the electric lights that were spaced evenly along the wall, mock candelabra filled with harsh glassy suns that hurt his eyes. The unwavering brightness of the light threw solid shadows and made even the darkest colors seem a species of pastel. Elaborate moldings and cornices, gilt leaf, rococo woodwork, the tapestries and curtains—all seemed brittle, as though glazed, spun from sugar.

At the entrance to his box Hay parted the curtains and stepped down inside to his seat. Adams lingered on the step. From the stage below, scarcely twenty feet away, he heard a male voice sing soothingly, lovingly. Hay took his seat and, when he noticed that Adams hadn't joined him, turned to gesture to the empty seat next to his. Adams shook his head. "Where is she?" he mouthed. With a discreet finger Hay pointed across the open expanse of the house and to the right, to a balcony on the other side that Adams couldn't see.

The woman next to Hay—an old dowager with an unlikely pile of dull gray hair on her head, surmounted by a tiara with a row of rubies fat as horse's eyes—noticed Hay's gesture.

She turned to stare at Adams from behind the shoulder flounces of her dress. Her thickly powdered face reminded him of a stale bonbon nestled in its fluted paper cup. When she snapped open her fan and fluttered it in displeasure her bracelets dangled on her thin forearm. Adams was repelled— not by the censure she intended, but at something else, the girlishness of her gesture, the delusion it suggested. Her companion, a sharp-featured old man with oiled white hair and sunken cheeks and a long mustache that drooped at either side of his mouth, framing it like parentheses, glanced back, then sniffed while taking Adams's measure out of the corner of his eye. Inside his jacket his shirt collar was several sizes too large for his veiny, wrinkled neck.

They were a matched set, he thought: the ancient dowager and the elderly Duke, the dried and wrinkled fruit of aristocracy. He attempted to nod graciously, in silent apology for his poor manners, but they turned back to the opera without acknowledging him.

Adams decided to edge down into the box until he could see Madame LeBlanc. But then he thought: When I can see her, she'll be able to see me. He didn't want to scare her off again. Slowly, hoping not to distract Hay's hosts, he squatted down. If he was low enough he could just peer over the rail at the front of the box and Madame LeBlanc would be able to see no more than the top of his head. Sitting on his haunches, he inched forward in little hops until he had gone far enough to have the full left-to-right sweep of the balconies opposite. Cautiously he raised his head. He didn't want to stand any higher than he had to in order to see her.

He found her on the opposite side of the house, in a box with a commanding view of the stage. She sat looking ahead, her hands folded in her lap, her attention focussed on the opera, in which a trio spilled out from two men and a woman. Madame LeBlanc wore a purple dress with a tight and low-cut bodice, which even at a distance Adams could see revealed a shaded line of cleavage. Onstage the soprano, dressed in the simple clothes of a country girl, fell to her knees in front of the baritone. As if sensing his gaze Madame LeBlanc stirred and glanced about the house, pulling her fox stole over her shoulder. Adams ducked down, waited a moment, then raised his head again. The two other women with Madame LeBlanc were slightly younger than she, and were dressed a bit more modestly. There were no men in the box. That stood to reason, Adams thought; whatever company she kept in private, no one would want to be seen with her in public.

When the soprano swooned the trio became a duet that ended the act. Adams watched Madame LeBlanc; as the curtain fell she joined the applause, delicately patting her gloved hands together. She turned to say something to one of her companions and he ducked again. From his position squatting on the floor he sensed someone looking at him, and he turned to see the Duke and the dowager glowering as they applauded. "Adams," hissed Hay from the Duke's side, "what are you doing?"

"Observing," Adams said quietly. He tried to inch his way back into the shadows of the box before standing and found that hop-stepping didn't work in reverse; he'd have to waddle. He worked his way back, and when he felt himself safely out of sight, he stood, stretching his legs.

"Your Excellency, my friend is . . . Excuse me a moment." Hay came to Adams in the back of the box. "Let me introduce you," Hay insisted. He pulled Adams toward the front of the box.

"No!" whispered Adams emphatically.

"Adams!" Hay whispered back. "You're in their box, you bloody well have to meet them. They're the Italian ambassador and his wife, for God's sake."

"She'll see me," he said, nodding toward Madame LeBlanc. "I can't step up there. The last time she saw me she ran."

"Adams, you have to meet them. What do you want me to do, bring them back here?"

To Adams, this seemed a perfectly reasonable solution. But he knew that Hay hadn't meant it; as the representative of the sovereign dignity of a foreign power, the ambassador in his box wouldn't have stirred for anyone less than royalty. The applause had ended, and from below the balcony rail drifted up the liquid burbling murmurs of intermission, a sound that swelled quickly to fill the hall.

Hay moved to stand alongside the ambassador and his wife, from which place he beckoned to Adams. "Mr. Ambassador, Madame, I would like to present to you Mr. Henry Adams." They turned to look at him and Adams could see no way out. Resigned, he stepped down to their chairs, stood next to Hay, and forced a smile. At least he could turn his back toward Madame LeBlanc; this required him to step down nearly in front of the ambassador and to nudge Hay aside. Hay had nowhere to go but to cross in front of the ambassador, a bit of clumsiness and a breach of protocol that couldn't be helped. Maybe, just maybe, he could do this without warning Madame LeBlanc away.

"A pleasure," he said to the Duke, nodding.

"Ehhhhrgh," the Duke said, either acknowledging the introduction or clearing his throat.

"*Enchanté,*" Adams murmured to the dowager as he bowed and brought her hand near to his lips. She made a slight mewing sound in response. Adams held his bow for an instant, then deepened it as it occurred to him he could get a glimpse of the far balcony behind him, underneath his arm, as he did so. He could, and did: in a moment he had found Madame LeBlanc, who was holding opera glasses in hand, looking his way. He straightened and imagined he felt her vision, magnified, boring into his back.

"Mr. Adams is one of our finest historians," Hay said. "He's recently finished a round-the-world trip, haven't you, Mr. Adams? Tell the ambassador where you've been."

"Oh . . . Hawaii, Tahiti, Burma, Ceylon." He glanced at Hay, trying to discourage this attempt to draw him out. "*Panama.*" Let the ambassador ask about that, he thought, and see what Hay does.

"And he's been touring cathedrals. Chartres, Notre Dame. And the monastery at Mont-Saint-Michel."

Hay might be struggling, grasping at conversational straws, Adams thought, but that was no cause to pull someone else down with him.

"Cathedrals? Cathedrals?" The Duke raised an eyebrow.

"Yes. A developing interest of mine."

"Hrrrgh. Try Italy. Great churches there. What have the French ever done? Their best works are all Roman." Next to him the dowager studied his face, ready for his reply.

"Well." Adams looked to Hay for a clue as to how to proceed. "Ah yes. I suppose . . ." He wondered how much polite conversation he would be expected to make. He tried to see, out of the corner of his eye, if Madame LeBlanc was still in her seat. "Italy has some fine architecture, true. I'm more interested in the Gothic, though." The Italian ambassador turned a beady eye on him; it was clear he thought Adams had revealed a defect of taste. He risked a quick glance, but couldn't find her.

"Did I tell you Mr. Adams is one of our foremost historians?" Hay asked. "Perhaps you've heard of his *History of the United States of America during the Administrations of Thomas Jefferson and James Madison*? A masterful work. Definitive."

Adams waved the compliment away with the back of his hand. "It's . . ." Damn, he thought, I will actually have to do this. "Ah," he said, "as nothing compared with real history. Gibbon, for instance—*The Decline and Fall of the Roman Empire*. There was a historian." He put a smile on his face and tried to decide if he felt Madame LeBlanc's gaze on his back.

"Gibbon! Phah!" the Duke said, meaning to sound as if he were spitting, and nearly doing so. He pulled a handkerchief out of his breast pocket and dabbed at his mouth as he went on in a gurgling, wet voice that set Adams on edge: "What did he know? Nothing! Not a thing! Christianity the downfall of Roma. Beh!" The dowager stared straight ahead and fanned herself deliberately.

Adams fought back the urge to bolt. If he could find just the right unexpected gesture, shout the right word or make the right sudden movement, the ambassador and his wife would disappear in a puff of smoke.

"There is certainly room for disagreement about Gibbon, wouldn't you say, Mr. Adams?"

He didn't understand.

"The ambassador apparently has some strong opinions about Gibbon." The warning was clear in Hay's voice.

Hay needed something from him. He tried to think. "As well he might." He took a deep breath. "I only meant to say that my own humble efforts do not even measure up in scope of ambition or execution to what Gibbon attempted so mightily. Attempted—and failed, I might add. Yes, failure. Gibbon—what should we think of Gibbon? Yes. He saw what he brought, and he brought the French Revolution. Limited. Very limited.'' Adams shook his head and did his best to look sorrowful.

The scowl on the Duke's face diminished a few degrees, and the dowager actually smiled at him. At close range Adams could see that her face was heavily layered with white powder, and she had drawn a dark blue line on each eyelid, for a strangely doll-like effect. He made himself stop staring at it. The Duke nodded. ''The Roman Church,'' he croaked. ''There's a subject. There's history for you, as—arrgh—you please. You . . . write . . . mmm . . . about that.''

Adams looked at Hay as impatiently as he dared, a brief instant of wide-eyed warning. ''Excellent advice, Your Excellency. Excellently said. I'll be sure to keep it in mind.''

''*Bene, bene,*'' the Duke said, nodding and smiling and raising one claw-like hand in a gesture of absolution. The hand stopped in midair as a look of sudden curiosity came over the old man's face; then he was leaning over, coughing hard, a wet, gurgling cough, and sucking air sharply through his nose with a whistling sound before coughing again.

''Catarrh,'' the dowager said primly, fanning herself.

''Adams,'' Hay said, ''the ambassador appears to be in need of a glass of water. Could you get one for us, please?''

''Certainly.'' But instead of turning to leave he walked forward, in front of the ambassador and his wife, toward Hay. As he squeezed past, Hay was pressed tight against the railing and Adams held his friend's shoulders for safety. As they shuffled to exchange places, Adams leaned forward— the whole point of the maneuver—and whispered in his ear, ''You owe me.''

''For getting the water?''

''No.'' He switched to Hay's other ear as he moved past. ''For what I said about Gibbon.''

Adams found the stairs and went down, then made his way quickly around the back of the hall: her box had been below them and three or four back from the front. The ambassador could wait. To be on the safe side he checked the whole row, pulling curtains back slightly, peeking through, seeing the backs of men and women in evening clothes as they chatted. One box in the row was empty. He opened the curtain wide; she had gone. From the back of the empty box he squinted across the width of the opera house, finding Hay, who still stood, ministering to the ambassador. Could she have recognized him from this distance?

He heard a step outside and drew back, trying to tuck himself into a fold of the curtain. Whoever it was had paused outside the box. As Adams watched, the curtains drew back and a head appeared thrust between them: oiled hair, no beard. The head rotated left, then right. The man's wide-set, bulging eyes stared right at him. Delahaye! Involuntarily Adams drew back, but it was no use. The deputy took his measure for a moment, and then as suddenly as his head had appeared, it was gone.

Adams waited for a moment, recovering his nerve, before heading for the lobby. He kept an eye out for Delahaye and for Madame LeBlanc. What had the deputy wanted with her?

At the top of the Grand Staircase he paused to survey the crowd and was promptly jostled from behind. He squirmed out of the line of traffic and stood at the red marble balustrade to look down on the lobby. Around him was the continuous slow rustle of intermission, women's skirts pumping languidly, men starched and crisp in their evening clothes. Below the staircase the lobby floor was a hummocky plain of heads and women's hats, spiked with feathers that pointed this way and that, with fumaroles of cigar smoke rising here and there from the black-suited men between them. The Culebra Cut, he thought, done as a costume party. On the ceiling Apollo in his chariot was blued by haze.

Adams didn't see her anywhere. Had she worn a hat? He couldn't remember, hadn't even noticed. He scanned the crowd for purple.

He turned to survey the staircase and saw a familiar face on the landing halfway down: Elizabeth, standing with the senator. She was striking in any setting; here, in evening clothes, she drew glances from nearly all who promenaded past her. He was about to duck away—the Camerons were a complication he didn't need—but Elizabeth spotted him and waved. He waved back. No choice: he entered the stream and was carried down toward them.

"Well, there you are!" Elizabeth said. "We waited and then looked for you at your rooms, but you were gone. Is something the matter?"

"No, no, some business came up. I'm sorry. An unexpected trip. Downtown. I had to leave in a hurry. An errand." From his new vantage he could see the people who milled about under the Grand Staircase.

"I'm sure it must have been important." She waited, expecting enlightenment, but he was looking past her. Donald Cameron stepped into the pause. "Good to see you, Adams. Glad you finally made it. Enjoying the opera?"

"Yes." Adams smiled automatically and met the senator's eyes briefly. "Magnificent." He pressed forward to avoid being entangled in the traffic that passed at his back. There—a flash of purple, at the base of the staircase. He waited for the woman to come back into view from behind the statuary on the newel posts, the draped nymphs who held candelabra in their upraised arms. No: not her.

"I don't think I'd call it magnificent," Elizabeth said, glancing sidelong at her husband. "I think it simple, musically, and a little too political for my taste. Who is this man Bruneau? Does anyone know one thing about him? This is the trouble with premieres. You just don't know, do you, what you're going to get. *The Attack on the Mill.* Give me *Rigoletto* any day."

"*Rigoletto*—that's the one with the clown." Donald Cameron eyed a man who eyed his wife as he descended past them.

"Mmmm," Elizabeth said, confirming her husband without looking away from Adams. "It's a wonderful opera. You've seen it, remember, Henry? There's that aria the Duke sings in the third act—*La donna è mobile.* Woman is fickle. Beautiful song, but I'm not so sure I agree with the sentiment. Do you?"

He sensed a subterranean import but he hadn't been paying enough attention. "Ah, no. Not necessarily." What was Elizabeth asking, what had he told her? Would an affirmation have better represented him?

"Ah, but '*Questa o quella*,' this one or that, you'd have to say the Duke is fickle himself," Cameron allowed. " 'Constancy, that tyrant of the heart. At husbands' jealous fury I mock.' Not a good neighbor, you'd have to say. No. Not a true friend." Cameron was looking at Adams.

"Definitely not," Adams agreed. The three of them stood silent for a moment until Adams remembered his mission. "You must excuse me. I'm on an errand for Hay. I have to get a drink of something for the Italian ambassador."

"Oh, that's where you are," Elizabeth said. "I thought we'd all be sitting together."

"Yes, we were, but my plans got changed," Adams explained. "I just arrived and I don't think I'm going to stay. More of this business. Is there any place to get a glass of water?"

"Here, take this," Cameron offered, digging into a pocket in his evening coat and producing a silver flask. "Best thing."

Adams thanked him, promising to return it when they got back to the hotel. "Don't like Italian opera," Adams heard Cameron announce to his wife. "Give me the Germans any day." From the top of the staircase Adams looked back. Elizabeth had watched him ascend and now smiled at him. He smiled and nodded before he headed down the corridor.

Back in the ambassador's box Adams uncapped the flask and handed it to Hay, who held it to the ambassador's lips. The ambassador took a draught, then stopped and spit it out on the carpet, coughing. "*Maledizione!*" he gasped. "Poison!" He glowered at Adams.

"*Che? Che?*" the Dowager asked, sharp and birdlike.

"*Liquore*," the ambassador growled.

"*Liquore? Liquore?*" The dowager was horrified. "*Temporanza*," she said to Adams emphatically. "*Temporanza*, no, no, no. Teetotaling. *O Stelle!*" she murmured, looking away and fanning herself.

"I couldn't find any water," Adams explained. "It was the best I could do."

"Adams," Hay said. "The man is a cornerstone of the

Italian temperance movement." He shook his head. "Where did you get this?"

"Cameron."

Hay rolled his eyes. "Perhaps," he said slowly, "you should excuse yourself. I think you've done enough for one night."

Adams looked at the Italian ambassador, slumped in his chair, smoldering at him; and at the dowager, who stared off at the curtain on the stage, her lips pursed in disapproval, which cracked her powder-caked wrinkles into clear relief, like the lines on maps that radiate out from mountain peaks. "I'm sorry," he said. "You're right." He nodded toward the back of the box. "Will you show me out?" He gazed levelly at Hay, impressing on him that he ought not to say no.

"Madame LeBlanc is gone," he whispered when they reached the hallway. "I need that address."

Hay looked at him before answering slowly. "One seventy-five, rue Lavoisier," he said. Adams started off. "Adams—" Hay called after him. "Oh, never mind."

"I'll be fine," Adams told him. "Don't worry. And I'm sorry, Hay. About that." He nodded toward the Italian ambassador.

"Don't worry. I can salvage it." Hay watched Adams's receding figure. "I always do," he added, speaking softly, so that his friend wouldn't hear.

9:30 P.M.

RUE LAVOISIER WAS a short, quiet street just off one of the broad boulevards that Baron Haussmann, Napoleon's chief city engineer, had carved through the heart of Paris, as straight and broad as the cut that Lesseps had meant to make in Panama. There was much talk of their benefits—the improved traffic flow, the sanitation, the water systems that lay beneath them, the benefits to commerce and industry—but on the whole Adams thought these boulevards ugly. They were too large, too wide; the human form seemed dwarfed between curbs fifty yards apart. People could talk all they wanted about the scientific and rational approach to public works but he suspected another reason, never given in public: the boulevards gave a clear field of fire for the Emperor's dragoons. In any civic tumult the citizens gather in the streets, and the boulevards would give them less protection than the knotted, twisting streets they had replaced. If Louis XVI had been able to give his soldiers this kind of tactical advantage, Adams thought, the Revolution might have had a different outcome.

The stone townhouses on rue Lavoisier presented a regimented succession of stoops and ironwork railings; a moistness in the air, a wet anticipation of rain, gave the street a riparian feel. Its end was framed by tall wooden poles that carried their burden of telegraph wires toward the stock exchange. In the other direction he saw the Chapel of Expiation, a church built to commemorate Louis XVI and Marie Antoinette, guillotined during the Revolution. As his cab wheeled toward it, he was struck by the thought that the chapel's moral influence did not extend very far into the surrounding neighborhood. On the Ile de la Cité Notre Dame stood clearly as the moral center of the city, arguably of all France; its towering spire and its sweeping buttresses carved the entire world of action and belief into right and wrong as clearly as the island divided the Seine. Or the cathedral with its stained glass was a kind of lamp, source of an invisible force, like the *epistemes* the Greeks used to believe in, only instead of carrying vision this substance carried moral knowledge; it made virtue possible in the world. A thirteenth-century lamp, one whose lights could dazzle, but which seemed unequal to the task of enlightening the modern age. You had to go inside to see the effects of the glass, and the world could not be made to enter. And below the church the very earth it stood on was riddled through, like a termite-weakened beam, with the chases and conduits of a different sort of power. Above the ground commerce and science had nearly evaporated the church's medium, the thin ether of conscience through which the church's power is propagated—invisibly, like the force that has a flock of starlings whirl in unison.

Maybe every church has its emanations, maybe every church stands as a symbol for something in the lives of those who live within its purview. He scanned the buildings as they passed. On this street, in one of these houses, women sold themselves to men—to powerful men who could not fail to see the chapel as they stepped out onto the curb afterward, their bodies sated by their indulgence of lust, their minds turning over some twist of policy or maneuver by which they hoped to outpace their rivals, and like as not, if Delahaye's accusations were correct, their pockets filled with the immoral largesse of the canal company. He imagined these men waiting for cabs, looking ahead to an appointment at the club or to dinner with their families, their souls small, wrinkled, and loose within them, rattling about like a raisin in an otherwise empty cup, too small to feel the forces that might act upon it.

There was a lesson here, he thought, about dedicating churches to mortals.

Outside 175 Adams told the cabbie to wait. "Certainly, monsieur." The cabbie shrugged and grinned, the broad, slack width of his lower lip curving out and nearly doubling over onto the stubble of his face. "It's early yet," he said. "The ladies might not be receptive."

Adams looked at the man for a moment, but decided that explanation was useless. He turned and walked up a flight of granite steps to the door.

He was about to ring the bell when he saw, through the sheaf-of-wheat designs etched into the glass pane of the front door, the back of a man standing in the brightly lit hall. The man gestured with a hat in his right hand: he was talking to someone, a woman whose dress showed like a purple corona in the eclipse of his dark overcoat. His voice came through the door, muffled and indistinct but unmistakable in tone. He was angry. He pointed with his hat, spoke a low, growling sentence whose cadences thudded against the glass of the door like hail on a carriage roof, and spun on his heel.

Adams stood back, out of the light. In the glimpse he caught of the man there had been something familiar: graying hair and a long, pointed chin. When the man passed on the stoop Adams recognized him: Monsieur Loubet, the premier.

First Delahaye, now Loubet. What was the connection? He waited in the shadows until Loubet was gone before ringing the bell. He was let in by a woman servant who asked him to wait. As he measured his shoe against the marble parquet in the floor, he thought: What had gotten Loubet so angry? Was her rendezvous with him what drew Madame LeBlanc away from the opera? He tested the polish on the newel post with a finger.

In a few moments Madame LeBlanc appeared, holding her gloves in one hand. She looked to be in her mid-thirties. With her high, wide cheekbones and almond-shaped eyes she was pretty, he supposed, in a feline sort of way. Without opening her mouth she licked her teeth, a gesture that might have been sensual had it not been performed with brusque efficiency. He thought to see if she had been crying, but could find no trace of it. "Yes?" she said.

"I am Henry Adams." He paused a moment to see if the introduction would be mutual. It wasn't. "I am looking for a woman named Miriam Talbott and I have reason to believe that you might be able to help me."

Madame LeBlanc stared at him before speaking. "Come with me." She swept through a pair of oak doors to his left, waited for him to follow, then shut the doors behind him. He saw couches—rather more than one might have expected in a sitting room—and smelled a scent, strong and flowery, too sweet to be genuine. It was the scent of mingled perfumes, as tight and lush as the cushioned backs of the couches, with something else mixed in; cinnamon, he thought, and some other sort of spice, and above these, like the dictates of moral truth transcending mere sentiment, the piercing, unmistakable smell of ammonia. Madame LeBlanc walked past him and didn't speak until she had turned to him from behind the narrow mahogany desk that faced the door. "What do you know of Miriam Talbott?"

"She is a friend of mine." Adams thought her tone abrupt.

"How do you know her?"

"I spent some time with her in the country. Chartres, Pontorson. We became friends."

Madame LeBlanc's face was impassive. "Miriam Talbott is dead."

"No," Adams said. "She isn't. The body the police have is not that of Miriam Talbott."

"Miriam Talbott has never been to Chartres. She died sometime late last night near the quai de Valmy," Madame LeBlanc said flatly. "I have seen the body. Believe me, it is a body that is known to me."

Adams was repulsed by the thought that this woman had an entrepreneur's interest in the female form. "I've seen the body, too," he insisted, "and it is not Miss Talbott."

She didn't respond. He felt at an impasse. "The woman I am looking for," he started over, "is an American woman, a young woman, a painter. She's an art student, she lives here in Paris. She has blond hair, dark eyebrows. She had a dimple in her chin," he said, his hand rising and nearly touching his own chin, "and her eyes . . . her eyes are blue. Do you know a woman of that description? Apparently there has been some confusion," he finished lamely.

"I know of no such woman," Madame LeBlanc said. "Now if you will excuse me, I have preparations to make." She did not move, but reached a hand beneath the desk. In a moment the servant woman opened the door behind him.

"I saw you at her hotel this afternoon," Adams said.

"Impossible. I was here, tending to my accounts, all day. Now, please. I have work to do. Avril," she called, "show our visitor out."

The maid moved toward him. Adams turned to go but stopped. Loubet had been angry at her. She had been at Miriam's—had most likely been the reason the concierge there grew uncommunicative—and was lying about it. What was the connection? Why had Loubet been shouting? Why this secrecy about Miriam Talbott?

She would deny everything. He could not, as he stood there, think of how to ask a question that might get him information he wanted. "They say that the Panama scandal has its roots here. Is that true? Was Miss Talbott involved? Who is the woman in the morgue, the one you claim is Miss Talbott?"

"Avril, please." The maid took his arm and he thought for a moment of resisting but realized it could do no good. He let himself be shown to the door.

"A bit too early, weren't it, monsieur," the cabbie said, spitting into the street. "Or was the service very efficient?" The cabbie grinned.

Adams glanced down the street left and right, but no other cabs were in sight. "Rue Christophe-Colomb," he said, climbing in. "No," he commanded when he had sat, "make that boulevard des Capucines." Back toward the Opéra; he'd find another cab there.

Adams paid the cabbie off near a news kiosk and, on impulse, bought an evening paper from the potato-faced man inside. If Madame LeBlanc proved to be a dead end, he would have to work with what he had: the body of a woman who had pretended to be Miriam Talbott, somehow connected to the body of one Jacques de Reinach, whose death had prompted a commotion in the Chamber of Deputies, where Loubet and Delahaye held office. The paper ought to have something on this man Reinach. He retraced his last few steps back to the kiosk, to buy a handful of papers. It would be best to have all points of view represented.

At a table in the window of a quiet, nearly deserted restaurant, he ordered a glass of wine and began. Delahaye's speech had occurred too late to be reported; it would be a front-page item in the morning. He began looking for Reinach's obituary. Dead at age fifty-six of cerebral congestion, *Le Figaro* said, noting he had been the chief financial officer and a director of the Compagnie Universelle du Canal Interocéanique. *Le Temps* had a long and respectful account of his life: founder of the Paris banking firm of Kohn, Reinach, et Compagnie; railroad financier and speculator; partner in the Türr syndicate, along with Cornelius Herz ("the distinguished inventor and entrepreneur"), Charles Cousin ("the well-known owner of France's largest railroad"), and "the Saint-Simonian financier," Isaac Periere. (The article explained that Periere, following the teachings of Saint-Simon, believed in industrial progress as a moral duty; for him technology was a kind of religion. Adams recalled vaguely that decades ago a group of Saint-Simonian pilgrims had, with more enthusiasm than planning, begun the work at Suez that eventually produced a canal.) Reinach's fortunes had turned with Panama, and he had been devastated by the bankruptcy of the company in 1889, a collapse that the paper implied was due to mismanagement and the manipulations of foreign financiers.

La Libre Parole (publisher, Edouard Drumont—Hay's good hater, he recalled) excoriated Reinach as part of the Jewish conspiracy to drain France of its lifeblood, and dwelt in some detail on "La Débâcle"—the crash of the Panama company, which "assaulted 800,000 French men and women, pensioners and widows, with the levelling hand of poverty as it wiped out the savings that they had so nobly entrusted to the cause." One and a half billion francs of stock had been sold in the company's ten years, which meant a hundred and fifty million francs a year had been taken out of France in order to move mud, to kill a small army of workers, and to leave machinery of Gallic design scattered, rusting, in the tropical jungle. Adams calculated: something on the order of thirty million dollars, a sizable chunk of their entire economy, year after year. Could it have been a tenth of France's annual investment? *That* would be a fine irony— a tithe for the new god of steam. And what had its priests accomplished? They had cut down some trees, scratched a line across the skinny leg of a continent, made twenty thousand not totally voluntary martyrs to the cause. And they had put a permanent crimp in the prospects of French power in the world: those billions were gone, billions not spent on factories or schools or ships or armies or any of the other engines of national power; France had lost ground in the race for industrial might, was behind the place she'd have had if Dingler and Reinach and Lesseps had never swaggered, metaphorically, into those grasping, malarial jungles. Adams spied a difficult lesson for the new industrial bourgeoisie, one that by nature they could learn only with difficulty, since it contravened their social experience: cash flow alone doesn't establish power—the spirit of national power, though partial to the wealthy, is not to be wooed through vulgar, spendthrift display.

He had been staring out the window. He picked up another paper and scanned it for its obituary, then another, and another. There was a depressing sameness to them. Drumont's gave the clearest voice to what apparently was popular opinion, an opinion that allowed the French, peasant and statesman alike, some measure of self-respect. Most of the money, Drumont charged, had never been brought to bear on the problems in Panama, but had "lined the pockets of corrupt politicians and greedy financiers. When the truth of Panama is known," it continued, "the Jew Reinach will be seen to have cheated not only the people of France, but Justice herself, by administering her inescapable sentence in advance of her inevitable judgment."

He shook his head. How was Miriam involved in this? He looked out at the street where a light drizzle had begun to fall. A liveried coachman unfurled the canvas side curtains of a carriage, protecting its passenger, and behind him little wisps of steam rose from the streetlamp as rain hit hot tin. The cobbles shone in the gaslight, scattering it in a hundred confusing directions.

Tuesday,
NOVEMBER 22,
1892

6:30 A.M.

THE RAPPING HAD been going on for some time. "Adams," a man's voice called. "Hello? Adams?" Cameron. Adams found his watch on the nightstand and clicked it open. The rapping continued.

"Just a minute," he called. The senator was up early; most mornings, Adams understood from Elizabeth, he didn't rise until eight or so. Adams pulled on his robe and looked for his slippers; he had wanted to be up and writing half an hour ago. "I'm coming." He made his way deliberately to the door, shuffling his right foot to get it seated in its slipper.

"Hope you'll forgive me," Cameron said when Adams opened the door. "I've got to be downtown soon, but I wanted to talk to you."

"I understand." Adams stood for a moment looking up into the composed, jowly sincerity of Cameron's face. The senator looked as though he had been up all night, and he smelled of alcohol.

"I woke you, didn't I?" He didn't wait for an answer. "May I come in?"

"Oh. Yes. Please." Adams stood back and Cameron wandered into the center of the room, his hands clasped behind his back.

"Can I fix you some tea?" Adams asked. "I'm afraid I don't have any coffee."

"Tea would be fine," Cameron called over his shoulder.

As Adams put a match to the burner in the small kitchenette, he saw Cameron come to a stop at the window, where he held back the curtain with a hand. "Wonderful view you have here," he said.

"Same as yours, I imagine," Adams said, shrugging.

"No," Cameron said. "You're that much higher. It makes a difference." Adams could sense Cameron looking at him but didn't glance up from spooning out the tea: two tablespoons, just so. "Well," Cameron said brightly, turning back to the window, "Paris after a rain. Magnificent. Makes you feel . . . Clean. New. Fit as a fiddle and young again, eh?"

"No coal smoke," Adams allowed, replacing the lid of the tea tin.

"Hmmm?"

"No coal smoke," he repeated, more loudly. He slid the tea tin onto its shelf and glanced at Cameron. "The rain cleans the air. Knocks down the coal smell." He found an extra cup in the cupboard and set it out on its saucer, next to his own.

"Oh." Cameron nodded and leaned closer to the window to peer up and down the street. "Well, a fine city. Sparkling. Jewel of Europe. Enjoying your stay?"

"So far. I've been keeping busy."

Cameron let the curtain fall closed and Adams saw his eye land on the writing desk where he had left Dingler's photograph. He had meant to put it away. Cameron was leaning over to study it. "Ah, the Tiger," he said, tapping the picture with a forefinger. "Clemenceau."

"You know one of those men?"

"This one. Met him once, a few years ago." Cameron picked up the picture and held it close to his face, then extended it to Adams with a finger marking one face. Adams moved over to see. "Visiting fireman, brotherhood-of-legislators sort of thing. Not a man you forget. Fierce. Quite fierce, forensically speaking. A duellist, too, I hear. Killed a man is the story I heard. Some sort of insult. Still, not a bad sort, for a Socialist." Cameron's index finger lay just above the second figure from the left, a tall, thin man with a shock of light-colored hair, gaunt cheeks, and a thick mustache. "Has an American wife, you know."

"No, I didn't."

"No, I didn't mean to imply that you did. I mean, why would you? No reason, no reason, no reason at all, really." Cameron licked his lips and set the picture down on the desktop. For an awkward moment the two men stood near each other, uncomfortable.

"So what do you know about Clemenceau?" Adams asked, moving back to the stove to stand by the kettle. "Is he involved in this Panama affair at all?"

"The Panama affair?"

"The scandal. You must have heard about it."

"Oh, oh yes. That. Well, won't that be the pickle. A vote of confidence today, I hear. It probably won't go well, not at all. A shame. Finally France has a government you can talk to, get along with, and first thing you know, it's going to go under." Cameron shook his head. "These Boulangists, I don't know about them. Can't do business with them. Too, too . . . charged up. The one true faith. Everyone else is wrong, stupid, evil."

"And Clemenceau? Do you think he's involved?"

Cameron shrugged. "Don't think so. Too shrewd. But who knows. Why?"

"No reason." He didn't want to explain about Miriam, about the possibility of her involvement, about his need to pursue any chance of finding her. "But you didn't come to talk to me about Clemenceau."

"Ah, no." Cameron tented a hand on the desktop, steadying himself, trying to look casual. "It's about Lizzie." He looked down at the desk as he spoke. Adams waited. He had suspected as much. Even so, at the actual introduction of the topic he felt a pit open in his stomach. He tried to close it through sheer will.

Cameron took a breath and began. "Last night was—difficult. After the opera. She was upset, very upset. I—that is, she; she didn't or rather couldn't—I mean, all that I could get from her was that you were somehow involved. She said, ask you." With his head tilted to one side, still looking at the desk, Cameron held a hand up to forestall an objection that Adams hadn't made. "I know. Presumptuous. But it's no secret that she's fond of you. Enormously fond of you."

Cameron seemed to expect a response. "Yes."

"And, well, I was wondering. Exactly how, ah, *reciprocal* this whole business is. You and she. Vis-à-vis this, this fondness."

"Am I fond of her?"

"Well, yes. In a nutshell."

"Yes," Adams told him. "I'm fond of her."

"Yes. Of course," Cameron said, looking up. "Everyone's *fond* of her. We're all very fond of everybody, aren't we? But I mean," he said, meeting Adams's eyes, "*fond* of her. You know."

Adams knew. But how could he answer? To a mind as evenly divided as his—a mind, his brother Brooks had warned him, that would never find a place in politics, where simplicity of vision was required; a mind to which evil never seemed unmixed with good, nor good unalloyed with evil; one to which no object appeared important enough to call out strength of action, nor absolutely necessary enough not to allow that its absence just might be possible to accommodate—to such a mind, the only accurate answer to bluntness was contradiction: yes and no. Need he count up the considerations that weighed on each side? On one side of the scale put Elizabeth's beauty, and her charm, yes, and the sympathy he felt for her—especially the sympathy he felt for her because of her attachment to this boor, this specimen of manhood before him, who had as much as paid for his bride (her brothers had insisted on the match, as the only means to salvage their father's business; and indeed, that enterprise had reversed direction remarkably, thanks to post-nuptial infusions of Cameron's capital), this fool whose family fortunes had been made on the shadowy ground where politics and railroads were joined, and whose own hereditary political claim had no greater merit, but much greater practical success, than Adams's. And, too, if he were to be frank with himself, there was his own need to find himself mirrored in the regard of a woman he admired. Elizabeth did this. Oh, she did this admirably. In the years since Clover's death he had found great solace there: in Elizabeth's slate-blue eyes he was engaging, clever, interesting, profound. And if at times he saw mirrored there his own ambivalent cast of mind—if she was moody and seemed now and then impatient or uninterested—that was only fair.

But, as against that, an equal and opposite heft, an amalgam: memory, inertia, fear, habit. Its shape was not so fully available to him; it seemed more an emptiness, a great vacuum that nevertheless had weight—an infinitely variable weight, for it adjusted automatically to whatever sentiments or thoughts could be arrayed in balance against it, exactly cancelling them, leaving him stymied—like Aesop's lazy donkey, who starved, equidistant from two piles of hay.

"Damnit!" Cameron muttered, exasperated with himself. "This is awkward. I suppose I have to be straight. What I'm asking—what I'm trying to get at here is, are the two of you in love, exactly, or what?"

Were the two of them in love? Adams wanted to answer exactly. But he could answer only for himself; he couldn't answer for another. For a moment he felt the possibility of a rhetorician's solution: "*Distingué!*" Master Tower would have cried. You must distinguish, must divide the question; and if the question is flawed, it need not be answered.

No. There was no room for sophistry, for an aggressive quibble about the letter rather than the spirit of what was being asked. Cameron's intent was clear. Put the question: Was he in love?

Yes. And of course, no.

Love is an unalloyed emotion, unmixed, unambiguous. He felt ambiguous. Therefore—

"Right. Well then. Good."

He must have moved his head. Cameron rapped on the desk twice, quickly, a gesture of finality, or perhaps of superstition. It seemed to Adams that as the breath of contained worry within him was expelled, Cameron lost an inch of height. "Lizzie and I, well, it's no secret. We haven't been that close. Lately. These last few years. I was just wondering. She seems so . . . so angry these days. Yesterday, mostly. I don't know what it is. I thought perhaps you and she . . . Some sort of argument, perhaps . . ." The senator shrugged, leaving open a range of answers he had no doubt imagined. His face was guileless, open to all possibilities. Delicacy, Adams thought, is a steep ramp, against which even the energy of possessive curiosity must falter. And yet Cameron had managed to suggest his question.

With his eyes on Cameron's Adams shook his head. "I don't know." He moved to the stove, where the kettle had begun to hiss. It would boil soon. Could he reasonably make tea with water that hadn't quite boiled? He didn't want to have to turn around, didn't want Cameron to see his face.

"Yes," Cameron said, somewhere behind him. "Well."

Adams busied himself setting out sugar and cream on a tray. When he was done he decided the water was hot enough. Neither of them spoke as Adams poured it into the teapot. These tasks done, he could think of nothing else to occupy himself. When he finally turned, Cameron met his eyes and studied his face coolly. The sustained attention was making him uncomfortable, but something told Adams that he would be telling Cameron the wrong thing if he looked away.

"It'll just be a minute." Then, as an afterthought, Adams added, "It needs to steep."

Cameron nodded and turned, strolling back to the window, where he fingered aside the curtain again to glance absently at the street. Had he, Adams wondered, seen his true thoughts?

"She is moody, isn't she? Lizzie."

"Yes," Adams answered cautiously.

"Hard to live with sometimes."

"I can imagine." Was that appropriate? Ought he to tell a man he could imagine living with his wife? "It must be hard," Adams went on, quickly, "living with a woman that other men find so attractive."

Cameron frowned and stared at him for an instant. "Yes."

"That tea's probably ready now," Adams allowed. "I'll just go get it."

Cameron stood at the window while Adams poured, waiting for him to finish before speaking. "Lizzie's fond of you," he said when Adams had set the pot down. "Very fond of you. And this makes me think that you are the one person of whom I can ask this favor." Cameron turned to face him. "Would you—would you be so kind as to spend some time with her today? If you could find out what is disturbing her, I would greatly appreciate it. I believe she wants to go to the Louvre. Perhaps you could take her.''

Adams stirred a spoonful of sugar into his tea. When he felt its grit completely disappear, he answered. ''I'll do what I can.''

The two men stood in the middle of Adams's sitting room, saucers in hand, facing each other. ''Well,'' Cameron said, setting down his full teacup. ''Thank you for the tea. I must be off now.'' With his hand on the doorknob he paused. ''I am pleased that my wife has a friend such as you,'' he said quickly. ''You amuse her; and I find you trustworthy. This combination is not as common as you might think.'' Cameron squinted at Adams, the sagging flesh below each of his eyes stretching upward as if gathered by a drawstring. Adams had the impression that Cameron was weighing him against an idea that was familiar and troubling, like an old bunion. ''I won't stand for a scandal in my life,'' Cameron said quietly. ''My wife bores easily, and ours was never really a love match. You know that, I know that. But I'm sure you're a gentleman.''

The senator's casual pose had been belied by his voice. Clearly he waited for some word from Adams that would demonstrate agreement; just as clearly, Adams knew, he could not fail to give it.

''I understand,'' he murmured.

7:00 A.M.

AT HIS DESK Adams tried to push Cameron's visit from his mind. It had been years since he had experienced the imposed discipline of writing first thing in the morning as a constraint, but this morning he was having difficulty concentrating. He looked through his notebook, finding a page he had written the week before:

Fenestration: one becomes pedantic and pretentious at the very sound of the word, but Chartres is all windows, and its windows are as triumphant as its Virgin, and were one of her miracles. One can no more overlook the windows of Chartres than the glass which is in them. That glass is the most splendid color decoration the world ever saw, since no other material, neither silk nor gold, and no opaque color laid on with a brush, can compare with translucent glass. Even the Ravenna mosaics or Chinese porcelains are darkness beside them. The claim may not be modest, but that is none of ours: the Virgin answers for all sins—including excessive celebration of works done in her glory.

He had written this while seated in the nave of the cathedral, a hundred feet below the center of the forty-four-foot-in-diameter west rose, Miriam next to him, binocle in hand.

He scarcely had to shut his eyes to picture her: the way she tilted up her face, inviting him to see how the light in the transept colored all it fell across, her skin tinted red and amber and gold and blue by turns, the coloring subtle, wonderfully subtle . . .

Idly he wrote her name in his notebook, finding pleasure in the rhythms of the up-and-down strokes, feeling the sheer mechanical movement of writing so much that he was led to corrupt the *r* into a narrow thing with hardly any hip to it; then up and down again and on into the round sweep of the *a*, back down and up for its rounded closure, and then, with a regular pace, the three equal strokes of the final *m* as a sort of return and consummation, a musical signature: ta-da-da. How close her name was to Clover's given name, yet how different it was to write: plainer, more direct, a solid metronome of pen scratches, not the medley of strokes and roundnesses that formed "Marian."

Miriam, he wrote again. Where was she? What could her absence mean? Why had a woman carrying Reinach's card been using her name?

He determined to do something. Quickly, with no thought for the texture and motion of the writing, he made a list of what he understood to be his choices, running down the page. The concierge at Miriam's apartment. Madame LeBlanc. Loubet. Delahaye. Reinach, at the morgue. Pettibois—the police. Another moment's thought brought him another possibility: "Scene of that woman's death," after which he wrote quickly, "Morgue"; then, below that, "whole Panama scandal."

Adams drew a vertical line down the center of the page, establishing these entries as a column. On the right side of the page, another column; he would need help. "Hay," he wrote. One entry to balance a whole list. In the lower right quadrant of the paper he began a new category, neither leads nor helpers but something else. He scratched onto the page the names of Elizabeth, Cameron, Amanda. Getting them out and onto the paper seemed to clarify things: he wasn't forgetting them, because there they were. He looked again at his list and made his choice.

The roofs of Paris, catching their first strong light of the morning, smoked with drying dew. As Adams left the hotel on rue Christophe-Colomb he noticed that with the aromas of sulphured coal smoke and sewage gone, the city smelled of open fields and pastures, as if the rain had washed the current character of the city off its streets and paving stones and freed them to expire the smells of an older Paris: sweet haymow and dung, damp earth and wood. The rain had accomplished a sort of olfactory archaeology: as he walked beneath the tulip and sycamore trees that lined the street, scuffling wet leaves, he half expected to meet a representative of some long-gone tribe of Franks, who, rudely clad and muscular, would nod in acknowledgment as he passed.

Once he had gotten a cab and was making his way on the boulevard, he noticed there was a peculiar feel to the city, one he couldn't quite place: in spite of the freshness of the morning, its inhabitants seemed distracted. He made a study: whenever he passed another vehicle and attempted to make eye contact, invariably the occupant stared back blankly or turned away. And then Adams realized what had thrown him off. There were no voices to be heard, not even at the intersections, where traffic usually sorted itself out with shouts and grumbles. The clatter of wheels, the hollow echoing clop of hooves on pavement, the continual jangle of harness and hitch, all these were an eerie counterpoint to the human silence. It was as though overnight a formal distance had been inserted between everyone. The traffic seemed slower, more deliberate in its movements, its general disordered tumult tamed somehow; every carriage and cab and cart, all the pedestrians, the pairs of policemen strolling side by side, each worker and walker and cabbie and horse, every person and thing he saw was part of this delicate treading on toe tips, a mood made of incipient intention, like a word caught in the throat.

It wasn't until he saw the headline on a paper in a passing carriage that he remembered: GOVERNMENT TO FALL, *La Libre Parole* was prophesizing in two-hundred-point type. Of course: the political culture of the city was under siege. It was a wonder that Paris hadn't slipped back completely to a state of nature, a war of all against all. He began observing the Parisians around him with a sharpened eye, looking for some symptom, some characteristic of a people forewarned of the dissolution of public authority. What he had seen as lethargy now appeared as caution: these people were moving more slowly, not because they were tired, but because they were afraid, fearful of energy liberated by an insecurity of form. Now the freshness of the morning seemed not a bright promise but a warning, and he felt an urge to instruct his cabbie to heed it, if only there were words to make it sensible.

At the morgue he was refused admittance beyond the double doors; he would not be permitted to see the body again, nor would he be allowed to view the personal effects that had been with it. The fat coroner behind his desk sorted stacks of files and kept an eye on him as he paced to the door and peered through glass with screen reinforcement embedded within it. He saw a white-smocked figure bending over the woman's body, holding a tape measure along its length.

"What's that man doing?" he asked the coroner.

"Bertillonage," the coroner grunted.

"And what is that?" Adams asked politely.

"Science." The coroner shrugged. "Identification." He continued shuffling through papers in a file folder and Adams thought that he would get no further elaboration, until without looking up, the coroner slid a sheet of paper out of the file and across the desk in Adams's general direction. Uncertain, Adams took it; the coroner did not object.

It was a form labelled "Bertillonage Report," and contained eleven boxes with numbers in them. He translated the categories: height, length of head, breadth of head, length of right ear, length of right lower arm (elbow to tip, middle finger), length of right middle finger, length of ring finger, length of left foot, length of trunk, span of outstretched arms.

"In combination, these measurements can be used to identify individuals," the coroner said. "That is the theory, at any rate."

Adams nodded. Each measurement in itself wouldn't be definitive, but added one to another, combined, they might have the power to distinguish. He looked at his own fingers, comparing them. "Why is it called 'Bertillonage'?" He handed the page back.

"Ask him," the coroner said, "in there." He jerked his head toward the double doors before burying his face in an open file folder.

Adams moved to the doors and was stopped by the coroner's throat clearing. The coroner frowned at him and wagged his pencil before pointing with it toward a bench on the wall opposite his desk. He watched until Adams sat down.

Seated, Adams ventured another question. "Could I see the file for a body you have here, a woman you have provisionally identified as Miriam Talbott?"

The coroner shook his head. "Our information is not public."

Adams waited about ten minutes before the double doors to the mortuary swung open and the white-smocked figure, a young man with curly hair, emerged. He handed the coroner a folder and spoke quickly and quietly, saying something Adams couldn't catch. Adams rose to stand behind him, then cleared his throat. The young man's face was round and smooth, yet held a suggestion of the sort of knowledge that morgue duty might bring; or perhaps what Adams saw was less a positive mark of understanding than the residual sign of a retreating naïveté, some quality of muscle tension and thickened skin left in the wake of his ignorance, like a foam line left by a retreating wave. The tightness at his eyes contrasted with the milky plumpness of his cheek and the smooth beardless skin of his jaw. It was difficult to tell how old the young man was; he could have been anything from twenty to thirty-five. He was, Adams thought, a man whose looks would improve with age.

The young man could offer Adams no help. No, he could not let him see the body again; the coroner was about to begin the autopsy. No, he could not show Adams the Bertillonage report. No, he could not discuss the circumstances of the death. Behind his desk the rotund coroner rolled his chair toward the wall and leaned back, the chair's spring-loaded hinge protesting; he stretched his hands to lock them behind his head, taking care not to disturb the oily smoothness of his hair when he rested it against his palms. A darkened spot on the wall suggested that he wasn't always so careful to use his fingers as an antimacassar. He smiled at Adams, a smile genuine and, Adams thought, malicious.

The young man had also seen that smile. "Tell you what," he said. "I can't give you this information, but my superior can." The chair squeaked again as the coroner rotated into an upright position. The smile was gone, replaced by bureaucratic impassivity. "It's a short walk," the young man said, sliding some papers into a briefcase and fastening it. "Care to come with me?"

8:00 A.M.

TO GET TO the prefecture of police from the morgue one must walk downstream along the Seine past the Cathedral of Notre Dame. To a tourist at the top of the Eiffel Tower, the cathedral in the light of a November morning would appear to rise above a misshapen sea of partially defoliated trees. Motionless in the quiet air, compressed by distance, their limbs become a false base against which to measure the structure. The flying buttresses are robbed of some part of their height and no longer soar as daringly; they seem a frail afterthought, a decorative element unrelated to the architectural problem of enclosing a vast chamber with stone. From the path on which Adams and the young man walked, the height of the cathedral was effectively disguised by foliage. When, out of the corner of his eye, Adams first registered the building through the shifting gaps in the leaves, its size led his reasoning mind to unreasonable explanation: he first thought the sky itself had been fractured into the grays and slates of building stone.

He had introduced himself to the young medical examiner and learned in return that the man's name was Michel DuForché. "Tell me," Adams asked, "why are those measurements called 'Bertillonage'?"

"Oh, that," said DuForché. "It's a system invented by Monsieur Alphonse Bertillon, the director of the Service of

Judicial Identity, who stubbornly clings to it, even though it's not that effective.''

"No?"

"No."

Adams had hoped to elicit more information. "Why is it not effective?"

"Well, you have the inconvenience of all the measurements. They must be exceedingly precise, and even then I, for one, do not feel confident that they identify one unique human being. The cataloguing of this information is extremely difficult, as you can imagine. Besides which, most horribly, we are seeing an increase in dismemberments and disfigurements. Many thieves in Paris have cut off their middle fingers—it figures in two measurements, and they choose this pain over the likelihood of getting the increased penalty that comes to repeat offenders. And murderers have learned how it is we identify their victims. We measure the size of the head—the head is taken off. We measure the length of the finger—the hand is chopped off. These," the young man said gravely, "are some of the problems."

Grisly problems, Adams thought, for a science of measurement.

"There is an alternative," DuForché allowed. "Something suggested by your own Francis Galton."

"Who?"

"Galton. One of your scientists. Had a chair at Oxford, I believe."

"I'm American," Adams said.

"Sorry." DuForché gave him a long sideways look. "That's not a mistake I usually make." He studied Adams another moment before proceeding. "Galton suggests that fingerprints—these patterns on the tips of our fingers—are different for every individual. He's studied them for quite some time, and so far he has found no two alike. I don't believe anyone will. Dactylology, he calls it, and I think it's the best, most scientific way to identify people. He even has a classification system in place."

Adams studied the lines on his fingers. He had, of course, seen them before; but now they seemed to be his own in some different way.

"They have one added advantage," DuForché continued. "Unlike Bertillonage, fingerprints can generally be found at the scene of a crime." He went on to explain this to Adams, describing finger oils and how a light dusting of fine powder could make them visible. If what this man says is correct, Adams thought, these swirls and patterns could betray me to anyone who knows how to read them: some key element of identity has become alienable. We leave a sort of calling card everywhere we go. While DuForché spoke, Adams saw that the effect of this discovery must be enormous: the very nature of police work must change. The world would have less room for anonymity, just as people were becoming more and more numerous, more mobile, more anonymous. Police would need to rely less on what witnesses had to say, less on what neighbors and family might be able to tell them, less on the difficult comprehension of particular criminal nature than on sheer, physical, mechanical evidence. The Progress of Science! No more reconstruction of the logic or the story of a crime; no need of narrative, of understanding human motivation. There would be fingerprints. These little swirls, he thought, represented the rationalization, the *industrialization* of police work. "Of course," DuForché was saying, "if either of them are going to be useful, you need a big bank of fingerprints and measurements on file. That's why police take measurements from everyone who comes before them. And why I go to the morgue and do the corpses there before the coroner does the autopsy."

"Will I be measured? Fingerprinted?" Adams asked.

"We can't require it," DuForché said. "Not if you don't want. Strictly voluntary. You're a visitor. Bertillonage would help the police, though. And fingerprinting would help me— I want to build up a bank of prints, for comparisons. One of these days Bertillon is going to appreciate the virtues of fingerprinting, and when he does, he'll thank me for having begun the files."

The conversation had carried them out from the shaded walk and into the parvis, the open square in front of the cathedral, where pigeons bob-stepped in low parade behind patrons of the food carts, and the tourists distinguished themselves from the customary pedestrian traffic of the city by walking slowly or stopping, mid-stride, to admire the cathedral's façade. Around DuForché and Adams the pigeons were in constant motion, busy as surf, retreating from them, closing behind them. "Bertillon's obstinate," DuForché judged, "but he's reasonable. So I'm working to marshal the evidence. Eventually he must be convinced. Just last week I received clippings about a murder solved last year in Argentina, I believe the first murder ever solved with fingerprints." The young man was warming to the story, and to the larger subject; as they passed the equestrian statue of Charlemagne he slowed, wanting to make sure he got it all in before they reached the Prefecture. "A woman had killed her two sons, stabbed them, then claimed a neighbor did it. She even stabbed herself a little, to make it look as though she was lucky to get away. But she left bloody handprints all over. This was in some small coastal town, south of Buenos Aires. A detective in Buenos Aires, a transplanted European, knew about Galton's work, and he read about this case and the handprints, and he wired the local police. He said: Get me those handprints, and get fingerprints from her. He was very precise about what he wanted. They did what he said, and sent it to him. He found they matched, and he wired back, and the police went to her with this and said they knew she had done it. And she confessed. This detective solved the crime *from miles away*, thanks to fingerprints."

Adams wasn't sure that was accurate: fingerprints had scared the murderer, true, but they hadn't convicted her; her own confession had done that.

They had crossed the place du Parvis and now stood curbside opposite the Prefecture. DuForché showed no interest in crossing the street, but continued: "I think Bertillon has to pay attention to this. No more trying to convince with fiction. Dactylology is an accomplished fact."

"You mean you were trying to convince this Bertillon with made-up cases?" Adams took on the task of gauging traffic, looking for their opening, and stepped from the curb, but DuForché didn't follow.

"Yes, yes, with possibilities. And with fiction—with literature. Your own Mark Twain—he is American, isn't he?" DuForché smiled—"had a murderer trapped by fingerprints in one of his books. *Life on the Mississippi*. Ten years ago he was predicting this. Of course, no one minded him—your own police least of all.''

''Fascinating.'' Adams glanced toward the Prefecture, anxious. When and if he did get access to the morgue records, there was no guarantee it would help, and maybe he'd have to talk to other people on his list.

''It's my thesis at the Sorbonne.''

''Shall we cross? Ready?''

''I'm not a medical student, but I want to be.'' DuForché darted ahead of Adams and led the way. ''But first I have to convince them that there's a good reason for a detective to know medicine. I want to be a police detective. Right now they have me in the category of 'temporary student.' ''

''And the morgue is your laboratory work?'' Adams asked when they had gained the far curb.

''No, what I do there I do on my own. I take their Bertillon measurements, just to check them against our records. I fingerprint all the cadavers. Bertillon frowns on it, but he hasn't said I can't.''

A pair of priests heading for the cathedral approached them, and Adams waited until they were out of earshot before asking his next question. ''That woman in there—the one they say is Miriam Talbott—did you find out anything interesting about her?''

''The suicide? No.''

''Anything to show that she might have been a, ah, lady of the evening? A prostitute?''

''No. I didn't examine her.'' DuForché eyed Adams carefully. '' 'The one they *say* is Miriam Talbott'?''

''I know Miriam Talbott. That's not she.''

DuForché nodded. ''A shame. Some fingerprints would clear that right up, wouldn't they? But your woman probably wasn't ever printed. Have you got anything you know she touched?''

Adams pictured her using her brushes and reaching into her valise in the field outside Pontorson. Her easel—she had folded it up, carried it. Any of her supplies, yes, but where were they? With her. And at Chartres: her clasp purse, her binocle, the sleeve of his coat. "Can you take prints from clothing? From this jacket?"

"Sadly, no. Have you a book, a letter? I've been having some success in reading prints on paper."

Had she handed him his journal once? He was sure she had, but then he had carried it, held it himself. He explained this.

"Not good. The overprints will have smudged hers."

They were at the top of the steps to the Prefecture, a huge five-story rectangle occupying an entire city block; Adams wondered at its size, at the obvious dedication of material and personnel to the business of policing. Hadn't this building been a palace for some past king? He tried to remember.

"Wait a moment, will you?" DuForché asked him. The young man led him toward the wall of the building and glanced around. "I forgot this," he said. Quickly he stripped off his white smock, folded it neatly, and placed it in his briefcase. Underneath he wore the distinctive cape-less uniform of a junior police officer. He pulled a policeman's cap from the case, and Adams could see that the case contained little else. "Best not to be caught out of uniform," the young man said, tugging the cap into place. "There." He led them into the building.

The three uniformed policemen stationed at the front desk had been talking, but interrupted their conversation to examine Adams and DuForché. Behind the desk, on the far side of the lobby, rose a large marble staircase. DuForché nodded at the men and Adams could see them relax. Still, one surveyed him minutely and skeptically as he passed.

"That's new," DuForché said over his shoulder as they climbed the stairs. "The guards, I mean. Since that anarchist incident two weeks ago, we have men on all the doors. It's really cut into our manpower, protecting all the stations."

"Anarchist incident?"

"A bombing," DuForché said. "A precinct house. Messy. Two policemen killed. It's got everybody on edge. No more solitary patrols; everybody's doubled up. That's one reason I wear this smock outside," he confided. "I travel around the city alone a lot, and, well . . ." He shrugged. "You'll want to see Bertillon himself, if you can," DuForché mur-

mured as they walked down the long corridor. "I'll take you
there. It's near my office."

"Could I get fingerprinted first?" The idea of seeing the
whorls and ridges on his fingers come out on paper intrigued
him.

The presiding officer at the fingerprint station was all efficiency, but even so it was awkward to have one's finger
held so firmly by another person, and Adams did not immediately understand how his finger was to roll on the print
card, and so caused a smear. They started over. The final,
clear set had a certain abstract beauty to it; he wished he
could have kept it as a memento or conversation piece. It
would have been just the thing to show to his friends back
in Washington.

From the fingerprint desk DuForché led him down the
wide hallway to the stairs. They passed an open door and
Adams could see that the interior offices had windows that
looked onto a courtyard: the building wasn't nearly as large
as its façade suggested but was hollow at its core. The offices
were small and cramped. Inside one, a workman bent over,
busy with something on the floor; down the hallway a few
yards, another stood on a ladder, banging nails into the wall.
As they got closer Adams could see a spool of thin black
cable at the foot of his ladder. A few unspooled coils of the
cable snaked around on the marble floor before darting up
the wall to where the man was attaching it to a molding.

"Wonderful new thing," DuForché explained. "Telephones. You know of these, yes? The entire building is being
wired. We're supposed to get ours tomorrow. When they're
in, you'll be able to call the Prefecture from any post office
in Paris." He said this with obvious pride. "It should do
wonders for crime control. Very modern." Yes, Adams
thought, very modern. Very modern because it would be
more abstract, more anonymous, to be talking to someone a
great distance away, someone whose face you couldn't see.
Of course they were the next logical step after telegraphy,
but that didn't mean they were a good thing. He'd seen telephones in some of the government offices in Washington,
but hadn't actually used one.

On the fourth floor DuForché paused before a door marked

SERVICE OF JUDICIAL IDENTITY. "The secretary is going to
tell you that Bertillon is very busy. Have you got any
weight?"

Adams didn't understand.

"Weight—influence. You know, connections."

"I'm a historian . . ." Adams said.

"Not very good," DuForché said, shaking his head. "Unless . . . Look." He narrowed his brown eyes. "We'll tell
him you're a journalist, that you're reporting on methods of
scientific detection and identification. I've already told you
a lot, and you can use that, sound like you've done research.
Yes—a journalist. He always has time to talk to people like
that." Adams started to object, thinking that perhaps a discreet mention of Hay might be more effective, but stopped
himself: why involve Hay if he didn't have to?

DuForché was already talking to the secretary in a rapid
French that Adams couldn't follow, pointing to Adams and
gesturing toward the other door, next to the secretary's desk.
The secretary, a young man with oiled hair and a uniform
similar to DuForché's, rolled a cigar in an ashtray to loosen
the ash, then slowly raised it to his pursed lips while looking
at Adams. He drew on the cigar, exhaled slowly, nodded;
DuForché smiled and moved to open the interior office door.
"Remember!" he whispered, "a journalist!" Then, with his
hand on the knob of Bertillon's door, he said out loud, "Wait
here. I'll introduce you."

8:30 A.M.

THE OFFICE WAS large but plain in its furnishings: a desk on one side faced a wall of bookshelves on the other and in the center of the room three straight-backed chairs faced the desk and the pair of windows behind it. To the left and right the painted plaster walls were filled with unframed photographs thumbtacked in orderly rows. Behind the desk stood a handsome man, mid-thirties, Adams guessed, with strikingly clear gray eyes and a sallow, unweathered complexion. In his hand he held an object wrapped in a cloth. "I am Alphonse Bertillon, chief of the Service of Judicial Identity. Good to meet you," the man said. A vaguely familiar smell, no longer masked by cigar smoke: Adams started to feel uneasy. "Do please sit down." With the cloth in his hand Bertillon gestured toward a chair across from the desk. "I would shake your hand, but . . ." He shrugged. Adams could see that the object he held was a lens of some sort: on the desk between them lay other camera parts, including a large black bellows and frame. "I save this tinkering for when I have talking to do," Bertillon explained, sitting down. "More efficient that way."

"I . . . I . . ." Adams began. The sharp, acrid odor of chemical fixative—he feared he would be physically ill. Ever since Clover's suicide he had found the smell of it intolerable. "You take photographs," he managed to say, swallowing hard.

"Yes. The single most effective and underutilized crime tool in the world today." Bertillon smiled broadly, choosing to ignore DuForché's throat clearing. "Our whole staff is trained in the techniques—even Michel here. Nothing like a photograph to explain it all to a judge—to fix, with precision, the relationship of the body, the weapon if there is one, the blood, the personal effects . . ." Bertillon, satisfied with the lens, began putting the camera back together, an activity that necessitated close attention; he hunched over, using tweezers to slide some small part into a cranny in the camera frame. "Each of the pictures you see here on my walls was involved in a capital case of some sort. I could tell you about them, if you wish."

Adams glanced at the pictures. His eye caught on one that showed a room with a rumpled bed, seen from an unlikely position high above. On the bed were two forms, lifeless, sprawled, tangled in the bedding; a dark black stain spread in the center of the bed. "Ah, no. No, thank you." But he was supposed to be a journalist. "Later, perhaps." He thought that he ought to ask a question, but he was finding it difficult to think. He felt dizzy.

"I make the exposures myself, for certain cases," Bertillon volunteered. "I don't trust anyone else, you see." He glanced up and smiled at Adams, who managed a weak smile in return. "There is a certain satisfaction to it. Setting up the tripod just so, lights, proper settings, focus just right, and the crime scene is fixed forever. Have you ever done any photography, Monsieur Adams?"

Adams was concentrating on his breathing, trying to take in the shallowest possible doses of air. "No. Once but not anymore." He didn't own a camera. He had thrown Clover's away. Somewhere, near this office, Bertillon had a darkroom. Adams felt a bulb growing at the top of his stomach. Not just potassium cyanide but any photography chemical did this to him.

"So you will write about me, eh, Monsieur Adams? What will you say?" Bertillon didn't look up, but was attending to something inside his camera.

Seven years, Adams thought, I really ought to be able to control this. How am I going to get what I want? "Actually," he began, "Monsieur DuForché has been very helpful in explaining the operation of your department." He almost retched and hoped Bertillon didn't notice. "I have almost everything I need. I simply wanted to meet you in order to describe you for the article."

"I could have given you a photograph, eh?" Bertillon said from behind the camera. Adams couldn't tell if he was joking.

"And," Adams continued, "I needed your approval." Adams glanced nervously at DuForché, who looked back with a puzzled expression. "I'm describing your identification method, and I thought it might be interesting to report an actual case. Show the method in use, as it were." Now DuForché nodded encouragingly. Adams continued. "There's a body in the morgue that Monsieur DuForché has just measured. I'd need your approval to review the records."

"My approval," Bertillon murmured, as he slid a thin bracket onto the camera frame. He began to tighten it with a screwdriver.

"Not so much approval," DuForché broke in. "Your authorization."

"My *authorization*," Bertillon murmured. "Oh, that's different. My *authorization*." He paused for a moment to glare at DuForché, then contemplated his camera. He slid the screwdriver into a different crevice, then looked up. "Tell me. Why not take a case that is completed? Aren't you gambling on our success? What happens if we do not identify this body?"

Adams and DuForché looked at each other. "Actually, sir, we've thought of that," DuForché said. "What he's doing is a different sort of article. It has to be current. He's going to follow me around, report it just as it happens, very contemporaneous. It hardly matters whether we're successful or not." When he saw the look this idea brought to Bertillon's face, he added, "I mean for his purposes. For the article. Of course it *matters*."

Bertillon grimaced and returned to his camera to adjust something down in the bellows mechanism. "Nevertheless," he said, "it does represent a bit of a challenge. Identifying a body while a reporter—excuse me, a journalist—is watching.'' Adams heard a crisp *click* from the camera, and Bertillon sat up with a look of satisfaction on his face. ''There,'' he said, sliding the bellows back and forth, ''clean and done.'' He admired the camera for a moment and then set it aside. After slipping the tweezers into an inside jacket pocket and the rest of the tools into a desk drawer, he looked at Adams, directing his complete attention to him for the first time. ''Monsieur Adams,'' he said quietly, ''I have half a mind to throw you out of my office. Coming here with a story like that. A journalist! Tell me the truth. What is it you want?''

''I . . .'' Adams felt a red flush well up out of his shirt collar to heat his ears. He gambled on a deep breath, steeling himself against the pungent aroma. His stomach was building a glutinous knot inside. He tried again. ''I want to identify a body. In the morgue. I want to know who it—she—was.''

''Identification! Well! You have come to the right place.'' Adams couldn't tell whether Bertillon was being sarcastic. He glanced at DuForché, to get a second opinion, but the young man wouldn't meet his eyes.

''Let me guess. Michel put you up to this story.'' Bertillon looked from Adams to DuForché and back, and was evidently satisfied by what he saw. ''Regrettable,'' he sighed. ''Leave us now, Michel,'' he said with a wave of his hand. ''Wait outside. I'll talk with you later.'' DuForché offered a noncommittal shrug in response to Adams's recriminating glance as he turned to leave.

''My sister's son,'' Bertillon said when DuForché had closed the door behind him. ''A detective needs a good imagination, but that boy . . .'' Bertillon shook his head. ''At any rate. You are interested in a death. Particulars, please.''

After Adams explained, Bertillon leaned forward. ''Who took you to the morgue?''

''A man named Pettibois.''

''Just so.'' Bertillon thought a moment. ''Could your address have been mistaken?''

''I had it in her own hand,'' Adams told him.

''Even so, even so . . .'' Bertillon swivelled his chair to gaze out the window. ''Have you filed a missing-persons report?'' he asked after a moment. He turned back to face

Adams. "It seems you are more interested in the living Miss Talbott than in the dead, is this not so? Such a report is the first step. It's another department—my secretary will direct you there." Bertillon stood, indicating the interview was over.

"And the morgue—will I be able to see the file?"

Bertillon studied Adams for a moment. "Certainly," he said, "if you think it will help." He bent to scribble a note. "You will also have access to the autopsy report when that is done, if you wish. I don't see that it can do any harm."

Adams hesitated. It was clear he should go, but he felt sheepish. He did not want his moral failure to pass unremarked; Bertillon might think that untruth was, for him, unremarkable. "May I ask," he said softly, "how you knew that I was misrepresenting myself?" He had a sudden urge to explain everything to this man. "If you thought that I was lying because I acted nervous, I must tell you something. I feel physically ill. Photography chemicals—they always do this to me. My wife—"

Bertillon held up a hand. "I wish I could pretend that it was my detecting skills. That would be something, wouldn't it? No newsprint smudges on the heels of your hands, no bloodshot eyes from meeting deadlines, no characteristic squint from too many nights spent reading proof . . ." Bertillon smiled and shook his head. "No, Monsieur Adams, there are no Sherlock Holmes miracles here. I know that you are no more a journalist than I am—though I suppose you *were* a journalist, some years back, if you count the time you spent at the *North American Review*." Bertillon smiled again, pleased with the look he saw on Adams's face. "Ah. You see. I am an avid reader of American history. Of course your name is known to me. Wonderful tale you made out of the whole Battle of New Orleans—very compelling. Now if you will excuse me . . ."

In the stairwell Adams breathed more deeply. The knot in his stomach began to relax; the clean air was clearing his head.

"Monsieur Adams!"

Inspector Pettibois looked down on him from a few steps above. "What brings you here? Not still detecting, are we?"

"Well, actually—" The experience with Bertillon smarted; he would tell the truth. "I am. Yes. I've just been to the Service of Judicial Identity."

"Ah, Alphonse! Well, his men are just the ticket. They'll find out who our mystery woman is, if anyone can." Pettibois was generous, smiling. "So. You are on your way back to your hotel? Perhaps you could drop me—I have some business out that way . . ."

"No, I'm going downstairs. Missing Persons. I'm about to file a report."

"Excellent decision. Excellent! You can return to your affairs confident the matter will be in good hands. Very wise of you." Pettibois nodded. "But this should not take long, should it?"

"I thought I would go over to the morgue after."

"Oh? Why?" Pettibois registered Adams's hesitation and descended the stairs to his level. "Come, come, Monsieur Adams. A good detective doesn't spurn help. I help you, you help me, perhaps we will find this friend of yours all the sooner. What have you got in mind?"

Adams took in the ruddy complexion, the round, soulful eyes. "My card. I never gave that woman a card. The one she had came from Miss Talbott. Unless the dead woman is a thief, Miss Talbott must have given it to her. So Miss Talbott knew this woman, somehow."

Pettibois considered a moment. "Yes. Obviously, then, they were acquainted, this dead woman and your friend. Have you any ideas how?"

"No."

"Mmmm. Well. That could prove important, couldn't it?" The two men looked at each other. "I have some news for you, Monsieur Adams," Pettibois said finally. "I have been thinking about the matter, and it seems to me that circumstantial evidence—the papers, the personal effects—well, these should not count for as much as the testimony of a single reliable witness who knows what he's talking about. So: I have amended my report; the cadaver is officially an unknown." Pettibois frowned slightly when Adams didn't respond. "Really, I thought this would please you."

Adams shrugged. ''It's a good idea. But it doesn't help find Miss Talbott.''

Pettibois nodded sympathetically. ''You really must let me know how your investigation proceeds. If you turn up anything that you think would help me, let me know. My office is here, on the third floor,'' he said, pointing. ''Do stop by.''

9:00 A.M.

A STRANGE JUXTAPOSITION, Adams thought: Notre Dame and behind it, a scant two hundred yards away, the morgue. An irony, no doubt underappreciated by the pony men and the vendors and the cabbies and the tourists and the omnibus passengers who went about their business in the place du Parvis: here were two of the great social needs addressed in close proximity. Although if architecture were to reflect practical worth, the morgue would be the larger building, larger than any cathedral. Death, as a brute fact and as a social problem—even simply as a *sanitation* problem— was logically prior to the urge that had given rise to this cathedral.

Or maybe the cathedral and the morgue were paired, not so much in ironic contrast but as twin manifestations of the same thing. For wasn't the problem of death the original rise of both? One building was dedicated to the practical aspects of our mortality, the other to its consequences for theory, belief, consciousness. Yes, it made sense that both buildings would be here, on the Ile de la Cité, the exact heart of Paris, her place of historic origin. The disposal of the dead, the controlled disposition of spiritual longing: these were necessary in any culture.

As Adams walked, he wondered what other institutions were crucial to a civilization: the police, of course—the building he had just left; and behind it, the judiciary, the courts. Did geography recapitulate cultural ontogeny—did it betray the evolution of social institutions? For instance, the Chamber of Deputies, where laws were made, was not on the island, not at the center. Could that signify? Yes: society lived first under fiat, and only later evolved more public and participatory means of articulating its laws. Was there, had there once been, a school here? Every culture must teach its young—though of course the vast majority of the human race was born and died without ever entering a building specifically designated for instruction in the mores, habits, and beliefs of its tribe. For most of them education had been inseparable from religion. Churches as schools, then—Adams made a mental note to jot this down later—though of course the secularization of culture had denied them that function. Science, it was now, not faith; science cold, hard, lifeless. There could be no stained glass in the house of science, nothing to lend its color to the flat, clear glare of enlightenment. He wondered what would become of a culture that worshipped such a sterile god; would it become a kind of necropolis? Would it then school its young in its morgues?

In his small office the coroner sat behind his desk with his back to Adams, an open file drawer at his elbow. Adams cleared his throat, waited, then spoke a greeting. The man did not move. Bored into sleep, no doubt, by the finality of his task. His bulk hid whatever he had been reading. Adams approached the desk and called another "Hello," louder this time, but still the man did not respond. The desk was cluttered; Adams began to scan the papers there, trying to read them upside down. He cleared his throat and glanced around, embarrassed. He looked for a book to drop, thinking the loud clap would be just the thing, but saw only loose, silent papers. At last, uneasy, he walked around the side of the desk.

The coroner sat with a manila folder in his hands, and in the front of his shirt, above the folder, there were two ragged holes, from which welled up a steady flow of dark black blood. Before he shut his eyes Adams glimpsed flesh the color of uncooked pork. He made himself look again. The upper wound was in the exact center of the man's chest, just above the concavity where his belly and the rounded forms of his pectorals met. Adams saw white splinters in the wound, a shattered bone, which gave the hole depth and definition, like a grisly cross-hatching. As he watched, a tiny bit of bone floated free and was carried out on a trickle of blood, a rivulet that flowed to the top of the dead man's belly, spreading from there in a stain that soaked his shirt on either side.

Adams let out the breath he had unconsciously held. He had never seen a gunshot victim before, and some part of his mind was relieved that he was managing it so well. Perhaps he should take his cue from Pettibois: how would a detective think? He looked around, thinking, There must be a reason for this death, and that reason ought to be discernible in this room.

It seemed likely that the murderer had stood close to his victim: there was room between the attendant and the wall for a man to stand, though Adams had no intention of standing there. He walked gingerly around the desk, to the other side, where the filing cabinet stood with one drawer open. Had the coroner been interrupted or had the murderer left it open, perhaps after taking something? He looked down the row of labels, each one a name representing a soul who had preceded this poor attendant to whatever came after. Adams could sense nothing amiss in the file; you had to know what the order was before you could detect disorder. He glanced at the file folder in the dead attendant's hands, craning his neck to read the name on the tab, being careful not to brush against the body. Miriam Talbott, it said, with the date of admission: *21 Novembre 92.* There was the coroner's autopsy report in the folder, and—Adams moved the report slightly with a fingernail, mindful of what DuForché had said about fingerprints—nothing else. There was no sign of the Bertillonage report anywhere.

Adams stepped away from the desk and walked backwards from the office, fixing the scene in his mind, reducing it in scale as he retreated. This was no great concern of his. He would bring the police. Only when he was outside, in the daylight in front of the morgue, did it occur to him that the murder was fresh, and that the gunman might still be lurking nearby. He had to lean against the building for a moment: he might want to think it no concern of his, but his body knew differently. Hadn't he been making inquiries about Miriam Talbott? Hadn't he gone to her apartment? Hadn't he talked to the concierge and to Madame LeBlanc, either of whom might well know all sorts of unsavory types? Without actually deciding to, he was running, away from the morgue and past the cathedral, into the plaza and past the vendors, where pigeons splayed up in a great feathered wave with a sound like the shuffling of cards. He darted between carriages and cabs on the rue de la Cité. He didn't stop running until he reached the door of the Prefecture.

As his older brother Charles once told him, sharing wisdom gained in his service in the Civil War: "Given a choice, stick with the generals." Thus, Adams sat waiting in Bertillon's outer office, even after the first detachment of officers had left for the morgue. DuForché was nowhere to be seen, and Bertillon, when he at last appeared, rounded up a half dozen assistants from a neighboring laboratory, then led them to the courtyard, where they entered a pair of horse-drawn wagons, each with the word POLICE painted on its side. The men took their places quickly, silently, as if by prior arrangement. Bertillon himself swung up onto the driver's seat of one wagon and surveyed the courtyard. "Well?" he said when he saw Adams hanging back. "Are you coming?"

At the morgue, Bertillon went immediately inside with Adams close behind. "Damnit, stop!" Bertillon shouted, and Adams flinched. "You! Out! Out of my sight! Leave!" He almost turned to go, but then saw the object of Bertillon's attention: a patrolman busily examining the desktop, picking up the papers and the folders there. "You try to train them," Bertillon muttered, "but they won't learn. They won't read the notices you post. They get to a crime scene, they are like monkeys, always *at* everything." He sighed. "All right, Louis," he said to one of his men. "Let us preserve this scene as our oblivious colleague has seen fit to leave it to us. Jean-Pierre, give him a hand, please."

As one man set up a tall tripod, extending its legs until the back of the surmounted camera touched the ceiling, another placed metal stands with narrow pans atop them around the room, while a third filled the pans with flash powder. Yet a fourth unpacked a small leather kit bag and began using a rubber bulb to squeeze bursts of fine powder over the papers on the desk. Adams tried to remember if he had touched anything. "I thought you didn't believe in fingerprints," he said.

"Believe in them? There they are," Bertillon replied, gesturing at one hand with the other. "How could I not believe in them?"

"I thought you didn't collect them from crime scenes."

"Who told you that?"

"DuForché."

Bertillon turned his head to the side and stretched his neck out in a sort of rolling shake. "No. For the record: I remain unconvinced that each print is unique. Time will tell. In the meantime, I would be a fool not to employ every method that offers some chance of success."

"Including your own."

"Including my own."

"Someone," Adams said, "thought enough of your method to steal a Bertillonage report." He indicated the folder in the morgue attendant's lap. "DuForché was filling it out when I first came here this morning. Now it's gone."

"What's he holding?" Bertillon asked the man working at the desk.

The man examined the folder without touching it. "One manila folder, dark brown, unbleached fiber. Government issue, made in Paris. Contents: one coroner's report, signed and dated today. Label: *Miriam Talbott, 21 Novembre 92.*" He went back to his dusting.

"Well, Monsieur Adams. It appears you have discovered the motive," Bertillon said briskly. "Thank you. Now, if you would just—"

"Inspector Bertillon," one of the crew called from the door to the morgue. "You'd better see this."

Adams followed him in, and his eyes were drawn immediately to the slab where, the night before, the body of the woman who was not Miriam had lain. There, partially covered by its drape, was a cadaver, its stomach opened wide by a long cut from chest to pelvis. Someone had systematically disemboweled the body. Reflexively Adams looked away, down, only to see that the steady stream of water that

gurgled in the tiled channel at the foot of the table was pink
with blood. When he looked up, there was that white, bloodless flesh of the incisions again. ''Oh my God,'' he said out
loud. Bertillon, too, couldn't look, nor could the detective
who called him in; both of them were bent over near the
table, weakened with nausea.

But then Adams realized that the policemen were not
bending in disgust; they were stooping to examine something. He craned his head to see. In front of Bertillon he saw
the cadaver's arm hanging down. Its hand was misshapen,
the fingers too stubby, as if some trick of perspective had
foreshortened them. No, Adams realized, it wasn't perspective; the ends of the fingers weren't rounded anymore. They
were blunt, too blunt, a little . . .

''Hmmm.'' Bertillon fished in his overcoat pocket for a
moment and brought out a magnifying lens and tweezers in
a smooth motion. ''Fingertips missing. That's not part of the
autopsy.'' He weaved his head about, examining the hand
from different angles, using the tweezers to lift it into position. ''Some bone fracture here. They were cut, not sawn.
Quick. Sloppy.'' He squatted down a little lower, peering up
at the hand. ''Whatever they used was pretty sharp.''

10:00 A.M.

BACK IN HIS office, the Chief of the Service of Judicial Identity offered part of his lunch to Adams. Something wrapped in butcher's paper—Adams shook his head and moved his chair an inch closer to the window, which he'd opened a hand's width. In came a slight breeze, faintly dispersing the residual smell of chemicals and the odor of onion. "Find Pettibois," Bertillon commanded an aide. "He'll have a fit if we start without him."

As the aide left, Bertillon shook his head. He glanced at Adams, whose blank gaze he misread as the reserve of judgment. "Pettibois is a different sort of policeman than I," he explained carefully. "Less appreciative of the need for dispatch." There was no implication in his tone: he was simply stating a neutral truth. He reached into his butcher paper again, bringing a chunk of sandwich to his mouth, which he clipped absently, precisely. Adams turned away. Outside, in the courtyard, he saw the desiccated leaves of a poplar tree rattle in a gust of wind, turning together like a school of fish. The running, the excitement, the horrible sight of that woman's body opened up, the chemicals, the smell of strong food—he was feeling tired and old and more than a little anxious. He wondered if his friend Hay was in his office at the Embassy.

"This is a waste of time," Bertillon announced. He wrapped up his sandwich and placed it at the edge of his desk. "Let's start. Suppose you tell me, Monsieur Adams, what you did when you entered the morgue."

Adams recounted his movements.

"Why didn't you leave to call a patrolman when you first noticed he had been shot? Why walk around the desk to look at the folder?"

"I didn't see he was shot until I walked around the desk."

"Yes, yes, but you just said you leaned over to look at the folder in his lap, then examined the premises. Why not just leave immediately and get help?"

"I was curious."

"*Curious.*" Bertillon repeated the word as if he were testing its strength, its truth. "Mmmm." He arched an eyebrow at Adams. "You didn't touch anything?"

"I might have touched the file cabinet. And the coroner's report."

"Why that?"

"To see what was in the folder. To see if the Bertillonage report was there."

There was a knock at the door, and before Bertillon could answer Pettibois opened the door and swept into the office. "Alphonse," he said cheerfully, with a slight nod. "Sorry I am late. I have something for you." He smiled, revealing a row of teeth dominated by a pair of spatulate incisors. His cheeks were pink with excitement; he held out for inspection a large pair of bolt cutters, heavy and new. "No sign of a gun, but these were found in some bushes just beyond the morgue. Obviously the thing that removed the woman's fingertips." He held them close to peer at the cutting blades. "Harder to carry than a gun, I suppose. Not that much blood on them, considering. But then she was dead already, no?"

Bertillon eyed the bolt cutters. "I don't suppose," he said slowly, "you've had the handles examined for fingerprints?"

Pettibois stared at him in disbelief. "I am truly an idiot," he finally said. "Truly I am, truly, truly. No, regretfully, no." He shook his head. "Forgive me."

Bertillon sighed. "Well. That's as it is, then. Please. Sit down; I was just starting with Monsieur Adams."

Pettibois pulled up a chair. "Go ahead. Please. I'm sorry."

Bertillon asked about the body, whether Adams had

moved or touched it; and then he asked Adams to tell them just how he had found the body. He let Adams answer, nodding, encouraging him. "Did you hear any sound from the cadaver room?" he asked when Adams was done.

"No," said Adams. "If there was any, I didn't notice."

"Did you see anyone leave or enter? Anyone at all?"

"No."

Bertillon nodded. "Yes. That'll be all." He swivelled toward his desk and faced Pettibois. "You have to figure that someone doesn't want the identity of this woman known. The Bertillonage report, the fingertips."

"Mmmm," Pettibois murmured in agreement. "Did you see the autopsy report? It's done. Whoever killed the coroner must have got him just after he finished."

"Yes," Bertillon said. He glanced at the desktop where the folder from the coroner's lap now lay. "Suicide."

"Adams thinks she was mixed up in this Panama affair," Pettibois said, glancing between them. "Did he tell you?"

Bertillon turned to face him. "No. Why—what makes you think that, Monsieur Adams?"

Adams told Bertillon about Reinach's card on the effects table. "It might not mean anything," he added, out of deference to Pettibois.

"No, no, you were on to something there," Pettibois said. He stroked his mustache with the tip of a finger as he spoke. "At the time I thought the coroner had made a mistake, had mixed up his things with hers, but I think it's worth investigating." He pulled at his earlobe with the thumb and curved finger of his right hand.

"Both dead at once," Bertillon said, nodding. "A coincidence that strains credulity."

Pettibois shrugged. "He's dead of apoplexy. She's a suicide. Perhaps what is, is."

Bertillon sat silently for a moment, then leaned back in his chair. "I can see taking the Bertillonage report. We can't get good measurements from an autopsied cadaver. But the fingers, that's different. Why chop them off now? Her prints have already been taken. Michel!" Bertillon called to the outer office. "You took that cadaver's prints and filed them, didn't you?"

"Yes, sir," DuForché said from the doorway. "Just this morning. It will be at least a day before they find out if we have a match. To anything we already have. Sir."

"At least a day," Bertillon murmured. He looked to Adams with his eyebrows raised, a glance that seemed to indicate some quality of joint sufferance, of mutual understanding, but Adams couldn't tell whether Bertillon had in mind the slowness of the fingerprint examiners, or the tone of dutiful officiousness DuForché was now affecting, or perhaps his indulgence of his nephew's theories. When Adams smiled back, Bertillon stood, extending a hand. "Monsieur Adams, thank you for your time. You have been very helpful. I am very sorry that you found yourself in such unpleasant circumstances."

On the street the cabbie who answered his hail had such a broken-down horse that Adams thought to dismiss him and find another. But the cabbie himself was even more broken down—small, round-shouldered, with stubble growing unscathed in the deep lines of his face—and seemed in desperate need of business.

"No, stop," Adams said, once he was seated and the cabbie moved to unfurl the curtains. "It's not raining. Leave them."

"I am sorry, monsieur. Customers they prefer it, monsieur. Because of the anarchists." The man nodded again and again, to some obscure rhythm, an involuntary movement. When he smiled his lips disappeared with that peculiar inward enfolding of the toothless. He held himself stiffly; couldn't turn his head without moving his shoulders as well. "Those ones, they're all about. Shot a man, they did, just as I am to you. Jump onto his carriage and a gun to his ribs and there you have it." He pointed a finger like a pistol and grinned, showing dark gums.

"When was this? Where?"

"On the Champs-Elysées. Yes! Climbed up, shot him, ran away. Just Wednesday a week." The old man clambered onto his perch behind the roof of the cab with some difficulty; Adams felt the vehicle tremble with his shaking. "Don't you think that changed some things. Yes! 'Purrr-romm-n-aid?' you can ask them. *'Ah non, non, merci, non!'*

they're saying now. No sir, don't want to go out, they don't. Can't blame 'em, no, can't blame 'em.'' With a big shake of the reins the horses started.

"The American Embassy,'' Adams called out. "Was there a reason? Whom did they shoot?''

"A rich one,'' the cabbie answered, a disembodied voice from above. "He was a rich one, that he was.'' Adams settled back against the leather seat. The reins, slicing into his view from the top of the cab, continued to quake slightly. "Reason enough for them,'' the cabbie called down as an afterthought.

What had become of Paris? Bombings, random shootings, a sullen and wary populace, the police under assault and the government about to fall, a coroner murdered, an American disappeared—the Paris of the Panama scandal seemed like an impostor, a surly, belligerent stranger that had usurped the place of the city he had known in his youth.

As the buildings crept past and the horse's rump swayed rhythmically in front of him, Adams let himself remember: he had first come to Paris thirty-some years ago, on his way to study the legal institutions of Germany, part of a negotiated hiatus from paternal expectations. It had been good for him to be away; Boston was too full of brothers. Alone, he discovered by crossing them the limits of Trinitarianism and the moral vision centered in the old house in Quincy. Even the loneliness had been tonic: an exercise in keeping his distance from the family. Sometimes their presence in the world worked a corruption on him—he knew, with a confidence he struggled to resist, that his name commanded respect.

Paris had been his first exposure to a culture in which his name could signify little, except among a very narrow circle, who were in any case precisely those from whom he meant to break free. He was drawn to the poets and painters and writers, to those whose muses rarely spoke to them of matters civil or political or juridicial. And in those circles the codes of behavior and fashion and dress had been wonderfully new and alien. The women, in particular, were different—bolder, more provocative, with a forwardness unknown in American women. This characteristic cut across all levels of French society; it was most disconcerting to be flirted with by women dressed in the harsh dark cloth of pauperdom. At the time he had marked the phenomenon down to France's radical egalitarianism, one of the legacies of the Revolution. Now he wasn't so sure: there was, he thought, some pre-existing tendency in the French character, some basic disinclination to temper their sheer physicality with restraint, and this allowed women and men to understand each other, no matter the social situation, first as physical bodies, as sexual beings. No matter how civilized they were otherwise, the French were never far from their animal nature. This explained the egalitarian urge in French life, rather than the other way around.

And of course it helped explain the violence, the rapidity with which political difference became civil disturbance. Bombings of police stations were one thing: now there were random murders in the street. That an anarchist should light upon such a resolutely anonymous target as a Parisian burgher taking his ease in his carriage was a sign that political symbolism had evolved along with the power of the state. No longer did only the great and the near-great have reason to fear the assassin's bullet; society had been so thoroughly transformed in the image of factory production that it stood as a single piece, a large, clanking, obstreperous machine, and the anarchist was right—an attack on any part of it was an attack on the whole.

His cab took him past a park whose gravelled bridle paths with their casual traffic made him think of Clover; they had gone riding nearly every day in Rock Creek Park, late in the afternoon when he was finished with his *History* for the day. He knew it was likely to be a trick of memory—memory, that great sentimentalizer—but it seemed to him that when they rode they had always been happy. Clover had moods, yes, difficulties, her inherent weakness of temper, which his family thought any proper god-fearing woman with the mettle of Concord in her ought to be able to overpower, but when they rode together they were happy, her mood was bright, and his family was far away.

It didn't make him sad to remember how they had been, but he couldn't fully recover the happiness he had known then, either. He wished there was some way to possess those moments again, wished that recall didn't gloss with every use, so that what got recalled was not the hard gritty kernel of event itself but the pearlescent memory of it, encased in layer upon layer of recollection. Not enough blue in this light, Miriam might have said: no wonder it refuses to come to life.

And then, as if coming onto a familiar road from an un-familiar angle—just as one might on horseback when trail jumping through the woods, so that the road when you find it is, in an instant, both strangely familiar and strangely, bril-liantly new—he remembered Dingler shooting his horses in that ravine.

Thumping the roof of the cab, he called out a new desti-nation to the driver.

12:00 P.M.

AT THE NATIONAL Library Adams set to work tracking down Jules Dingler. He expected no help from the main catalogue but instead turned immediately to the indexes for newspapers. The man's obituary would be the most obvious account of his life. He found a half dozen listed in the index to 1885—the year Clover died—and jotted down the citations on call slips. Dingler's notices were dated early November, which meant he had died a few months after returning from Panama. He hadn't faced a life alone for very long, had not carried on without his wife for anything like the seven years, coming up this December, that Adams had. But still, he had shot those horses. Adams recognized in that act the desire of a man to exorcise his fate by seizing control of it and asserting it. It was the same peculiar logic that impelled acrophobes to jump, the logic that said the answer to the uncontrollable assaults of vertigo is a willful leap. The more startling the gesture, the less it would seem to be an act of acquiescence, a lame and futile seconding of a matter that had already been decided. What he most hated, what Dingler must have hated, was the feeling of being powerless. Dingler had shot those horses, and he himself had burned his diaries and letters, anything that spoke of Clover.

He wasn't sure what he expected to find.

Adams turned in his call numbers at a long oak counter across from the main entrance, then took a table near a window. He waited, pleased to be warmed by the large squares of sunlight that bathed his back.

The clerk approached with a single large, leather-bound ledger, which he placed delicately on the table. "Ah, the others . . . ?" Adams asked. "Are they . . ." He tried to remember the word for "checked out," then settled for "engaged."

"One at a time," the clerk said, pursing his lips and frowning slightly behind his silver-framed glasses. He had deep circles under his eyes, although otherwise he looked quite young. He stays up too late reading, Adams guessed.

Adams sighed. "*Merci.*" He opened the ledger quickly, releasing motes that swirled up to define the shaft of light from the window, making it seem liquid with roiling movement and solid with rectilinear precision. The volume contained a month's worth of *Le Temps* from 1885, its cheap paper already yellowing. With the sun behind him as he sat in the light, his shadow fell onto the swirling motes, becoming a three-dimensional, extended silhouette of himself, a man-shaped tunnel that slanted down from his body to the table and the page in front of him.

The page that should have contained Dingler's obituary was missing. Adams double-checked the page numbers and the date to make sure. No doubt about it: it wasn't there. He bent to examine the binding. It had been ripped out.

Adams took the book up to the desk and explained the situation. The young man in glasses looked at him suspiciously, but agreed to bring him another volume.

When the clerk placed the November 1885 volume of *Le Figaro* in front of him, Adams thanked him and checked immediately for the issue that held Dingler's obituary. This volume, too, had been vandalized. The clerk raised an eyebrow but said nothing. Adams persuaded him to take the other call slips and bring all the remaining volumes out at once. Together they flipped through them, looking for notice of Dingler's death. Without exception every page that contained material about Dingler was missing.

Adams left the clerk to his consternation and returned to the indexes. Why had someone systematically removed all information about Dingler from these volumes? What was it that was being concealed? He searched through the indexes for stories on the canal company and its failure, and jotted the titles and citations down on call slips. Perhaps the history of the company might provide some clue.

As his volumes came, one by one, he learned that the company had floated a succession of bond issues in the eighties, with progressively poorer results as capital became scarcer and scarcer, and that it had then lobbied for legislation to permit the issue of lottery bonds, by which a portion of the money raised would be returned to bondholders as prizes. There seemed to have been an inordinate number of confident articles on the company; the general consensus was that the canal was all but done, the work proceeded smoothly, and all talk of difficulty was unpatriotic pessimism. Finally, in April of 1888, the Chamber of Deputies had approved a lottery bill—the bill, if you believed Delahaye, for whose passage the Chamber had been thoroughly bribed.

When he took the volume back, the clerk with the night-owl eyes accepted it and then cleared his throat to speak. He looked up for a moment as if remembering something. "Monsieur is interested in the canal company?" he asked slowly, in English. "Perhaps he would like the Micros articles from *La Libre Parole*?"

Wasn't that the paper Hay had mentioned? "The Micros articles?"

"Ahhm, yes, the series that is of the scandal."

"Yes. Very much."

The clerk walked to a filing cabinet behind the desk and in a moment returned with a clipping file, which he wordlessly placed in front of Adams. They were all from Drumont's paper, *La Libre Parole*, and all were published under the pseudonym "Micros."

The first, dated September 10, charged that the petitions presented to the Chamber in 1886 asking for approval of lottery bonds for the canal company hadn't really been the spontaneous effusion of stockholders that they appeared; they had been organized by the officers of the company. Not exactly an earth-shaking revelation, Adams thought, though the paper treated it as one. Maybe he was missing some nuance of the French political system. Either that or the French were more naïve than he thought. The second article charged that the company had bribed up to twenty members of the Chamber in order to get the lottery bill passed. Now that was scandal, Adams thought. Jacques de Reinach was named as the briber; a man named Henri Cottu, the article said, had been involved as well. The third and fourth articles focused on Reinach, repeating the bribery charge, questioning his patriotism. He was German; he was an "evil presence" in the canal company offices. Throughout the month, every day, there was an article on the affair, usually centering on a vague charge: one day Micros allowed that "some senators" had also been bribed; another claimed that the company's money had been mismanaged, that thousands had been frittered away on useless or extravagant things; yet another charged that there had been corruption in the way contracts had been let, and said that Gustave Eiffel, whose firm had built the tower for the International Exhibition of 1889, had won large contracts without submitting bids.

As he paged through the articles, Adams saw that Reinach's name came up often. He was always identified as "the German Jew, Baron de Reinach." After a time the articles were repetitive; it was obvious that Micros was milking the subject, stretching out a few hard facts in this thinning series. By late September there was no new information in them at all; the series had become hysterical editorials about the contamination of France by German financiers.

Then, in early October, there was a change. The focus was different, and the articles became more explicit. Every day there was some revelation about the workings of the company, some detailed account of a morally repugnant transaction: the chairman of the committee that reviewed the lottery bond law in the Chamber had received a thirty-thousand-franc donation from the company. The chairman was named. The company had given money to a long list of newspapers, which had then editorialized in favor of the lottery bond. Adams read through the list: every newspaper of note was there, and many others. (*The Bee Keeper's Journal*? Adams thought. Why in God's name would anyone spend money to influence the editorial policy of *The Bee Keeper's*

Journal?) Micros named one editor who, he said, had suggested to the Panama company that they pay him for *not* writing about the work in Panama; so bribery had spawned a sort of equal-and-opposite blackmail. And on and on, with dates and amounts and, usually, names. One article stated that no fewer than 150 members of the Chamber of Deputies had received cash or other considerations from the company; here, however, Micros gave no names.

What intrigued Adams was the question of sources. Obviously, in October this Micros must have gotten himself a new one. It would have had to have been someone very well acquainted with the company. He had a hunch and flipped back to the beginning of the series to test it. Reinach, Reinach, Reinach: the man's name was everywhere, every day, always as "that German," "that Jew," "the German Jew-Baron," "the German financier." But then, in October, it was gone. There was no mention of Reinach that month. None at all. The last time the dead baron was named was in the article on September 24. After that he just dropped from view.

Someone, Adams thought, had started protecting Reinach. Someone had started feeding this journalist information that led away from the baron, and the material was too good not to use.

What this meant for his search for Miriam he could not begin to decipher, but he made a note of it.

Adams was ready to quit. He flipped a clump of pages, about to shut the file, but stopped when he saw a headline: PANAMA BUILDER DIES. On June 19, 1888, the day before the new lottery issue, Ferdinand de Lesseps had been found dead. With this event, the paper editorialized, the fate of the company was sealed: without *Le Grand Français* there was no hope of a canal. The company could no longer command the confidence of the public. The bond issue was expected to fail, indeed *should* fail; the directors could no longer expect to raise capital, not even with the device of lottery bonds.

Actually, Adams thought, the fate of the company had been sealed the moment Lesseps had plunked a finger on a map and said "Dig here." He wouldn't have been so confident if he had first sweated in Panama's heat, or felt the pressure of its inescapable sun, or stepped in any of its rainy-season muds, or breathed its malarial airs, or seen with his own eyes its dense, grasping jungles. Its carnivorous jungles, he remembered Miriam calling them.

He stretched, then shut the folder. The sunlight that had warmed his back had long since moved on to the table, then fallen from there to the floor, where, reduced to a thin parallelogram, it hugged the wall, as if cringing from the intensity of his concentration, or from the dust that his researches had released into the room. He checked his watch. Well after three; if he meant to see Hay, he should pack up and get on with it.

4:00 P.M.

"GOD, ADAMS, ARE you all right?" Hay asked when Adams had told him about his visits to the morgue. Adams waved a hand. "Does this man—this Bertillon—does he have any suspects?"

Adams hadn't thought to ask. "I don't know."

"Whoever killed the coroner was after the fingertips," Hay speculated. "The coroner was just in the way. Don't you think?" He stood next to the floor globe in its oaken rack in a corner of his sitting room, spinning it lightly. Hay thought better on his feet; Adams knew from his years of scholarship that he thought better sitting down. He sat now in a wing chair near the window, toes resting on the floor.

"I guess. Yes, most likely. And the Bertillonage report," Adams reminded him. "Someone wants to disguise her identity. This makes me think it's crucial to find out who she is. And then there's the Dingler material, the attempt to hide information about him." Adams shook his head; it all seemed too confusing.

"There's something else, too, Adams. I've been asking around and I've found out something you should know." Hay looked somber.

"What?"

"I know how important this young woman is to you, this Miriam Talbott. But things aren't always what they seem. I

mean, people can be . . .'' He paused, and the pause length-
ened into a silence.

"Just tell me."

Hay exhaled a deep breath and drew another. "Miss Talbott was Reinach's mistress."

Adams sat, head cocked to one side, as if still waiting to
hear him. "I've talked to a good many people," Hay added.
"It seems to be common knowledge." Adams's posture and
visage didn't change, except for a shift in his eyes: he
glanced sidelong, toward the floor. He was silent for a long
time—long enough that Hay, concerned about the effect of
this news on his friend, was relieved when he cleared his
throat to speak. But he was surprised by what Adams said.

"Do you know this man Clemenceau? The deputy? He
was a director of the canal company." He had been there in
Dingler's photograph of the directorate, Adams was thinking,
and that made him some point of intersection between the
canal company and the Chamber of Deputies. He was excellently situated to know something.

"Georges Clemenceau. Chamber of Deputies. Socialist.
Ferocious debater. I know a little about him. But—what
about Miss Talbott? Aren't you . . . aren't you a little . . .''
He couldn't finish the thought, for Adams stared at him impassively.

"She is who she is," Adams said quietly. "I enjoyed her
company."

"But—don't you think she's . . . Reinach was certainly a
repulsive type, wouldn't you agree? The man who bribed the
Chamber? And she, his lover . . . ?"

"We don't know that for certain. And if she was, what's
it to us? Whatever she has done she had her reasons—reasons I couldn't presume to judge. Not," he said pointedly,
"without first hearing them." His frown made it clear that
he would brook no further comment on this subject. "Now
this Clemenceau. He knew Reinach. If what you say is true,
then there's a good chance he knows Miss Talbott. How do
I go about getting in touch with him?" He had taken a risk
in allowing that Clemenceau and Reinach were linked, for
his only evidence of this was the photo and he didn't want
to have to admit to Hay that he had had the opportunity to

study it. But the risk seemed justified, and he waited to see
its result with the calm detachment of one watching an al-
gebra equation being worked toward a solution: would it go
this way or that?

"At the Chamber, no doubt. He must have an office. In
there with the *chéquards*."

Good. Hay hadn't noticed. "The who?" Adams asked.

Hay explained: The French didn't have the sangfroid to
bribe themselves with cash; instead, deputies had traded their
votes for checks made out to bearer. The endorsements, of
course, left a trail. "They are a dear race, don't you think?
The term is all over Paris. There's even a ditty, just heard it
today: 'Who Hasn't Had His Little Check Today?' "

"So somewhere there's a pile of checks with all the
names?"

"Quite possible. Likely, even. They'd all have come back
to Reinach, and he might have had his reasons for keeping
them."

Adams mulled this over.

Hay shrugged. "I don't know how helpful this man Clemenceau would be. He's arrogant. And ambitious. There's
talk of him for prime minister someday, if the Socialists ever
get called on to form a government. That could only happen
if he manages to put together a coalition against the Boulangists—a circumstance that this whole scandal might speed
along."

"Why?"

"Well, look at it. You've got a republican government
here, a government of the center"—Hay's hands cupped an
invisible melon—"which is really a motley group holding
off the Boulangists and all the others—the Bonapartists, the
royalists, all of them—on the right and the Communists and
Socialists and radicals on the left. Now, if it turns out that a
republican-centrist government was corrupt, all the deputies
and ministers with their hands in the pie"—he wiggled his
fingers—"then the parties at the extremes are going to benefit from that. Clemenceau is going to do his damnedest to
make sure that the Socialists are the ones who gain from this
scandal, Delahaye the same with his Boulangists. Clemenceau has the tougher job, because of his connection to the

company, but both of them want to see this thing blow up in the republicans' face.''

Adams fixed an image of Clemenceau and Delahaye as antipodes: paired and opposite forces, as alike and as distant as those verandas at Dingler's Folly. ''Which will happen soon, I expect. Loubet will call for a vote of confidence, correct? Cameron says so, at least. And I would think the longer Loubet puts it off, the more information will come out.''

Hay shook his head. ''If Cameron says Loubet wants a vote, he's got better information than I do.'' Clearly, Hay didn't think so. ''And about putting it off: no. Not necessarily. Loubet called in a few favors and got an amendment added to the investigations bill before it passed, which may explain why he didn't fight against it harder. The committee's powers of subpoena expire at the end of the week.''

Cunning, Adams thought. ''If Delahaye doesn't produce that list he was talking about by Friday, then the Chamber will have to let the whole thing drop. It'll seem that Delahaye was just grandstanding. And Loubet will have taken his public stance on the side of getting the truth out.''

''Precisely.''

Ah, legislation, Adams thought; unacknowledged kin to theater. A kind of puppetry, really, when you thought about it: each legislator was both puppet and puppet master, manipulating the public presentation of himself to advantage, in order to suggest the story he wants told. Who knew what Loubet's private, puppet-master motives were? Why had he set a limit of a week? Adams pictured the long, sallow face, the graying hair, the smooth neatness of the man. What lay behind it? Setting a limit and waiting it out would make sense only if he knew that Delahaye didn't have the list ready at hand—and knew it would be difficult for him to get. An idea was growing in him. ''I saw him at Madame LeBlanc's last night,'' Adams said. ''Loubet, I mean. I think he wanted something from her and didn't get it. She lied to me about not being at Miss Talbott's apartment. I have this feeling that she knows where Miss Talbott is.'' And then, suddenly, he saw it: ''Miriam has the checks—or at any rate the list of deputies who took bribes. That's why she's in hiding. She was Reinach's mistress, he did the bribing, she'd have access to all the names. That's got to be it, Hay.''

Hay thought this through. Idly he walked his fingers across the globe until the Isthmus of Panama came into view. ''Possible. You're making some assumptions, but it's possible.''

''Of course it's possible. Not only that, it's likely. This explains everything. You've got to help me find her, help her get that list out.''

Hay gave the globe a soft spin. It was impossible to read the small triangle of mouth that showed below the white, long-handlebarred mustaches, above the swirling strands of his white goatee-patch. Nor could Adams find a clue to Hay's thoughts in his eyes; these remained unfocused, fixed on something far from the globe in front of him. ''So,'' Hay said finally. ''You want to help Delahaye and the rightists.''

''No, that's not the point.''

''But that will be the effect.'' Hay looked up from the globe and turned his dark eyes directly on Adams. ''I can't help you. I don't really think advancing the cause of the Boulangists would be in the best interests of the United States.''

''The list could be given to this man Clemenceau. Hay, you have to help. She's an American citizen and deserves the protection of her government.''

''There's no proof that she's in trouble, no proof that she needs protection.''

''Proof! What do you want, bloody fingerprints all over a message in a quaking hand, begging for help? Of course she's in trouble!''

But Hay was resolute. ''I have no authority to intervene.''

''Authority! The girl is in *trouble*.''

''That's as may be.'' Hay shook his head. ''I'm sorry, but I have duties here.''

''And what, exactly, are they?'' There was a querulousness in Adams's voice that he wished hadn't been there.

''Adams, we've never had secrets, because you've been tactful enough not to pry.''

''Yes. But now I want to know.''

Without speaking Hay walked to the window and stood there, looking out. ''You're putting me in a difficult position.'' His fingers rested on a mullion, which he noticed was dusty; he wiped his hand on his trousers. ''I can't tell you.''

''No?'' said Adams. ''All right. I'll tell you.'' Hay was still at the window and Adams couldn't see his face. ''You've been asked to feel out the French on what they think is the value of the work they did in Panama. There is interest at the highest levels in Washington in purchasing their concession. You'd love to get a treaty assigning the French rights under the concession over to us. But it's a bit problematic right now, isn't it—the scandal, the government changing? Whom does one negotiate *with*? And if you are too interested, that sends the value up—or makes the French think that they would be wrong to let the concession go. And if word is spread too far that the concession is for sale, other countries might get interested. That would bid the price right up, wouldn't it? For the railroad, especially. It's a money-maker, just the way it is. The main link between two oceans. And it's crucial—you can't build a canal without it.'' Adams paused, wanting to gauge the effect of his words, but Hay stood at the window with his back to him. ''It's all too obvious, isn't it?'' Adams asked.

Hay finally turned. ''Yes, I suppose it is.'' He sighed and seemed relieved. ''Don't you go running the railroad stock up on me now, you hear?'' Hay grinned at him but could not force a smile from his friend. ''Look, I'd like to help, but I can't. It wouldn't look good. I can tell you I'm involved in some extremely sensitive negotiations, and if these people I'm talking to get word that I'm prowling around, prying into their precious Panama secrets, well, that might be the end of it. I've already risked a great deal just finding out what I have about Miriam Talbott. If I keep at it, these people are going to think I'm trying to undercut their negotiating position. And they'd be right. The more the scandal is revealed, the more obvious it is that France is done with Panama—and the weaker their position is. I wish you success. But I can't help. I can't be seen to help, and I can't risk trying to do it on the sly. Of all the people you could have asked to help you, I am undeniably the worst.''

''Something new,'' Adams said. ''A moral argument.''

''All right,'' Hay said, a note of warning in his voice.

"Even if I wanted to, even if I were authorized and even if it weren't a mistake, I couldn't." He shrugged to indicate his helplessness. "This Panama business is taking all my time. For instance, today I had to call on the Italian ambassador. I had to leave the office, get in my carriage, go across town, and call on him. Someone, it seems, has done him a major disservice by giving him alcohol."

"He's a fool."

"Nevertheless. He's an important fool. I still had to go." Hay shook his head slowly, then tried another smile. "You were pretty wild-eyed."

"What's he got to do with Panama?" Adams asked.

Hay's smile disappeared. "Who said he's got anything to do with Panama?" His black eyes were half-lidded. "There are some things it's better not to know. I wish I could tell you, but I can't. Someday—later. Back home. Believe me."

"Yes," Adams said, shaking his head so slightly that Hay might not have noticed. "Back home."

He ran through it for the tenth time as he jounced along in the cab. The body of a woman—Not-Miriam, he had begun calling her, needing some name, but aware that in letting her existence be defined negatively he did injustice to who she had been—turns up dead, drowned in the river, a suicide. Someone wants to hide her identity, and so chops off her fingers—and kills the coroner to do it. But prints had already been taken. The woman was acquainted with the baron, who has himself committed suicide in order to avoid prosecution for his crimes, and who kept as his mistress Miriam Talbott, an American artist, who in all likelihood is in hiding with a list of *chéquards*. While at Hay's he had tried to assimilate his friend's news of Miriam as just another fact needing to be accommodated, but he was beginning to feel its force. Miriam, a mistress. A Frenchman's mistress. If anything it made her seem . . . more compelling. Hers was a social position defined by sex, by the fact of a sexual relation. It seemed particularly bold of her. He thought of her walking in front of him, in her mannish painter clothes, the shapeless wool pants that she had worn, the way he had enjoyed watching her legs swing with each stride.

She would have had her reasons. He was certain of that.

How did the dead woman fit into this? Why had she been trying to pass herself off as Miriam? What did that have to do with it?

He remembered the cleft in Miriam's chin, the clear blue of her eyes and those remarkable dark eyebrows. She had been Reinach's lover. And he only just realized: that meant she had been abandoned by a suicide.

God, he hoped she was bearing up.

There had been some strength of character visible in Miriam's face; there was about her no hint of deference, but some quality of solid determination, the will to make her way in life, to do what was right. This was the quality that had first drawn him to Clover twenty years ago—Clover with her penetrant wit, she who seemed free of the tyrannies of propriety and the regard of others, weights he always feared he himself felt too keenly.

There was a lump in his throat that he couldn't swallow. How wrong he had been! He had failed her. He had gotten her out of Boston, away from his family, and had cultivated friends capable of appreciating her, but it hadn't been enough. There was too much of the world in the world he had placed her in, and he hadn't been able to protect her from it, hadn't been able to make it a world that needed her. He hadn't seen her clearly, not at all: the strengths that drew him to her, the qualities he thought were deeply rooted aspects of her character, were in fact something else, a shield which, perversely, the more comfortable she had felt with him, the freer she had been to drop, revealing herself in all her weakness. Her strengths seemed to lie on the surface, to be impressed on her from without. Far from being bold and confident, she seemed to value herself only for her worth to her family, most especially to her father. It was as though the confusing emotional tangles of the Hoopers, the tragedies that seemed to plague the family, were the trellis upon which she displayed herself. And these had been the very relations he had taken her away from. Alone, she had been too weak to hold herself erect. Her letters to her father were written not just out of filial duty but because they had been her one narrow means to replenish and affirm her being. A letter a week, every Sunday—more often on their honeymoon; a letter a day she wrote then, a thin papery trail that extended all the way down the fat Nile, across Europe, across the ocean to home, like bread crumbs, an epistolary trail meant to mark her way into exile in the land of marriage. And even that hadn't been enough; at Aswan she had asked, and he had agreed, to cut their honeymoon short. She needed her father that much.

He began to cry, quietly. Are all tears tears of self-pity? He felt sorry for Clover, for Miriam, and yes, for himself.

5:30 P.M.

AT THE HOTEL he found a visiting card from Delahaye in his mailbox. He marked the fact of this but was too tired to think about it. All he wanted was to sit down in his own room with a comforting cup of tea. There was also a letter in a familiar script, as familiar as his own—Elizabeth's. With a pang he remembered his promise to Cameron that morning. He had completely forgotten. He opened the envelope as he crossed the hotel lobby, preparing himself for the guilt. She had waited all morning for him. Oh God. He'd have to smooth it over.

The stairs were so formidable that he decided to go straight to Elizabeth's, instead of climbing first to his rooms and coming back down. When he knocked at the door he was admitted to the sitting room by Amanda, who offered him tea and a kind of reprieve: Elizabeth was resting. Such a lovely young woman! Graceful; sweet. She was happy to see him, and eager to tell about her afternoon in the Louvre. He settled into a soft couch to listen. She had already made the tea; she poured him some, relishing, he thought, this chance to preside as hostess, and doing so with as much grace as her stepmother. As she spoke, he listened with part of his mind, the part behind his eyes that was warmed by the tea; the deeper part of his attention was engaged not by this moment but by memory, by all the moments he had ever spent with Amanda and Elizabeth; and in that larger moment, which stretched back to Amanda's girlhood and Elizabeth's arrival in Washington as the new, fresh-eyed wife of the senator, he felt a pang of sadness. Everything changed, everything changed.

"But, Uncle Henry," Amanda said, "you must tell me where *you've* been. Mother said you would join us today, and we waited and waited, but . . ."

"Yes," said Elizabeth coolly. She was standing in the doorway, wrapped in a dark blue embroidered dressing gown. How long had she been there? "Amanda worried about you."

"All that talk about anarchists and the government falling. Isn't it exciting? You weren't in trouble, were you?"

"No, no."

"Where were you?"

"I—" Adams began, then paused to find his purchase on the day. What could he tell her? "I've been looking for Miriam." That would have to do. "No luck yet. I spent the better part of the day at it," he added, thinking to avoid a detailed accounting.

"Oh? And how is your work progressing?" Elizabeth pulled the belt of her dressing gown more tightly about her and strolled into the room. "Are you getting much writing done? I thought perhaps you were too busy with your researches to join us. Or even to get word to us."

"I am sorry, Elizabeth." He thought that if he could tell her about the coroner she would understand, but he didn't want to upset Amanda with gory tales.

"What? You can speak in front of her." Elizabeth sat in a wing chair across from Adams and reached to pour herself some tea, wrinkling her nose at the bitter last of the pot.

"No, no," Amanda said, rising. "I was just leaving. I have been meaning to study my French magazines." Graceful, sweet, and socially astute, Adams thought. When she had taken her leave, Adams gave Elizabeth a rundown of his day, not overplaying its difficulty, but not stinting, either, in the presentation of his troubles. He left out the part that Hay had told him; it was not the sort of thing he wanted Elizabeth to know about Miriam. "So—I'm very sorry that I wasn't able to join you today. But you have to admit, it's not every day that you walk in on a gunshot victim and get dragged into the inquiry.''

"Oh God, no,'' she murmured. "That sounds horrible. Of course I forgive you.'' She smiled and shook her head. "And of course I was put out with you; it's not every day that I can arrange for Donald to invite you to squire me around.'' She moved next to him on the couch and smiled again, pulling her legs under her to sit sideways, facing him. "We could try again for tomorrow. Would you like that? I've been promising Amanda I'll take her to the Tuileries, and I know she'd love it if you came.'' When Adams didn't respond she added airily, "I've been promising quite a bit lately, and I think it's time I came through on some of it.''

Had Adams been more attentive he might have sensed the subterranean import that Elizabeth intended; the casualness of her voice was undercut by her wide-eyed, questioning gaze and the way she gently pinched her lower lip between her teeth. But Adams had been distracted by a thought, a comparison: Elizabeth was to Clover as Miriam is to Not-Miriam. Clover and that poor Not-Miriam had been suicides; and wasn't Elizabeth a species of kept woman, not quite a mistress, but not in substance different from one? Cameron kept her as certainly and completely as a baron might keep an impoverished art student.

"Henry? I said, do you want to go with us to the Tuileries tomorrow?''

And he saw other permutations: Miriam and Not-Miriam were linked by that name, a half-shared identity, while Clover and Elizabeth were linked by the fact of his love for them. But what if you paired them the third way? Clover and Miriam were artists; did Elizabeth and Not-Miriam have anything in common?

He couldn't say. Elizabeth was his closest female friend, the woman he knew best in the world; Not-Miriam was some tragic, anonymous wretch of a woman about whom he knew nothing.

Elizabeth was looking at him expectantly, her soft, full lips tensing a bit with concern. Hers was a wide mouth, wider than some would find attractive, but she used the corners of it to good effect. Very expressive mouth corners, he thought.

There was where you could see her sense of humor, her sense of irony in play: it would tug there, curving her mouth in subtle, delightful ways. It wasn't tugging now.

"Yes," he managed. "Yes. I'd be pleased. Certainly." But he couldn't shake the thought: A kind of mistress. Like Miriam. He found himself growing angry at her.

"Henry? What is it? You're still troubled about something, aren't you? Was it seeing that body?"

"No."

"Miriam, then. She's got you worried. I don't think you need be," she said, matter-of-factly. "The police will take care of everything. It's their job." She leaned against the back of the couch, her elbow up over the crest of it; with a finger she stroked the soft velour pile, plying its nap back and forth.

Her reassurance seemed dismissive. "They have a lot to do. They're trying to find out about the dead woman, and of course they're investigating the murder of the coroner. They have better things to do than to worry about some American painter whose friend can't find her."

"You went to Missing Persons, didn't you? You can't do anything more."

But he could, Adams thought. If everyone knew that Miriam Talbott had been Reinach's mistress, then perhaps the dead man's business associates might be able to tell him something about her. Anything might be useful, anything might provide a clue to her whereabouts. Clemenceau, to be sure—but what about this man Lesseps, the one in the picture? If he could be found—

"Have you spoken to Hay? Can he help?"

"I thought of that. No. Says he's too busy."

"If it would help, I could talk to Donald. If you'd like me to, that is. I don't know what he could do—"

"No. Let's leave him out of it." This had come out more sharply than he intended. "I don't think it will be necessary," he said, moderating his voice.

"If you think not." Elizabeth reached out her hand to him along the back of the couch; she might have stroked his temple, had he not moved.

"I must be off," he said. He set down his teacup and stood. "It has been a pleasure."

"Oh yes, by all means. Don't let me keep you." Something in her voice made him turn to her, in time to see her hand make a dismissive wave. "And don't bother telling me what you're doing. I'm used to being kept uninformed. Alone and ignorant, that's the motto, isn't it? You and Donald should form a club."

There was no cause to put him in the same category as her husband. "Elizabeth," he said sharply. He looked at her, down into her face, seeing in her blue eyes the delicate rim of black around each iris. She glared at him and leaned back on the couch, one leg bent beneath her and the other dangling carelessly to the floor, bare from calf to toe, and even though she was glaring at him, he thought: Half the men in Washington would envy me this, just this. At whom was he angry? At Miriam? At Cameron? "I'm sorry." He was about to explain, but it suddenly seemed too hard, with too many dangers to steer around: Miriam's status as Reinach's mistress, his concern for her, and his confused feeling for her, a confusion he wasn't sure he wanted to examine, let alone examine in concert with Elizabeth; and then there was his own feeling for Elizabeth, crosscut with the mixture of envy and distaste he felt for Donald Cameron. And there was his promise to the senator as well. It was too, too complicated. "I'll tell you all about it later," he promised. "Back home." Hay should hear him.

"Certainly." Her voice was ice.

He thought out a plan while climbing the stairs to his room. He'd find the cabstand nearest the canal company offices, find there a cabbie who knew Lesseps and remembered driving him home. He had washed up and was rinsing his face when he saw something strange: a black smudge on the white enamel of the sink. Ash. And there was a black-hypotenused triangle of paper, an inch on each side, in the drain. Someone had burned something, then run the water. He started to pick it up, stopped himself, and bent to examine it. A photograph. From his desk he got a pair of pens and with the nibs of these he carefully picked it up. He carried it over to the desk, holding the two pens out in front of him like a dowser's witch. Only when he set it down did he notice that Dingler's photograph of canal company officials was missing from his desktop: someone had entered his room, burned the photograph, and taken the frame. Nothing else was missing, nothing else had been disturbed.

He sat down. What could this mean? His room—his desk—had been violated. He looked about. The room no longer appeared to him as the comfortable haven it had been just a few minutes before. Someone had come here precisely to destroy that photograph, someone who knew him and knew what he was about.

Well, if fingerprints could be lifted from paper, maybe he could find out who. He slid a sheet of clean paper under the burned corner, then fished an envelope out of a drawer with his other hand. He jockeyed the scrap into it, then folded it and put it in his breast pocket. Perhaps Bertillon or DuForché could make something of it, though it was too late to catch them in the office. Tomorrow, he decided; tomorrow the police. Tonight Lesseps.

The cabbie had to talk to five other cabbies before he found one who knew the address: all the way out in the mansions near the Bois de Boulogne, the great park in the northwest quarter. "Are you sure you want to go?" his driver asked. He stood on the curb, an old bowler mashed low on his head, his whip tucked under one arm.

"Of course," Adams said. "Why wouldn't I?"

"Fine by me." He clambered up and gave the reins a shake. "The anarchists haven't been after cabbies yet." His voice, coming from his perch above and behind the cab, was indistinct against the clatter of the wheels. "Thugs, thieves, anarchists, that's what you've got out there. It's gotten out of hand. The general'd have cleared it up—never would have let it happen, in the first way."

"The general?" Adams leaned forward and turned in his seat, to hear better.

"General Boulanger himself. Finest man who ever breathed French air. He'd have set them straight. Not like these nine-pins we have now."

"But he's dead."

"That he is, yes, and it is a cold-stove pity. They say he did it himself, but I know, I just know *they* got to him."

"Who?"

"The government. These damn republicans. He was too strong for them. Too popular. He would've been premier, would've shaken them right up."

"He's still got quite a following, doesn't he?"

"He has, he has. Anywhere the people love France, anywhere they are the real Frenchmen, why, that's where they love the general. He's a real patriot, you ask me."

And that's where, Adams thought, you'll see political beliefs locked in the armor of patriotism. On both sides of the Atlantic this was the new disease of the body politic: political power, no less than economic power, tended to monopoly. Partisans on all sides proclaimed that they alone were virtuous. Washington, Paris, London, Berlin—it hardly mattered, you could see the process eat away at the common ground of a political culture until all that was left were the extremes. Or maybe one couldn't even call them extremes: the term implied distance from a center that no longer existed.

"Your general—didn't he want to restore the King?"

"He did, he did. He was going to get us back on track, that one."

So he was talking to a bona fide royalist. "What did your general think of the Panama Canal?"

"He'd have blasted 'em, that's for sure. Jail's too good for them, that kind there."

Adams puzzled on this. "I meant the *canal*. What did he think of it, of the Panama Canal?"

"Why, he was all for it. Greater glory of France, path between the seas, all that. He would have had something to say about these goddamn Jews who ruined it, I'll tell you."

To this, Adams did not reply.

8:00 P.M.

LESSEPS'S HOUSE WAS protected from the street by an iron fence and a yard so densely vegetated it seemed impenetrable. Bushes and low trees hulking together in the twilight hid the lower story completely. Adams asked the driver to wait for him and stepped down from the cab. He wondered for a moment what Parisian etiquette suggested for an unannounced evening call; at home, certainly, one did not do this sort of thing. He swung open the gate and tried to push aside the feeling that he was trespassing.

From the gravel walkway he could see that the yard had been landscaped, that it had in fact been a garden at one time, on the English model—its design, by avoiding symmetries, obscured the hand of the designer—though it was now overgrown and tangled from neglect. Small wooden plaques, their paint peeling, identified the species of each tree and bush. He pushed beneath an overgrown lilac bush and faced a dark tunnel that curved through the shrubbery, its end—if it had any—obscured from view. Beneath his shoe the slate walkway was covered with a soft bituminous scum, a litter of wet decaying leaves. Ducking down with his arms over his head, elbows high to fend off unseen branches, he feared he would lose his balance and fall. He was relieved when he reached the wide and tractive expanse of porch.

He found the bell and rang it. In a few moments a light came on—suddenly, without the usual soft glow before the wick is fully lit and trimmed. It revealed in the translucent glass of the front door the silhouette of a man, a servant. Adams presented his card and was wordlessly escorted to the foyer. Thick carpet covered the stairs, and the newel post supported a crystal-globed lamp, whose white glare washed the foyer clean of shadows. Electricity: nothing but the latest for the house of an engineer, Adams thought. To the left and right of the stairs were matching mahogany doors, the wood polished to a dark sheen, each with a large panel of frosted glass, and in the center of each panel some sort of etching. Adams moved to examine one: a dredge.

Eventually a tired-looking man in a dark business suit descended the stairs. Adams recognized him from Dingler's photograph as Charles de Lesseps, which the man soon confirmed by identifying himself. His hand rested lightly on the banister as he came down, erect and graceful. There was a familiar quality about him that went beyond Adams's acquaintance with the photograph; with his short, trim beard and balding head, in bad light he might have been mistaken for Adams's own brother Charles. "Can I help you?" he asked.

Adams introduced himself and bowed slightly. "I would like to have a few words with you about the Panama company, if this is at all possible."

"I'm afraid that is out of the question." The man seemed to preside over him; Adams glanced quickly at the bottom step to reassure himself that Lesseps was not still standing on it. "Our solicitor recommends otherwise."

Adams was about to say that his questions wouldn't be complicated, wouldn't reach to the ground a lawyer might want his client to avoid, but of course this wasn't true. And as the impetus for his assertion faded, a new thought supplanted it: this man was in the picture. Maybe he would have some idea why someone had broken into Adams's rooms to burn it. While these thoughts occupied him, he could see Lesseps looking at him expectantly, then resolving to speak as it became obvious that Adams had fallen silent. "I want to know about Jacques de Reinach," Adams said quickly. "Not his business dealings, but something more . . . personal.

His private life. You knew him, didn't you? May I ask you a few questions?''

Lesseps's face was inscrutable. "No," he said evenly. "I cannot help you. And you will have to go, Monsieur—Monsieur . . ."

"Adams. Henry Adams."

"Yes, fine, then, Monsieur Adams. You will—"

"Charles!" came a voice from behind the door to Adams's right. "Who's there? Who is it? Damn you! Answer me! I will have my visitors!"

"Excuse me," Charles de Lesseps said with dignity, and moved deliberately to the door, shutting it softly behind him. In a moment he returned. "You'll have to go now," he said to Adams.

"Who's there?" came the voice again. "Don't let him stop you, goddamn it! Come in here where I can see you! Who are you?"

Adams spoke despite the warning he saw in Lesseps's face. "Henry Adams," he called, loudly enough, he hoped, to be heard.

"Henry Yaddams?" the voice responded, testing the English pronunciation. "Get in here!"

Slowly, watching Lesseps as he did so, Adams moved to the door. Lesseps did not protest. "Don't tire him," he advised as Adams opened the door and slipped past.

Adams entered a study that had been made over into an invalid's room by the addition of a bed in one corner. The light was dim, emanating from a shaded kerosene lamp on the desk; bookshelves and pictures on the walls seemed to swim up, on the verge of assuming form, before retreating back into darkness. A pool of light on the desk revealed a tray with supper dishes on it, clean except for bones and a crust. Two windows opened onto the porch, and Adams could neither see through them nor find in them any reflection of the room: the darkness inside was matched exactly by the gathering darkness without, behind the enclosing wall of shrubbery.

It took him a moment to locate the white-haired figure in a rumpled suit sitting in an armchair immediately to his right. Despite the deep bags under his eyes and the general dishevelment of his clothing, Adams recognized him: *Le Grand Français*, Ferdinand de Lesseps himself. He still had that full head of white hair, unkempt now, spraying out from its part like pages of a book. He saw in the father's face the same resemblance to his own lineage that he'd seen in the son; despite the full head of hair, there was some essential relationship of features, something between his eyes and nose and cheek that evoked parental authority. "Henry Yaddams," the old man said in a deep gravelly voice. "American. Your father, he is Charles Francis Adams, ambassador to England?"

Adams nodded.

"As I thought. I met him. I, too, was an ambassador, you know."

"No," said Adams. "I didn't know." I didn't know you were alive, he thought.

"Yes," the old man said, looking steadily at Adams, who returned the gaze, expecting the elder Lesseps to continue. He didn't. "Sit," the old man said finally. "Sit!" He pointed to an armchair across the room, then to a spot in front of him. "Over here where I can see you."

Adams pulled the chair up as he was told.

The old man waited for him to sit, then leaned forward in his chair. "Oh, they set me up," he said, shaking his head. "The bastards! I had everybody happy. I was busy. Negotiate here, negotiate there, flatter flatter, soothe, reassure, talk, talk, talk. But I had them. Me! Mazzini, Garibaldi, the Pope—all of them were going to do what I said. But then what?"

Adams was confused: he had thought Lesseps was talking about Panama, and he couldn't imagine what Italian nationalists and the Pope had to do with the canal.

Lesseps's pause had been purely rhetorical. "That damned rat-sucker sent in more troops. Me, I negotiate a peace for him and what does he do? He attacks!" Lesseps threw up his hands and sank back in his chair, his story finished.

Adams felt a need to clear up a few points. "The, ah, rat-sucker—was he a general? The commanding officer?"

"Nooo!" Lesseps looked impatient. "Napoleon III. *Before* he made himself Emperor. Just Louis Napoleon. Louis. The Prince President." He leaned forward again and dropped his voice. "I tell you, he couldn't hold a candle to his uncle. Not fit to feed his uncle's horses, if you ask me." He smiled with satisfaction.

"That was the end of your diplomatic career?" Adams tried to recall: When would this have been? 1849? He'd been eleven years old then himself, too young to have a memory of the time. If Lesseps had been in his forties, he must be in his eighties or nineties now. Although he didn't look that old.

"Yes, yes, of course," Lesseps answered impatiently. He spoke quietly, but even so managed to communicate a sense of force, of will, strength of command. Wild white hair, eyebrows full and wiry, eyes deeply lidded but bright—add a beard and he would pass for a biblical patriarch. Or a prophet. Which, Adams thought, he was, in a manner of speaking: a prophet who had made good the promise the Saint Simonians heard in the desert at Suez, a prophet of the coming age, the age that worshipped the secular gods of coal and steel.

And then in Panama he had failed. In the Church, failure might mark you for martyrdom, if it was spectacular enough, because elevation came through faith, not works; but in the church of industrial power, beatitude came through success and success alone; failure could know no forgiveness. Not because failure established an ineradicable guilt, no, failure was not a sin. But failure revealed you to have been falsely elevated; failure sent the entrepreneur back down to that mass of men whose numbers grew with each passing year, men who were subjects, not actors, men from the great anonymous mass whose motions and purpose and very lives were not generated from within but were impressed from without—stamped into them by circumstance, like so many pots or trigger guards or lamp bases or pen nibs. And who could find virtue—or fault—in a pen nib?

Looking at the man before him, Adams could imagine him with the borrowed youth of that great passion upon him, could imagine what he had looked like when he was known the world over as *Le Grand Français*, the Great Frenchman, the personification of the power of an entire nation. That had been his revenge on Napoleon III! Yet here he sat in this quiet room, his passion long since spent, his energies and reputation darkened into ash. "It was a matter of honor," Lesseps said, drawing himself up in his chair.

Adams nodded. "I thought you were dead. I read it in a paper."

"Bah! They tried to ruin me."

"Who?" Adams pressed forward.

Lesseps did not answer immediately. "The world," he said finally. "The world and everything in it."

It wasn't surprising, Adams decided, to find this man alive, for in this darkening room he was complete and unchanging, beyond the pushes and pulls, the wants and desires of humanity. The old man sat quietly, his eyes resting on his visitor, in a darkness thick enough to breathe, a darkness Adams feared might be contagious. No! Adams thought. With a feeling bordering on impatience and not completely innocent of anger, he wanted to break the spell; he wanted to see the world flood in, wanted to see *Le Grand Français* move, act, react. The historian stifled an urge to reach across the space that separated them and poke the entrepreneur in the stomach. You can't protect yourself, he thought. "I was in the diplomatic service once," Adams heard himself saying. "I worked for my father in the Embassy in London. But I left. Had to leave, really." The old man made no response—did not even indicate interest. "Some articles I had written—anonymously, for an American paper—were traced back to me by . . . by someone in the Home Office. I hadn't been very discreet in my descriptions, in my judgments of British society and officialdom. It caused a big stir. It, ah, caused my father great embarrassment."

Lesseps sat impassively.

"I was foolish, I know. I should have known that I would be found out. There was no one else in London who would have—who *could* have—written those articles." Why, he wondered, was he telling Lesseps this? Adams noticed his own hands, the hands of a stranger at the end of his arms, nervously twirling his wedding band. *My wife killed herself seven years ago this December*, he wanted to say. Wouldn't Lesseps understand how the world had gotten too complicated? Wouldn't he understand how it felt not to achieve the greatness one felt called to achieve, not through any malfeasance of one's own, but because some slot, some enormous unseen mechanism in the world, had shifted, foreclosing this path, opening others that were too distant, too strange? Lesseps was nodding gently, as if, having read his thoughts, he was indicating agreement. He did not seem to be waiting for Adams to speak. They understood each other perfectly. A question presented itself to Adams and he asked it without hesitating. "What would you do if you were my age? If you were fifty-four?"

"Me," the white-haired Frenchman said emphatically, "I would build a canal. Through *Panama*."

In response Adams could only nod, slowly; for a moment he felt the man's asseveration as a moral injunction. Yes. A canal; through Panama. It needed to be built. Then Adams remembered himself, remembered the pathetic sight of the broken machinery that had been hauled out of the Culebra Cut and left to rust, having proven itself insufficient to the task pressed upon it. The mud, the disease, the army of workers sacrificed to malaria, and everywhere the grasping greenery, the mute, lush, indifferent vitality of the jungle: it hadn't changed. What made him think anything had changed? "Nature beat you," he said slowly to the old man.

The Great Frenchman shook his head slightly, holding one hand to an ear, folding it forward until it looked like an albino fig. Adams knew what he wanted. He repeated the phrase, leaning forward, and on repetition it seemed the wrong thing to say.

"Nature beat me!" the old man shouted when he understood. "Nature did *not* beat me!" He thumped the arm of his chair. "Bankers beat me. Lawyers. Jackanape accountants! Cowards for shareholders, goddamn greedy politicians! Not nature! Never!"

Adams glanced nervously over his shoulder at the door, worried that the son would hear the commotion and pull him away. "Yes, yes, I understand," he said, as soothingly as he could. Still, Adams thought, nature *had* beaten this man; his machines had been too weak for the jungle and the mud, had proved incapable of joining two oceans. Joining two oceans: the phrase itself gave some sense of the sheer hubris of the effort. No one spoke of hubris anymore, Adams thought. The catechisms of industrial progress disallowed the very concept, as a heresy on the name of Power.

When Lesseps quieted, Adams remembered his purpose. "I've come to ask you something about your company," he began. "Actually, about an officer of your company, Jacques de Reinach. And a woman, Miriam Talbott. Can you tell me anything about either of them?"

"Who?" Lesseps said.

"Jacques de Reinach and Miriam Talbott."

Lesseps smiled and shook his head.

"You don't know them?"

Lesseps gazed at Adams and sat motionless, except for the tip of his index finger, with which he slowly traced a tiny *s*, backwards and forwards, on the arm of his chair. "Charles!" he suddenly bellowed. He remained silent, frowning, until his son entered the room.

The younger Lesseps stood in front of Adams and held an arm out to encourage his movement in the direction of the door. "You've been asking about Panama, haven't you? Under advice of legal counsel my father and I are forbidden to talk about the Panama affair."

"I understand," Adams said. His instinctive reaction had been to rise, and he had pulled his feet together in preparation, but then saw that further conversation was possible only as long as he remained seated. He settled himself back into his chair and began to explain. "I am not here in any official capacity." He tried to speak calmly, slowly, but could see that the patience of the younger man was wearing thin. "At any rate, I am an American and will be going home soon. My interest in the affair has nothing to do with politics or law or justice." Tactical mistake, that, he thought: the implication was that these men had something to fear from justice. Maybe they wouldn't notice. "I am looking for a woman. The police think she is dead, but she isn't. She was acquainted with one of the directors of your company, Jacques de Reinach."

"Miriam Talbott?" Charles de Lesseps said sharply. "What do you know of Miriam Talbott?"

Something in the man's eagerness pushed Adams back,

and he determined to think before answering. The younger Lesseps held up a hand toward the door. "Come with me," he said. In a louder voice he said to his father, "I will show Monsieur Adams out." Adams glanced at the old man as he rose, and paused to offer a slight bow, one that he abbreviated when he saw the intensity with which the old man was glaring at him.

8:25 P.M.

AS HE FOLLOWED Charles De Lesseps out, Adams realized that what had sparked his interest was the possibility of gaining information. He should have played that angle from the start. Lesseps shut the door to the study behind them and pulled Adams away from it, toward the stairs. He turned and spoke. "What do you know about Miriam Talbott?"

Adams cleared his throat. "There are two women, actually. Miss Talbott is a friend of mine. She is missing. The other woman is dead." This information held Lesseps narrow-eyed with attention: Good, Adams thought. "The police think that my friend is the dead woman."

"Mmm-hmmm. But you are saying they're mistaken."

"Yes. I know that the body the police have, the woman they have in the morgue, is not Miriam Talbott."

Lesseps nodded. "Because she was a friend of yours."

It seemed Lesseps was about to go on, but he didn't. "What can you tell me?" Adams asked him. "About this man Reinach."

"You didn't know him?"

"No."

"Mmmm." The son of *Le Grand Français* paused to choose his words carefully. " 'This man Reinach' bled my father white. Bled the company. There's a good chance we'll go to jail for what he did."

"He was blackmailing your father?"

Lesseps looked insulted. "My father has never done anything for which he could be blackmailed. No. Reinach was embezzling from the company. Took millions. Millions of francs. He was a disgusting, underhanded, weak-willed thief. They're going to say we should have known."

Adams thought it wouldn't hurt to establish himself as a sympathetic listener. "But of course you didn't."

"No." Lesseps appraised him carefully for a moment. "No, we didn't. But I will tell you who did. I might as well. You're bound to run across him soon enough. Cornelius Herz." Adams nodded to let him know he'd heard the name before. "My father and I have made mistakes. You must understand that, to us, the canal came before everything. We had to hold the company together, had to keep the work going, had to find more and more money for it. Reinach knew a man he said could help us. This man, Herz, was hired to ensure the success of the company's financing—the bond issues."

"He was a banker, then?"

"No, no. A—what would you say—publicist? I believe you have a word for it, lobbyist, yes. We had a contract with him: he was to publicize the company, prepare a good reception for us in the Chamber of Deputies and the Senate." Lesseps narrowed his eyes. "We gave Reinach a free hand. Too free. I was extremely surprised to learn the amounts he had authorized to Herz, the ways the money had been spent."

"The money went for bribes."

Lesseps shrugged and eyed him solemnly. Adams hoped he would not be able to read the thought that crossed his mind: he ought to have known. "I can tell you what is common knowledge. Herz is under indictment for having passed money to a deputy at the café in the Bois. The prosecutor says that from among Herz's hundreds of transgressions he has picked the one that he can most readily prove. I suspect politics—the deputy in question is a syndicalist, with no friends in the Chamber. Be that as it may. It is likely that some of the money also went for Reinach's vices, which included women. Which is why I am interested in speaking to this friend of yours, this Miriam Talbott. Our lawyer should pay her a visit.''

Adams hadn't considered that his inquiries might set other events in motion, and the reality of this possibility made him a little queasy. ''I—I don't know where she is. She is missing.''

Lesseps smiled a thin smile. ''Obviously my lawyer can't talk to her, then. Not until she is found, eh?''

''I was hoping you might be able to give me some information, something, anything, that might help me find her. Perhaps you know of some habit of hers, or perhaps she and this man Reinach had a favorite pastime, a favorite restaurant . . .''

''How well did you know her?'' Lesseps looked puzzled. ''Aren't these things a friend would know?''

''I know she has the list of *chéquards*.'' Adams wasn't certain of this, but wanted to re-establish a kind of standing. And it wouldn't hurt to test the idea.

''Mmmmm.'' Lesseps arched an eyebrow. ''Yes. And what are her plans for it now? Does she have any more blackmail in mind? Or is it just for sale to the highest bidder?''

Miriam a blackmailer? How?

''You don't know what I'm talking about, do you? Really, how well did you know this woman?''

''I—we—'' He began again. ''She and I . . .'' Lesseps stared at him, waiting. ''She was my friend,'' Adams said simply.

Lesseps shook his head. ''I suppose she didn't tell you about her blackmail attempts. No, I don't suppose you knew her well enough for her to tell you about the blackmail she had done.'' Adams didn't like the sarcasm he heard, but couldn't do anything about it.

''Whom could she blackmail with the list? Somebody on it?''

''Yes—or anyone, on it or not, who didn't want it revealed, for whatever reason. Your Miss Talbott paid some visits to various deputies with the idea of getting their assistance for her baron. Call off the papers, get him some sort of deal for giving evidence. It didn't do much good. And so now she is in hiding.''

''Yes.'' But it had done some good: Reinach's name had disappeared from the Micros articles, the series that broke the scandal, starting sometime in October. Had she succeeded? Is that why she was out of sight now—she had to keep the list hidden, to honor the agreement? He tried to decide if Miriam could have made such an agreement. There was a hardness there, a quality of determination . . .

''God willing, and if there is ever to be a French canal company again, she will *stay* in hiding, along with that list.'' Lesseps stepped toward the door. ''Enough. Our interview is at an end.'' Adams protested, but his host shook his head. ''No.'' He held up his hands. ''Please. No more. You must go.'' He put a hand under Adams's elbow and encouraged him along.

''What about Micros?'' Adams asked quickly. ''How does he figure in this?''

Lesseps stopped. ''What do you know about Micros?''

Adams calculated. He knew only what he had read in the papers; he had no idea who Micros was or who had fed him information. But the subject had gotten Lesseps's attention. He did his best to remain stone-faced as Lesseps stared at him, waiting.

''You know nothing,'' Lesseps said, dismissing him after a moment. ''Whoever your Micros is, I hope he can sleep at night. He drove Reinach to suicide.''

''Suicide? I thought he died of apoplexy.''

''So some say. Others, not.''

The two men looked at each other a moment. ''Micros must have had a good source within the company,'' Adams said levelly. ''Was it you?''

''Hardly.''

''Herz?''

''Really, monsieur—what did you say your name is?— Adams? You'll have to go.'' He reached behind Adams for the doorknob and opened it.

''Herz made a great deal of trouble for you. And yet he wasn't let go; you stuck with him.'' Adams let himself be backed into the threshold but went no farther. ''Why? Why, if he wasn't blackmailing you? What was in it for you?''

Lesseps stared at him for a moment. ''I will tell you this. He is very well connected,'' he said slowly. ''A friend of Clemenceau's.''

Adams felt his heart beat faster. Were Clemenceau and Herz together in this? Did Clemenceau help bribe other deputies?

Lesseps held up a hand. ''No more! Monsieur Adams, really, you must go. Goodbye.'' Firmly, leaving no room for resistance, Lesseps began to close the glass-paned door, pushing it against Adams. It shut with a clank, leaving him alone on the porch.

Scarcely had he taken a step down the path when the lights within the house were extinguished. In the darkness, nothing could prevent the encroaching vegetation from screening out an entire world.

Wednesday,
NOVEMBER 23, 1892

5:00 A.M.

HE HADN'T SLEPT well at all. In the quiet hours of the morning, when fear is most likely to masquerade as certainty, he'd awakened to the idea that whoever burned Dingler's picture would return. Lying there in bed, his eyes wide in the darkness, his nerves sensitive to every sound from the city below, he knew it was too late to do anything else—too late to pack up and mend things with Hay, too late to creep down the stairs and prevail upon Elizabeth to give him refuge. Much too late for Elizabeth, he thought. He held his breath every time he heard horse clops approach in the street.

His search for Miriam led inexorably into the Panama scandal. At first it had seemed to circle a bit, to move warily on the periphery, like the wrestlers he'd seen with La Farge in Japan, the immense, fat men who slowly revolved around a common center before leaning in to meet with a slap of flesh and a low grunt. But although the sense of visceral menace was appropriate, the image of a wrestling match wasn't right: no, it was more like a kind of brachiation of possibility, a confusing, interlocking web of alternatives that threaded through the central, substantive matter of his ignorance, as though the Panama affair were a sodden clump of jungle soil he could see around, but whose substance, held together by a thousand tiny roots, was opaque. A line from Schiller came to him: "Natural necessity has entered into no compact with man." The world is under no obligation to make sense to us. One stumbles along as best one can, subject to correction from anyone who knows better.

"Schiller." Adams said the name once, out loud, lying on his back. Schiller was a romantic, more romantic than even he had been, even years ago when he was young. He winced to remember how much he had loved Schiller, how he had introduced Clover to his work, how on their honeymoon the two of them had taken turns reading aloud to each other from his history of the Thirty Years' War. They read in German, his own schoolboy's familiarity with the language coming back to him, Clover surprising him with her fluency, with the easy way she rolled the gutturals up from her throat.

Remembering this, Adams suddenly felt disgusted with himself. Miriam Talbott! Miriam Talbott, *blackmailer*, he thought. Another man's mistress. Just what did he intend to do when he found her: take her to his home, sit her down on a couch, get a fire going in the grate, lean back and read poetry to her in German? God! He was little better than some love-struck freshman, mooning about, ready to attach himself to anything in skirts. He should honor the memory of his wife and leave it alone, leave the whole thing alone.

He tried to picture Clover, tried to construct an image of her as he had seen her so many times: astride a horse, booted, with that jacket she used to wear and which he could see as clearly as if it were there before him. What remained obscure, what always remained obscure, was her face; he could never really see it, and because of that couldn't even try to recall it without simply aggravating his sorrow.

A strange light through the window drew him out of bed. The street below was quiet, its gaslights carving the dark cobbles into soft pools of stone. Behind the building across the street, on the horizon of city roofs, there appeared the tip, the first golden wedge, of what revealed itself as an illuminated obelisk. It was far too large to be a human invention, too large at that distance and the wrong shape entirely to be a hot-air balloon—even if (unlikely, he thought) a balloon might be aloft at this hour and could be made to give off light from every atom of its being. For an instant he had been filled with wonder and fear and an intense excitement: now here was miracle, here was the work of some agency or being unknown and unimaginable. Anything was possible! But scarcely had he felt the flush of this idea before he knew better. The obelisk was the first thin wedge of a crescent moon, a narrow tail slicing upward, beautiful, yes, but an ordinary marvel.

If his search for Miriam had the outward form of a pathetic thing, perhaps that was a sign that the controlling hand here was not entirely his own: circumstances had bent his life these past two days in ways he hadn't foreseen. This did not mean he shouldn't continue, didn't mean that the desire that moved him was small and mean-minded. True, ever since he had walked behind her to the field where she painted the Church on the Mount he had known that his attraction to her had some component that was irredeemably physical. And his sense of her had been changed by learning she was Reinach's mistress, and that she had attempted blackmail in aid of his cause. But he was seeking her not because she was beautiful or intelligent, not for her moral rectitude or because he sensed that he might have things to learn from her; not even because she reminded him of Clover, though he saw that this had counted for more than he had realized, and had sharpened his disappointment when he'd learned that she was a mistress and a blackmailer. No, he was looking for Miriam because he had known her and liked her and she might need him.

A sound in the hallway made him sit up, tensed, listening. After a moment he was reassured that it had been nothing— wood creaking in the night. But the fear, the alertness—this was intolerable. He was more fearful here, in the dark city of Paris, than he had been in Dingler's Folly, when he had lain awake listening to the eerie calls of nocturnal animals. The jungle of Paris was the more chilling for being a human construct, completely a human construct: there was no stick or stone or brick of it that hadn't been part of someone's plan, though like the jungle of Panama, the whole lacked any order, any pattern, any design. Who knew what harm was meant for him out there in that blank, anonymous night? It was horrible to face it alone. In the morning he'd pack a few things and move in with Hay. If, that is, he could smooth things over with him.

Here he was, he thought, a poor imitation of Saint Michael, the soldier angel of the Mount, who surveyed the sea, the immense tremor of the ocean. Like the archangel, Adams himself faced a danger that could come from any quarter. Saint Michael was on the whole less fearful than a pathetic old historian alone in his rooms, but no less keyed to circumstance, to environs, to enemies. Adams lit his lamp, found his pen, a fresh sheet of paper, and began writing.

The warrior angel was a force for unity, binding his minions into a whole, but it was a unity that could never find peace. And what do we in this century have in his stead? A belief in coal? In steam? In the probity of a human nature that had such powers at its beck and service? The Panama affair gives a definitive answer to that question. Given the chance, and the empowering hubris of industry, humans prove themselves to be corruptible, vengeful, greedy, crazed with the prospect—the burden, which they covet—of controlling things, of holding nature and themselves in check. Individually, perhaps, they had always been so; and this, one might even say, was part of their charm as a species, and the challenge that the angel called them to surmount. But today's polity is different from that of a half a dozen centuries ago, and so then are its gods, its saints, its acolytes: steam and coal encourage the elevation of men born in their likeness. Fanatic, amoral, incapable of perceiving ambiguity. Unconscious.

In the stillness of the night he looked at what he had done and thought: I have begun to describe how the world has become at this moment.

He continued: "There is no depth, no profoundness to the rottenness they carry. Their evil does not achieve greatness, even as evil; it is shallow, all surface, all appearance; that is its substance."

He read this over, pen in hand, and a final thought came to him. "But that will not," he added, "prevent it from engulfing any number of innocents."

8:30 A.M.

"MONSIEUR ADAMS?" THE man who spoke had a face like a shovel, with high cheekbones and long, flat cheeks. The other, with blue eyes and a sharp beak of a nose, stood a half step behind him at the hotel desk, motionless. "Could you come with us, please?"

"Why?"

"Chief Inspector Pettibois wants to see you," the officer explained. He was standing next to Adams, exerting a gentle pressure at his elbow, encouraging him along. The blue-eyed officer took up a position on his other side, and Adams saw that he had to go along. "May I leave my bag with you?" he asked the clerk, heaving it up onto the desk. There wasn't time to make arrangements about the handling of his mail. With a backward glance to make sure that the clerk was stowing the bag safely, he walked out of the hotel, flanked by the two officers.

He was surprised to discover that they did not have a carriage or a wagon waiting at the curb. Apparently they were walking; but the Prefecture was a mile away. At the head of the street they turned away from downtown and the Prefecture and instead walked him toward the boulevards, through a street filled with shops. "Here now—shouldn't we go that way? The Prefecture is that way. And where's your carriage?" Adams asked.

"We're just down the street here a bit," the blue-eyed

officer said. "Commissioner Pettibois wants to see you. There's been a . . . an incident."

"What? What happened?" Adams asked, but the officer just shook his head. Neither man spoke to him again. Passersby gave them a wide berth, turning to look at him as they passed. He tried to walk casually, not like a man being detained by the police. When he let himself imagine why Pettibois wanted to see him, what sort of incident there might have been, his stomach felt numb and sodden: maybe he was being taken to another identification, another body; maybe this time it would be familiar . . .

He tried to calm himself by looking at the shop windows along the way, but the gadgets and devices he saw there were disturbing in their unfamiliarity. The very furniture of life was changing—when had the objects and appliances of this world begun to look so strange? Wheels and levers and hoppers, or blades and whirligigs, or sleek rounded forms with handles; all of them, cumulatively, were sinister, the more so for being so new and shiny. What dangerous things were Parisians doing in their homes that they needed contraptions such as these?

People were still staring at him, but as long as he looked at the shop windows he could feign ignorance of their attention.

They walked past a tobacconist's, a cobbler's, a bookstore. In a doorway past the bookstore he saw a placard announcing an art school one flight up. *An art school.* Of course, Adams thought. That's where Pettibois has found her. She said she was a student . . .

He was confused when they passed the doorway. Then he thought, Maybe he's found her and has taken her somewhere for questioning. If Pettibois had found Miriam, it would be perfectly natural for him to want Adams to come and talk to her; and he'd want to question Miriam about the dead woman, too. But then he thought, This would happen downtown, at the Prefecture, unless there was a good reason . . .

Half a block past the art school Adams saw a knot of people gathered on the sidewalk and a police wagon in the street. A tired baritone voice addressed the group from somewhere near the doorway of a pneumatique office. "Here now," it said, "move back, move along. Go on about your business. There's nothing to see here." Through a gap in the crowd he caught a glimpse of uniform and the red face of a sergeant in the doorway. Most of the crowd did not accept his judgment but obliged him by stepping back. The blue-eyed officer took his elbow and led Adams through the crowd until they came into the clearing that the sergeant had made. Adams could feel the eyes of the bystanders on him, and was thankful to be out of view when they went inside.

The small office looked familiar—they were apparently built to a standard plan. In a quick survey he saw no dead body but wasn't sure that there might not be one, hidden somewhere, perhaps behind the counter. He looked more carefully: to his left he saw a row of uniformed messenger boys waiting on a bench, nervous and shy, no dispatches to deliver; one of them slumped loosely in his seat, eyes closed, head tilted at an uncomfortable angle. He was being attended by Pettibois and another policeman who held a jar of smelling salts. He saw that there was no space in which Miriam could be hidden and began to breathe a little easier. Behind the high counter where customers stood to write out their messages was a small workspace. Part of it was given over to a desk with a rank and file of pigeonhole cubicles above it, but most of the space was taken up with the office's reason for being, the iron pipe of the pneumatique, its large loop cresting up into the valving system, all shiny brass and copper and nickel.

"Monsieur Adams! So good of you to come." Pettibois left the young boy to greet him.

"I was under the impression I had no choice."

Pettibois ignored this. "Most curious, most curious. I thought you should be consulted."

"What is it?"

"Here," Pettibois said, steering him to the end of the counter, where a section was hinged to allow access. "Let me show you something."

Behind the counter Adams saw a bin that held a few dozen of the message carriers, brass cylinders about eight inches long with felt-and-leather gaskets at both ends. On the desk, centered on the clerk's blotter, was a single message carrier, opened along its longitudinal hinge. Pettibois stepped back toward the valving mechanism to allow Adams room. "Take a look."

Adams peered at the cylinder, approaching it slowly. There, nestled inside on the dark felt lining, were a number of small white sausages. With a start he recognized them: fingertips. Human fingertips. He turned away.

"They arrived in the pneu just"—Pettibois consulted a clock on the wall—"thirty minutes ago. We have no idea at which station they were entered, and there's no way to tell. Bizarre, isn't it? Gruesome, really."

Adams stood back where he couldn't see into the message carrier. The thought of those bloodless fingers, those lifeless, bloodless fingers, detached from their owner, sickened him. "Why did you send for me?" His head felt airy.

"Ah, now, that's the most interesting part." Pettibois reached onto the desk and picked up a slip of paper that lay there. "*To Henry Adams, Esquire*," he read, "*Hôtel Vendrielle, 56, rue Christophe-Colomb, Paris.* They were addressed to you."

"To me?" Adams asked. He thought fleetingly of the smelling salts. "Why were they sent to me?"

"That is what we were wondering," Pettibois said, smiling a terse, paper-thin smile. "Exactly what we were wondering."

9:30 A.M.

AT THE PREFECTURE Adams was shown into a room furnished with an unused desk pushed against a wall and half a dozen hard-backed chairs. The policemen departed, leaving the door open. Adams sat in a chair, then immediately rose. Looking out the door, he saw that his escorts had taken up positions in the corridor. He sat again. From the window he could see the rue de la Cité, a corner of the place du Parvis, and the hospital—the Hôtel Dieu—which obscured any view of Notre Dame.

He was left alone and distractionless for half an hour.

When Chief Inspector Pettibois finally arrived, he flashed a broad smile at Adams as he came through the door. "So! Monsieur Adams! I am sorry to have kept you waiting. I had another minor matter to deal with. I trust my men treated you courteously."

"That they did," Adams said. "Unless you count the discourtesy of wasting my time."

"Regrettable, very much so. Please," Pettibois said. "Don't get up." Adams had made no move to rise. Pettibois sat casually on the edge of the desk, next to Adams. "I heard about your episode with the Italian ambassador the other night. Difficult man, that." He shook his head. "You gave him liquor?"

"By mistake."

Pettibois nodded, with a sly smile.

"Really, it was a mistake," Adams repeated. He still wasn't sure he had been believed.

Pettibois leaned over and spoke amiably. "If you don't mind my saying, the Italian ambassador is a dry pill. Hard to take. All that sanctimonious teetotalism! I myself have had occasion to—"

"Is there a point?" Adams interrupted.

Pettibois was taken aback, but recovered well. "Forgive me. You are a busy man. Let's begin." He rose and stood in front of Adams. "Before joining you I thought it wise to detour through our friend Alphonse's fingerprint files. The fingertips do indeed belong to the unfortunate woman who drowned herself, the woman you viewed in the morgue. I think we both would like to get to the bottom of this, no?" Adams nodded. "Well then, let us begin."

"Certainly," Adams said, shifting in his chair. It had grown uncomfortable during the wait. "By all means."

Pettibois opened the door and called out to someone, and two men entered the room. One moved quickly to a chair and sat, placing a notebook and pencil at the ready on his knee. The other was an elegant older man, with short, graying hair and deep-set eyes, the large lids of which he held open with apparent effort, which gave him an air of permanent surprise. His expensive suit supported the impression that he was a stranger to the world of police work; he looked continually startled by his encounter with it. "The prefect will join us," Pettibois said. Although this hardly counted as an introduction, Adams caught his eye and nodded toward him, but received no acknowledgment in response.

"Now," Pettibois said, "why don't you tell us what you know of this woman, this body in the morgue I asked you to identify?"

Adams recounted the story, presumably for the benefit of the stenographer, or perhaps the prefect, since Pettibois already knew it.

"And this other woman," Pettibois prompted, "this other Miriam Talbott? What does she look like?"

"The real Miriam Talbott? She's about my height, five feet three inches, about twenty-five years old. She has blond hair and blue eyes, dark eyebrows. She has a pointed chin with a cleft in it, here.'' Adams pointed, touching his face, remembering how he had thought the cleft looked like a suture.

''And how did you meet?''

''In Pontorson, when I was visiting Mont-Saint-Michel. She was there, painting.''

Pettibois nodded. ''Did you see her with anyone else?''

Adams shook his head.

''For the record, Monsieur Adams.''

''Pardon?''

''The stenographer. You have to speak. Was there anyone else you saw with her?''

Flushed at his own obtuseness, he shook his head again and said, ''No.''

''You didn't see her at her hotel, didn't see her talk to anyone else?'' the prefect wanted to know.

Adams shook his head. ''Just the people I was with. Elizabeth and Amanda Cameron. They spoke to her.''

''Is there anything else you can tell us about her?'' Pettibois asked. ''Anything unusual, anything at all that you can remember?''

''No. She's American, that's all I know. She's been in Paris for a year, I believe she said.''

''Mmm-hmm.'' Pettibois tilted his head back and scanned the ceiling. ''Now, Monsieur Adams, I want you to help me imagine. What is the story here, what role do these fingertips play in our little drama?'' When Adams did not immediately respond, Pettibois levelled his gaze at him. ''You are unfamiliar with this method? To my mind this is how police work proceeds: take the senseless and make it sensible. Any set of facts can be made sensible if given the right explanation, the right origin in character and circumstance. You find your sensible explanation and it points right to your criminal. Of course,'' he added expansively, ''if you believe the philosophers, anyone who disrespects the law is already a little senseless, no? Certainly you've read Rousseau? He is so convincing about the law as the expression of the social good, about law as the product of reasoned self-interest, that it is hard not to think of any criminal as being a little, well, deranged, no?'' Pettibois smiled. Adams thought he was playing to the prefect. "But that is just theory. In actuality crime is perfectly sensible. This is what we must find, this sense of the matter at hand. Let us try to imagine. Why would someone send you those fingertips?"

Adams waited, thinking the question was rhetorical. When it became clear that it wasn't, he answered, "I don't know."

Pettibois nodded sagely. "Would it be to cast suspicion on you?" He looked at Adams, his eyes wide to read whatever he could. Adams stared back, trying to regulate the thoughts that came to him, fearing their betrayal on his face: he was revolted by the thought of those fingertips, pale and bloodless, and felt a degree of panic growing at the idea that their appearance somehow implicated him in events he didn't understand. Without knowing the complete shape of what had happened, the coherence of these events that were drawing him in, he was afraid that he couldn't present his innocence effectively. The facts of his life might misalign, might inadvertently match up in too many particulars to some pattern he couldn't yet sense, suggesting his guilt. And he *felt* guilty—not just about Clover and now Elizabeth, but here, now, about these fingertips. Out of all the millions of residents of Paris they had come to him. Why? Why had he been chosen? He felt a sinking sense of responsibility and failure. He mustn't let it show. How does one look innocent? Certainly innocence does not hesitate, isn't nervous. He swallowed, preparatory to speaking—what was wanted was a soft, controlled "I don't know"—but before he could speak Pettibois shook his head slightly. "No," he said. "If you *received* them, it's clear that you didn't *have* them."

Adams nodded.

"Perhaps," Pettibois said, putting his palms together and tapping his fingertips together, "they were meant to frighten you, to scare you."

"That could be."

"Are you frightened?" Pettibois took what he saw in Adams's face as assent. "Let us assume that this is the effect your unknown correspondent desired to achieve."

If that was it, Adams thought, the message was a bit ambiguous; he was unnerved, yes, but if someone meant to get him to stop doing something, he had no idea what he was supposed to stop doing. "If it's a threat, it isn't very clear."

"The criminal mind is not a complex thing, Monsieur Adams." Pettibois glanced at the prefect. "But an alien one. We must penetrate it, reconstruct it." Pettibois leaned forward and spoke in a voice that Adams thought the stenographer would have difficulty hearing. "What does the criminal want? He wants this thing or that thing, it hardly matters, because the important thing is that he is willing to step outside the rules of the nation to get it. What he wants, ultimately, is that his will should prevail. He wants his desire satisfied, his passions indulged, he wants to be the protagonist of his own story. And this, I think, is the key to his derangement, the thing that brings him into conflict with society—with *us*, Monsieur Adams. Because every nation insists on being its own protagonist, yes? Can there be room for these individual tales in a society ruled by law? This, this is the epic question, this is the epic struggle, between the self and the necessity for abnegation of the self in the larger whole. It is the whole that survives, flourishes, gives life, is it not? This is my purpose, as policeman—to secure this life of the whole." Pettibois paused and shook his head. "You see, there is philosophy in law enforcement," he added with a wry smile. "But our job, what we must discover, is the story our man is telling himself. I have a strong presumption that whoever sent these fingertips killed the coroner. This is sensible, obvious even, wouldn't you agree?"

Adams nodded. "What about fingerprints? Did you try the notepaper for fingerprints? DuForché told me that he's been experimenting with lifting prints from paper."

Pettibois stared at Adams for a moment before frowning. "That is a good idea. I should talk to Patrolman DuForché. Though I'd be surprised if we found any. No, I think we're dealing with a very cunning man here, Monsieur Adams. Very cunning." He shook his head slowly, then stood and walked to the window. "Perhaps our criminal seeks to create a mood, a sense of danger. In that case the threat need not be specific."

"No, I suppose not."

Pettibois nodded gravely. "Then again, perhaps the criminal means to discourage you in some pursuit. You have been detecting, have you not?''

Adams nodded.

''Do tell me what you've done, whom you've seen.''

Adams recounted the substance of what he had learned: Miriam Talbott had been Reinach's mistress, she was in hiding with a list of *chéquards*, she had, according to the younger Lesseps, attempted blackmail, Reinach was an embezzler who had sucked the life from the canal company . . .

Pettibois smiled, pleased. ''Very impressive. And of course you were going to come to me to tell me all this, no?'' Adams nodded and swallowed. It hadn't been his first thought. ''Now, there is one thing I find very puzzling, Monsieur Adams.'' He stood and slowly began to circle behind Adams's chair. ''Especially in light of your friendship with Miriam Talbott, and given that you were the one who found the coroner dead.'' Pettibois paused behind Adams, who tried to crane his neck to see him. He felt the pressure of the policeman's hands on his chair. ''My men tell me they found you this morning, suitcase in hand, prepared for departure. And yet a check with your hotel reveals that your registration was paid through the middle of next month. Leaving in a hurry, perhaps, Monsieur Adams? Why the sudden departure?'' Pettibois's eyes were cold: congenitally, professionally suspicious.

''It's not what you think.''

''No? What do I think, Monsieur Adams?'' Slowly he completed his circle of the chair and stopped in front of Adams. He leaned forward, bringing his face uncomfortably close.

Adams resented having his fears dragged out of him. ''I didn't want to stay there anymore, that's all.''

Pettibois smiled and straightened. ''This wouldn't have anything to do with a jealous husband, perhaps? Nothing to do with Madame Cameron and the, shall we say, affection that passes between you?'' Pettibois pursed his lips and looked patient.

''No!'' This interview was unimaginably horrible. To

whom had Pettibois been talking? "What in the world are you talking about?"

Pettibois shrugged. "Why, then, Monsieur Adams? What has you leaving for parts unknown?"

Adams took a breath. He could tell them. Yes. "I was on my way to stay with a friend. Hay. John Hay. I didn't want to be in my rooms anymore. I didn't feel safe there. Yesterday, sometime in the afternoon, someone broke into my rooms and destroyed something. A picture."

"A painting?"

"No, a photograph." Adams described it.

"And how did you come by this picture?"

"It belonged to Jules Dingler. I—I took it. From his abandoned house in Panama. I didn't think anyone would mind."

"Dingler, Dingler. I don't know the name."

"He was chief engineer for the canal company in Panama for a time. He died a few years ago."

"Chief engineer," Pettibois said slowly. "Hmmmm. Very interesting." He looked at Adams thoughtfully. "Well," he said after a moment. "Not someone you have seen in Paris, then, at any rate. Correct? Can anyone confirm your story? Did anyone know that you had this picture, did you show it to anyone?"

Adams shook his head, then remembered. "No—wait. Donald Cameron saw it on my desk. You could talk to him." He was relieved that Cameron had been nosy, that he himself had been forgetful enough to leave the photo in plain sight.

Pettibois nodded. "Let us speak of other things. You might be interested to know we've begun to piece together the movements of your friend, Monsieur Jacques de Reinach, on the night of his death. A very complex man, Monsieur Adams."

It was clear that Pettibois was speaking ironically, but there was, after all, a stenographer present. "For the record," Adams said firmly, leaning toward the stenographer, "Jacques de Reinach is not my friend." The stenographer made no indication that he had heard but continued to write furiously, head down. Adams was about to repeat himself when Pettibois distracted him by handing him a slip of paper.

"He stopped at this address. It is familiar to you?"

Adams read it. It was familiar. "It's Hay's address. John Hay. Special envoy to the President. My friend." The feeling that he had somehow let Hay down with this admission was replaced by a growing disquiet: what had Reinach wanted with him? And if Hay knew Reinach and hadn't ever mentioned it to Adams, what were the chances that he knew something about Miriam Talbott?

Pettibois, it seemed, had read his mind. "Why did Reinach go there? What was the nature of his business with Hay?"

"I don't know. You should ask Hay. I intend to."

"We shall, we shall. No harm in asking you, I thought. But I see I've upset you. Does Hay have any idea about this woman, this Miriam Talbott you seek?"

"I'm sure I don't know. I'm not privy to Mr. Hay's secrets."

Pettibois nodded sympathetically. "Yes, yes, I understand." He waited a moment, as if in respect for confidence lost, before changing the subject. "Another address, Monsieur Adams. Latin Quarter this time. Do you know it?" He showed it to him. "A very large concierge," he prompted. "A very large concierge with phossy jaw. Surely you noticed."

"I think so. Phossy jaw?"

Pettibois ignored the question, but stroked his own jawline, below his plump cheek. "Monsieur Reinach spent some time at this address the night he met his unfortunate end. We have talked to a cabbie who remembers taking him there. This is consistent with what you have learned—that Miriam Talbott was Reinach's mistress. She never mentioned him to you?"

"No."

"Did she speak of any of the men she knew in Paris?"

"No, no. The subject never came up. We spoke—" Adams stopped himself, thinking their conversations would seem comic, given what he now knew of Miriam.

"Yes? What did you speak of?"

He fought off a sigh. "Art. Stained glass. Cathedrals, things like that. She is very knowledgeable," he added, responding to Pettibois's skeptical glance. The chief inspector squinted at him, watching him carefully. Adams thought perhaps the man was waiting for him to continue. Well, he wouldn't say more. No.

After a moment Pettibois spoke. "Were you the man who asked for her?" he asked softly. "Monday afternoon?"

"Yes."

"Mmmmm. I thought as much." Pettibois nodded, then turned to the prefect, who had remained so motionless and silent throughout that, for all Adams could tell, he had been doing sums in his head. "Monsieur Adams is our mystery man," he said, rising from his perch on the desk. "I don't think we need go any further. Monsieur Adams, you don't know how close we were to putting your description on police bulletin boards all over Paris. Thank you for your patience and your trouble. You may go."

At this, the prefect stood. "Phossy jaw," he announced. "A debilitating bone disease. From phosphorus. Chronic in match-factory workers." He nodded to Adams without seeing him and moved out the door.

"May I ask something?" Adams turned to find Pettibois behind him. "Have you any news of her? Miriam Talbott, I mean?"

Pettibois shook his head. "No. And I do not hold out much hope, Monsieur Adams. This friend of yours is excellently situated to give evidence in the Chamber's inquiry. I suspect that if she were able, she would come forward. And I believe our experience with the coroner shows that we are dealing with unscrupulous men, men who will stop at nothing."

"Maybe she wants no part of the inquiry, but will turn up after Friday, when it's over."

"Perhaps, perhaps. That is certainly better than the alternative, eh, Monsieur Adams?" Pettibois moved to the door but paused to look back. "You may go, but please—do stay out of our way."

Adams nodded silently. The stenographer completed a few last marks on his pad and then shut it quickly. With a brief, round-eyed glance at Adams, he, too, left the room.

Adams was exhausted. Gathering himself, he walked into the hall. He felt alone in the world. There were some things it was best not to know, Hay had said. Back home, he had said, back home. Which was fine if you were Hay, with a rotund, iron-willed hausfrau of a wife anchored to the hearth, waiting, defining with stolid lack of imagination the unshakable base from which to journey. Even when Clover had been alive, Adams hadn't had that—hadn't wanted that. He had wanted a partner. And now . . . now he knew himself to be more portable in the world, less rooted to a particular place.

What else had Hay kept from him?

He took out his watch: nearly noon. The entire morning was gone. But perhaps his detour here had not been totally impropitious. He glanced right and left, up and down the hall, and walked to his right, where he could see a widening of the hall into another, smaller lobby. He presented himself to a man at a desk there, a receptionist. "Could you tell me," he asked, "where I might go to find a list of art schools in the city?"

An hour later he was descending the steps of the Ministry of the Interior with just such a list in his hands.

5:30 P.M.

AT THE BELL desk he retrieved his bag from the clerk. In his room, alone, he checked his belongings. All was in order. He had been unable to find Hay at the Embassy or at his home, and he had decided against leaving a note: what he had to do had to be done in person. And as a consequence of his failure to find Hay he would be spending another night in his own room; he had thought to forgive Hay quickly enough to become an overnight guest. After heating some soup and eating it, he got his paper, pen, and ink pot out and set them carefully on the writing desk. It had long been his habit to think on paper, and his faith was that this practice could serve him now.

"The difficulty," he wrote, "is that I have no control over the information that comes to me. I seek and do not find; and yet I have no lack of material for cogitation. It is information that does not inform, facts that do not clarify or cohere. Who in this morass is to be believed?"

The effort to encompass what lay before him, to render it reasonable, was formidable. Where to begin? Perhaps it would be best simply to describe.

"The art schools so far have yielded no trace of Miss Talbott. It is incredible to think that half the population of Paris is enrolled in one art school or another, but this appears to be the case. It is equally incredible to think that this reflects truly the distribution of talent for plastic representation among the populace . . .'' This wasn't the direction he had meant to take, but he decided to let it stand. He put his pen down and rubbed his eyes to think; he needed to see how Reinach, Herz, Lesseps, Dingler, LeBlanc, and Miriam all fit together. And Hay—where did Hay fit in? But the art schools . . . there was something bizarre about so many art schools. The new bourgeoisie wanted art, and what the bourgeoisie wanted it could call forth, like the mythic Chinese emperor whose magic staff caused armies to spring from the ground. Would the production of art become as industrialized as the manufacture of gun parts or shoes? He could picture it, long rows of students painting the same painting, being goaded on by an instructor who rushed up and down the aisles, desperate to make some quota. The students would be paid by the painting, would be driven to work long hours, would stop and start and eat their meager lunches to the sound of a steam whistle. Each of them had a brilliant electric light and a telephone next to his or her easel, and many of them were trying to speak into the mouthpieces while painting. The building was cavernous, empty, receding into dimness. Was this the night shift? There was the throbbing grumble of some immense source of power, the power that drove—what? The trolley-like carts that brought paints to the workers? Artist-drones slapped and spread the color on their canvasses, slathering it on, not spilling any, each of them miraculously forming under broad, hurried brushwork the same painting, over and over—a pastoral, Hudson River School. With one motion the workers stood, picked up a finished canvas, and put it on a moving belt that ground off into the darkness. He drew closer to look at one of the paintings where it lay, and the moving belt turned into a large glass tube somehow, with each painting sealed inside its own felt-ended container. The painting, he saw, was of a picnic, a grassy scene on the flank of a rock-bound cathedral. It was flat, perspectiveless, and like one of Miriam's paintings, each mass of color was outlined by a dark border. In the center of the painting sat Elizabeth, a nude Madonna on a field of blue, hamper at her elbow, motioning him in, holding out some delicacy that he couldn't quite see, inviting him to join her. She was in the painting, but also real and alive somehow. He was embarrassed by her nakedness and had to look away. He knew he couldn't join her, could not step into the world of the painting, and was about to tell her this when there came a whoosh of compressed air and the containers rattled in the tube and were gone.

He awoke slowly, trying to orient himself. His first conscious thought was to stay still: he did not want to spill the ink pot. When he wiggled the fingers of his right hand, he felt pins and needles; taking care not to move his arms, he drew his head up slowly, feeling strangely mechanical for this isolation of body parts, one from the others. A bit of drool from his mouth had smudged some of his writing. He blotted it, rocking the wooden handle back and forth. His left eye wouldn't focus: his knuckle had pressed it out of shape. Where was his pen? He found it, made an experimental scratch with it, and then tapped it on the desk to bring the ink down before capping it.

How long had he been asleep? He fished out his watch. Nearly seven o'clock! Should he light the lamps and continue, or get himself to bed and start early in the morning? He rose to stretch and was still debating the point when a knock at the door sent a clench of alarm through his neck muscles. He reminded himself that an intruder with ominous designs would not be likely to knock first. Still, he was cautious as he approached the door.

It was DuForché, vague and indistinct in the wan light, his police uniform blending with the shadows of the hallway. Adams squinted and motioned the young man in. "Oh, I'm sorry," DuForché said on entering. "Were you asleep? I woke you up." He moved to the center of the room, cap in hand, looking around.

"No, no," Adams replied. "I was just, ah, writing." Some sheepish part of himself hated to admit to napping.

"In this darkness?" DuForché asked.

"Thinking, actually." Adams still felt a little groggy. He should offer something—tea or coffee. Not coffee: he didn't have any. Squinting made his eye hurt; it would come into shape soon enough. He sat down.

DuForché nodded. "I know what you mean. I think in the dark sometimes, too."

"Do you want something?" He meant to be curt, but DuForché took him wrong.

"No. No, thank you. I'm fine." The young man turned to look at him, squaring his shoulders. "I came to apologize. For yesterday in my uncle's office. I let my imagination get the better of me."

"Yes. Well. Thank you. Apology accepted."

DuForché smiled and made no move to go. "Is that it?" Adams asked. "Or is there something else?"

The young man reached into his cap. "I have something for you. I picked up your mail."

It was hotel stationery, sealed with wax. Adams unfolded it and scanned it quickly, shutting the eye that wouldn't focus. That was much better: no binocular vision, but at least he wasn't straining.

"What is it?" DuForché asked. Adams was put off by this: a gentleman's mail is private. He weighed an admonition, then decided against it. There would be no harm in telling him. "It's from Deputy Clemenceau."

"What does he want?"

Rude, Adams thought, before realizing: this is part of the case. "He wants to see me." Adams turned his head to the side to focus on the paper. "Very polite. Apologetic. 'I should call on you, but duties keep me near the Chamber.' Asks me to come to his office in the morning. First thing." Delahaye and Clemenceau, political antagonists, both interested in him. There was a symmetry to it. "I bet he thinks I know something. Something about this scandal."

"Are you going to go?"

Clemenceau had been a friend of Herz. Maybe he knew enough to explain to him how Miriam was involved. "Yes."

"You might miss something," DuForché said, and he smiled, pleased with himself, pleased that he knew something Adams didn't.

Adams didn't have patience for this. "What?" he said sharply.

"A funeral."

It took Adams a moment. "The woman in the morgue— Not-Miriam? Her funeral?"

"Yes."

"Why should I go?"

"Oh, you always go to the funeral." DuForché affected a knowledgeable air. "That's where you've got the best chance of finding the killer. They almost always come. All you have to do is stand there, watching the mourners, and you get a pretty good idea of who did it."

"She was a suicide."

"Not *her* murderer. The coroner's. Whoever killed him wanted to get into the morgue and mutilate her body. He's bound to show up at her funeral." Adams's skepticism must have shown on his face. "Well, we might get a good lead, anyway," DuForché said. "It's worth a try. Look, I'll go with you to Clemenceau's, then we'll go to the funeral. It's at ten o'clock, in Père-Lachaise. Do you know where that is?"

Adams knew. Père-Lachaise, named for the Jesuit priest whose country estate the cemetery had been years ago, before the city expanded, contained the grave of Peter Abelard, the twelfth century's foremost logician, the Church's fiercest disputer, the philosopher condemned by the Pope and banished from his Parisian school for his heterodoxical defenses of Christian belief, the man who had been castrated by Canon Fulbert for his love affair with Fulbert's niece, the beautiful Héloïse. Adams had visited the grave his first time in Paris, in homage. "Clemenceau didn't say he wants to see you. I'll meet you at the cemetery."

"Suit yourself." DuForché shrugged and moved toward the door. "Maybe you'd like to come with me tonight. If you wanted to, I'd let you," he said pointedly.

"Where are you going?"

DuForché narrowed his eyes at Adams. Slowly he drew a folded document from his breast pocket. "This is a warrant," he said solemnly. "A search warrant." He held it, folded, in the air in front of him before replacing it, keeping his eyes on Adams. "I am going to pay a visit to the dead woman's apartment."

8:00 P.M.

ON THE RIDE to the Latin Quarter Adams told DuForché about the burned picture and the disturbing business with the pneumatic tube. "Who do you think did it?" DuForché asked when he was done.

"Whoever cut those fingertips off sent them to me," Adams said testily, annoyed that the boy's response wasn't a bit sympathetic but was entirely analytic. "And I have no idea who burned that picture." The only one who had seen it was Donald Cameron. Could Cameron have burned it for some obscure reason? To punish him? He rejected the idea: Elizabeth's affections had been alienated for a long time, and Adams had given him what he wanted when he called. Still, the senator hadn't been very clear about the nature of his business in Paris; could he be involved in the scandal somehow? Something to do with the railroad, something that had him and Hay in Paris at the same time? Not likely, but possible, possible. That still left the puzzling question of just why the picture had been destroyed. What could it have shown? "I saved a corner of it," he told DuForché. It had completely slipped his mind. "Maybe there's a fingerprint on it. Could you check it?"

"First thing tomorrow."

"And the paper that came with the fingertips?"

DuForché said he would look into it. "Do you know why

I think the same person did both—the photograph and the fingertips?''

''No.''

DuForché smiled. ''My theory,'' he announced, ''is that the picture didn't show anything worth hiding. The only reason to burn it was to scare you. If that's true, then it's obvious: the fingertips are supposed to frighten you, too, and they were sent by the same person.''

Something about this reasoning seemed flawed to Adams. He tried to trace it. His strong feeling was that the photograph had been burned because of something it showed. But he couldn't just assert this; this was the thing that was at issue. He tried to identify his reasons for thinking it showed something. First, if someone had wanted to frighten him, there were dozens, maybe hundreds of other things he could have destroyed once he had access to Adams's rooms. His journal, for instance: much more personal and threatening. And destruction to the point of disappearance wasn't nearly so threatening as defacement—if someone wanted to scare him, they could have shredded everything on his desktop and he would have been frightened, very frightened indeed. And someone had destroyed information about Dingler, information he had wanted; maybe this was the same sort of thing. DuForché's theory tried to make sense of one event in the light of another that happened later; it assumed a connection between two events that might not be connected, when finding out if there was a connection or not was the whole problem.

But, as DuForché pointed out when Adams said this, Adams' alternative assumed the same circle the other way, beginning with the assumption that the picture held some meaning.

He was stymied.

Adams had paid little attention to their route, and so was surprised when DuForché drew his cabriolet to the curb in front of the building with the fat concierge, at the address that Miriam Talbott had given him on the train from Pontorson. ''Why are we stopping here? What is this?''

''This is the dead woman's address. Why?''

His stomach seemed to be tightening around a cold, hard

pellet of iron. Had this dead woman swallowed Miriam completely, taken over her name, her apartment, the very idea of her? "It's Miss Talbott's address," he mumbled.

Inside, DuForché spoke to the concierge, who, with an infuriatingly slow waddle, found the key and motioned them to follow. This time his clothes signalled gender: a badly cut blue suit of some distinguished material that fell across his bulk loosely, like sailcloth in the doldrums. Adams forced himself not to stare at the man's misshapen face. DuForché took the stairs immediately behind the concierge, who trailed an aroma of sweat and scraped animal skin, the raw unwashed smell of poverty. Adams concentrated on the odor of dank plaster and dust, an innocuous, breathable smell in comparison. Maybe, he thought, Miriam hadn't been swallowed by this woman; maybe there was a better explanation. "When are you," the concierge said when he had bested the stairs and caught his breath, "going to clear this place out." It was not so much a question as a lament. His bulk blocked the narrow hallway, and Adams and DuForché were forced to pause on the stairs. "I've got a business to run," he added. "Or are you going to pay the week's rent?"

"You are doing a service to the Republic," DuForché replied, glancing back at Adams. "We appreciate your sacrifice. Believe me, it will be noted. It has already achieved widespread comment downtown. Just the other day the prefect himself was holding you forth as an example of the sort of selfless cooperation the force needs if it is to succeed in holding the criminal element in this city at bay." The words had tumbled smoothly from DuForché without a moment's pause. Adams wondered if his words were true, or a standard recitation, or made up on the spot. He seemed to have a special talent for this sort of thing. The concierge grunted, unimpressed.

He bent to work the key in the lock and swung the door open for them. Breathing heavily from these exertions, he stepped down the hallway, past the door, to get out of their way. "Please," he said as he turned to face them, "lock the door after you and return the key when you leave."

DuForché entered the room, but Adams held back, wanting to test a theory. "Of the two women who lived here," he began, "at least one was a painter. The one with lighter hair. You would have seen her carrying canvasses, paints, easels, back and forth." Adams stood in the center of the hallway, blocking it.

"She may have been a painter, but I saw no such thing." He hadn't denied that there were two women. It seemed so obvious now. How could he have forgotten? Miriam had said she had a roommate. That explained how the dead woman had his card on her; she had got it from Miriam. "You saw her come and go?"

"Yes, but she didn't carry anything like that in or out of here." The concierge shifted from one foot to the other.

"When did you last see this woman? The painter."

The concierge glowered at Adams and was silent. Adams met his gaze with a steely patience. "I don't know," the concierge said finally, not glancing away. "A week ago, two weeks ago. I don't ask questions, I don't pay much attention."

"The last time I was here, you had never seen her," Adams said, darting a significant glance at DuForché, who had come back to the doorway to listen. "Why have you now changed your story?"

He got no answer. He tried another tack: "Was there a lease? Who signed it?" Adams wanted to know if circumstances had thrown the two women together, and if so, which one was the temporary resident.

"No, no lease."

"Which one paid for the apartment, then? Who brought you the rent money?"

"The rent check came in the mail. Very regular, no problems, I didn't ask questions. Now, if you don't mind ..." The concierge sliced a hand upward and held it out, palm vertical, indicating his desire to pass; his words and gesture had the form of politeness, but in his face there was a growing impatience.

DuForché growled a question: "And which of them wrote the check for the rent? Or did they take turns?" Adams was pleased that DuForché was following his thinking here, but he wished that the youth hadn't given the concierge a possible answer. The concierge made no reply.

"Answer the man," Adams said, working to put a deep note of warning in his voice.

"Neither," the fat man said slowly. "It was always a check from some man. Some friend of the ladies. I never met him, I never asked questions. I don't even know what he looks like."

But you know the name, don't you, thought Adams. "Reinach. Jacques de Reinach."

"No. He was a frequent caller, but no." The concierge enjoyed telling Adams this.

"Who was it, then? Whose name was on the checks?"

The concierge didn't answer.

Adams opened his mouth to guess another name but stopped himself. To be wrong again would only reinforce his status as an ignorant inquirer, a supplicant in need of help, and it would not serve their purpose to appear weak.

"You can answer our questions here," DuForché said conversationally, "or we can take you to the Prefecture for questioning."

The concierge swivelled his gaze slowly toward DuForché and sneered at him.

"It's rather late to get a cab, don't you think, Monsieur Adams? I think we would have to walk. Exercise is good. Perhaps we'd all enjoy a little walk. A brisk walk. Maybe even a run. Just a little run, oh, say a mile, over to the Prefecture. Wouldn't that be just the thing, Monsieur Adams?"

"Yes," Adams said slowly. "Just the thing."

DuForché began to reach for the man's sleeve to pull him along. The concierge shrank from DuForché and spoke to Adams.

"Herz. Cornelius Herz," he said slowly.

Of course. Reinach had brought him into the Panama company, into what proved to be a very lucrative arrangement; maybe Herz had returned the favor by picking up some of Reinach's expenses here and there, especially the ones he might want to hide from the prying eyes of family. "Now can I go?" the concierge asked in a bored voice.

"One more question," Adams said. "What have you got to do with Madame LeBlanc? Why did she come here on Monday?" Adams was pleased to see a reaction this time, an involuntary tic of an eyebrow before the gaze hardened again.

"She takes a proprietary interest in the accommodations."

"You don't mean that women—that the women who stay here are . . ."

"No. I mean she's an owner of the building. But sometimes her girls stay here. Her, mmm, employees."

Employees. "Was either of these women her 'employee'?"

Perhaps the concierge sensed how keenly he wanted the answer. Adams braced himself for it, anticipating it, thinking there were situations in life from which the move to being a man's mistress could be considered an improvement, yes, a discernible improvement. The concierge's face did not change, his gaze did not waver, but his head rose slightly with the inhalation of a breath. Adams found himself growing angry at the sight of him. "No," he said. "They weren't."

"But they had male callers." DuForché moved closer.

"Just the one—Reinach." The concierge shrugged. He looked from Adams to DuForché. "May I go?"

Adams could sense DuForché looking at him, but didn't turn to see. The young man had to tug on Adams's sleeve to get him to step through the doorway and allow the concierge to pass.

"You weren't bad, you know, with your questioning," he told Adams when the concierge had gone. "Maybe you've got another career in you, waiting to get out."

Adams didn't hear him. He was stuck on how ready he had been to think of Miriam as a prostitute—or not so much ready as open to it as a possibility, as a possible part of her history. He had been certain that he knew her essentially, knew who she was in the central matter of her being; but this periphery . . . Could something like that *be* periphery? His sense of her was fluid, too fluid, and this disturbed him.

DuForché, on the other hand, seemed exhilarated. He rattled on as he prowled about the small dim room, squatting to look at things in the light from the doorway. "It's a difficult business, being a detective. Pressing your questions, always on the lookout for lies or inconsistencies, having to know when to be pushy, when to be chummy, all the while trying to think ahead. Not like being a historian, is it? You can sift and sort at leisure, you can go back again and again to the sources if something bothers you. But you know— every time a detective talks to someone, it's different. At the Prefecture they have a saying: You can't interview the same witness twice. The second time it's a different person. You made them different with what you asked. You've got to have your wits about you, because you only get that one chance to catch them the first time.''

Dully Adams watched DuForché examine the apartment. It was small, two rooms, trim enough in its appointments and furnishings, but dingy somehow, as if the best efforts of its occupants had never succeeded in overcoming the aged paint, the cracked plaster. Or maybe it was what he knew about the apartment's occupants—one a suicide, the other the mistress of a man in power—that made it seem dirty and pathetic. ''Sometimes the second time is better,'' DuForché allowed, ''as with this man. It makes sense. You talked to this man, he tells you nothing. Now he's ready to talk to us. Who knows what happened in the meantime? Your asking him things set him off, set him to thinking, and he changed his mind, decided to be helpful.''

''Yes. Or perhaps someone has frightened him.''

''Usually that works the other way,'' DuForché said absently. ''Shuts them up.'' He examined the gasolier, and, hearing a functional hiss when he opened the valve for a moment, began patting his pockets for a match.

Adams, seeing what he wanted, produced a boxful.

''Maybe whoever had convinced him to keep quiet about Miriam Talbott has lost his grip on the man. Maybe they're gone, or dead, or they've given up.'' He had gotten the gasolier lit, and by its sibilant light they could see the room mirrored in the two windows that overlooked the street. There was a small daybed, which doubled as extra seating for the table in the center. In the kitchenette dirty dishes lay in a sink filled with grimy, grayish water. There were no canvasses or paints in sight. Adams thought to examine the floor: no paint spots, either. He supposed the concierge had told the truth—they hadn't used the apartment as a studio, unless they had been particularly, impossibly fastidious.

He had seen enough. He wanted to go.

"I, personally, don't think so," DuForché said, squatting to unpack his kit bag on the floor. He produced squeeze bottles of powder, fine brushes, clean sheets of white paper. "I can't say why, but I don't think so." He turned to Adams and said quickly, "Please don't touch or move anything. Everything here has been catalogued, but I want to get some prints. For my collection."

Adams smiled to himself. DuForché probably wasn't authorized to admit him to the scene of a police investigation, and now the boy was getting nervous. They had come together and they would have to leave together; he'd wait until the boy was finished.

In the kitchenette Adams imagined Miriam standing in front of the small two-burner gas stove, cooking for herself and her roommate, wearing that same boyish cap he had seen her wear while she painted. She, a painter, partner to a corrupt business dealer. It all seemed too sad.

He surveyed the bedroom from the doorway. There wasn't much to see: two beds covered with blue spreads, a wardrobe, a bare plank chair. When he opened the wardrobe, he saw that it held a few dresses on hangers; there was a pair of women's shoes on the bottom. He looked at the clothing carefully, trying to identify something she wore in Pontorson, but ultimately couldn't say if any of it was Miriam's. He tended not to notice what people wore. He shut the wardrobe carefully.

Back in the main room, DuForché knelt in front of a narrow bureau that Adams hadn't noticed at first; it was tucked between the foot of the daybed and the door to the bedroom. He had a squeeze bulb of powder in one hand and several sheets of paper on the floor next to him. "I'm not getting any prints," he said. "Nothing at all."

"Oh. Too bad." Adams had gone to the window to see what sort of view the apartment had. Not much: the windows were a half dozen feet from the blank brick wall of the building next door. When he leaned forward until his face was almost on the glass, he could see a thin slice of gaslit street.

"I don't think you understand," DuForché said. "I'm not

getting smudged prints, I'm getting no prints at all. None on the stove, none on the table, none on this bureau. None.''

''That's a problem?''

''Everyone leaves fingerprints, Monsieur Adams. If there are no fingerprints, that means someone wiped them away.'' He picked up his paper and moved to examine the knob of the exterior door. ''Troubling, very troubling. The evidentiary value of this apartment is close to zero.''

''Can I see what's in the bureau?'' Adams asked.

''Go ahead and look, but use a handkerchief,'' DuForché advised. ''Don't leave any prints.''

The top drawer held women's clothes, white underthings and stockings that he felt a little sheepish to be seeing. Still, he poked through them, looking for anything of interest. In the bottom, tucked in the back, he felt something smooth and round and metallic.

''What's that?'' DuForché asked when he held it up with the handkerchief.

It was a round tin container, about three inches across and a half inch deep. ''Bettleman and Sons,'' Adams read from the lid, ''purveyors of pigments and oils. Orpiment.'' He stood to see it better: his knees hurt from squatting. ''She's a painter,'' he said, holding the tin out for DuForché to see. The tin was smooth and slippery beneath the handkerchief. He turned it over to examine the underside, trying not to wipe it on the cloth. The bottom was smooth, white-painted tin. ''There's only one of these. That's peculiar. There should be a whole set. Why just one?'' He tried to open the tin, but the painted metal was too slippery beneath the handkerchief.

''You'd better put it back,'' DuForché said. ''If my uncle knew we were handling evidence . . .''

The second drawer wasn't a drawer at all but a false front that folded down to form a writing surface, revealing compartments for papers and the like. There was a stack of blank pale-blue writing paper next to a wad of envelopes. In another compartment were letters received, envelopes ragged from being torn open. With his hand shrouded in the handkerchief Adams pulled these out and laid the small stack on the writing surface. There were about half a dozen envelopes addressed to Miriam Talbott. He ticked their corners with a fingernail to reveal the return addresses.

"We've looked at all of those," DuForché said at his elbow. "Nothing much there, I'm afraid."

Adams stopped at a familiar name: Mme Dingler, with an address in Sablonville, just outside the city. He felt the skin on his neck prick up. "This is something," he allowed. The postmark was a week old; the envelope was empty. Why would, how *could* Miriam be getting mail from the engineer's dead wife long after she died?

"What?" DuForché pressed in to read over his shoulder. "Madame Dingler? Who is that?"

"Jules Dingler was the chief engineer of the Panama company. Lost his wife and children in Panama." He looked back at the young man. "I didn't tell you, but I got interested in this man Dingler, tried to look him up in the library. Everything about him in the papers has been cut out." He looked at DuForché significantly.

"Meaning?" the youth asked.

"Someone is hiding something," Adams said, impatient. He picked the envelope up, holding it through his handkerchief. "His wife died in Panama, years ago. This makes no sense."

"Maybe your engineer remarried," DuForché said.

The idea surprised Adams. He hadn't thought that possible. True, there was a period after Dingler returned to Paris before he, too, succumbed to malaria; perhaps he had met someone . . . had known someone from before . . . But it had been only a matter of months. "No. I don't think so." He handed the handkerchief and the envelope to DuForché. "Write down this address. We ought to pay her a visit."

10:00 P.M.

AT THE HÔTEL Vendrielle the stairs seemed steeper than before. Adams had fallen asleep in the cab after dropping DuForché at his apartment on the Ile St. Louis; the driver had had to shake him awake. Climbing the stairs he was thinking only of his room and his bed until he came to the third-floor landing and realized: Elizabeth. The Tuileries. Amanda. He had completely forgotten.

He knew himself to have no choice. Numb, with no sense of anticipation or dread, he made his way quietly down the hall to the Camerons' door. A soft splash of light escaped beneath it, visible in the night-dimmed gaslight of the hall. Carefully, gently, he rapped. He put his ear to the door. No sense waking anyone he didn't have to wake. "Elizabeth?" The door was cool to his cheek. Please let it be Elizabeth. Although, as he thought about it, he wasn't sure but that it might on the whole be easier to talk to Cameron. He rapped again, just a little louder, and listened: he heard the rustle of movement inside.

The door opened six inches and there, slightly above him, was Elizabeth's face. Startled by her closeness, he drew back. She wore a dressing gown, blue to match her eyes, different from the one he had seen her wear the day before. Her dark, shiny curls fell across its lace bodice: she had let her hair down, ready to retire.

"May I come in?"

"No, you may *not* come in, *Mister* Adams." Her eyes were wide and fierce under those fine, long brows, and her voice, a whisper, was harsh. She opened the door and reached a hand out to push him back, then slipped out into the hall after him. She pulled the door shut softly behind her. "What I have to say to you I'll say out here." She was hissing her words at him. "I am angry. What happened?"

"Elizabeth—I—I'm sorry. The police came this morning, they took me to—I saw—" He struggled to stitch together an excuse out of the elements of his day, thinking for an instant that the sympathy he had gained the day before by having stumbled onto a dead body might here be duplicated (Yes! There was the business of those fingertips, and the ordeal of being questioned), but he stopped himself. In truth he had forgotten completely about her. He was guilty of that and there was no sense in denying it. He deserved her wrath. He shut his eyes and swallowed, and held up his hands to signal submission. "I'm terribly sorry."

"It's more of this Miss Talbott business, isn't it?"

He nodded.

"What happened?" Her eyes were sharp, but interested. A paler, grayer blue than Miriam's, he thought. He told her about being taken to the pneumatique office, about what he had seen there, about being questioned, about searching the art schools of Paris.

She appraised him for a long moment before speaking. "I don't know if you want to hear this from me or not, but I must say it. You are being foolish over this woman. You are using her for something."

"She needs my help, Elizabeth." He could see her try to read answers in his face, but he had no idea what she found.

She nodded. "I know she needs help. But there's no law that says it's got to be you who helps her." She didn't like the effect that this had. "That sounds ungenerous, I know. But listen to me." She leaned forward a little. "I am trying to tell you this as a friend. You're using her to run away, Henry. You aren't facing your life. Your life is right in front of you, not out there getting mixed up with all manner of grisly things, or wasting your time crisscrossing some city you don't even know, looking for someone you're not even sure wants to be found.'' She leaned back, pausing a moment. ''An adventure. That's what you're after. A younger man's adventure.''

He was listening hard; had heard her every word; but somehow individual words which were each in their separateness well known and comprehensible to him were refusing to cohere into anything like an idea that he could grasp. He saw her see this, saw her begin to draw away.

''Elizabeth? Please. Forgive me.'' He reached out to take her hand in his. It was soft; white; warm. He held it in both of his, cupping it. He looked down at it, saw it there in his hands. It moved and he thought, absurdly, *like a caged fish*. He shook his head, drew a long breath, and exhaled slowly. ''I'm—tired. I'm sorry. I just . . .'' His tongue felt thick in his mouth and he couldn't think of words. He shrugged to indicate his helplessness. Words were slippery, and thought, thought was so viscous! She would have to understand without them. He tried to let her see his heart. Regret. Contrition. Affection. Goodwill.

She looked down to her hand, then into his face. Slowly she pulled her hand away, nodding. ''You look horrible,'' she said. ''Get some rest.''

Thursday,
NOVEMBER 24,
1892

8:00 A.M.

OUTSIDE THE CHAMBER of Deputies the marble steps were smooth and slick with rain. Despite his umbrella the shoulders of Adams's overcoat were soaked through, and this was putting him in a foul mood. He had slept badly again; he was tired. The rain was a relentless drizzle, stronger than a mist but still fine enough to be carried on the air. Behind him as he climbed the steps, out of sight in its channel, the Seine rolled on behind the gray veil of the weather. Somewhere down there a steam launch whistled, sounding close and foreign in the rain. Adams shook himself off in the lobby. He furled his umbrella and consulted the directory: Clemenceau's office was on the third floor.

Upstairs, he prowled the corridor. He saw no one. Whether this was usual at this hour he couldn't say. Perhaps it was a normal morning emptiness, made more pointed and cold by the rain. Light from a window at the far end of the hall reflected on the floor, revealing its subtle, nacreous ripples. At a corner he glanced back and saw that his wet shoes had left prints.

Clemenceau's door was open. Adams entered a small office with an uncurtained window, through which he could make out the grand dome and spire of Les Invalides, its final, surmounting cross indistinct in the mist. A lanky man he recognized from Dingler's photograph was bending in front of a bookcase.

The deputy sensed his presence and glanced up, then pulled a book from a lower shelf before straightening. "Yes—may I help you?" His hair—short, a ruddy gold—was the only bright color in the room; against the dark paneling of the office and the gray drizzle of the morning it made him seem uniquely alive, the recipient of some special dispensation.

"Monsieur Clemenceau," Adams said, "Henry Adams."

"Ah! Monsieur Adams! Splendid to see you! Thank you for coming." Clemenceau smiled a smile broad enough to be signalled through his thick mustache. "It's certainly a gray morning," he added amiably. "One of those mornings that make you feel tired and thick of limb. Do you know what I mean? Does that happen to you? Please, please, sit." He gestured toward a leather-upholstered chair facing his desk and sat in a matching chair behind his desk. "Obviously you got my letter. Thank you for coming."

Adams accepted the thanks. "What is it you want?"

Clemenceau eyed him a moment, evaluating this bluntness. "Yes. Well then. I want to talk to you about the list of *chéquards*. I want to make sure that you understand how crucial that list is to the political future of France. It must be made public before Friday. I want to convince you to make it available to me for this purpose."

"I don't have it."

"I didn't think you did."

Adams reasoned: He must expect me to have it soon. Does he think I am close to finding Miriam? Why? Which among his actions had constituted progress? He tried to think: The letter from Clemenceau had arrived at the end of the day, sometime while he was napping. Had he tripped over a clue at one of the art schools? If he had, how had it been reported here, to Clemenceau, so quickly?

And: If it had, why didn't Clemenceau, himself, investigate?

More likely: Clemenceau was protecting himself against possibility. And maybe—a possibility he couldn't rule out—Clemenceau's name was on the list. Maybe he wanted the list, and maybe having it made public by Friday was the last thing he wanted.

Clemenceau was leaning forward, attentive to his expression, waiting. "It is not my intention," Adams said carefully, "to interfere with your country's system of justice."

Clemenceau's head ticked sideways, a brief impatient reflex, then he leaned closer to speak. "Monsieur Adams. Surely you appreciate that justice and politics are completely separate matters. Justice is blind. Politics is not. At law it does not matter how or from whom evidence comes to be delivered into court. Each case is decided on its merits. Politics, electoral politics, is quite different. Whoever produces that list, his party will be the heroes of the hour. They will have the opportunity to leave their stamp on France. I don't know if you can sense it, Monsieur Adams, but we are at a turning point." Clemenceau paused, gauging his effect. When Adams said nothing, he continued: "The Panama failure affects us profoundly. How will we go on? Will we move forward, or will we spend ourselves trying to scapegoat the past? I am interested in seeing us move forward."

Adams thought he understood what Clemenceau meant, and disagreed: "Justice should be done."

"Yes, yes, of course." Clemenceau shook his head dismissively. "But *after* justice is done, after the *chéquards* have been named and punished, what then? That is what concerns me, Monsieur Adams. I fear . . . I fear that many deputies believe that the only tonic for the French character will be some sort of glorious victory, a military victory. Hogwash, pure hogwash, of course. I aim to head it off. That list would be a boon."

"And what of the possibility," Adams said carefully, "that your name is on that list? That would give you a different reason for wanting it."

"I most assuredly am not on that list. I am untouched."

"And your friend Cornelius Herz—is he untouched?"

Clemenceau looked dyspeptic, curling his mouth in distaste. "No. Herz is not 'untouched.' He has been indicted; I hear he has fled. Good riddance!" Clemenceau gazed at Adams's eyes without flinching. "You will think what you will think but I can tell you this: I disconnected from him immediately on seeing his dishonesty. I showed poor judgment, I know, in allowing him anywhere near me. An error of youth. It seems so long ago.'' Clemenceau shook his head, then gave a little laugh and spoke familiarly: "It's strange, isn't it, here I am defending myself to you and you aren't a constituent, you aren't even a French citizen. But with that list you represent the power to affect multitudes.''

"I am not interested in the list so much as in the woman I believe has it,'' Adams allowed carefully. "Miriam Talbott. Can you tell me anything about her?''

"She's dead, no?'' Clemenceau's eyebrows rose.

"So the police said—but they were mistaken. A case of mistaken identity.''

Clemenceau nodded thoughtfully. "I don't know her. Never saw her. Reinach, yes, but her, no.''

"You have no idea where she is?''

"No.''

"What about a picture, a commemorative picture, taken in January of 1883, of a ceremony honoring Jules Dingler? You are in it. Do you have any idea what it shows that would lead someone to want to destroy it?''

"One moment.'' Clemenceau opened a desk drawer and after a few moments of rummaging produced a framed photograph, identical to the one Adams had taken from *la folie Dingler*. He glanced at it and handed it over. "I see nothing remarkable about it.''

Adams asked for the names of the men in the photograph and got a list: the two Lesseps in the background, and in front Istvan Türr, one of the founders of the Türr syndicate and a director of the company; a director named Lévy-Crémieux; Clemenceau himself; the banker Emile de Girardin; then Dingler shaking hands with Henri Bionne (the secretary general of the company); Henri Cottu (another banker-director); a man Clemenceau didn't know; Reinach; and one other he couldn't remember. "As you can see, it's not a remarkable picture. The occasion was Dingler's installation as chief engineer. I was there as a friend of the company. I believe I was the only non-director.''

Adams studied the photograph, looking for a clue, any clue, to a meaning someone wanted to remain hidden.

"I had a visit yesterday from your friend Monsieur Hay,''

Clemenceau said. "He was very convincing about the canal works."

Adams looked up from the photograph. "And what does Monsieur Hay have to do with me?"

"I just thought you would like to know this. I think the United States should take over the French concession in Panama. It would be good for the United States, and good for France. If the price is right."

"That's of no interest to me."

"It is of interest to Monsieur Hay. And I am trying to indicate to you that anything you could do to bolster my position in this Panama affair is likely to gain the approval of Monsieur Hay."

Adams wasn't sure he needed or wanted the approval of Monsieur Hay. He frowned. "The list of *chéquards* is not mine, and when I find Miriam Talbott, it still will not be mine. I have no claim over it whatsoever."

"I understand. I speak to you as a friend of your friend."

Adams resented the cozy tone. "And as an ambitious man who prepares for different possibilities?" He rose to go.

Clemenceau gazed at Adams coolly and spoke softly. "I want to make sure we understand each other. I believe we do."

"Yes, I believe we do." Adams held Clemenceau's eyes long enough to exhale once, slowly, before he turned to leave.

"Thank you for coming," Clemenceau said before Adams was out the door.

He had thought to tell Clemenceau about the visiting card he had gotten from Delahaye Tuesday afternoon, but once he had met him, that confidence seemed ill-advised. In the entryway he paused to look up Delahaye's office number but didn't go back upstairs. He checked his watch: he would have to hurry to make it to the funeral.

Outside, the rain had lifted.

9:30 A.M.

AT THE CEMETERY the gravel path crunched under his tread—wet, lugubrious, like oats in a horse's mouth. A signboard at the gatehouse had shown him where to find the site. Père-Lachaise wasn't exactly potter's field; he wondered who had paid. To the left and right he passed the monuments and mausoleums of the well-to-do, the noteworthy, the honored: Dantan, a sculptor; Fould, a Minister of Finance; Rossini, the composer; Arago, an astronomer; Auber, a composer, whose bust was by Dantan; Clément-Thomas and Lecomte, the first victims of the Commune in 1871.

I am in a cemetery, he thought. Of course. It hadn't registered when DuForché had encouraged him to come to the funeral, but of course a funeral would be held in a cemetery. There was little about this one to remind him of the cemetery in Rock Creek where Clover lay, but still it was a cemetery, had the same sorts of monuments, the same expanses of green, the same trees turning bare-to-bones in the autumn chill. He felt strangely close to Clover, felt her presence with him, as strongly as when he sat gazing upon what St. Gaudens had wrought, the monument that endured as a tribute to her memory, the hooded figure of a seated woman lost in some reverie of grief or understanding. Maybe, he thought, what haunts us isn't the literal shade of the departed but our memories of them, and in the effort to keep those memories pinned in place the weight of stone is a great help.

He remembered how Clover looked in the morning, rising from bed in her nightgown, and felt a pang of longing so strong he had to stop walking.

From the seat of a bench he could see a small slice of city between the trees. It lay dank and gray in the late morning, under a high winter-ocean sky smudged by smoke from thousands of chimneys. Down there, out of sight, ran the curving meanders of the Seine, sinuous evidence of the river's oblique path to the sea. Water seeks its level, yes, but it is capable of enormous patience, even cunning misdirection. Why had Paris grown on this loop in the river rather than any other? He supposed that two paths had crossed here, long ago, in some otherwise trackless wood. All the rest was inertia—the force that had carried him for seven years come December.

He made himself continue up the slowly rising avenue toward a manicured sward that surrounded a small chapel. The grass there was thick and uniform and clipped extremely short. He paused at the crossroads in front of the chapel and turned to look behind him. He could see no one. He turned to face the chapel again and then took the path that led off to his left, toward a pair of monuments to war dead. A hundred yards ahead he could make out an undertaker's carriage on the path. It moved slowly, the white shroud on the coffin a limp signal in the distance.

She was to be buried within sight of the bronze bust of Bizet, halfway down the avenue de la Chapelle. By the time he arrived there, the hearse was standing just off the gravelled walk, and the horses snorted steam and pawed the ground uneasily. Three men in pallbearer black were making an awkward business of unloading the coffin. Their rough features and cheap dress told him they were cemetery employees. From behind the hearse Adams surveyed the gravesite. He didn't see DuForché anywhere. The boy had said he'd be there; where could he have gone off to? There were only two other people in evidence: two men standing, facing him, in front of the pile of damp earth mounded next to the hole. The handles of three shovels stood erect from the dirt; they hadn't even bothered to move the shovels, Adams thought, and it made him sad.

He immediately recognized one of the mourners as the fat concierge from Miss Talbott's lodgings, dressed in the same large, ill-fitting suit he'd been wearing when Adams had last seen him. A few feet away stood another man whose pale round face had the starchy plumpness of a poor diet. His nose was large and bulbous, and a red dewlap of flesh fell over his collar. His shirt and black coat looked to be several sizes too small. Both men glanced at him as he came around the hearse to take a place opposite them near the grave. The stranger's boots were cracked and scuffed and showed signs of many mendings. Could he be Cornelius Herz? Adams didn't think it likely. The man looked as though he had been crying. The concierge stared at Adams warily. Adams nodded back, his own eyes narrowing.

The pallbearers hoisted the coffin over the grave and laid it on the waiting ropes, which were secured to stakes on either side of the hole. Their work done for the moment, one of them, tall and rangy, pulled out a pipe and proceeded to light it. One of the other pallbearers scowled at him and gestured him away from the graveside with a sharp jerk of his head; the three of them retreated a respectful distance, back by the hearse, to wait. They hadn't put any skirting around the coffin—nothing to disguise the great gaping hole below it, nothing to deny that while these poor humans said their few words over it the box was suspended above emptiness. At Clover's funeral there had been carpets on the ground and the coffin had been lowered on velvet ribbons, and there had been a sort of flounce rippling softly all about it, hiding the raw earth below. She had sunk smoothly into a bed of flowers and beautiful fabric, so that the earth that was thrown on top of the coffin seemed something alien, reduced for the moment to a purely symbolic thing. But here there were no flowers, no disguise, no illusion whatsoever, nothing to soften the hard fact that death was a return to soil.

A priest (where had he come from? Adams hadn't seen him arrive) took his place at the head of the coffin and with a solicitous glance at the three of them began reciting the service from the small, leather-clad book he held in one hand. The Latin was familiar, comforting. Adams remembered why he had come and kept an eye on the concierge, who stared back at him blankly once or twice, and the other man, who looked nowhere but at the shrouded coffin, sniffling audibly now and then. The man was too young to have been this woman's father, and didn't look at all like a brother. Who was he? By the time the priest was done and had signalled the pallbearers, Adams had decided he would speak to the man and find out. The pallbearers folded the shroud and undid the ropes on one side of the grave. With the silent coordination of familiar routine they lowered the coffin into the hole—quickly, undramatically; like workmen, Adams thought. He turned to go—he had heard the sound of dirt thumping against buried wood often enough that he no longer needed it to remind him of the finality of death—but the priest held up a hand. "Each mourner," the priest said, "will turn a shovel of earth."

Adams glanced at the concierge and the other man. Neither had moved. The priest leaned the handle of a shovel toward the concierge, who took it and dutifully applied the tool to the soft pile. Gingerly the concierge held the loaded shovel out over the grave, then rocked the blade back and forth to sprinkle the coffin. This looked like more work than the fat man had done in a long time. The sound was distant and metallic, like a sockful of coins being set softly on a table, slowly, over and over.

The concierge handed the shovel to the man with the ruddy dewlap, who took it mechanically and shoved it into the dirt with the instep of his boot. Without any wasted motion he hefted it and swung it into the hole, where its thud resounded like muffled tympani, the beat of a drum with no resonance or body, all stretched head and impact.

The man gestured with the shovel, as if to hand it to Adams across the grave. Adams walked around the open hole and took it from him. He felt he was there under false pretenses; he hadn't known this woman, and hadn't really come to mourn her. The handle was smooth in his hands, worn by who knew how many funerals, and the blade bit into the soft earth with ease. He didn't need to use his foot. Suspending the shovel over the open grave for a moment, he pictured the dead woman as he had seen her, not the last time, mutilated, but the first time, when in death her features had seemed to regain their habitual set and he had wondered what in her life she had feared. This moment seemed to him the least he could offer in the way of tribute. He had never known her. No one knew her name.

Where the hell was DuForché?

He turned the shovel and then saw it shake once. This surprised him. He hadn't willed that; something had made him let go for an instant. He was close enough to watch the dirt fall, to see it thud against the top of the coffin and spread out. The sides of the grave were amazingly straight, cut through bands of soil with subtle shadings. About a foot down from the top there was a perfect little half-sphere concavity in the wall of the grave, two inches across, where a stone had fallen out. Off to one side of it was a bright round medallion of palest yellow rimmed in black, the size of a silver dollar: a sawn-through tree root. At the bottom of the grave he saw that his shovelful had landed on top of the stranger's, and together the two of them made a lumpy cone. Around this, clods of earth and bits of gravel lay distinct upon the lid. Everything seemed too distinct, too real and separate, and as if in response to his judgment, everything blurred, ever so slightly, as tears rose in his eyes.

Adams felt a hand on his arm. The priest nodded solemnly, solicitously, and pulled him away. He was done. Adams smiled weakly at him. He wanted to explain the tear on his cheek but didn't: let the priest think what he would. He remembered the shovel in his hands and handed it to him.

Over short grass and then to the sound of an animal munching, past trees and most of all the monuments, each thing particular and distinct and rimmed, somehow, with an invisible border, their edges refracted by tears he didn't want to blink away, Adams walked. What were seven years? Apparently they could be as nothing. A meander you pursue that brings you back within hailing distance of where you were, downhill, yes, but not much farther along, not much farther at all. He heard the crunch and jangle of a vehicle behind him and stepped aside to let a coach past. In the years without Clover what had he done? He'd finished his history—*his history*, he thought, stumbling on the irony of that double meaning—travelled some, moved into the house they had meant to share. What else? Nothing that mattered. None of it, none of it since Clover, mattered at all. Seven years ago he had begun the epilogue to his life, and all that remained was to see how long it would rattle on.

He had been standing alongside the chapel for some time before he remembered his plan to talk to the stranger. With a start he looked around. He hadn't even noticed whether the man had stayed at the gravesite or not. Where was he? Had he gone?

He caught sight of him, down at the gate, and hurried to follow.

10:15 A.M.

THE MAN WAITED for an omnibus on the rue de la Roquette, in front of a florist's shop, and by hurrying Adams was able to board it just before the driver jogged the horses into motion. There were no empty seats. Adams stood a few passengers behind the man and watched him, trying to read his character from the soft pink flesh at the back of his neck.

At the place de la Bastille the man got off and transferred to another line for the rue de Rivoli. Adams hung back while doing the same.

At the place de la Concorde the man got off. Adams waited until the bus started again before pushing his way out, not caring about the angry stares he received. It had begun to rain again, softly. He realized he had lost his umbrella somewhere. No matter: the cold clamminess of the air felt good, like an expiation of sorts.

They passed the fountain and then the obelisk in the center of the plaza—two pedestrians, apparently unrelated, paired invisibly by Adams's purpose. The man headed directly for the river. Beyond him, above the curving hump of the pont de la Concorde, Adams could see the columned façade of the Chamber of Deputies. Was this man a *chéquard* in disguise? Adams reminded himself to keep his distance.

But instead of taking the pont de la Concorde, the man turned down a set of steps to the quai. Adams glanced upstream, toward Notre Dame. There was no one on the bridges, no one in sight anywhere. Something in the air above the river—the smell of garbage, the shriek of a bird—made it seem as if the ocean itself lay just out of sight, as if a minute of floating in the river's lead-colored water would bring him to the ocean, the vast, indifferent ocean. He pulled the lapels of his coat closed and walked down the steps. His gloves, he noticed, were soaked through; he'd have to dry the leather carefully or they'd be ruined.

The man had turned left, heading upriver along the quai des Tuileries, and was about forty paces ahead of him, nearing one of the landings for the taxi launches that plied the river. Along the banks the rain-darkened elms and chestnuts had released the last of their leaves overnight, and this damp litter, collected in the corners and along the base of the wall and balustrade, softened the harsh stone angles of the quai. A launch was approaching, moving quickly downstream on the current though its engine, thumping languidly, gave it barely any headway in the water. On its prow a man held a coiled rope and eyed Adams as the boat drifted past. With a sputtering the engine increased speed and belched black smoke; the boat turned upstream and angled toward the quai. Adams hurried to close the distance between himself and the man in the shabby clothes, worried he'd lose track of him when the launch discharged its passengers. He saw as he drew nearer that the boat was nearly empty, and no one rose to disembark. No one approached it to board. The hands didn't even bother to tie up but, after holding the boat at the quai for a moment with the engine, swung it back into the stream.

Ahead, twenty yards beyond the landing, Adams saw his man approach a white shack that stuck out from the wall. The man fiddled with something at the front, then opened a door and entered.

As Adams drew closer he saw that the shack was deeper than it appeared, built into a niche in the crannied wall, its entrance flanked by a pair of short, badly espaliered trees. On the wall next to one of these was a sign announcing rates for swimming. Hadn't Pettibois said they took her out of the water at a swimming concession? Could this be it? The front of the shack was hardly wider than the door—a Dutch door, he noticed, where the concessionaire probably took in the money. In the summer for a few francs you'd get a place to change, a towel, and maybe a seat at a little table on the quai when you were done, and the comfort of knowing that in the netting you wouldn't be nudged by any fish. Opposite the shack, a set of steps led down to the river. The netting was gone: stored away, he imagined, for the winter.

He began methodically to examine the quai and the river. He wasn't sure what he expected to find. Certainly nothing so telling as a footprint: the stone paving was immune to impress, the river too fluid to capture a mark. He stared at the water spooling past. It had borne witness; it had received the body, touched it intimately, and then had given it up; but all that it had known had been swallowed and carried away. These weren't the waters that had held the poor woman's body; that river, the river as it was, had long since gone to sea. This, Adams thought, is what Heraclitus should have said: You can't drown in the same river twice.

He walked about, studying the area from different perspectives, examining the quai to make sure that a stray— what? earring? matchbox?—hadn't been left behind. He saw nothing. The shack was shut up tight. He was standing at the edge of the quai, staring at the grimy, rain-pitted face of the river, when he heard a creaking sound behind him. The top half of the shack's door swung open and clattered against the wall, revealing the face and torso of the man from the funeral. He hadn't changed his clothes. Adams looked away, then back. There was no escaping: he'd been recognized.

The man gestured him over, apparently pleased to see him, for he smiled and nodded at his approach. Close up, Adams could see that his nose was veined through like a ripe cheese. "Coffee?" he asked, then, beaming, raised a full cup and saucer from somewhere below the door opening. He looked off at some place across the river, not meeting Adams's eyes, and there was something faintly dog-like, puppyish, in the gesture: Adams half expected the man's body to quiver, driven by a wagging tail.

"No. No, thank you." A steady trickle from the roof of the shack was landing on his shoulder and he leaned back to avoid it.

·

"You're here about the girl," the man said. He raised the cup and sipped, watching Adams over its rim. Adams nodded. "Horrible," the man said.

"Did you see anything?" Adams tried to look past the man, into the contents of the shack, but couldn't: the interior was dark, and the man filled the doorway. Was he standing on something? He seemed taller here than at the gravesite.

The man just shook his head.

"Are you the concessionaire here?"

The man nodded, still smiling. "Marcel Desmondes," he said, saucering his cup in order to hold out a hand. "Pleased to make your acquaintance." He spoke the phrase in French as a child might recite it, with care and pride, as a difficult formula recently learned. Adams took the man's hand in his, shaking it, feeling the flesh wet and soft against his own. "I hope," the concessionaire added, "it doesn't put business off." His smile seemed incongruous. "Coffee?" he said again, holding the cup out. Adams shook his head, glad that he had declined the original offer, if the man had meant to share the one cup. He felt a slight breeze on his face, and noticed that the steam from the cup wafted toward him. There must be another entrance, Adams thought.

"Did you know her?"

"Oh," the man said, looking away, "she swam here. Swam here all the time. All summer. A pretty one, that one. I see them all." He raised his eyebrows. Guileless and open, but inquisitive as well, he gave the impression of being a conspirator in some innocent, childish prank. Something in the man's manner suggested that he thought Adams should envy his line of work.

"Is that why you went to the funeral?"

"Yes." Adams waited, and perhaps because this didn't seem like enough, the man volunteered something else: "She was my favorite."

"Did she bring anyone with her?"

"Two men. All the time. Until August. Then no more swimming. Then—dead." The man shrugged.

"What did these men look like?"

"Beards, mustaches, big men, important. Like men." The concessionaire saw that he wasn't pleasing Adams with his

description, and his smile faded. "They stuck her." He
shrugged, apologetic. "The men, I don't see the men as
much."

"Would you recognize them if you saw them?"

The concessionaire shrugged again, then opened his eyes
wider and tilted his head to one side. If he had been a dog
Adams would have scratched his head. He sighed. As a
source of information, this man left a great deal to be desired.
"So," he said. "Do you live here?"

"Back there." When he turned, Adams could make out
another doorway in the back wall of the shack.

"I might be in touch."

The concessionaire nodded, pleased. "Always happy to
help the police," he said.

The police? "I'm not the police," Adams told him.

"Oh." The concessionaire accepted this information amiably.

"Have the police been here to talk to you?" Adams asked.

The man's eyes broadened and he tilted his head. "They
came and took the body and then they go. No one talked."

Adams nodded: they hadn't investigated, hadn't looked
into this poor woman's death at all. "Thank you."

The concessionaire nodded too, his face solemn, reading
Adams's concern. When Adams glanced back, he saw that
the concessionaire was still watching him: he leaned out of
the door frame and gave a careful wave, a brief, shy flash of
his palm through the rain.

11:00 A.M.

SABLONVILLE IS A village beyond the city walls on the rue de la Grande Armée, along which the leaves of half-bare elms gave little shelter from the rain as Adams's and Du-Forché's cab clopped beneath them. They left the city proper through the porte Maillot, and the houses they passed became older, closer to the road, mixed with shops catering to the trade that travel brings. DuForché had missed the funeral but talked to the man in the cemetery office, from whom he learned that the woman's burial at Père-Lachaise was not as unusual as it seemed. Burial space in the cemetery could be rented for one, two, three, five years, whatever was desired; at the end of the rental, remains were removed to a companion ground outside the city. As an American citizen she had been buried on account, as it were; city law required burial within four working days, no other arrangements had been made. The Embassy would receive a bill.

Adams described his interview with the concessionaire. "He mistook me for the police."

DuForché murmured sympathetically. Adams feared he was missing the point. "Shouldn't someone have gone to collect evidence, collect his story?"

"For a suicide? There are hundreds of them every year, Monsieur Adams. Lonely, anonymous people. They come from far away, looking for work, and when things don't go well, they feel they are out of choices. It's not unusual. It sounds heartless, but investigators are more wisely occupied elsewhere, on cases with some problem, some question—some *mystery*.''

''But this *is* mysterious. Who was she?''

DuForché nodded. ''As questions go, this is not so momentous. No prosecution turns on it. It is important to *you*. And to me,'' he added, when he saw the way Adams looked at him.

The house was two stories, of whitewashed mortar and stone, an old farmhouse; the city had grown around it, filling its fields with tenements and streets. From its size Adams judged that it had once been a rich farm. He stepped down and asked the cabbie to wait.

DuForché led him to the arched tunnel that served as an entryway into the interior courtyard of the building. On the left wall there was an address board: the farmhouse had been broken into apartments. Dingler, number 8. The left and the back of the courtyard were defined by a Palladian portico, a tile-roofed overhang supported by round columns, with arches in between; on the right the wall of the farmhouse rose two stories to a tiled roof. There would have been stables along the back, there beneath the portico, and the cows and goats and maybe a pig or two would have been kept under the other. In the center of the courtyard were a pump and a trough and bare ropes strung from poles for the hanging of laundry. The courtyard was empty.

In the back, on a narrow passageway off the courtyard, they found number 8. ''Who is it?'' asked a female voice when Adams knocked.

''Henry Adams, calling on Madame Dingler.'' He glanced at DuForché, to let him know that his failure to mention him wasn't neglect.

''Who are you? What do you want?'' The voice, abrupt and high, was displeased and perhaps a little frightened. It sounded old.

''I'm American. A historian. A friend and I are interested in talking to you. We're acquainted with Miriam Talbott, from whom we got your address.'' This wasn't exactly a lie, he thought. He heard the bolt being drawn back and then the door swung partly open.

Before him was a dimly lit room piled high with boxes and cartons and bales of papers. Whoever had opened the door was bent over behind it, fussing with something, leaving her wide, full-skirted hips jutting into the entryway. "Mind the cat, mind the cat," the woman said, from behind the door. Adams looked, but saw no cat; all he saw were stacks and stacks of papers and boxes. "Well, are you going to stand there or not? Do you want to let the cat out? Come in if you're coming!" The woman remained bent over. There was hardly enough room for Adams and DuForché to squeeze by her skirts, or to stand in the room once they did. Stepping sideways, Adams managed to get in. To make enough room for DuForché to enter and shut the door, he had to squeeze by her; by drawing himself up to his thinnest, he did so with what he hoped was not an unduly immodest contact. "Well, finally," the woman said, straightening and turning to face him. She pushed her hair back and scowled. She was white-haired and hollow-cheeked; gravity working through time had pulled her face into deadpan sadness. She held a thin Siamese cat at bay behind the door. "I always say: Come if you're coming, go if you're going, but don't stand in my door." Her face was nearly level with his, and he was close enough to smell her breath, pungent with fish. Adams still held himself in; the boxes and crates stacked shoulder-high around both of them kept him from stepping back. "She fights," the woman said, pointing at the cat. "Don't you, you little ferocious one. Can't let her out. All the other cats want to come and fight with her."

Adams introduced himself with a nod of his head, a further compression of his chin into his chest, in lieu of a proper bow. "And this is a friend of mine, Michel DuForché. You are . . . ?"

"Bernice Dingler. Bernice, Madame Dingler, I don't care." She waved a hand. "Friends of Miriam Talbott, you said?"

"Yes—"

"Who is she?"

Adams and DuForché glanced at each other. "You wrote to her," Adams said. "Not too long ago. We found your envelope among her things."

"Is she in some kind of trouble, then?"

Before Adams could answer she smiled at him and reached out to push him, gently, on the shoulders, leaning him back into a stack of cartons. "Follow me." She squeezed past him.

There was a sort of aisle between the cartons and stacks of newspapers and books, and he followed her down it, noticing that other aisles branched off it, reaching sometimes to the walls on either side, sometimes dead-ending in a confusion of boxes and papers. Nowhere was the stacked material less than waist high; in some places it touched the ceiling. He followed her toward a window, where a small clearing held a skirted wing chair and a table. A brightly colored afghan was draped on the chair. "Care for some tea?" Madame Dingler asked, seating herself and flipping the corner of the afghan expertly over her lap. "You—what's your name? Adams? You pour." She waved a hand at the table, which was piled with magazines and books; on one pile there sat, precariously, a teapot; on another was an oil lamp.

Adams nodded and moved to the table. There was just the one cup, resting on a months-old copy of *La Rive Droite*. He held the saucer by the edge, puzzled; the cup had tea in it, was in fact half full.

"Oh yes. That's mine. You need your own. Through there, in the kitchen." Adams nodded, as if this too made sense, and turned to find his way through the papers. DuForché had to lean back against them to let him pass. "You'll have to wash one, probably," Madame Dingler called after him. "And you—DuForché?—you'll have to clear some chairs, there." From his place in the stacks of paper Adams could hear her muttering: "I don't know. I just can't keep up. Find it?" she called out to him. "That's right—straight in front of you, through there." Adams couldn't see her; how the devil did she know where he was? He stood in front of a doorjamb, its pair of glass-paned doors held open by a round, smooth rock on one side and a fat book on the other. He bent to read its spine: *Minutes of the Proceedings of the Academy of Civil Engineers, New Series*. Volume XXXIII. "There you are now," she called, "right in front of you."

The kitchen, free of printed matter, was buried under a clutter of utensils and dishes and white-enamelled pots and pans. It had no window, and the piles of papers closed it off from the sitting room so completely that hardly any light entered. A single candle over the sink gave a wan and stingy light. Something gray eyed him from the table: the cat, which leaped down and padded off. There was not a square inch of the kitchen table or counter space that did not have something, if only a dried stain, on it. He found a teacup in the sink and examined it, deciding that with a quick cleaning it would do, then found another for DuForché.

On his way back he saw that there was actually furniture beneath the burden of paper: a table straddled old newspapers and was buried under others, so it seemed less a table than a layer of mahogany in a sedimentary deposit of newsprint. On the wall behind the table he noticed strange legends in blue chalk. *66 27a ecr*, one of them said. And *Trav de Feu, 1879*. And *Ponts, 18 à 47*.

"Here now," Madame Dingler called when he came into view at an intersection of aisles. In the clearing DuForché had unearthed one chair and was moving a stack of papers from another, putting them in the aisle next to a wooden vegetable crate filled with fat manila folders. Adams stepped over this to take his seat.

"Nice tea," Madame Dingler said, sipping. "I get so few visitors. Really, it's not worth the bother, straightening."

"What are the markings on the wall for?" Adams asked her. He poured two cups of tea and handed one to DuForché, taking care not to spill it. Not that she'd mind, he thought; but there was something sacrilegious about spilling tea on paper.

"Those; oh, those." She took a hand off the side of her cup to flash it back and forth. "Those are my cataloguing system. Everything in its place, you know. I have it all organized, really."

Adams and DuForché exchanged a skeptical glance. "Are you related to the man who was the chief engineer of the Panama works?" DuForché asked. There was no cream or sugar, Adams noticed; he'd drink it black. He didn't want to go back to the kitchen.

"That I am. My son. Worst mistake he made. It killed him." The cat materialized from some private passageway through the clutter and climbed up the side of the wing chair, its claws popping the frayed fabric. It pulled itself to the top and then sat just behind Madame Dingler's head on the back of the chair.

"Malaria," Adams said. That disease the body never completely defeats, but which, after one's first exposure, can erupt again and again in a life, asserting the claim of the past over the present, until, ultimately, it wins. His tea was bitter and lukewarm. He put his cup down on a pile of newspapers.

"You can say so if you want to." Madame Dingler shook her small head in reproach, a movement that made the cat open its half-closed eyes for a moment. "But I don't think so. He was good. He knew what he was doing, and he was a good man. Good men don't just up and get sick like that. No. I don't believe that malaria business for a minute. I think it was something else. I think they got him. Killed his wife, didn't they?" She looked at both of them for reaction to this idea.

"The Panama company," Adams said, as much because an answer seemed required as for any other reason.

"Yes, yes," she said quickly, as pleased as if he had agreed with her.

Apparently Dingler had gotten his peculiar theories about disease directly from his mother. "The reason we came," Adams began, "is that we were wondering how you know Miriam Talbott, and if you might know where she is."

"Miriam Talbott, Miriam Talbott." She rolled her eyes to the ceiling as if her memories could be read there in the yellowing plaster. When she spoke again, she kept her face turned up and looked at Adams out of the sides of her eyes. "I know the name. Why?"

"She's missing."

"Don't know any missing people," the woman said, shaking her head, as if this settled the matter.

Adams glanced at DuForché. "No," the young man said, then cleared his throat a little. "We don't know how you know her, but you do."

"We thought you might help us find her," Adams added.

"Well, I can't. I have no idea where she is. What is she, missing?"

"You wrote to her," DuForché said gently. "What about?"

Madame Dingler looked at the young man a moment before answering. "I had a letter from her sometime back. Oh, this memory! What was it?" She bit her lip and turned to look at the ceiling again, and Adams noticed that the flesh of her neck, when stretched tight, was almost smooth. "Political things, I don't know what-all."

"It's very important," DuForché prodded. "Can you remember what exactly it was?"

The woman eyed them both warily. "I remember," she announced after a moment. "Jules had written to a man she knew, years ago, about some accounting thing or other, for the company. I don't remember exactly. I think she wondered if I still had his books, could she come and see them sometime."

"Did she come?" Adams asked.

"No."

"Do you have her letter? Perhaps, if we might see it, it could help us find her."

Madame Dingler stared at Adams without responding.

"I just thought," he said. "If you had it."

Madame Dingler laughed a short laugh, throaty and broken. "Oh, I have it." She waved a hand toward the material that filled the room, though her eyes stayed locked on his. She leaned close. "I have it. Don't be a goose. I keep it all." She sat back and surveyed the room from beneath the afghan. "I've got every piece of paper that ever had anything to do with my boy, as far as I could. Every paper he ever set pen to, every letter he ever received. That's what's got the house a mess, if you ask me. But I have to. I couldn't just let them all go. No sir." She adjusted herself under the afghan, pulling it up to her throat, her hands making serpentine shapes beneath it. "And it keeps me busy, you know. Very busy."

"It keeps you busy?" Adams asked.

"Organizing them." She looked surprised that he hadn't thought of this. "Cataloguing them. No good having them if you can't find them, isn't that right? Want to hear about my system?''

''Ah, well, no. I don't think that will be necessary.'' Adams could scarcely suppress a smile. He felt a kind of admiration for this woman's obsession, but she was clearly disturbed. From the look of the clutter that buried her apartment, it was hard to believe that there was any system to it at all. ''If you could just show us her letter, I think that we—'' He saw DuForché frown at him.

''Not necessary, then. Oh no. Of course not. Not necessary,'' Madame Dingler said. She had seen that smile, and it had been a mistake. ''Certainly. I'm not going to force you.'' She pulled at the afghan and worked her shoulders against the back of her chair, back and forth, the way a cat cozies up a place to lie down. The cat was no longer on the chair; Adams hadn't noticed it leave. ''This is a private collection, you know. Not some public library. I don't have to let you look at anything. I don't even have to let you in.''

''Madame Dingler,'' DuForché said smoothly, setting his teacup down on a pile of newspapers, ''I think it admirable the way you have managed to collect your son's papers. It shows the instincts of a true archivist. And I think you can appreciate that men such as we, Monsieur Adams and myself, are thankful for those instincts when we run across them, because talents such as yours are so necessary for the success of our efforts. We haven't been exactly forthright in describing our project, I'm afraid.'' He looked at Adams in reproach. ''Monsieur Adams and I are trying to unravel this Panama scandal. There are malefactors at work out there, malefactors who were on the payroll of the Panama company, and it is our intention to see these men brought to justice. We think they've done something to this girl. We want to find out who did it.''

''Oh, fine,'' Madame Dingler said curtly, clearly not meaning to assent. ''A little sweet talk and everything is fine.'' Before either of them could speak she continued: ''That's not the way you do it. Just come in here, as you please, almost let my cat out. God only knows what could happen to her. They fight with her, you know. Then you start pushing things around, getting everything out of place.'' She pointed at the piles DuForché had moved into the aisle. "No. No, no, no," she recited, as if to a willful child or an errant cat. "You come here, I look at you, we sip a little tea, we talk. We talk about this, we talk about that, we have ourselves a visit. And you go away and come back. We get to know each other. *Nicely.*" She smiled a thin smile at him. "That's it. Then we see. We see if we like each other, see if I find you agreeable. That's what we see." She paused, looking at them with a blank face. "Come back tomorow."

"Could I—" Adams began.

"Tomorrow! Maybe then," she said abruptly, and reached for her tea. Adams glanced at DuForché. The young man shrugged, a gesture of helplessness. "What did you say your name is?"

"Adams. Henry Adams. I'm American—"

"Fine. Monsieur Adams. And you?"

"Michel DuForché."

"Monsieur DuForché. Tomorrow, that's all I'm going to say." She closed her eyes and compressed her lips, a pose that, on a younger face, might have been demure; on hers, the effect was that of a death mask. "Do please show yourselves out," she said after a moment, without opening her eyes. "And mind the cat."

As Adams closed the door, blocking the animal's escape with a foot, the animal looked up at him and produced a single, complaining cry, weirdly human in tone.

"Michel," Bertillon said with some surprise, "don't you have something you should be doing? Or is this your assignment—hanging about in my anteroom?"

"I was waiting with Monsieur Adams," DuForché said innocently.

Bertillon glanced at Adams and back at the young man. "Are you on a case? Have I assigned you to our American visitor?" The questions appeared rhetorical. DuForché started to say something to Bertillon, then changed his mind. "I'll be in the laboratory," he told Adams.

Bertillon sighed as the door shut behind him. "My sister's son. Or did I tell you that already?" He shook his head. "Monsieur Adams, today I am very busy and I haven't any news for you, if that's what you're here for. I expect to receive some reports soon, maybe this afternoon, but—'' Bertillon shrugged, his hands wide, gesturing behind him toward his office, where his work waited. ''So if you will excuse me—''

''I have just one question . . .''

''Yes?'' Bertillon asked matter-of-factly.

''Well, several, actually. How much of a fingerprint is needed to identify someone?'' Adams knew this was a question DuForché was better equipped to handle, but asked it anyway. ''Did anyone question Cornelius Herz before he fled? And who is in charge of the investigation of this woman, this Not-Miriam-Talbott's death?''

Bertillon nodded thoughtfully. He looked behind himself and moved some papers on the secretary's desk before perching on the edge of it, one leg up, the other foot still on the floor.

''From whom did you learn that Cornelius Herz is gone?''

''Clemenceau.'' To Bertillon's raised eyebrow Adams elaborated: ''He sent me a note and I called on him this morning. He's interested in the list of *chéquards*.''

''Yes.'' Bertillon's gaze fell and he looked through Adams a moment before continuing. ''The answer to your question is no. I understand that his summons was never served. Unfortunately. If the truth could have been gotten out of him, a great deal could have been made clear.''

''He was the briber.''

Bertillon nodded. ''Enormous influence. Not just money, though of course there was that, but an appeal on behalf of an institution. The canal company, *Le Grand Français*, French pride and honor—these were inseparable. For a time it was a matter of pride in France to own Panama stock. Herz played on this, this chauvinism. I believe a good many people would describe his ends as worthy and his means as flawed but necessary.'' He shrugged. ''Knowing this doesn't help, does it? Now, your first question—is it a theoretical one, or practical at all?''

Adams pulled the envelope from his jacket pocket and, after opening it, tapped it with his finger to slide the corner of the photograph onto the flap. ''Do you think this has a fingerprint on it? Whoever burned it obviously held it by this corner.''

"Ah, a matter of identity. Now this, this is the ticket.'' Bertillon fished his tweezers out of his jacket pocket and carefully picked up the charred fragment. "I don't think we'll get much here. No, not much,'' he said, examining it. "But we shall try. Come with me.''

Bertillon left his office, tweezers raised in one hand with their fragment of photograph, and Adams followed him down the hall a dozen steps to a laboratory, at whose door he paused before entering. "I must ask you not to touch anything, Monsieur Adams, and to stay by my side. We have no unescorted visitors to the laboratories. There have been some difficulties with materials disappearing. Photographs used in evidence—a whole case collapsed.'' He began to enter, but had second thoughts. "Not that I would suspect you capable of such a thing,'' he said carefully. "But I hope you understand.''

"Of course,'' Adams answered.

Bertillon nodded to a white-smocked attendant who glanced up from some activity at a table near the window. Still holding the tweezers before him, he led Adams to a central oak table arranged for fingerprint work. Here he pulled up a stool and placed the piece of photograph on a small glass plate. "As to this other question of yours, Monsieur Adams,'' he said, reaching for a rubber squeeze bulb held in a rack on the table, "I have to say that I am unaware of any investigation. Why?''

"Today I met the concessionaire—the man who works where the body was recovered.'' Bertillon puffed a delicate cloud of powder onto the paper triangle and then, using the tweezers, lifted it to tap the excess free. "He mistook me for a policeman, because no one had ever come to talk to him.'' Adams glanced around, looking for DuForché, but didn't see him. Wasn't this more in DuForché's area? Why was Bertillon handling this?

"Mmm-hmmm.'' Bertillon turned the bit of photograph over and repeated the dusting procedure, then held it up to look at it. "No, I don't think so,'' he muttered to himself. "But let us try.'' He covered the glass plate with another,

sandwiching the fragment between them. "And you are naturally concerned about this."

"Well, yes, I am. Wouldn't you think a thorough investigation would have led to this man? He should have been
questioned."

Bertillon glanced up at Adams before bending over the
microscope to insert the slide. "Yes," he murmured. "The
powder came out nicely. Just one problem," he added, leaning back and motioning Adams forward to look.

"What's that?" Adams asked, putting his eye to the eye-
piece. At first he saw nothing, just blackness, but motion of
his head made a white disk flit across his vision. He moved
his head again slightly, zeroing in on the disk, which darted
in the opposite direction. In a moment he managed to get the
disk centered and still. In it he saw fuzzy gray lines, roughly
parallel to each other, curving downward.

"What we're getting isn't definitive. The central whorl or
arch—that's the part you want to see. This, this came from
the very tip of the finger. Not very good."

"So you can't tell whose it is?" Adams straightened.

"Oh, I don't know," Bertillon said. "Maybe. *If* this fragment turns out to be enough. *If* we have this person's prints
on file. It's not very likely." He pulled the slide out, turned
it, reinserted it. "Same story on this side, I'm afraid," he
said when he had it in focus. "Makes sense. You hold a
burning piece of paper very gingerly, no? Like this—" and
he held out one hand with the nails of his thumb and index
finger pinched together while keeping his eye to the microscope. "Do you have any idea whose print it might be? So
we could collect a complete set from them, for comparison?"

Adams had no idea—none, that is, that he wanted to divulge. His suspicion that Cameron had done it was based on
nothing more certain than Cameron's having been the only
one to know that he had the picture. As telling as that was,
it was mere circumstance; and he'd be embarrassed to name
Cameron, to have Cameron know he suspected him, however
marginally. Unless of course it *had* been Cameron. Maybe
he could collect a set of Cameron's prints himself, for comparison, and bring them in. No—Bertillon wouldn't permit
it. Unprofessional.

He shook his head. "I can't think of anyone. I can't think of a reason for anyone to burn it."

Bertillon tilted his head back, putting his chin in the air. Adams could see a small star-shaped scar on the tip of his chin, which showed lighter than the surrounding skin. "Four reasons," Bertillon said after a moment. "Four *types* of reasons. One, because of what the picture showed. Two, because it was a picture in *your* possession." He glanced at Adams through narrowed eyes. "This is rather a small fragment. Still, perhaps you were meant to find it. It was damp, no? Perhaps your burner saved the corner, to make sure that you would see it."

"But there are other things he could have burned or destroyed, if the idea was simply to frighten me." Adams had thought this through with DuForché.

"True, true. Which makes this second category unlikely. Three: something attached to the picture, something on it, or some quality of its existence as an object, but not actually in the photograph. This we are unlikely to discover, as we no longer have the object for examination."

"And four?"

"Four: something the picture doesn't show. This, too, we cannot now discover. But I have an idea." Adams waited as the policeman removed the slide from the microscope. "Whoever left this print might have left others in your apartment. This one is too small to use, but perhaps we'll find others that aren't."

Of course! Adams had fixed on the object, the tiny triangle of paper, forgetting that the object was but the most obvious result of an action, an action that might have left other physical marks in its wake. Bertillon taped the two pieces of glass together and slid them into an envelope marked EVIDENCE, then put the envelope in a drawer of the oak table. "Tell me—what does this photograph have to do with your mysterious missing friend?"

"I'm not sure. She corresponded with one of the men in the picture—Jules Dingler, the chief engineer of the Panama works. And the woman who turned up dead Monday—she had Reinach's card on her. He's in the picture, too. It's a photograph of company officials, on the occasion of Dingler's appointment as chief engineer.''

"Who else is in it?''

Adams listed them as well as he could from memory.

"That's eight. You said there were a dozen? So there are four others.''

"Yes. I don't know who they are.''

"Twelve men, four unknown.'' Bertillon shook his head. "Pity I didn't get to see it. I might have recognized them. They're likely to be prominent men. Do you think you could describe them?''

"Maybe I can do better than that,'' Adams said.

1:30 P.M.

AN HOUR LATER Adams was inside a cab, examining the picture. Of the dozen figures in the photograph, he knew eight and had seen four in the flesh. Now he made out the Lesseps, *père et fils*, on the steps to the Panama company's offices; second from the left was Clemenceau, tall, commanding, his shock of hair showing light in the photograph's black-and-white; and several places to the left of the unfortunate Reinach, the equally ill-fated Dingler. Adams looked at Dingler, trying to read his expression. Had he some inkling of his future? When he'd departed for the isthmus, French workers had already been dying by the boatload there. Perhaps what Adams had seen as solemn pride in his face was actually troubled concern. The elder Lesseps stood at attention, but there was a hint of a scowl on his face; he seemed ready to move up the steps, eager to return to his office and his work. Charles de Lesseps stood, expressionless, dutiful, beside his father. Clemenceau, whose photograph it was, stared at the camera, angry or impatient. In exchange for the loan of it, Adams had hinted broadly, he'd do what he could about steering the list of *chéquards* to Clemenceau.

In Bertillon's office, Adams handed over the photograph: "Better than a description: the faces themselves."

"Hmmm. Yes, yes." Bertillon bent close to the photograph and scanned it, back and forth, peering at the men. Then, flipping it over, he expertly removed it from its frame and repeated the examination. "I don't recognize them. The four you can't name. This of course is Clemenceau, this one Lesseps, and Lesseps Junior, but these others you'll have to show me."

Adams connected names to faces for him. "You must return this, no?" Bertillon asked. "I think it would be useful to have a copy of it, for our own purposes." He led Adams back into the laboratory, to a different table, one that held a large apparatus with a leather bellows pointing downward. Adams recognized it as similar to a piece of equipment Clover had owned.

"Could you make two copies?" Adams asked. "One for me? And can you enlarge it somehow? I have another idea."

After positioning the photo, Bertillon slid the wooden-handled, tin-plated film caddie into a slot in the machine and then pulled it out, counted the exposure in slow, clearly enunciated numbers, then slid in the tin caddie to remove the film. He repeated the procedure with another caddie. When he was done, he turned, wordlessly, and made his way across the laboratory. Adams followed.

Only when the door had shut behind him did Adams realize his mistake. He was in Bertillon's darkroom. At eye level, on a stave of parallel clotheslines, glossy eight-by-ten photographs of crime scenes had been set swinging by Bertillon's passage. In the dim red light he recognized the fat coroner. What was troubling about the darkroom was not the photographs but the smell: chemicals. Sharp, acrid, stomach-churning chemicals. He should have known. Now he was stuck; the door couldn't be opened until Bertillon was finished. He moved beneath the photographs and took a place at Bertillon's elbow. No—too close. He moved back to the door, where he thought he might have a slim hope of finding fresher air. Was there a keyhole? He knelt to see.

"Monsieur Adams? Are you all right?"

Gamely Adams nodded. "It's the chemicals." No keyhole, but kneeling felt good. He heard bottles clinking, running water, silence: a familiar sequence. "I'm sorry," Bertillon said over his shoulder. "I'm so used to it. One forgets the effect on others. I rather like it—sharp, astringent. It clears the mind."

And the stomach, Adams thought. He concentrated on breathing shallowly.

"I will let you know the minute it's done." The water ran again, then stopped. Out of the rinser, into the fixer. Soon. Another minute. He could last that long. His stomach was in his throat; his esophagus was burning with bile and acid. Half a minute . . .

The moment he could, he opened the door and fled.

Back in the office, waiting, breathing deeply at the open window behind the desk, Adams's eye fell on paperwork that lay exposed on Bertillon's blotter. "The search you requested 22 November 1892 is complete. The fingerprints in question are indeed those of Miriam Talbott. This is a positive identification. She is an unmarried American subject, born 23 June 1870, in New York. Her passport was issued in November 1889, at Washington, and she has been resident in Paris for two years."

How had Bertillon been able to find her? Why hadn't he been told?

When Bertillon returned with two large copies of Clemenceau's photograph, holding one in each hand by a bit of corner and balancing on one foot to swing the door shut behind him with a toe, Adams didn't wait.

"Where is she?" he demanded.

"Pardon?"

"Miriam Talbott. You got her prints somehow, so you must know where she is." Bertillon looked at him uncomprehendingly. "I know you didn't get her prints from her apartment—it's been wiped clean. I was there with DuForché. Where did you find her? At an art school? I thought of that. But I haven't had enough time to track her down."

Bertillon stood for a moment, waving the photographs slowly, to dry them, and looked at Adams blankly. He moved to set the photographs on his desk. "Ah," he said, following Adams's glance at the papers on his desk. "That memorandum." He didn't seem surprised. "I believe I mentioned to you that I would be receiving some information today," he continued, walking around his desk. He took up a position next to Adams's chair, leaning lightly against his own desk, and picked up the paper. "This is a report on the fingerprints from the cadaver," he said, tilting his head back to read. "I have found Miriam Talbott, yes. She is dead. Your friend . . ." Bertillon shrugged. "Your friend is someone else, Monsieur Adams."

"Are you certain?"

"I would say I have confidence approaching certainty." Bertillon raised his eyebrows. "The fingerprints match. We do not, of course, know the likelihood of this being a coincidence, but mathematically it would have to be extremely small." Bertillon continued, explaining the precise ambivalence he felt about fingerprints, giving Adams a short lesson in statistics and the mathematics of probability as he did so, but Adams wasn't listening: he was trying to assimilate this new information. The story she had told, about names she had been called in school, was that all made up? If Miriam wasn't Miriam, who was she? He tried to find in his memory a hint that she had been lying about her name, but couldn't discover any. His memories of her now looked different, very different. The woman with whom he had stood in the shaft of stained-glass light at Chartres, when he felt the force of that belief in whose service this and so much other art had been made: not Miriam. The woman whose profile he had secretly memorized as she stood before him, painting the bay and the cathedral rock of Mont-Saint-Michel: not Miriam. The woman with whom he had laughed on the train, the woman who had slept on his shoulder, the woman whose company had helped him, however briefly, to find pleasure in life: not Miriam. Everything he had thought about her could be wrong, he realized. She had played him false.

Bertillon had asked him something. What?

"I was saying, as to why your friend felt it necessary to lie to you about her name, have you any idea?"

"No." Adams said this loudly, for Bertillon seemed to have gotten smaller and farther away. The smell of the chemicals was back. He bent closer to the window and shut his eyes, inadvertently fixing an image of the courtyard: pigeons roosting on the entablature below the eaves on the other side, below them the building streaked with their droppings, the poplars small and fragile against the great mass of the building.

"What was that you said about an art school?" Bertillon asked.

"She's a student at an art school," Adams responded without turning around. "Didn't you know?" He could hear the burbling sound of pigeons as if they were in the room with him. False, all of it false. How much of what he knew of her did he know of the wrong woman? He began to realize that among the consequences were ones he liked: could this mean she hadn't been Reinach's mistress? That she wasn't the blackmailer?

"How could I know if you haven't told me? Really, Monsieur Adams. This presents us with some possibilities. Some interesting possibilities." Adams saw him, far away, move paper on his desk. "Perhaps . . . well, I shouldn't speculate. But this could prove useful. Tell me, is there anything else you know that you haven't told me? Anything at all?"

He considered. With each breath the pressure in his chest subsided. But he had a residual dizziness: the floor seemed not quite horizontal. He tried to think. Was there anything he knew that he hadn't told Bertillon? The past few days weren't a series of discrete events and information but a roil of experience, all present at once to his memory and in no order, churning together like a thick stew on the boil, animated by his one new fact: Miriam had lied. No, no, she wasn't even Miriam. Now she, not that other woman, was Not-Miriam. She had lied—not to just anyone, but to him. He wasn't sure but that this was worse than when he had thought she was Reinach's mistress.

Bertillon was waiting, small and trim, his hands folded in front of him. He was looking at Adams curiously. "I went to look up some information on Jules Dingler at the library a few days ago," Adams said. His own voice was familiar and soothing to him, though it sounded hollow in his ears. Talking made him feel better. He would speak some more. "Somebody got there before me and removed it. Sliced it out." Adams tried to think: Who had known he was going there? Was he being followed? Anticipated?

"Dingler. In the photograph."

"Him," Adams said, putting a finger on the photograph, surprised to find it within reach. He felt a little better to see his own hand at the end of his sleeve, out there, moving in the world. "The chief engineer in Panama. Shot his horses after his family died." It seemed so abrupt, compressing Dingler's tragedy that way, but he hadn't the breath for a longer explanation. "He died years ago. Malaria, like his family. A relapse. Out of his past." He shook his head: a vulnerability any historian could understand.

"You suspect that he is—was—connected to this Panama affair?"

Adams tried to think, searching his mind for what he thought, like an overworked clerk at inventory. "I don't know. His mother thinks he was murdered. What for? Maybe he knew something important in the scandal. He would have seen the money, seen how little ended up in Panama, could have figured out that vast sums were disappearing somewhere along the line. And I had a copy of this picture— Dingler's copy of this picture—and someone broke into my rooms and burned it."

"Yes. You told me. When did you learn about this list of *chéquards*?"

Adams paused to remember. He had to count the days backward: today was Thursday, yesterday was Wednesday . . . "Tuesday. Sometime Tuesday."

Bertillon stood and walked to the other window, where he stared at the courtyard. Adams couldn't see his face. The Frenchman rocked on his heels. "Puzzling," Adams heard him murmur. In a moment Bertillon turned. "Well, Monsieur Adams. On to the matter at hand. Would you be so kind as to tell me what is your intention in regard to this photograph I have made for you?"

"I want to take it back to the concessionaire, show him these men. Maybe he can identify them. He said there were two men who came swimming there, all summer, with this woman. The dead woman. With Miriam Talbott." He didn't like using her name. "Maybe the men are in this picture."

"And what would that prove?" Bertillon asked.

"Why, that they knew her. That she's mixed up in this Panama thing."

"And this would be a consolation to you?"

Adams was puzzled. A consolation? Why was Bertillon saying things like this? "No, of course not. But it might help you figure out why she killed herself, and how she's connected to this Panama affair. And that might help find Miriam. My Miriam, I mean. The other one. Not-Miriam. They were roommates—did I tell you that? They lived in the same apartment."

Bertillon shook his head. "No. I don't believe you did tell me that." He sighed and looked out the window. "It's all tangled together, no? And you want to be the one to untangle it." He smiled at Adams. "I am sorry if I seem difficult, Monsieur Adams," he said gently. "Let me be clear with you: I am interested in your missing-persons case. Because it involves a question of identification it is an appropriate matter for this office, and because it is personally interesting to me I am willing to devote more attention to it than is customary for cases of this kind. But I am not empowered to help you unravel the Panama affair, or to investigate any sort of corruption, murder, bribery. That is most definitely beyond my authority; that sort of case belongs, oh, I don't know, to the prefect himself and the Civil Tribunal. Or to the Chamber—they're running their own investigation. None of it has anything to do with me, unless they ask for my help, which I certainly hope they will do if they need someone identified. Am I making myself clear?"

Adams nodded.

"Now, the question is, shall we conceive of your problem as a matter for the Service of Judicial Identity, or not?"

"What are you saying?"

Bertillon turned to look at the courtyard again, his back to Adams. "The identification of the dead woman as Miriam Talbott is based on fingerprints, a method which, to my mind, is not yet fully proven. They have not yet failed, but I am permitted, in my discretion, to doubt them if I choose. So: I have these unproven fingerprints saying one thing, and an eyewitness, sitting in my office right now, who has said another. A witness who has said she can't be Miriam Talbott, because he knows Miriam Talbott and this is not she." Bertillon turned to Adams, his face a bureaucrat's mask, his hands clasped behind his back. "Because of this discrepancy we may say that the matter of the dead woman's identity is not fully resolved. Until it is resolved to my satisfaction, I have authority to pursue whatever lines of inquiry I believe likely to produce results." Bertillon arched an eyebrow at him, reading his face. "I believe you understand me, do you not?"

Adams did, and said so.

"Good." Bertillon's mouth formed a thin smile that disappeared quickly. "Now, inasmuch as this question of identity would be a great deal easier to solve if we had this other woman to talk to, your Miriam Talbott—or Not-Miriam-Talbott, as the case may be—I think I can be of some assistance with your missing-persons case. I shall set one of my men out to visit art schools with a description of this woman, this Perhaps-Miriam-Talbott, to see what he can find. I understand that you and Michel have engaged in certain inquiries?" Adams nodded. "I trust you will keep me apprised of any interesting and relevant findings. I will do the same for you." Bertillon paused, meeting Adams's gaze, and Adams felt that it would have been a moment for shaking hands, except that they were too far apart. "And now," Bertillon continued, "I have a suggestion for you." He picked up the original of the photograph he had copied. "The provenance and circumstances of this photograph remain unclear to me. If someone burned it to destroy information it contained, these circumstances might help us deduce the sort of information it holds." He turned the photograph over. "Don't you think it would be interesting to talk to the man who took this picture?" He placed a slender forefinger underneath the legend that had been stamped on the back, in a delicate blue script framed with a geometric border.

Adams stood and leaned away from the window to read it: *St. Cyr et Fils, Photographie, 348, rue Ventadour.*

2:00 P.M.

ADAMS FELT ILL. He needed to think.

For a time the Panama affair had seemed, if not clear, then at least orderly: each fact had suggested an action, a next step, an appropriate and logical further inquiry. But as he stood outside the Prefecture, his questions branched as confusingly as lines of descent in a village of polygamists, until he was no longer exactly sure what had begat what and where anything was related. His conversation with Bertillon, besides revealing that the woman he sought was a liar, had also forced him to see something he ought to have seen all along: everyone involved in this affair had their own motivations, their own perceptions, their own angle on events, their own limitations. The interests of some were necessarily antagonistic to the interests of others. And yet there were also alliances, near congruences of interest, based on desires so similar that the subtlety of difference between them might not be fully apparent until they were brought, like the swatches of cloth a tailor displays, into juxtaposition in the good broad light of day.

Clearly, Bertillon worked within practical and political limits. Clearly, he was worried about those limits. His work ought to have been constrained only by the limits of the human mind; but in the end the chief of the Service of Judicial Identity had to accept his place in a bureaucracy. Maybe he did this with as much dignity as he could, but still:

his life was shaped not by a complete commitment to the search for truth but by the forces that bore in upon him. He, like everyone else, wore the impress of external compulsion. What was it that Clemenceau had said? Justice is blind, politics isn't. He had thought Bertillon an officer of justice, blind to political context. He wasn't.

And in seeing this Adams had lost the center somehow, the confident hub upon which all else had turned. There was no milepost from which all other mileposts were measured. No, the affair would look different to each participant. Clemenceau, Reinach, Madame LeBlanc, Miriam Talbott—both of them, Miriam Talbott dead and his Not-Miriam-Talbott, the liar!—Lesseps, father and son, the concessionaire, the fat concierge, the dead coroner, Herz, Dingler, Delahaye, the *chéquards*, the broken investors, the Boulangists, the whole damn Chamber of Deputies as a matter of fact, and the Türr syndicate and those crazy Saint-Simonians who had first dreamed of a canal, and Hay and Cameron and maybe even Elizabeth and Amanda, all of them: each had a specific place, a unique place, in the thing.

So did he. And the position that made the most sense to him, the idea that drew him with its seductive promise of simplicity, was to see them all aligned against him, all part of a vast conspiracy. Yes. They wanted to keep him alone, uninformed, frustrated, scared, lonely. Well, if there was to be no central milepost, then he would be his own—he, Adams, the measure of all things! Everyone his own measure— *that* was modern life, that was the result of history being spun in the whirligig of progress, spun end-around over and over by pure Force: coal and steam.

Across the boulevard stood Notre Dame, emblem of a different sort of energy. On the train back from Chartres Miriam (no, not "Miriam": *Not*-Miriam) had been *so* interested in his idea about churches, about the evolution of architecture: Mont-Saint-Michel was the Church Militant, built by the energy of expansion, while the cathedral at Chartres was the product of a different Church entirely, the Church Forgiving, the Church built not on rock but on the promise of the Virgin, on her promise of pure ennobling grace. Ha, he thought; should he have known then? That she had lied? The Virgin was Force, too, sufficient to animate an entire culture; she had been the gathering point for all the disparate arts and sciences the twelfth century knew. But her day had long since passed. New powers—steam, electricity, telegraphs and telephones, factory production, even the vacuum pipes under the earth in which grisly messages could whoosh here and there, and especially the political groupings that these inventions brought into being, the syndicates and corporations, the new alignments of wealth and interest, greed and design— these were beyond her reach. They let men accomplish their ends in the world, gave them more control over natural forces, yes, but for all that, none of these powers could hold together a world, not as she had done. None offered more than a partial vision.

He found a cab and gave the driver the photographer's address. And what if the world could know a unifying power again? There was no reason to hope that such a power, today, would have a reign as benign as that of the Virgin. It was more comforting to reject the problem entirely—to refuse to see the fragmentation, to accept the idea of conspiracy, the idea of society controlled by some dark syndicate that intended harm and pain. This made sense of the world—certainly it explained the world of politics, the dense jungle of the Panama scandal, the increasingly brutal treatment of man by man!—without requiring one to lose faith in the very idea of order. And it was, he saw, a way of asserting the self, a way of valuing, for once, the self's emotional response when it said (as selves have always said), *I* am the zero mark, the only milepost worth trusting, the center from which all is measured and around which all revolves. This *must* be so, because I *feel* it to be so, I *want* it to be so! What would such a self need with reason and evidence? And where would be the harm? Whom would he hurt if he did that?

He had never felt his loneliness more sharply. He was slipping, losing himself in this new and confusing world, where even a matter as simple as identity became an uncertain thing, less a matter of knowledge than surmise, a vague distribution of probabilities, as discomfiting and as difficult to grasp as a cloud of tropical mosquitoes, buzzing, lighting, flitting away.

This image, strangely, was reassuring. A cloud of mosquitoes shares a purpose, a more or less conscious intent. And he thought, Even if Not-Miriam had lied to him, she would have had her reasons. He ought to trust her. He didn't want any harm to come to her through anything he could control, anything he should do and didn't, or shouldn't do and did. And he sensed that somehow, in some way he couldn't describe, he would be harming her if he allowed himself to be seduced away from difficult truth by the easy logic of paranoia. He ought to do right by her. Liar or not, she wasn't part of the world that was arrayed against him.

And once he had cut her out of the aggregate, once he began that process of distinction, he saw that it was of course a process he could not stop. No, they were not all of a piece. Each participant in this affair had his or her own separate motivation, his or her own vantage point. Only egotism, his own selfishness, could make them appear the same. He knew that he wouldn't get anywhere if he didn't recognize that and think it through.

He was delivered to the photographer's without quite expecting it. When he looked up from the cab, he realized he had been there before: the burned-out building gaped open to the weather like a sunken-eyed waif too dim to seek proper cover. Dismounting from the cab into the light drizzle, Adams felt the small hairs on his neck stand up. Here, as if to mock him, was either a coincidence ripe for misinterpretation or further evidence of a malignant conspiracy, the idea of which he had only just rejected. It had been a few days since the fire—three, he realized when he counted—but he could still see the distinct crystalline trail of the steam-breathing behemoth that had passed, clanking, down the street. The trail only seemed to emphasize the point: there were modern powers loose within the city, indelicate powers whose energies and ambitions had little historical precedent.

He climbed the steps to the building, past where he had seen a fireman arrange his unlikely salvage of bottles. There was no trace of them now. The charred door was open. Adams peered into the studio, where the smell of ruin was damp and sharp and sour.

The interior had been gutted. Far below, on the cellar floor, a pile of trash had been scraped together, broken bottles and partially burned wood, oddly shaped remnants and sundry other objects coagulated together by dampness and ash. Adams thought, for some reason, of a palimpsest, an abrasion on old parchment where a word has been removed and replaced by another. A scholar might dedicate his entire life to reading the implications of one such ambiguity, proposing possibilities into its void. Now, here, architecturally, Adams might do the same.

And for some reason he thought of the photography studio Clover was to have had in the house on Lafayette Square. The room waited for her, waited for her still. What if he hadn't encouraged her photography? The chemicals wouldn't have been close to hand. What if he hadn't gone to the dentist that Sunday morning, but had remained with her through that hour in which she had, by long custom, written to her father? Sundays were always difficult since her father's death. He had known that.

In the past seven years he had avoided her studio and the painful questions it posed. In its way it, too, was a palimpsest: beneath its bare walls and floor was the undeniable truth of its purpose, which he could not recall without sorrow.

He might have made inquiries; he might have asked neighbors about the cause of the fire, and the fate and current location of the photographer; he might have tried to puzzle out the meaning of the remains before him. But this had been Bertillon's curiosity. He wasn't sure what he was after, and the fact of the coincidence—more precisely, his virtual certainty that it wasn't a coincidence, this fire at the studio of the photographer who had, years before, taken a picture of some men on a set of steps—told him as much as he wanted to know.

Lifting a hand to the back of his neck, he turned to walk back to his cab. The rain was falling more steadily now, and on the sidewalk it carried a thin scum of ash into the gutter.

4:30 P.M.

THE EMBASSY SECRETARY was a dour-looking young man with oiled hair and a sharp chin. He watched Adams carefully and with obvious mistrust, as if by letting Adams wait for Hay he was being asked to play some sort of confidence game that he could lose if he wasn't attentive.

Adams sighed and surveyed the anteroom for distraction. Having finally grown uncomfortable with the damp solitude of a cab, and wanting to find a way out of the funk he felt descending on him, he had decided to find Hay. To feel at peace with him, to feel once again welcome in the bosom of friendship, would be a comfort. But Special Envoy Hay wasn't in; he was expected shortly; would Adams be pleased to wait?

Yes. And no. Adams was unambiguously pleased, though, to spy a copy of that morning's *Le Temps* on a chair across the room. He rose to retrieve it, forcing a smile at the secretary, gratified to find that the paper hadn't been read: he liked the crisp flatness of fresh newspapers, all their pages aligned. Clover had known this, and had always seen to it that he got the papers first.

He scanned the Panama story on the front page. Loubet was promising to bring the *chéquards* to justice, no new warrants had been issued, and the Chamber was selecting its investigating committee—the Socialists were agitating to have the matter taken up by the courts (a more thorough, non-partisan investigation, they argued), and the Boulangists had abstained, saying no investigation run by the Chamber itself could possibly be legitimate. They had a point, Adams thought. The paper went on to note that there was no word on who, exactly, the *chéquards* were, and it opined that in the face of this ignorance the responsible citizen could only reserve judgment.

Adams had begun reading correspondents' reports from the Crimea by the time Hay arrived. "I'll see Mr. Adams now," he told the secretary, motioning Adams to follow him. "I hope you don't mind," Hay said when they were seated, a silver-handled, ebony-bladed letter opener in his hand. "I have to deal with this." He pointed at the stack of afternoon mail on his desk. More of his officiousness, Adams thought: it will make it easier for him to hold me at arm's length. "Have you seen Lizzie today?" Hay spoke absently, without even looking up, as he sliced an envelope. Adams watched him glance at the letter, then set it and its envelope into the wooden tray on the left side of his desk.

Finally Hay looked at him. No, he hadn't seen her. "Not since last night." He would keep the details of their talk to himself.

Hay nodded. "She and Cameron had a visit from the police. She's very upset by it. Apparently the police were rude. Abusive, she said. Perhaps she exaggerates, but still."

"I'm sorry to hear that."

Hay unfolded another page, glanced at it, and set it in the tray. "Yes. Well. Something about a burned photograph? The police said they were there on your complaint."

"No. They have it wrong." He hadn't complained. "Hay, I have to ask you something. Why did Reinach visit you the night he died?"

Hay finished slitting open an envelope, but it seemed to Adams that his movements slowed for an instant. "You've been busy, haven't you?" When Adams didn't answer, Hay set the letter opener down and looked across the desk at him. "Railroad business." But simple answers were no longer sufficient, and Adams waited, gazing at him. "All right, I'll tell you. I am sounding out the possibility of an offer for the railroad, separate from the canal concession. There's some interest in it; we shall see. It's a key to the canal—the canal can't be built without it—and I would be very surprised if they let it go, so I'm holding my breath. Reinach was one of my contacts with the company. He gave me to understand that if the company is re-formed after a bankruptcy, it may be so hungry for capital that it would be willing to sign it over. Sell one asset to protect the other, the concession. We talked for twenty minutes—he thought it best that I not meet him in his office—and he was gone.''

This began to mollify Adams. "How well did you know him?"

"If you mean, did I know him at all, the answer is no. I met with him a few times. Corresponded with him before I got here."

"Did you know Miriam Talbott?"

Hay shook his head. "Never heard of her. Didn't know she was his mistress until I asked."

"Whom did you ask?"

"Adams, really. I can't—" Hay's dark eyes evaluated his friend's mood and he reconsidered. "Henri Cottu. Another director I know."

"Yes." He was in the photograph.

Hay watched Adams think this through. "Are you satisfied? I'm on the up-and-up, honest." He smiled, pleased to see Adams agree. "Now, what about this police visit to Cameron? What happened?"

Adams explained about the photograph, about the fingertips that arrived in the pneu, about being questioned at the Prefecture. He had hazarded a guess, that was all. Cameron had seen the picture. Maybe Adams shouldn't have said anything. No, he shouldn't have. It was a mistake to voice even a suspicion. But he had been disturbed, frightened really, by those fingertips. He had been thrown off balance. He wasn't thinking clearly. The whole affair had him off balance—tired, feeling low. Did Hay know: Miriam wasn't even Miriam, she was Not-Miriam? So she had lied. He didn't know what to make of that. And then there was the photographer's studio, the coincidence, if that's what it was. Put that alongside the Dingler material being gone and those fingertips and the murder of the coroner and it began to look like some sinister conspiracy was shaping events . . .

Hay heard him out, then spoke gently. "This picture—it's the one from Panama? *La folie Dingler?*"

Adams nodded. He had forgotten; his ears burned with embarrassment. He tried to will it away. Hay gazed at him, silent for a moment, then reached for another envelope. "Lizzie is pretty angry with you." Above his dark eyes his eyebrows asked a question.

"I'll have to make it good with her." Maybe he should go to her now. He had ignored her, chasing this woman, this Not-Miriam around. What was he letting this do to his friendships? Of course she felt bad.

Hay was studying the contents of the envelope, unfolded in his hand. "Here now. This is something." He handed it to Adams.

It was a form, a death certificate, in French. At the top was a seal with the words *Coroner, Paris*. The name of the deceased was Miriam Talbott. Inked in next to *Cause of Death* was the single word: *homicide*. Hay handed him another page: *Coroner's Report*. He glanced at the bottom, at the signature and date: Tuesday, November 22. The day the coroner had died. How to explain this?

"She was an American citizen," Hay reminded him. He held out his hand for the papers and got them back. "When a foreign national dies and there are no local relatives, the coroner sends the death certificate to the Embassy."

Adams nodded. "It says homicide. But the report they found on his desk at the morgue says suicide. By drowning."

Hay drew the obvious conclusion: "Whoever killed the coroner switched reports, but didn't know that this one, and the death certificate, were in the post."

"Yes." He reached for the certificate. "Bertillon and Pettibois need to see this."

Hay stopped his hand. "I'll let you take it," Hay said, "but I need it back. I have to mail it to her family. And you must promise me something, something unrelated."

"What?"

"When you find that list of *chéquards*, give me as much

notice as you can before turning it in. It would be a great help to me not to be surprised.''

Adams nodded—a lesser order of assent, he thought, than an outright promise. ''I'll do my best,'' he allowed.

5:30 P.M.

"YOU FOUND THESE where?" Bertillon wanted to know.

"At the Embassy. The American Embassy. She was an American national—the coroner sent the Embassy a copy."

Bertillon held the paper close to his face, scrutinizing something. "Is that an established fact, or your surmise from evidence?"

"My surmise," Adams said.

"It's best to identify your guesses as such."

"Yes." Adams had almost added "sir." "It's standard procedure. Diplomatic courtesy." He corrected himself: "Hay says it's standard procedure—the coroner sending a report to the Embassy."

Bertillon seemed not to be paying attention to him. "Homicide. As I thought," he allowed, putting the paper down.

Adams frowned. "What do you mean, 'As I thought'?"

Bertillon leaned his head back to look at the ceiling and took a long draught of air through his nose. "She didn't have her glasses with her. Suicides, if they wear glasses, always have their glasses with them. It's probably the last thing they do—fold their glasses, put them in a purse or pocket."

"How do you know she wore glasses?"

Bertillon did not look at him. "A deduction from evidence, Monsieur Adams. Two very faint red marks here, on the bridge of the nose." He held the bridge of his nose with thumb and forefinger, twisting his hand down low so that he could still focus on the ceiling. "Also, if this was not enough, she had a card from an optometrist in her purse. Her optometrist assures me she wore glasses." Bertillon allowed himself a smile.

"So you knew she wasn't a suicide all along?" Adams asked, a touch of annoyance creeping into his voice.

"I did not *know*. I had suspicions; this confirms them."

What else does he suspect that he doesn't say, Adams wondered. "And it confirms the motive for the coroner's murder, doesn't it?" Adams said. "He was killed to hide his report. The problem is, this copy was already in the mail. Whoever shot him was too late to get it. But they switched the other report, in the file. So the purpose of killing him wasn't to mutilate her body, to prevent her identification. She had already been identified—" except, he thought, his own participation must have confused matters somewhat. "Whoever mutilated her was her murderer, and he was trying to hide his tracks, but he was doing that not by trying to hide her identity but by trying to establish her as a suicide. The identity issue, the mutilation, was a show, a red herring."

"A what?" Bertillon eyed him without turning his head.

"A red herring. From fox hunting. They used to drag a fish across the trail of the fox, when the hunt was over, to call off the dogs. The dogs would take the trail of the herring instead of—"

"Oh." Bertillon stopped him with a hand and returned his gaze to the ceiling. He didn't say any more, nothing about the deduction Adams had made, and Adams was disappointed. He ought to be quiet, he supposed, and let Bertillon go at his own pace, but he couldn't. His mind had been racing since he read that single word at the bottom of the report. To her murderer, it didn't matter who the law thought she was as long as she was thought a suicide. And so far, it had worked; no one had investigated, no one had even spoken to the concessionaire. He would change that. "So her murderer is also the coroner's murderer. And the person who sent the fingertips to me in the tube. Which means they want me not to find Miriam—I mean Not-Miriam, my friend. He's trying to scare me off. So somehow Not-Miriam is threatening to him. If she has the list of *chéquards*, then it's clear:

some member of the Chamber of Deputies, some deputy, is doing this. Whoever it was must have some knowledge of police forensic procedures. That should limit the field of suspects. A stake in the scandal plus knowledge of police business. Can you tell me, do you know, does this man Clemenceau know anything about police business? How about Loubet?''

Bertillon rolled his chair forward and leaned to his desk for something: he took the coroner's report up and studied the seal. ''This certainly looks genuine.'' It was as if he hadn't heard Adams at all. ''We'll check the signature and make sure, but I think it's genuine.'' He leaned back again and wiped his face with the palm of a hand, down from his forehead over the bridge of his nose, until he held his cheeks with thumb and fingertips. For the first time, Adams noticed a wedding ring. Bertillon looked tired.

''It's been a long day, hasn't it?'' Adams asked. He himself was tired, and in his wet shoes his feet felt cramped and formless. Bertillon was looking at Adams sidelong, with his hand still holding his face, and to Adams it seemed he weighed Adams's inconsequential remark for hidden meaning. Adams shifted in his chair.

''Yes,'' Bertillon said finally. ''It has.''

''Ah, I was wondering,'' Adams said, leaning forward in his chair. He pointed to the coroner's report. ''I don't think I followed all of this. The medical terms are unfamiliar. What does it say? In there, in the technical part?''

''It says,'' Bertillon answered, sitting up, ''that we had better be careful. It says that Miriam Talbott's murderer went to the morgue and killed the coroner in order to protect himself. It says the killer is familiar with police procedures, and in all likelihood was someone known to the coroner. That's what it says.''

Adams nodded, uncertain. ''And the, I mean, ah, there are some things there . . . What's this word here—''

''Let me translate.'' Bertillon picked up the paper. ''The subject, oh, let's see. You don't want word for word, no. I'll skip the routine.'' Bertillon scanned the page. ''Tissue and organ damage indicating presence of toxins. No certainty but a likelihood of arsenic. Mmm-hmmm. Water present in the lungs, both sides, not suffused, and as a slight pleural embolism, left side. Pleurocentesis between the fourth and fifth ribs, each side, entrance through the areola, apparently postcardial arrest. No significant loss of blood from these wounds.''

''She was stabbed? Poisoned and stabbed?''

Bertillon shook his head. ''Poisoned, yes, but not stabbed. Not as you mean it.'' He put the report on the desk and looked at it there for a moment. ''The coroner is—was—a good man, never went beyond description. He always left purpose and motive where it belonged. Still, you can see how his mind worked. He always asked the right questions.'' He sighed. ''Someone poisoned her, Monsieur Adams, then injected water into her lungs. Through the nipples, to hide the entry.''

Adams blanched. ''Why?''

''They wanted it to look as if she drowned herself.'' He shrugged and stared thoughtfully at Adams. ''Ever hear of *aurum pigmentum*, Monsieur Adams? A bright yellow pigment? It's made with arsenic. Arsenic trisulfide. Orpiment, you'd call it. I believe this missing woman, this friend of yours, was a painter, was she not? She would have had such a pigment?'' He reached a hand down to do something to his foot that Adams couldn't see. When he straightened, Bertillon had a shoe in his hand. Adams thought he might use it to demonstrate something about arsenic, but no: he turned it upside down over his desk blotter and tilted it until a small pebble fell from it.

He bent over again, slipping on his shoe, while Adams stared at him. ''All right, Monsieur Adams,'' Bertillon said softly when he had straightened. ''Tell me what you know. And tell me what you think. Identify both, and don't leave anything out.''

8:05 P.M.

NIGHT HAD COME to the city. The rain had stopped, bringing on a sharp-edged breeze, crisp and cold, a portent of the winter to come. It carried a smell of fish and sewage up from the river. Around him the buildings of the Ile de la Cité, familiar enough by day, combined their vague hulking forms in unlikely ways, disorienting him. The gas streetlights seemed ineffective against the damp night. He made his way not toward home but toward the river, the right bank, across from the looming Chamber building, where his day had started. He was alone on the quai.

At the swimming concession Adams pounded the door with the heel of his palm. The wind was moving the trees above the quai against each other, and he thudded hard to be heard over their squeal and squeak. The shack looked abandoned. Adams moved his head from side to side, trying to discern in the darkness a hint of light at the edge of the door, but could find none. Either the door was tightly fitted or it was dark inside. There was a large padlock on the lower part, but since it was a Dutch door, that didn't necessarily mean anything. And there was another entrance; someone could still be inside. Adams rapped again, glancing up and down the quai, wishing the man would answer, wishing he himself were someplace warm and dry.

Finally Adams heard the sound of a bolt being drawn. He stepped back to allow the door to swing open. The concessionaire stood before him, framed in the upper half of the door opening, smiling the same vapid smile Adams had seen earlier. Adams couldn't tell if the man recognized him or if a day's span of memory was beyond his capacity. Pointing toward the lower half of the Dutch door, which remained shut, Adams asked, "May I come in?" The man stretched to find a key somewhere to his left and then reached over to undo the padlock, letting Adams see past him into the room. It was dark, the sole illumination being two wall-mounted candles whose flames squatted in the draft, softly thup-thup-thupping, threatening to go out.

The candles stopped guttering when the door was shut behind him. Adams stamped his feet a bit to drive out the chill. "I've come to show you some pictures." The room was warm, in spite of its bare stone walls. Adams found the source of the heat—a stove directly to his right—and turned his back toward it, lifting aside the tails of his overcoat to let the heat penetrate. The concessionaire, latching the door, nodded at Adams and, smiling, gestured him toward a small round table in the center of the room. There was a shadowy doorway beyond it. On the table was an unglazed bowl. When his eyes adjusted to the dimness of the light, Adams made out the things it held: a small brown tuft of fur; a patch of white bone of complex shape and improbable delicacy, such as might come from a bird's skull; an undistinguished stone or two; a folded piece of decorated paper; a small silver photograph case.

The concessionaire saw his eye light on this latter object and he reached out to take it up. He clicked it open and showed it to him: "The Virgin Mary. The Mother of God." He nodded, offering it, indicating Adams could take it.

The case was rectangular, no more than two inches high, with a raised fleur-de-lis on its front and back. In the right-hand portrait oval was a miniature of the Virgin, a tiny reproduction of Parmigianino's *Madonna with the Long Neck*, apparently cut from a Mass card. The left oval was empty.

"She'll come back, you know." The man pulled a chair up opposite Adams and nodded at him.

"She will?" Adams asked, handing the case back. What manner of Christianity was this?

The man accepted the case and nodded. "The dead one. I've been calling her." When the concessionaire smiled, his lower lip protruded, spilling out of his face. "Maybe you could talk to her?"

"Ah . . ." Adams was at a loss for words. He had no brief for superstitions, seeing them as the desperate faith of the foolish and disempowered; but there was now, in the muscles of his back, a chill the stove couldn't warm. He knew that such a thing as spiritualism existed, that certain people claimed to communicate with the dead; but understanding that a phenomenon exists doesn't prepare you for experiencing it directly. The concessionaire was talking about communication with the dead as if it were perfectly natural. Adams glanced quickly around the room, wanting some evidence that the laws of the world as he understood them hadn't been suspended. A sink, shelves above it with some few things (a pair of water-spotted glasses, a soup bowl, a white enamelled pot), next to this a plain pine cupboard. The walls of the room were stone. Reassured by their solidity, he faced the concessionaire and was about to answer curtly, when he thought better of it. Whatever it was this concessionaire believed, he seemed to believe with certainty; and his beliefs were no business of Adams's. "No," he said gently, "I don't think so. Thank you, anyway. I've come to ask a favor. Will you do me a favor?" He reached into his breast pocket for the packet of photos. He had taken the enlargement that Bertillon made and cropped it into individual pictures, each roughly the size of a calling card.

"Here are pictures of some men," he said carefully, holding the packet up. "I want to ask you about them." Adams laid the pictures on the table in an orderly row, one by one, right side up to the concessionaire. "Were any of them the ones you saw with that woman—the dead woman?"

The concessionaire glanced at the pictures, then rose, took a lumpy stub of a candle from one of the holders on the wall, and brought it to the table. Silently he pored over each of the portraits, returning to Reinach with his high forehead and small, deeply browed eyes after he had examined them all. Adams hoped the man wouldn't spill wax on the pictures.

"This one," the concessionaire said finally, tapping Rei-

nach with a dirty fingernail. "Maybe. The other I don't see."
He looked up at Adams to see if his words had pleased.

" 'Maybe'?" Adams repeated. "You're not sure?"

"Can't be sure." The man's smile faded when he saw
Adams's face. "Well," he said, looking again to the pictures.
He examined them closely, putting his face near the table,
where the weak and yellow light from his candle gave his
flesh the color of spoiled dough. "Yes," he said finally.
"Him."

"You're sure?"

The man looked again, then shrugged.

Adams nodded. "The night they found the woman—the
dead one—did you see anything?"

"Yes," the man said.

"What? What did you see?"

"Two men. They brought her. She was asleep."

"Was he one of the men?"

The concessionaire shook his head. "No." Not Reinach.

Adams pointed to Clemenceau. "Him? Yes? No?"

The concessionaire leaned close again, examined the photograph, then looked up to Adams. "Maybe. The men, I
don't see the men so well."

"Do you mean you couldn't see the men, or you don't
see them here?"

"I saw them. They're not here."

"What did they look like?"

The concessionaire shook his head. "Can't say." Something in the way he said this made Adams think there was
more.

"But you know who it was?"

"No," the concessionaire said, and looked afraid.

"You have an idea who it was?"

"Nooo," he answered, drawing it out.

Come on, Adams thought. He took a breath to calm himself. "Look. I can't guess what you're thinking. Is there
something else? Why don't you just tell me? What is it?"

The concessionaire hesitated, then leaned forward. "They
undressed her. In one of the tents. She didn't mind. The man,
he had something, a doctor thing, he stuck her. She didn't

say anything, didn't move, didn't mind at all." He shook his head in wonderment.

"She was already dead."

The concessionaire squinted at Adams, mulling this over. His squint became a stare. "You have to go," he said abruptly, and Adams wasn't sure if this was a question or a command or a plain statement of fact. "But first, I have to show you." He stood, picked up the candle stub, and gestured to Adams from the doorway at the back of the room.

Adams scooped up his pictures and followed.

They turned sharply after the doorway, and made their way down a stone passage that must have run parallel to the quai. After a few yards, the concessionaire turned and put his finger to his lips. "Here," he whispered. Adams stood next to him. The concessionaire gestured to the wall. "I watch here," he said, pointing to a small iron grille, about six inches across, at breastbone height. "She was my favorite."

"Watch what?" Adams whispered back.

"Swimmers. Ladies." The concessionaire smiled. "Dress and undress." He put a hand to his throat, as if to undo a button, and gave a little shimmy, miming the removal of clothing. The changing tents, Adams realized; this pathetic little man always made sure that one was positioned in front of this hole. "You look," the concessionaire whispered.

"No," Adams said.

"Go on! You look!"

With a wary glance at the man, Adams bent his face to the grille. He wanted to be gone, to leave, but for some reason this would make the man happy. He'd do it and go.

At first he could see nothing; then the blackness gave way to a lighter darkness, the gaslit night of Paris. Had his eyes adjusted or had something obscured the opening? As he watched, he heard a slight cough, then saw a shower of sparks as a cigar landed on the quai near the edge. Adams pulled back.

"There's someone out there," he whispered.

The concessionaire nodded. "You have to go," he said.

8:22 P.M.

THE CONCESSIONAIRE LED Adams farther down the passageway, away from his room. The candlelight pulled strange, motile shapes from the wet stone: the constant change was making Adams dizzy. He concentrated on the light the candle threw on the floor. A dozen yards, then another; they walked in silence. Finally they came to a set of steps. "Up here," the concessionaire said. "There's a door. You have to kick hard. It sticks." He stood aside to let Adams pass.

There was indeed a door, and it was stuck, and Adams kicked it. So much for a quiet exit, he thought, as the door clattered open. He looked back down the stairs and saw the concessionaire's face in candlelight mouthing the word "Goodbye." Next to his cheek the fingers of his hand curled in a childish wave that made Adams shiver.

Outside, the darkness was not absolute; the soft light of gas lamps on the boulevard above shone through the rain-washed air. Adams glanced both ways quickly, did not see anyone, then concentrated on the stretch of quai downriver near the shack. Was that a figure slouching against the wall? The stone of the quai was shiny in the dark and this made it difficult to tell. He gave a thought to running away. No: he couldn't run quickly, and he was too far from the stairs and the nearest brightly lit street. Damn this, he thought. He flushed with sudden anger. He'd had enough of these skulky, shadowy threats. He was ready to face this one. He took a few steps down the quai, his hands unconsciously forming fists. "Who are you? What do you want?" He stamped his foot against the stone. "Show yourself, damnit!"

He thought he saw the figure move. Yes—a darkness separated from the stone wall and moved quickly onto the quai. Was it coming toward him? Good! Adams moved closer. No; the figure was receding. He heard footsteps, rapid footsteps: it was running. Adams gave chase, forcing his legs to move quickly against the damp bulk of his overcoat, which lapped at his knees with every stride. He could not catch up. He made himself run faster. The cobblestones were wet and slippery, and Adams had a fleeting premonition that he would wrench an ankle and crumple to the pavement.

By the time he got to the concessionaire's shack, he realized it was hopeless; the figure was still running, and he hadn't gained any ground on it. His quarry disappeared between the abutments of the pont de Solférino and was lost among the shadows.

Adams stopped. He thought he heard the regular pattering of someone walking; the sound faded in and out on the wind-blown air. Or was it his imagination, working some other sound to its purpose?

Breathing deeply a few times to slow his heart, Adams walked to where the interloper had stood and examined the cobblestones for clues. There had been a cigar; perhaps, if the end was still here, Bertillon might lift some fingerprints. But he found no trace of it on the quai.

He looked up and down the river. What he wanted, right then, was to be safe at home in his house on Lafayette Square, with a fire in the grate, a book in his lap, and a cup of tea at his elbow. He shivered, then patted his pockets, looking for the paper with DuForché's address. With a last deep breath, a sigh, really, Adams turned downstream, toward home. Next to him the Seine moved on, featureless and silent in the Paris night. Its oily black bulk seemed to drain the city, pulling all its warmth and vitality out and into the night, leaving just the dry husks of the buildings behind, their brick and stone enclosing empty air.

And then under the pont de Solférino his eye caught the

flash of an overcoat behind a pier before he felt the blow
crash into his stomach. He doubled over and the world tilted
crazily, the image of it disconnecting from the pull of gravity
and turning from the horizontal, way off, slipping over so
far he knew it could never go back the way it ought to be,
horizon and gravity at right angles; for an instant he felt
regret but no real surprise that the world had broken in this
way. Then his face met the unforgiving hardness of stone.

He snorted through his nose. The effort brought a sharp
pain deep in his sinuses. He was floating and something was
pressing down on his face. Woozily he tried to push whatever
it was away, but he couldn't raise his hands: they were tied
or blocked by something, stuck in place by whatever pressed
down on him. It pressed so hard it hurt. He couldn't step
away from it. He pulled his face back and felt an immediate
strain in his neck. His cheek had been against cobblestones,
wet cobblestones. He put his head back down, feeling the
damp and grit against his face. Rolling his head to one side,
he saw the formless gleam of a gas lamp down the quai. In
the cone of light beneath it he could make out a blobby
shape. A man.

His face was throbbing.

He stood carefully, wobbling through vertical once or
twice and managing to catch himself before he fell over.
Under the streetlamp the figure was now in better focus. He
saw it discard a lit match, which bounced once and went out.
Adams was overcome by a wave of nausea and he staggered
a few steps to lean against the wall. As he stood, his ears
filled with something like the sound of hoofbeats on turf and
he thought to look for its source before he recognized his
heart. His stomach seemed too full and too empty at the same
time. Slowly he put a hand to his face and winced as he
touched his nose. When his hand came away, it was red.
Adams felt for his handkerchief and retrieved it from a
pocket without taking his eyes off the figure on the quai. The
man was moving into the darkness and Adams would have
to follow now or lose him. His hands weren't working quite
right, and his handkerchief fell from his grasp. When he bent
to pick it up, he almost pitched over. Holding the handker-

chief to his face, he took a step, then another. With practice, remaining upright became easier.

He followed the figure from the streetlamp because it was all he could think to do.

After a few dozen yards his head had cleared enough for him to realize that he ought to hug the wall, to remain unseen in case the man turned around. When he took the handkerchief away from his face, he smelled cigar: the aroma was strong, almost painful, in his nose. The feeling in his stomach wasn't hunger. A soreness infested his muscles there, and he felt a rope of pain with every step. From the back the man who had hit him seemed supremely unconcerned; he strolled down the middle of the quai without looking back. Adams thought he saw a swagger in his walk.

The man climbed a set of stone stairs off the quai. Adams waited until he had disappeared before hurrying up as quickly as he could. At the top of the stairs he caught sight of his quarry crossing into the place de la Concorde. Adams followed him through the plaza, taking care to keep his distance, and on out to the boulevard Malesherbes. He could have followed him by the aroma of his cigar, which was sharp and strangely medicinal through the blood in his nose. Not until they passed the Chapel of Expiation did Adams begin to suspect where he was going. He slowed, then paused behind a tree while the man climbed the steps to Number 175: Madame LeBlanc's.

The man let himself in without ringing.

Adams followed up the steps and peered in through the door. In the glimpse he'd had of his assailant before he disappeared Adams hadn't been able to see his face. Suddenly furious, he contained himself long enough to ring the bell, then ring again; but this was not nearly enough, so he began to bang the flat of his palm impatiently against the door, harder and harder. Sensibly, he realized that the glass of the door might break; he moved his point of impact to the doorjamb, satisfyingly solid.

The door was answered by Madame LeBlanc's maid, who seemed surprised and afraid to see him. He paid her no attention but pushed past her, and then instead of waiting to be received he strode into the hallway and yanked open the door to the sitting room. Inside he found Madame LeBlanc and three men: Loubet, the graying, long-faced premier; the wiry, dark-haired Boulangist Delahaye; and Clemenceau, the lanky Socialist with tiger-colored hair.

"One of you will know the justice of the law!" Adams shouted at them. "Which one of you? Who did it? I'll hale you into court! Assault! Battery!" He was shaking his fist and when he noticed it there at the end of his arm he thought: A weapon. A shame he didn't know which one to use it on. He advanced, registering with satisfaction their expressions of surprise and fear. Loubet, the nearest, shrank away; Adams concentrated his wrath on him. "I ought to wallop you! All of you! Just whom do you think you're dealing with?" He was screaming. But before he was within striking distance, the heart went out of him; the scream had hurt his throat, a pain that released him. He knew he sounded like a crazed old man. He was relieved when Clemenceau, suddenly at his side, held his arm to stop him. He gave his fist another threatening shake at no one in particular and then stood back, away from Clemenceau's grasp. He felt like crying.

"Careful, Monsieur Adams," Clemenceau advised. "You are an intruder here."

Adams glanced about the room. Delahaye, Loubet, Clemenceau. Three deputies. None of them had on an overcoat. None of them was the right height or shape to be the man who hit him. No one was smoking a cigar.

"Monsieur Adams," Madame LeBlanc said calmly from an upholstered chair by the fireplace, "you look dreadful. Please sit. You must be in pain. Avril, can you attend to our visitor? A towel, perhaps? Whatever he needs."

Adams allowed himself to be seated on one of the sofas. With his anger ebbing, his legs felt powerless and limp. He tilted his head back on the cushion and could feel the blood in his nose drain down the back of his throat. There was blood, his own, on his coat, his suit. Where had his assailant gone? "I think we need proper introductions," Madame LeBlanc said grandly, before he could ask. "Deputy Delahaye, may I present Monsieur Adams."

"Delighted." Delahaye scowled in Adams's direction.

Adams kept his head tilted back, glancing at Delahaye along the length of his nose, and lifted a hand in response. It was heavy; Adams was suddenly tired. Delahaye's dark hair, smoothed close to his head, was shiny with pomade.

"I believe you know Deputy Clemenceau. And this is Prime Minister Loubet. Monsieur the Prime Minister, Henry Adams." The Prime Minister nodded in Adams's general direction without quite looking at him, then turned away, finding some element of decor on the far side of the room more compelling. Adams thought to tell him he had seen him before, on the steps to this very building, but thought better of it immediately. "Someone hit me," he said unnecessarily. He tilted his head back again. "I followed him here. I mean to find him."

Madame LeBlanc, still seated by the fireplace, exhaled a sigh. "Monsieur Adams." He heard in her speech a slight sibilance, caused by a mild overbite he had not until now noticed; her front teeth protruded enough that her lips, covering them, were held forward, as if pursed. It was not unattractive and made her seem girlish. "By long custom my house is a political neutral zone. A man is freed of everything when he enters here. No grudges, no antagonisms, no past, no prospects or purposes beyond the obvious, the ones that draw him here." She smiled, but above her high cheekbones her eyes were cold. "I have found this custom conducive to business. Do not violate it, Monsieur Adams."

The maid arrived with a large bowl of warm water and a cloth, and began ministering to Adams's face. He tried to keep the company in view over the moving cloth. "The man who hit me—" he began, but couldn't finish: Avril and her cloth made speech impossible.

"Might as well be gone." Madame LeBlanc finished his sentence for him. "Think no more on him. Really, I must insist. This is a safe haven."

Adams pushed the maid's hand away. "And thus this meeting?" He tried to sit up, but his stomach muscles hurt too much. There was a cut place on the left side of his tongue: his teeth felt sharp against it. His own mouth, an alien and dangerous place! He winced as the maid wiped the bridge of his nose. Something felt broken in there. She wasn't being very gentle. Adams looked at her face as she bent over him, the natural reaction to having another human face in close proximity, but she ignored him. Neither solicitous nor angry, she did her job, mechanically cleaning something that needed cleaning. When she rinsed her cloth, he saw that the water in her bowl had turned pink. He waved her away before she could hurt him again.

Some unspoken communication had passed between them. Why were they all here? Delahaye and Clemenceau, political enemies; Loubet, the centrist, atop a corrupt government that was falling apart. He had a guess. "The *chéquards*," he said. "The list. Each of you wants it. Madame LeBlanc knows how to get in touch with"—he couldn't call her Not-Miriam, not in front of these people—"the woman who has it."

"Monsieur Adams," Delahaye said, "it would be best if you did not pry. Get cleaned up and go. This doesn't concern you. Go home. All will be taken care of."

"It *does* concern me. I want to know where my friend is. The American woman. Just tell me where she is and I'll go."

"I'm afraid we can't do that," Clemenceau said.

"Can't, or won't?"

"Can't," Madame LeBlanc murmured. She gave a little laugh. "Louise is being kept safe. Everyone wants to know where she is. She's become a very popular young woman these days."

"Her name is Louise?" Adams asked. Louise, he repeated to himself. Louise.

"Yes," Clemenceau said. "Louise Martin—"

"Now really, Léonide, if you please." Loubet cut Clemenceau off. "He must go. I insist. I am most distressed by this breach of our privacy. You gave me your word. No one was to know of this." His glance at Clemenceau made clear the nature of his distaste for publicity.

"Ah, there, Monsieur le Premier," Clemenceau said in a soothing tone that the premier might well have considered condescending. "The presence of this Monsieur Adams can hardly be laid to Madame LeBlanc. She is formidable, yes, but not, I think, omnipotent. An unforeseeable event, neither positive nor negative in its nature. Isn't that the case, Mon-

sieur Adams? We shall see what he makes of us. Perhaps we
can prevail upon him to remain discreet.''

To one side Adams heard Delahaye exhale a brief, quiet-
voiced ''Ha!'' of dissent. When he rolled his head to look
at him, Delahaye spoke directly to him: ''This is no business
of yours.''

Wanting instinctively to prove Delahaye wrong on both
counts, but wanting even more to gain information, Adams
was unsure how to proceed. There was knowledge in this
room, knowledge that would help him find Louise, knowledge that might be his if he only knew how to win it. All of
a sudden he remembered the photographs in his pocket. Clemenceau, he thought, is vulnerable. ''I have something that
might concern *you*.'' He drew the photographs out and dealt
them, one by one, onto the table in front of the sofa. ''Lesseps Senior. Lesseps Junior. Reinach. Türr. All corrupt. More
corruption. More, more.'' He began saying this to cover
names he didn't know, and kept it up. The photographs
formed a ragged pile. ''Another. Another.'' Dingler's picture
fell. ''Another.'' A pang of regret: Dingler wasn't corrupt.
But the need of the moment, the dramatic force of repetition
. . . ''Another. And this one.'' He had contrived to make Clemenceau's photo fall last, for effect. ''You may have them,''
he said, dismissing them with a studied wave of his hand.
''There are more where these came from.'' He almost added
that a copy was in the possession of the police, but thought
it best not to divulge that; the implicit threat of disclosure
might prove to be useful. ''These come from one photograph.
Someone broke into my rooms and burned it. One of you?
Who?''

He looked from face to face, but found no one to answer
him. Loubet chewed his lower lip impatiently, gazing at the
wall, while Delahaye smirked and slowly shook his head. No
one spoke. Finally Clemenceau sighed. ''Monsieur Adams,
you have no reason to trust me. I wish you did. Because if
ever there was a moment in which your own interests would
be served by trusting someone, that moment is now. You are
involved in something you don't understand. Your presence
here is becoming less and less useful. It would be better if
you left us and let us continue. This would, in fact, hasten

your reunion with the young woman you seek.''

Adams stared sullenly from his place on the couch. A small part of his mind wanted to entertain the possibility that Clemenceau spoke truthfully, but this cautious voice was lost against the larger tide of his anger and distrust. Adams felt to a certainty that he was right: Clemenceau's assurances were self-serving, Clemenceau had been lying when he said he didn't know where Not-Miriam—no, Louise—had been, and he couldn't be trusted. ''I want to see Louise,'' he said. ''I insist on it.''

Delahaye snorted. ''We would all like to see this young woman, Monsieur Adams. You may join our club.'' Loubet looked at Delahaye with disgust.

''I'm not leaving,'' Adams assured them.

''That's that,'' Loubet said. ''Woman!'' he called sharply to Avril, who had retreated to stand discreetly by the door. ''My coat. My hat.''

''A compromise, a compromise,'' Clemenceau suggested, holding a prohibitory hand up to Avril. He turned to Madame LeBlanc. ''Monsieur Adams could prepare a message for Louise. Perhaps this would satisfy him. If she wants to meet him, or to divulge her whereabouts to him, she can say so in a reply.''

''I just want to help her,'' Adams explained, thinking Clemenceau's suggestion needed support.

''You'd do that best by leaving her alone,'' Delahaye said sharply. ''If you find her, how do you know you won't lead someone right to her, someone who intends her harm?'' He seemed, at that moment, to look pointedly at Clemenceau.

Adams saw that this concern had merit. He took a deep breath and considered. Yes. His attention might bring her harm. Did Clemenceau want that list badly enough to hurt Louise in order to get it? Did Delahaye? Did Loubet? Nothing he could see in any of their faces told him anything one way or the other. No. He shouldn't go to her, shouldn't meet her. Not yet. But—''There would be no harm in a message.''

''I agree,'' Delahaye said. ''A message from Monsieur Adams would be appropriate.''

''As long as there is no following of the messenger,'' Clemenceau said, eyeing Delahaye.

"Agreed," Delahaye said slowly.

"Loubet?" Clemenceau asked.

"Well then," Loubet said. He looked at Delahaye, Clemenceau, Madame LeBlanc, then stared at Adams. Working his jaw, he kneaded the inside of his lower lip against his upper teeth twice, then turned away. "If you wish it. Agreed."

"It's settled, then," Clemenceau announced.

"I'll do what I can," Madame LeBlanc said. "It's not completely in my hands."

Adams looked from face to face, from Clemenceau's mottled complexion to Loubet's long-chinned profile to Delahaye with his oiled hair and aura of waxy predation. Madame LeBlanc alone met his gaze. Lips pursed, eyebrows arched, she seemed amused and expectant. She waited for him to speak.

9:04 P.M.

HE CLEARED HIS throat. "Writing materials?" he asked. "And how do I know she'll get it?"

Madame LeBlanc was not amused. "Monsieur Adams, if you are suggesting that I would take a message from you and fail to deliver it, and then invent an answer, I am insulted!"

Of course, there would be an answer. That's how he would know. He wasn't thinking clearly.

"You could ask her to tell you something that only she would know," Clemenceau said, casting a glance at Madame LeBlanc. "Then you will be assured that her reply is genuine."

Adams thought it a good idea. "And when do I get my reply?"

"Tomorrow. Tomorrow afternoon, here," Madame LeBlanc said. "Two o'clock. That should be plenty of time."

"A sealed letter," Adams said.

There was a seal with the writing things that Madame LeBlanc showed him, in the desk she had stood behind when Adams had first spoken to her. He sat and took out paper, pen, and an ink pot from the drawer. When she hovered too closely he stared at her, forcing her retreat. *Dear Louise,* he wrote in his square, regular hand. *I am writing to you to . . .* To what? To say I finally learned your name? To tell you I miss you? To tell you how well I know that too much blue makes for a life as flat as too little?

He was unused to having an audience for his composition. He tried to block them out. Not wanting anyone to know he was beginning over, he didn't crumple the page but slid it quietly underneath a fresh page. He began again. *Madame LeBlanc tells me that this note will be delivered to you. If you receive it, please reply, and begin your reply with a description of the painting you were working on when I first met you. That way I'll know that the communication is genuine.* He paused to think. *I have been looking for you, and have grown concerned about your safety. Is there anything I can do to help?* He wanted to make the note personal; he wanted to communicate some part of the urgency he felt, some sense of his perseverance through the week. Come out of hiding, he wanted to say. Reveal yourself to me!

He couldn't say that either. *My offer of help is sincere. I remain, Your most obedient servant,* and he signed it simply "Henry." Then, thinking that after all he had met her two months ago, and it had been nearly six weeks since he'd seen her, he added "Adams." The full name seemed too formal, too distant. But there was no middle ground, and no undoing it without copying the letter over; he decided to let it go. He blew on the paper to dry the ink, then folded the note and tucked it into its envelope. In the drawer he found a bit of wax and a seal. In a moment he was done. Pocketing his false start, he rose and handed the note to Madame LeBlanc.

"Tomorrow afternoon. Two o'clock."

Adams nodded.

The stairs to DuForché's apartment were steep and dark. His feet felt cold, wet, and formless inside the tightness of his shoes. The exertion of climbing made his bruised face throb, and when he breathed too deeply, he felt that fist in his stomach again, a round hard knot below his diaphragm.

"Oh God!" DuForché said when he let Adams in. "What happened to you?" His curly hair was sleep-flattened on one side.

"A hard day." He glanced up to see if DuForché appreciated irony, but couldn't tell. He let the young man take his coat off. "I need to rest. I can't sleep at my place. May I stay with you?"

"Of course, of course." DuForché steered him to a chair, where Adams immediately untied his shoes, anticipating the relief to be had by releasing his feet.

In a few minutes DuForché had a cool damp cloth on his face, his coat and jacket hung up to dry, and a cup of hot tea at his elbow. When Adams complained about his feet, the young man soon produced a basin of warm Epsom salts. "This is the best thing," he said, rolling Adams's socks off. Adams protested—no one should have to remove someone else's socks, he thought—but the boy moved quickly, too quickly, and besides, it felt good to be taken care of. DuForché was pattering away soothingly. "I do this after I've been on my feet too much. The policeman's friend. I think that the police are responsible for half the sales of Epsom salts in this city. Here now, just so. How's that?"

Adams had to admit it felt good. DuForché had even brought a pair of thick books to place under the basin, lifting it, so that his feet were fully immersed.

"Thank you, thank you."

"It's not too hot, is it?"

"No. Perfect." His tongue still felt thick in his mouth and he didn't want to talk.

"Tell me what happened."

Adams moaned a little. But how could he deny him? He took a sip from his tea, cradling the cup with both hands, and began. "I went to the swimming concession. The concessionaire saw Miriam Talbott's murder. Oh, Miriam Talbott was murdered. It says so in the coroner's report—the one that her murderer killed the coroner in order to switch. I saw it at my friend John Hay's, because the coroner mailed a copy to the Embassy. It must have been in his mail basket when he died." The tea was sweeter than he usually took it, and its warmth felt uneven in his mouth. He tested his tongue and found it getting numb on one side. "I guess somebody followed me there. To the concession. When I chased him, he hit me. In the stomach. I hit my face when I fell." He reached a hand up, but the swelling of flesh there dissuaded him from any firm contact, and he didn't press it enough to hurt. "I think I broke my nose." Where was he? "So I followed him—the man that hit me. Very interesting."

"Why? What? What happened?"

Adams recounted the meeting he had interrupted and his arrangement to receive Louise's answer the next day.

"Well, there you have it. Murder, suicide, blackmail, extortion, corruption," DuForché said. He had brought a chair from his kitchen table into the living room and straddled it, leaning his chin on the back as Adams spoke. "It lacks nothing. Disgusting! They sell their votes for money, then kill to keep the sale secret." He shook his head. "And there's your motive. Reinach kills himself, but you could say Herz drove him to it. And Miriam Talbott has been trying to blackmail these deputies, so one of them kills her. Or maybe several of them do. Like a joint-stock venture," he added, sardonically. "Loubet, Clemenceau, and Delahaye, Incorporated."

"No. I don't think so."

"Right, yes: Delahaye and Clemenceau stand to benefit if the list of *chéquards* comes out. She wasn't blackmailing them, of course. What am I thinking. Of course not. Unless she tried and they laughed at her, told her, 'Don't be stupid!' " He thought a moment. "Your friend, this Louise woman, she gets this list of *chéquards* from Miriam Talbott. They're roommates. Miss Talbott had gotten it from Reinach; he had this list, maybe even tried to use it against Herz, said to him, 'I'll go to the papers with this list, bring the whole government crashing down, get you indicted for bribery if you don't kick back some of this money.' It's a good threat, and Herz makes the payments, but maybe Reinach gets too greedy and ultimately Herz sees a way out: he just kills him. But Miss Talbott—she gets the list, she's a different story. Scrappier. She sees how it happens with Reinach, and she goes into hiding, they can't find her when they kill Reinach or they'd have killed her right there, too. And she wants revenge, retribution, against these evil men who killed her lover. She's going to punish them. But she makes a mistake, and they find her, and they kill her, too."

Adams shook his head. "Is this all a fantasy, or have you got something?"

"Have I got something?" The youth smiled. "I have something all right."

Adams waited. "Michel, please. I'm tired."

"It's obvious, isn't it? Lesseps said that Reinach sucked the company dry. This is the story that makes sense. Herz bribed all those deputies, and he had secret money to do it, and Reinach saw how he could get some of it. A kickback from Herz."

"What if it went the other way?" DuForché didn't understand. "What if Herz was blackmailing Reinach? And Reinach covered the payments out of the 'publicity and lobbyist' accounts that funded Herz? You're right—the money was secret, so he could have dipped into it as much as he needed to." Adams didn't think this likely, but wanted to show DuForché that the facts were ambiguous.

"I like that. I like that better. And that explains something."

"What?"

DuForché smiled and held up a finger. "See, I have learned a few things. Such as: the visit she made just before she died, the visit she and Clemenceau made to Cornelius Herz right before Reinach died. That was her mistake. She came out of hiding long enough to meet with Herz. She must have threatened to expose Herz and the *chéquards* if Herz didn't stop. But of course it's a threat without any punch: Herz is German; he doesn't care if the government falls, if France goes to hell."

Clemenceau! Did he know more than he allowed? Or was DuForché giving his imagination too much rein? Adams's mind was beginning to feel the way his feet felt, mushy, formless, incapable of going on. He started to yawn, but caught himself before it could hurt, swallowing it with jaw down but lips resolutely closed. Maybe he should go to Loubet and find out what he thought Clemenceau's interest in this was. Or to Delahaye first, to ask him about Loubet, so that he wouldn't walk in cold, and could correct for any bias Loubet might have. Or to Clemenceau himself, to ask about Delahaye . . .

"But do you know what this means? This means that Reinach didn't kill himself. No—"

Adams held up a hand. "I'm sorry, Michel," he said softly. "I'm falling asleep. I have to go to bed. Let's talk about it tomorrow."

Friday, NOVEMBER 25, 1892

6:15 A.M.

ADAMS AWOKE IN DuForché's sitting room to the ominous sound of a murmuring voice. At his own insistence Adams had slept on the couch; DuForché would have given him the bed. He opened his eyes and lay still, trying to tell where the voice was coming from, though he couldn't see anyone. The murmuring was low and monotonous, indistinct except for the hiss of the sibilants, which cut through the air with an off-cadence rhythm. There was no way of telling how long it had been going on. He sat up warily, an effort that made his stomach hurt, and peered over the back of the couch. DuForché was kneeling in the corner of the room, facing the wall.

Adams lay back down. Once he knew its source, the muted speech was soothing. With a slight turn of his head on the pillow he could see out the window where, on the dull copper of a neighboring roof, the shadow of a chimney had shielded the night's frost from the morning sun, leaving a fat band of white. Above the roofline the sky was a clear light blue. His body ached and he felt tired, but also simply, childishly excited: he was going to hear from Louise. He wanted to be outside, in that crisp morning.

When DuForché went into his kitchen Adams got up. He slipped into his clothes and folded his blankets quietly. There was nothing he could do about the blood on his shirtfront. As he fastened his cuffs, regretting their limp, soiled condition, he wandered over to the corner where DuForché had knelt. There, on the wall, facing each other in the corner, were two old music-hall posters. Their colors clashed: one had black letters on a yellowish-orange background; the other, with an illustration of a woman singing while suspended from a trapeze, was mostly pink. They both advertised the same singer. On a table below them was a single candle and a silver-framed picture of a young woman holding an infant. He bent to examine it. A professional-quality portrait, done in a studio, and the woman was clearly beautiful. She stood in a formal gown against a perfectly white, featureless background, her face preternaturally serene, assured, kind. The infant was slightly blurred: it had moved during the exposure. Clover had always been able to communicate some quality of her own concentration to her subjects, capturing them informally but in perfect stillness; but then, she had never done children. Children would be hard.

"My mother," DuForché said behind him. "She was a singer."

Adams straightened. "Oh." It seemed more was required. "She's very pretty."

"Was pretty. She died when I was a boy." There was no complaint in his voice; he was just stating a fact.

"Is that you?" Adams nodded at the photo.

"Yes."

Adams's cuff was done, but he continued to fiddle with it, wanting the distraction. There was no man in the picture; he wondered if DuForché had been orphaned or if he had been raised by his father. "It must have been hard on you." He glanced back.

DuForché tilted his head to one side and stared at him wide-eyed. Had his comment been offensive? Too personal? DuForché looked as though he was trying to find in Adams's face some clue to his audacity. His stare was making Adams uncomfortable.

"Your eyes, right there around the nose?" DuForché asked. "An amazing shade of purple." He shook his head in wonder. "You should see it."

He looked in the bathroom mirror and saw that it was true. The bruise was a mask, spreading out from the bridge of his nose, darkening the flesh above and below each eye. It made him look tired, and dangerous.

"Come to breakfast," DuForché called out. "I have something to show you." Breakfast was strong bitter coffee, cheese, and chunks of stale bread broken from a long loaf. Adams sat down. "Look." DuForché indicated a newspaper clipping near Adams's plate. "You were too tired last night, but I thought you would want to see this."

Adams read the clipping. It was an old story on the Panama affair; he wondered what paper it had come from, for its interpretation exculpated Cornelius Herz. He was being charged with one count of bribery—the one the prosecutor thought he could prove, Adams remembered, against a syndicalist deputy—but at the exact moment he was supposed to have been in the Restaurant de la Cascade passing a demand note across the table he was in fact miles away, at a canal company luncheon, and could prove it. "So?" he asked DuForché, handing the clipping over.

"See? The motive for burning your photograph."

Adams didn't see.

"What's the date on your photograph?"

"I don't recall."

"I do. It's the twenty-fifth of January 1883. What's the date of Herz's meeting in the Bois de Boulogne?" He handed the clipping back.

"January 25, 1883?" He hadn't paid any attention to the date.

"Exactly."

"So the photograph proves what?"

"That Herz wasn't at the luncheon, the send-off for this man Dingler. If he had been there, he'd have been in the picture."

"He doesn't need to destroy the picture. He could concoct some story, some explanation as to why he was there but not in the picture."

"Yes, yes, but why take chances? He's counting on people's memories being faulty, and if there is hard evidence one way or the other, it will tend to pin things down."

"But he couldn't have burned the photograph. He has fled."

''Either he hasn't or he's got a pony. Slang,'' DuForché explained when he saw Adams's puzzlement. ''How would you say it? Agent, perhaps. Minion. Loyal helper. Someone who executes your will at a distance. That the coroner was killed by someone trying to prevent the identification of the dead woman is reason to think that his murderer is such a pony.''

Adams took the long loaf of bread and broke a piece off, thinking about this as he chewed. Why did Herz want Miriam Talbott killed? Who was Herz's pony?

''So they are negotiating with this woman, this Not-Miriam, for the list of *chéquards*?'' DuForché asked between mouthfuls.

''Her name's Louise. Louise Martin.'' Adams didn't want her identity to be lost in the confusion. He felt a kind of loyalty to her, even if she had lied to him. ''Yes. Apparently.''

''Louise Martin.'' DuForché said the name before taking another large bite of dry bread, and when he opened his mouth to put it in, Adams glimpsed half-chewed cheese. He looked away, down at his own plate. ''You know,'' DuForché said, ''that meeting''—he swallowed—''is extremely annoying. It's a very bad thing. A bad sign.'' The young man reached for his coffee.

''What do you mean?''

''Back rooms, secret decisions, little cabals and conspiracies. We fought a revolution to do away with that kind of business.''

Adams had no stomach for a political discussion this morning. ''Yes. Look, I think we should get over to talk to your uncle as soon as we can. About the burned photograph, Miss Martin, Herz, this meeting, all of it.''

DuForché agreed.

Outdoors, the morning was crisp and clear. On the pavement the frost lay not in a solid sheet but only in some few lines and bands that angled here and there across the street. In some places it was only inches wide and in others fully a yard across. What weird condition had caused this effect? Adams wondered. It was too geometric, too precise to be accidental. Why would dew falling just here turn to frost, while inches away it didn't?

"You know what did this? The sewers and drains," DuForché said when Adams expressed his wonder. "The cold air got into them overnight. So the pavement above them is colder than the rest of the street."

It took Adams a moment to understand. Given the right conditions, the entire subterranean network of pipes and tunnels could be limned in ice, painted on the surface for all to see. And then, as the day warmed, the revelation would melt away. He bent and touched the whiteness and saw it begin to disappear; around each fingertip grew a bloom of moisture on the cobble.

He sent DuForché along because he wanted to think. He was remembering a scene that had flashed by his train window in Panama, thinking, To see only surface, but to understand that he saw no deeper, might be the best that could be achieved. How had DuForché seen right away the cause of the frost lines and he not? And ponies—the idea seemed so typically French. Like a stalking horse, only not; the complement, the negation of a stalking horse. Someone unseen who acts for you, rather than someone who, being seen, serves your interest. What he remembered was how, on a siding outside Colón, at some distance from his train, he had seen a half dozen abandoned steam engines, their every edge traced in a slow, vegetable fancywork of vines. As sometimes happens with the products of a foreign industrial culture, they had the disconcerting aspect of being both familiar and unfamiliar at once. They were recognizable, obvious as to function, but alien in some important way. This mild dissonance he had found intriguing: he had turned his head to keep the engines in view as long as he could.

Given: the problems of steam engine design are of course the same everywhere. Given: there was something idiosyncratically French about the solution he saw abandoned in the jungle. Speculation: could all the differences between two peoples be condensed into the three-dimensional language of form? The French machines were made of rectangular boxes of sheet iron, one for the boiler and another for the engineer's cabin, and above the running gear and trucks there had been no extraneous details—no pressure lines or pipes, not even a handrail along the firebox, nothing to mar the broad expanse of flat metal that the machines presented in profile. Obviously, the French value form that denies its function. Americans want honesty from their machines, want to see the gears and wheels and levers exposed for all to see; the machines hide nothing, even exhibit a kind of beauty in their disclosure. Was it too much to see in the French machinery both a taste for elegance and a willingness to cede knowledge to experts? Because there was something democratic about exposing inner workings for all to see. What mistaken romance led the French to deny the truth of power, the truths of steam coursing through pipes and gauges and valves? Perhaps the same urge that led them to disguise its sources had kept them from discerning its limits clearly. Understand the machines, not just their limits but their design, their beauty, and you would understand the reasons for the French failure in Panama. To the French, form—surface—was all; and a man was better off to put his finger on a map in a show of bravado, as *Le Grand Français* had done, than to mount an expedition to survey the most economical, feasible route.

The corresponding danger to the American taste would be to mistake the extraneous shapes of a complex form for that form's content, to see pipes and gauges and levers and believe that one had spied the motive power of fire itself, which must always remain a mystery. Or, more simply, to see frost lines on a city street and to think that their explanation lay above, in the open, out in the air. Or even more simply: to think that each acts for himself, none for another. Every man a milepost, or part of a cabal—which was it?

Each could be an error, and on the whole he wasn't sure which was the greater. France's infatuation with surface had led to defeat in Panama, with results that rippled about him now. America was a younger nation; perhaps the direst consequences of her habitual cast of mind lay in the future. What idiosyncratic sort of defeat would befall those who, distracted by gears and levers and wheels, thought themselves immune to the romance, the camouflage, of form?

On the Ile de la Cité he passed alongside Notre Dame, walking in the long shadow it cast in the morning light.

Above the leafless trees he saw wisps of steam rising toward
the heavens, thin ribbons of evaporating frost lit from behind
by the sun, like lines of radiance. Inside, the great rose window on the eastern wall would be coming to life. Yes, it
would be good to hear from Louise again.

He dredged four bronze sous out of his pocket for the boy
selling *Le Journal des Débats* and scanned the front page as
he walked toward the Prefecture. The Panama committee had
finally been convened for its first meeting the day before;
the rightist members—with the exception of Monsieur Dér-
oulède, who was going to be replaced—had consented to
participate. Brisson, a former premier and a centrist, but a
man with no apparent partisan interest, was elected chair.
Today, Friday, they were scheduled to confer with President
Loubet on the extent of their powers, and on Monday they
were to begin sifting evidence collected and sealed before
the deadline this afternoon. There was, the paper reported,
still no firm information on who the *chéquards* were, or
whether an authoritative list of them would be produced. In
such circumstances speculation could not be held in check.
At least two separate shoving matches in the Chamber cloak-
room could be traced to mutual accusations between antagonistic deputies.

Adams folded the paper and tucked it away. What was
Louise waiting for? Would she hand the list of *chéquards* in
today and be done? Why hadn't she just given the list to
Delahaye or Clemenceau? Or even to some newspaper?

The officers stationed in the lobby of the Prefecture refused Adams admittance. His bruises; they didn't recognize
him, or he looked too unsavory. He sent word to DuForché
to come down and fetch him, then found a seat and glanced
through the paper. On page 7 he found an item headlined
DOUBLE SUICIDE NOW SEEN AS MURDER, POLICE SAY. The
story didn't add much: "Incontrovertible evidence delivered
to the police yesterday establishes the death of a young
woman, previously thought to be a suicide by drowning, as
a murder. Police pulled her body from the Seine Monday
morning. Sources close to the investigation say that a suspect
has been identified and an arrest is imminent. No other details were available, as police do not wish to prejudice their

chances for success.'' Adams smiled. It was gratifying to see
the work he had done mirrored back as part of the news. In
some small way, he thought, he had helped to set the world
on a truer course. He wondered if the police were actually
close to a suspect, or if that had been official optimism calculated to reduce anxiety.

What was taking DuForché so long?

The young man finally arrived and signed him in. ''My
uncle has some news for you,'' he confided when they were
on the stairs. He spoke in a low voice, after glancing around
to make sure that they were alone.

''What?''

DuForché put a finger to his lips and shook his head. ''Not
here. He'll tell you.''

''Did you tell him about Clemenceau, about that visit to
Herz? And the concessionaire? And my note to Miss Martin?''

''Yes, yes.''

''And?''

''And what? And nothing.'' DuForché shrugged, a definitive Gallic shrug. It must be taught to them as children. ''He
is of the opinion that none of this gets us anywhere. Herz is
gone, left for England the day the subpoenas were issued.
We have no idea who the other man was. Herz couldn't have
killed the coroner, so—'' DuForché looked at him with a
sidelong glance. ''There is still a murderer out there.''

''What about this Clemenceau connection?''

''Not his department.''

They trod the stairs in silence for a moment. ''The paper
says the police have a suspect in the Talbott murder.'' Adams
held up the folded newspaper. ''I suppose that means Herz.''

DuForché looked surprised. ''Must be Pettibois,'' he said
after he had read it. He folded the paper and handed it back
to Adams, who silently noted the sloppy edges. ''My uncle
hasn't done any work on this. He would have told me.''

When they got to the office DuForché opened the inner
door and ushered him in to where Bertillon sat at his desk,
writing.

''One moment,'' Bertillon said, rising. He walked to the
door to the outer office. ''I am in conference,'' he said to

DuForché. "No interruptions." He came back to his desk and motioned Adams to sit. "My receptionist may be out for two weeks," he commented, sitting and pulling his chair up to his desk. He looked at the closed door and sighed before bending over his writing.

Adams wondered if he should leave. But no; if Bertillon wanted him to go, he would say so. He sat quietly, waiting.

8:03 A.M.

FINALLY BERTILLON FOLDED the paper he was writing on, inserted it in an envelope, and faced Adams. "So. Do you have anything to tell me?"

"I understand that your nephew has already told you my news. About Louise Martin, about Herz, Clemenceau, the concessionaire. The meeting at Madame LeBlanc's."

"Yes. Good work. Thank you."

"And I believe he told you that I'm to receive a communication from Louise Martin this afternoon. We have good reason to believe she has a list of *chéquards*."

"Yes."

"I would think she'd turn it in to the Chamber today, to have it entered as evidence. I can't think why she hasn't done so."

Bertillon raised an eyebrow slightly. "Perhaps Miss Talbott's extortion was successful? And your friend feels bound to honor its terms?"

Adams didn't think so. Reinach was dead. "Michel says you have something to tell me?"

"Yes. Not tell. Something to show you. Have you ever seen this before?" He opened a drawer and handed a small round tin from it across his desk to Adams. Bettlemen and Sons, purveyors of fine pigments: orpiment.

"Yes, I believe I have. At Miriam Talbott's apartment.

Hidden in a drawer." He slid it back across the desk. "If it's the same one."

"It's the same one, all right." Bertillon picked it up and rubbed it thoughtfully with a thumb. "It had your finger-prints all over it."

Adams wasn't sure why, but this circumstance seemed to require explanation. "Well, as I said, I saw it before. At Miriam Talbott's. I tried to handle it carefully, through a handkerchief, but apparently I wasn't careful enough." And then, because this didn't seem sufficient, he added, "Sorry."

"Sorry," Bertillon repeated. In his hand he worked the tin with his thumb and fingers, turning it top over bottom over top over bottom, over and over, like a large fat coin. "I guess you're sorry. You really shouldn't have been al-lowed anywhere near a crime scene. Not your fault, I sup-pose. But: you are a foreigner, you have no business meddling about in our affairs. This isn't just playacting we do here, playacting at being detective. This is very real, *Mis-ter* Adams"—he emphasized the English honorific—"and having someone come in and falsify the evidence does not make my job any easier."

"Michel . . ." Adams began, thinking to excuse himself by appealing to the boy's complicity, but stopping himself when he realized how unseemly this was. No. He had gone of his own free will; he shouldn't blame the boy. But as he thought about it, he felt insulted: he had felt a kind of col-legiality with Bertillon, had felt his equal in some way. Ap-parently this was not so.

"I've had my talk with Michel. I wanted you to know what difficulty these prints of yours caused me."

"I appreciate that. I am sorry," he said curtly.

"You may go. Please. I do hope you are reunited with your friend soon."

"Thank you." He bowed slightly and turned to go, but remembered: "You have something I brought here that ought to be returned. The coroner's report."

Bertillon didn't look up from the letter he was writing, and for a moment the sound of his nib on paper was the only sound in the room. "The coroner's report is evidence. It is the property of the citizens of France."

"I thought you could photograph it . . ."

"No. I must have the original."

"But it belongs to Hay. He needs to send it to the woman's family."

"I'm sorry. The answer is no."

Adams saw that it was no use to argue. He sighed as he walked to the door. Bertillon looked up when he reached the door. "Sorry about what happened to your face. Do be careful."

"My uncle is in a bad mood," DuForché explained when Adams had shut the door. "I hope you don't hold it against him. He had a meeting with the prefect this morning. I don't know what happened, but the prefect is a spineless noodle of a man and talking to him always leaves Uncle in a very bad mood. And anyway," he said, leaning close, "*I* think you did right, bringing that coroner's report to him. I would have done the same."

"Thank you." He made for the door. "Good luck," he added as a parting thought.

" 'Good luck'? Why? Where are you going?"

"I want to be done with this. Your uncle is right. It's really none of my business. I'm going to get an answer from Miss Martin today. I've found her. That's all I wanted . . ." He let his voice trail off.

"So you're quitting?" DuForché looked angry.

"Well, maybe not quitting exactly." Adams didn't want to disappoint the young man. "Maybe tapering off." He could see this wasn't working. "I want to be less involved. It really doesn't concern me, you know. It's interesting, but . . . but I have other things to do."

"Of course." DuForché was sullen. "What if Miss Martin needs your help? What if she can't get the list of *chéquards* to the Chamber today? Did you think of that?"

"If she needs my help, she'll ask. I get her reply at two."

DuForché snorted. "That could be too late. Who picked the time? You? No. *They* did." DuForché shook his head. "I don't like the smell of it."

Adams leaned across the desk to touch the young man's arm and spoke gently: "What happens to that list isn't really my concern. Miss Martin is. And even that—" He straightened and smiled a thin smile. "I met her a few months ago," Adams explained. "She's just an acquaintance. Everything else . . . everything else is imagination, surmise, pretense. Understand?"

"So you wouldn't help her?" DuForché asked.

"Michel, Michel," Adams sighed. "It's just not like that."

8:54 A.M.

IN FRONT OF Madame Dingler's door stood her Siamese cat, alone, tail up, watching him with an all-consuming suspicion.

That's strange, Adams thought; what is the cat doing out? The sight of it gave him an uneasy feeling, and he began to think that perhaps DuForché had been right. The young man had prevailed on him to make this journey—a fool's errand, he thought, but it was important to the boy. What if, he had said, the reason Louise didn't turn in the list of *chéquards* was that she didn't have it? Assume that her rooms have been thoroughly searched. Then where could it be? We have the fact of Miriam's correspondence with Madame Dingler, and Madame Dingler's known archival predilections. Two and two: let us go see Madame Dingler.

Only, DuForché was tied to his desk. Well, the day threatened to drag itself interminably toward two o'clock anyway. An errand would speed the time.

When he knocked on the door, the cat bumped its head against his calf, then rubbed the length of its body along his leg. Not good. He waited, then knocked again. He tried the door, prepared to break it down if he had to. He didn't; it was open.

The cat darted in as soon as the door was open a crack. When the door opened wider, Adams had more reason to feel disturbed: the apartment was empty except for a few pieces of furniture—a pair of ladder-back chairs, the mahogany dining table. He could see bare whitewashed walls everywhere he looked. No crates, no boxes, no stacks of papers, not a single scrap. Slowly he stepped into the apartment. There must be some mistake. He glanced out the door, to the passageway. There was no mistake. That was the hall that had been there yesterday. And there by the window was her afghan-covered chair.

And her cat, which scratched at the glass-paned doors to the kitchen. Adams opened them. The clutter and mess there had disappeared as well. The cat went to the door of a cabinet below the sink and waited. Adams opened the cabinet, thinking to feed it, but found nothing. The cat walked into the cabinet and meowed once, loudly, and turned to look at him. "I know, I know," he said, trying to reassure it, then felt foolish.

He walked back into the living room. He could no longer see any of the cataloguing notations that Madame Dingler had written on the walls; with a finger he tested the whitewash. Fresh. Even the floor had been scrubbed. The only sign that anyone had ever lived here was the furniture.

He had to know what happened to her.

The first neighbor he talked to, a sullen young woman with a chubby-faced baby on her hip, took one look at his bruised face and shut the door hard. After that, he tried to keep his face turned aside, or humbly down, when he spoke. The second neighbor opened the door a crack and refused to speak, reading a slice of him up and down with an eye. A man in dark mud-crusted work clothes, whom Adams accosted as he crossed the courtyard, didn't live there and knew nothing. Methodically, Adams went door-to-door around the courtyard. At most of the doors no one was home; and when someone was, either they didn't admit knowing her or said they had seen nothing.

Finally, upstairs on the second floor, in a room that overlooked the street, he found someone who knew something. "Oh, the wagons," the old woman said, opening the door about a hand's width to his question. You could measure hospitality by these inches, he thought. "Seven of them. Seven! Incredible. Just incredible. Dozens of men. None too

soon, if you ask me. She was batty.'' The woman moved a
foot into the doorway and Adams saw that she was blocking
her own calico's exit. "She was always on about that cat of
hers. Wasn't she, Etienne? Thought she was the only body
in the world that had a cat, to hear her tell it. This is my
Etienne,'' she added, looking down. "I named him after my
husband's brother, because of the resemblance.'' The cat
turned its head sideways and smelled the edge of the door;
unimpressed, it turned and disappeared into the apartment.
"God rest his soul.''

"Do you know where they took her, Madame . . . ?''

"Cherdlieu. Same as the cat. No. No idea who, no idea
where.'' She sighed, to emphasize the moral.

"When? When did this happen?''

"Last night, about ten. Racket? I guess!'' A racket no one
else admits hearing, Adams thought. They're frightened.
"That's no way to live, mind you,'' Madame Cherdlieu was
saying. "All that mess and clutter. Fire hazard, if you ask
me.''

On the way back to the Prefecture he felt an anxiety he
could scarcely identify. Who or what was shaping this
world? What force was behind it? The degree of organization
needed to accomplish what had been done at Madame Dingler's was beyond the reach of an individual. He could think
of only one entity that had that sort of energy. "The empire
of force,'' Pascal had called it: "The empire of imagination
reigns for a while and is sweet and unconstrained, but the
empire of force reigns forever.'' Thus Pascal, explaining un-
knowingly why the Church Forgiving had been supplanted
by the State Militant. Was DuForché right—had the list of
chéquards been somewhere in that apartment? As he rode
by them, he did not find the monuments and houses and
pedestrians and traffic of Paris, the visual furnishings of ordinary city life, reassuring in the least. They seemed mere
façade, a regularity that masked malignancy; like an unwit-
tingly malarial host, they were being consumed from within
by a parasite whose purposes would not spare them.

At the Prefecture DuForché had to come down and sign
him in again. One of the guards eyed Adams's face, and
Adams stared back at him, a stare meant to discourage at-

tention. "What brings you back?" DuForché asked as he bent over the register. "I thought you were done with this."

Adams kept his eyes on the guard and shook his head. "I have something to tell you. Upstairs."

He waited until they were in the anteroom outside Bertillon's office. DuForché took his place behind the desk and Adams sat in the visitor's chair. "I thought you'd want to know," he said quietly. "Madame Dingler has disappeared. Cleaned out."

"Cleaned out? By whom?"

"I don't know. I thought you and your uncle might investigate."

"The Service of Judicial Identity? Investigate a disappearance?"

And why not? Before Adams could argue the point the door to Bertillon's office opened and Pettibois came out. "Monsieur Adams. So good to see you." He nodded and smiled, his pink cheeks riding up to narrow his eyes. "I understand from Alphonse that we have some very interesting developments, no? Identities fixed, finally, at any rate." He shook his head. "This must be a relief. For all involved. I, for one, am sorry that it took so long to establish the truth of what you so clearly testified to from the outset."

"I—yes. I'm glad the matter is resolved."

"Adams? Monsieur Adams?" Bertillon called from his office. "Please step in here for a moment."

Adams excused himself from Pettibois and rose, looking at DuForché, who shot his eyebrows up: he knew nothing.

"Monsieur Adams," Bertillon said when they were seated. "My apologies for the way I spoke to you earlier. I was boorish, which is, in my pantheon of sins, the least excusable. But I ask you to excuse me."

"I do."

"Thank you. This is what I wanted to see you about, this apology. But I have another thing as well, an offer. This woman, this Louise Martin. You are expecting word from her soon?"

"At two o'clock. I'm to pick up a message from her at Madame LeBlanc's."

"Do you want some help? An escort? Let me explain,"

Bertillon said, holding up a hand. "If you are correct and this woman has a list of *chéquards*, it is possible that malefactors will do what they can to prevent her from releasing it today. They may do this even if she doesn't have the list; it is only necessary that they think she has it, or that there's a reasonable possibility she has it. Maybe they know of your correspondence with this woman. Maybe they know of it but have mistaken it for something it isn't. Documents passing between people, one of them known to have sensitive information—it wouldn't hurt to have company." Adams's skepticism must have shown, for Bertillon said, "At least let me send Michel with you."

Adams wasn't sure if the dig at his nephew had been intended. "No, I don't think any help will be necessary." Bringing any sort of escort seemed a violation of the rules.

"Monsieur Adams, I think I should caution you—"

He stopped, because DuForché had opened the door. "Do you want me, Uncle?"

Bertillon stared at the young man for a moment.

"I thought I heard my name. I thought maybe you wanted me."

Bertillon's face was blank. "No," he said flatly. "Leave us."

"Ah, Uncle?" DuForché said quietly. "As long as I've already interrupted you, I might as well give you this." He smiled apologetically at Adams as he reached behind the door and produced an envelope. "It just came for you."

Bertillon waited until DuForché had shut the door before touching the envelope. Adams saw that it was sealed and marked both *urgent* and *personal*. Bertillon swivelled his chair to face the window, for privacy. When he had read what was inside, he turned back, dropped the letter in front of Adams, and swivelled once again to face the window.

Adams presumed he was meant to read the letter. "To all departments," it read. "From: The Office of the Prefect. A warrant has been issued for the arrest of Henry Adams, citizen of the United States of America, who is wanted in connection with the murders of Miriam Talbott, American citizen, and François Giradoux, lately coroner of the city of Paris. Any personnel who see this man are required to apprehend him and to notify this office at once."

10:17 A.M.

"HE COULD HIDE in my apartment," DuForché volunteered.

"This warrant appears frivolous," Bertillon said, gazing out his window, shaking his head slowly. "Unless there was some misunderstanding about the orpiment prints this morning . . . I believe I cleared you of that."

"I need to talk to Hay," Adams said.

Bertillon swivelled his chair away from the window. "Interesting possibility. The Embassy has extraterritoriality."

That had not been what Adams was thinking, but he saw that it was true: he couldn't be arrested there.

"It's absurd," DuForché exclaimed. "It's a mistake. Someone has made a mistake. Maybe he should turn himself in, be arraigned, get this all cleared up." He turned from his uncle to Adams. "They can't have any evidence that would let them hold you. Turn yourself in, get it straightened out. Then you won't have this hanging over your head."

"How long would that take?" Adams asked.

"The afternoon, at most. I don't think they'd keep you for the night," Bertillon said. "If there is indeed no evidence."

Adams shook his head. "No."

"What evidence could there be?" DuForché asked. "Unless the prefect signed a warrant without any. Would he do that?" Adams looked to Bertillon for an answer, but he had turned his chair again to look out the window.

"Michel," Bertillon said finally, without turning around. "I want you to do something. Go up to the prefect's office and find out what is behind this. Be discreet. Monsieur Adams, you wait here."

After DuForché left, Bertillon watched Adams with a steady gaze that made him uncomfortable. Couldn't Bertillon see what was happening? The warrant meant that Adams had gotten too close to something. The pattern was too clear to deny: he went to look up information on Dingler and it all had disappeared. He went to see the man's mother and *she* disappeared. Dingler's photograph had been burned in his room, someone sent him those fingertips in the pneumatic tube, he had been followed and punched in the stomach and left for dead. Now that he was about to make contact with Louise, someone wanted him arrested and kept away. Obviously someone was worried about what he'd find out from her, what he'd get. The list of *chéquards*. Some deputy, or this man Herz. Or maybe Delahaye—maybe he had heard that if Adams got the list he'd hand it over to Clemenceau. A dog in a manger—maybe Delahaye was working to make sure that if he didn't get the list, no one would get it.

Adams drew a breath in through his mouth, preparatory to speaking, but checked himself. If the prefect had issued a warrant for his arrest, did that mean the prefect was behind the burned photographer's studio? And the fingertips in the pneumatic tube? And the coroner's death, and Madame Dingler's housecleaning? Could Delahaye be behind all those things? This required careful thinking. And what, in fact, had he gotten close to? Maybe the warrant was legitimate. Not that he was guilty, but maybe the warrant was issued because he looked guilty: he was the one who had found the coroner dead, and then those fingertips had been sent to him. His prints were on that tin of orpiment, and Miriam Talbott had been poisoned. It was too confusing to sort through, and the case he had thought to make to Bertillon, the clear argument for Delahaye's guilt, began to dissipate.

"What?" asked Bertillon.

"Nothing. I didn't say anything."

"You were about to."

"No, no. Really."

"Monsieur Adams." Bertillon's tone was admonitory, but he did not look at Adams; his gaze was focussed on his desktop. He seemed detached, passing words idly while thinking of something else. "You were about to say something. You don't have to speak if you have changed your mind, but please. Don't deny it."

"Yes. I was about to speak."

This seemed to settle the matter.

After a moment Adams cleared his throat. "Thank you," he said.

"For what?"

"For not turning me over to the authorities."

"Monsieur Adams, I am one of the authorities." Bertillon looked up from his desktop. "I have you in my custody, don't I?"

"Yes, but—"

Bertillon held up a hand. "I know, I know. I am not inclined to take you downstairs for arraignment. And I have not notified the prefect. Let us just see what Michel turns up, shall we?"

They waited in an uneasy silence.

When DuForché returned, he made his brief report. "The prefect's secretary knows nothing."

"Did you think to ask who has been to see the prefect lately?" Bertillon scowled. "Did you?"

"No." DuForché smiled. "Better. I read his appointment book. It was open, right there on the desk."

"And?" The uncle was growing impatient.

"He had several visitors this morning. The mayor of the seventh arrondissement. Henri Cottu. A deputation from the Belgian trade mission, about that incident at the Embassy. Pettibois. Loubet."

"Cottu and Loubet," Bertillon repeated. Of course, Adams thought: Loubet has more to lose. Delahaye and the Boulangists have a chance to gain power in the next election, but Loubet and his coalition are going to lose no matter what. Loubet wants to control the damage; he's out to stifle that list.

He didn't share his thoughts.

Bertillon gazed at his desktop, which told him that the ink

pot ought to be moved a fraction of an inch to align it more perfectly with the edge of the blotter. He did this before he spoke. "Monsieur Adams, I am unsure why the prefect has issued a warrant for your arrest. I think perhaps the best course of action would be for me to detain you here until inquiries can clarify the matter."

"But, Uncle," DuForché protested, "you can't believe Monsieur Adams is responsible for those murders. The warrant is definitely politically motivated. It's a joke. You can't keep him."

"I would like to meet Madame LeBlanc this afternoon, to get my message from Miss Martin," Adams added. He realized he had no real bargaining position.

"Monsieur Adams," Bertillon began, leaning back in his chair, "can you imagine why this warrant has been laid against you? Assuming, that is, it is not to be taken seriously as a matter of criminal justice?"

"I—I presume it's because someone thinks I'm getting close to the list of *chéquards*. Loubet has been to see the prefect and convinced him of something, convinced him to arrest me, because Loubet doesn't want the list of *chéquards* to come out. If the list comes out, his coalition falls apart, and not only is he out of office but his party loses any role in forming the next government."

"Plausible, plausible," Bertillon agreed. "I tend to agree. Now, supposing that's true: can you see that this warrant is a tactical mistake on his part?"

"How so?"

"Wouldn't it make more sense to let you serve as, what do you say, a stalking horse? Is that the term? You are free to roam, they stalk you. You find the list, and they find you soon after and take it from you. Wouldn't that make sense? For this, you must not be under detention."

Adams thought. "But they can't be confident that the list won't come out anyway, without me. I'm in contact with Miss Martin, yes, but maybe she doesn't even have the list." Quickly he told Bertillon about Madame Dingler and her apartment. "The evidence that everyone's after could very well be with all of her papers, wherever *that* is." He took a perverse pride in being the bearer of this new complexity.

"Maybe they don't know that. But they do know that if they stop me from getting it, that doesn't mean that someone else won't get it, or someone else won't release it. So they have to act against me, while pursuing the list themselves." He suddenly realized something: "That's why they moved against Madame Dingler. Not because they *knew* she had it, but because there was a *chance* she had it."

Bertillon nodded. "This Miss Martin, who also might have the list—we can assume that Loubet, at least, does not know where she is. This is why he wants you arrested, to keep you from her. We can also assume that he seeks her."

"Yes."

Bertillon thought for a moment. "Monsieur Adams, because the warrant against you seems politically motivated, I am releasing you. But please—do not leave the city."

"Thank you."

Bertillon smiled. "You're welcome." He stood behind his desk. "The entire department knows you've been a frequent visitor here. I wish I could offer you the hospitality of my offices, but under the circumstances . . ."

"I understand." Adams rose to go. "Do you think I'll have any trouble at the door? Do you think they'll recognize me?"

Bertillon stared at Adams for a moment, in thought.

"Here," said DuForché. "I have just the thing." He left the office and came back with his briefcase. Opening it, he pulled out his laboratory coat. "Put this on. We can walk out together, and we'll look perfectly natural. A policeman and a doctor consulting." Adams rolled up the sleeves, squaring them neatly to look like cuffs. "You know," DuForché added, "maybe you should shave."

Adams frowned. "No." He had had a beard all his adult life. It was the way Clover had known him.

When they had crossed the plaza in front of the Prefecture, Adams took off the laboratory coat and handed it to DuForché. The young man tucked it into his briefcase. "I have some advice for you. You should let me pick up your letter from Miss Martin."

"Why?"

"Loubet knows you're scheduled to be there at two

o'clock. He was at that meeting, right? He heard the arrangement. It would be a simple matter to have you arrested then.''

Adams saw the reasonableness of this. ''But Madame LeBlanc won't give it to you. It's a message for me.''

''Give me a note with your signature.''

Adams scribbled Madame LeBlanc's address and a brief message on the back of a card and handed it to him. ''This should do it.''

He had taken his leave and gone a few steps before DuForché called after him. ''But where should we meet, after? Here?''

Adams looked up at the cathedral, at the great bell tower and the rose window below it. ''Yes. Yes, that would be good. But inside, in the nave.'' In the light.

11:15 A.M.

HAY WASN'T AT the Embassy, but was expected in an hour. "Do you think you could do me a small favor?" Adams asked the secretary outside his office. "An errand?" The man looked skeptical. "I need a few things at the pharmacist." He couldn't go back to his rooms, that was certain; the prefect no doubt had men there. The secretary agreed, and Adams gave him a ten-franc note and instructions to buy a razor—good and sharp, because he didn't have a strop—shaving soap, a brush, and a shaving pot.

When the man returned, Adams shut himself in the small washroom off Hay's office and began. It had been a long time; as he worked, he found himself curious about the result. The razor—bone-handled, he noticed; he wondered how much it had cost—was sharp, and once he had trimmed his beard back to stubble length, the work proceeded smoothly. When he was done, he cleaned out the sink, then stood high to see his face and neck in the small mirror. His nose and upper lip were still sore, so he had left a thick mustache, which drooped to either side, dividing his chin from the rest of his face. Without a beard his face looked unbalanced: his prominent forehead and weak chin made his head appear to grow in scale as it ascended. He didn't like it at all, but it suited his purpose. The bruises under his eyes really helped: he looked completely different. With a hat hiding his baldness he doubted if even Hay would recognize him.

As he folded the razor and tucked it inside his coat pocket, an idea occurred to him. Perhaps he could meet Madame LeBlanc himself at two o'clock. He placed the wet soap and brush in the pot and worked to fit it, right side up, into one of the large outer pockets of his overcoat. No sense leaving them behind. He wasn't about to buy new shaving materials every day. No, he shouldn't meet Madame LeBlanc, but he could be nearby, loitering a few houses away, when Du-Forché did. That would be safe enough, he calculated, and he'd get her reply all the sooner. The pot, in his pocket, was snug and bulky, but it fit.

He decided to wait for Hay outside. As quietly as he could, he slipped out of the office by the side door, without going past the secretary. No doubt the man would be confused when he didn't come out, but Adams didn't want anyone, even a secretary at the American Embassy, to be able to connect him with his new face.

For a time he worried that Hay was not coming, and then, just after one o'clock, a carriage pulled up, disgorging Hay and a man Adams couldn't see clearly, a short man in a dark coat. He waited for them to enter, waited another few minutes, and then crossed the street.

Adams was prepared to nod a greeting to the secretary, but the man seemed not to recognize him. "I'll announce you to Mr. Hay," he said.

"Very good."

"I don't believe I caught your name?"

The request caught Adams unprepared. "Mmm, caurrgh," he said, clearing his throat.

"Murtaugh?" the secretary repeated. "Are you an American citizen?" Adams nodded. "He's with someone just now, Mr. Murtaugh, but I believe he'll be free shortly. May I tell him what this is about?"

"A matter of law." He ought to say something that would get Hay curious, so he could get in more quickly. "The Panama affair."

"Are you in trouble with the authorities?"

"Well, actually, yes."

The secretary glanced sidelong at him, narrowing his eyes. I must look pretty disturbed, Adams thought. The secretary knocked on Hay's door, entered when bidden, and returned a moment later to his seat.

While he waited across from the secretary, Adams tried to bury his face behind the collar of his overcoat. Then, realizing that this hid the part of his face that was most unfamiliar, and revealed the part that still looked the same, he stretched his neck and jutted his chin out into the room. The secretary thought he was about to speak and looked up. Adams raised his eyebrows in return and tried to purse his lips in an unfamiliar way. He gave his head a shake to indicate he hadn't been about to say anything.

When the secretary returned to his paperwork, Adams looked around the room. He wished there was a newspaper he could unfold and hide behind.

After a few minutes Hay's door opened and the man from Hay's carriage walked out. He was no one Adams had ever seen before. Behind him was Hay, saying, "Don't worry, I'll attend to it as soon as possible." Adams realized he had the opportunity to test his disguise, and waited for Hay to see the man out.

"Mr. Murtaugh? To what do I owe the honor of . . ."

Adams frowned when he saw confusion on Hay's face. Quickly he pursed his lips and shook his head slightly. He would need some kind of hat.

". . . this visit? Come in," said Hay, recovering. "Come right in."

When he had shut the door behind them, Hay turned and stared at him. "You are beginning to make a habit of surprising me. What in God's name happened to your face?"

"I shaved. I rather like it. It reminds me of my youth."

"But that bruise!"

Adams had forgotten. "I was assaulted. Last night."

Hay shook his head slowly. "Have you seen a doctor? You should, you know."

"I'll be fine."

"Well, I am glad to see you. Where have you been? You didn't come home last night."

"Are you checking on me?"

"No. Lizzie is. She says she needed to see you desperately." Hay waited for Adams to speak, but continued when he didn't. "You don't know, do you? Of course. How could you."

"What? What don't I know?"

"Yesterday afternoon Lizzie and Cameron and Amanda were almost run over in the street. Lizzie and Amanda are all right—Cameron managed to push them out of the way, but he's been hurt. Not badly. Enough to put him in a hospital bed for a few days. He's got some bruises, too. I guess they about match yours."

"A runaway? God!" He felt his stomach sink with possibilities narrowly avoided: broken bones, tetanus . . .

"Lizzie's convinced not. She said she saw a man at the reins, aiming for them." Hay shrugged. "Who can say? The wagon and driver turned the corner and were gone."

"What does Cameron think?"

"He can't say. Didn't see." Hay walked around his desk and sat down. "They reported it to the authorities, but of course there is no chance of finding the man. Lizzie waited for you the rest of the afternoon and evening. When she didn't find you home this morning, she came to see me to ask if I knew where you were. She thinks," he said slowly, "that maybe you've found this Miriam Talbott woman, that maybe you spent the night with her."

"No." How could she think that? "That's not even her name. She's Louise—Louise Martin. I haven't found her." What sort of woman did Elizabeth think Louise was? He'd have to disabuse her of this prejudice next time he saw her. And Cameron—had someone been trying to kill Cameron because he'd seen Dingler's picture? Had he put the Camerons in danger by revealing that? "Hay, I'm in trouble. There's a warrant out for my arrest. It's totally trumped up. Can you do something about it? Anything?"

Hay examined his friend. "Do you feel all right? Have you been getting enough sleep?"

"Hay—"

"I can't get used to you without the beard." Hay shook his head. "It's not really you, you know. Much better the way it was."

Hadn't Hay heard him? He repeated himself.

"What's the charge? Fighting?"

Was Hay joking? Adams grew impatient. "Look. I'm being charged with murder. *Murder.*" Adams paused to let this sink in. "Of the coroner and Miriam Talbott."

"The woman who doesn't exist?"

"No. She exists. She did exist—she's dead. You gave me her death certificate, remember? Which," he added quickly, "I'm going to return. As soon as Bertillon's done with it. She's the real Miriam Talbott. I'm looking for Louise Martin."

"Oh." Hay frowned. "You *are* innocent, aren't you?"

Adams didn't deign to answer.

"Well, I don't know," Hay said, watching him. "You took that picture from Dingler's Folly after I asked you not to; you've come in looking very different, beat up, it's all very strange. I feel I don't know you anymore. What's happening to you?"

"Nothing. I am innocent, as a matter of fact. All right?" The anger was plain in his voice.

Hay nodded. "So you need help. What can I do? Do you want to stay here? At the Embassy?"

"Yes. No. I mean, not now. I don't know. I don't know what I want. I'm tired of all this." With an elbow on the arm of his chair he raised a hand to his forehead. Was he feverish? He felt limp, enervated. Maybe he had malaria. Sympathetic malaria. That would be fitting, he thought. Here he was, like Dingler, trying to plow a straight path through tangled terrain, through this jungle of a city, endangering his intimates at every turn. And failing. At least Dingler had cut down the jungle and moved some mud; at least he had always had a clear vision of what his success might look like. And when he left Panama he knew how far he had fallen short. Adams had no idea where he was or how far he had to go. There were connections, actions, machinations in this Panama affair that were invisible to him. "Who was that man who left here a few minutes ago?" he asked Hay suddenly.

"A member of the German mission. He wanted to discuss emigration quotas." Hay's eyebrows rose and he returned Adams's gaze with equanimity.

Adams looked at Hay for a long moment, then licked his lips. He had to believe him. He sighed. "I just want to be done with this." Which he would be, as soon as he got his note from Louise. "What time is it?"

Hay checked his watch. "Just after one-thirty."

"I have to go."

1:55 P.M.

HE DISMISSED HIS cab outside the Chapel of Expiation. He checked his watch: five minutes before two. Perfect timing. He walked slowly down the street, not purposefully but with a gait he thought would make him appear to be a local resident out for a stroll. He paused a few houses away from Madame LeBlanc's, in front of a low stone wall. He didn't want to be exactly at the door when DuForché arrived. He glanced up and down the street. There was no sign of DuForché, though there were a few carriages moving farther down. He sat on the stone wall and waited. A hansom clopped by, and he expected it to slow and pull over and discharge DuForché, but it didn't. After this, a large four-in-hand passed in front of him, its matched team cantering smartly under the light whip of a bored and liveried driver. The horses alone must have cost a small fortune. The carriage was buttoned up tightly—not so much against the weather, Adams was willing to bet, as against the possibility of anarchists. The bombing of that police station had been somewhere in this neighborhood. The carriage turned out of sight at the foot of the street. He looked at his watch: just after two.

Finally Adams saw DuForché walking up the street to his right, from beyond Madame LeBlanc's. He must not have come directly from the Prefecture. Adams saw him stop, double-check the street number from the sidewalk, then climb the stairs. The door opened. From where he sat, Adams couldn't see who answered. He felt an urge to move closer but resisted. He could wait.

As, apparently, would DuForché; whoever had answered the door hadn't admitted him but had left him on the stoop. After a minute the door opened again and a woman stepped out. As the door shut behind her, Adams could see that it was Madame LeBlanc, standing on the stoop with the boy. She had a piece of paper in her hand—the envelope. She did not hand it over right away. As they talked, she glanced once toward Adams, and he immediately looked away. Slowly, avoiding sudden movement which he thought might draw attention, he turned his head to look at the doorway out of the corner of his eye. She was busy talking with DuForché. Perhaps she had difficulty accepting his credentials. Finally, he saw her hand the envelope over. DuForché tipped his cap and departed.

Adams decided to catch him before he headed away, up the street, back the way he had come. Besides, it would be interesting to see how close he had to get before DuForché recognized him. It would be a way of testing his disguise. At his left he heard the clopping of a team of horses, and half noticed the four-in-hand returning, driving slowly. It must have gone around the block; the driver's looking for an address, Adams thought. At the sidewalk DuForché turned to his left and came toward Adams. Adams watched DuForché's eyes, now just ten yards from him, waiting for the moment of recognition. Maybe he could walk right past him. DuForché was looking not at him but at the carriage.

He saw DuForché's face transform itself an instant before he heard the report. The boy crumpled to the pavement, moving slowly, even as Adams felt his own face duplicate the astonishment he had just seen on DuForché's. With uncanny clarity Adams heard the slap of reins from the four-in-hand and the snort of its horses as it passed him. He thought he saw the muzzle of a rifle being withdrawn inside as it jounced down the street. For a fleeting moment he thought of chasing it, but realized it was hopeless.

DuForché was writhing on the sidewalk. At his stomach the deep blue of his uniform was being transformed into a shiny, wet black. As Adams watched, the liquid pooled onto the slate of the sidewalk. He knelt next to him, unsure what to do. "Goddamn, goddamn, goddamn," DuForché was crying through chattering teeth. His right hand held his stomach, and Adams saw blood seeping between his fingers. "Oh shit, goddamn, goddamn."

"Now now," Adams said, and immediately felt useless. "Here now, it's going to be all right," he tried again, more assertively. He was afraid it wasn't true. "Lie still. Let me see." He patted DuForché's hand gently. He put his other hand under the young man's head, thinking to pull him up, feeling some primitive urge to raise him, to get him standing again, standing up as a person, a living person, should, not lying on the sidewalk of a back street of Paris, but then he realized that the boy was better off lying down. Still, the pavement was hard. Adams put a knee, awkwardly, under DuForché's head to cushion it, holding him there, half in his lap. The look on the boy's face as Adams did this was wrenching. "Sorry. No, no, be still. I don't know, I don't know, I don't know," he murmured, responding to the question he thought he saw in DuForché's eyes. He stroked the boy's face, that face he had once judged to be innocent of the marks of experience. Already his cheeks were losing their color. "I don't know, I don't know. There there."

"Oh Jesus. Oh. I'm cold," DuForché said.

Adams realized that with DuForché's head in his lap he couldn't do anything to help him. Gently he lowered the head, then stood and whipped off his coat. He spread this over him. The blood that was spreading on the slate seemed obscenely thin and watery. DuForché tried to move and moaned sharply in pain. Adams realized he ought to try to stop the bleeding. "My legs, oh Jesus, my legs, oh—" Adams pulled his coat aside and tugged gingerly at the layers of uniform that covered DuForché's stomach. The hole in the jacket was smaller than he would have thought, from the quantity of blood. His handkerchief—he'd use that. He reached for it in his pocket.

"Oh my God—" a voice said behind Adams. He looked up. It was Madame LeBlanc, panting, out of breath. "Oh my God."

"Get help," Adams said. "Go." Remarkably he had a thought: "Find a telephone. That's the quickest. Call the police. Alphonse Bertillon, director of the Service of Judicial Identity. Tell him his nephew . . ." Adams couldn't finish the sentence. He took his handkerchief and placed it on the wound, pressed it in, trying to stop the blood. The pressure made DuForché wince and a whimper escaped him.

"Here, let me." Quickly she tugged up her skirt and ripped a swath of cloth from the petticoat. With this she fashioned a bandage, which she knelt to apply with brisk efficiency.

"We need help," Adams said, yielding ground.

"You go get it," she said without looking up.

Adams stood. His hands were covered with DuForché's blood and there was a large stain of it on his pant leg. He looked up to see the horrified face of Madame LeBlanc's maid. "You!" Adams shouted at her, as if she were far away. "Don't just stand there, get help!" She continued to look from Adams to DuForché, uncomprehendingly. "A telephone. Find a telephone. At the pneu office. Call the police." She made no move to go, and Adams, holding his hands dripping in front of him, thought of slapping her, not in anger but out of a practical need to get her going. "Go! Now!" he shouted. Slowly she began to move, looking back. "Call his uncle. Alphonse Bertillon. At the Prefecture." He waved her on; she moved slowly, as though she had no energy of her own, but could be moved only by Adams's impetus. "Yes, yes, go! Go!" Finally she turned and began to run. "Director of the Service of Judicial Identity," he called after her. "Bertillon!"

2:27 P.M.

WHEN THE POLICE arrived they were mercifully efficient, photographing, measuring, holding back the crowd that had gathered around the stretch of sidewalk in front of Madame LeBlanc's. Adams was dimly aware of the crowd as a ring of solemn faces surrounding him. A ring of witnesses. They contained the scene within their sight, surrounded it, so that no glimpse of it, no angle on it could escape and be forgotten. The surface of the street seemed to hold his feet when he tried to move. Men were milling around him—uniformed policemen in their blue capes, medical people in white smocks, other men, cabbies, teamsters, who knew who they were, all of them moving slowly, stepping here for something, standing there to talk, walking back and forth singly and in pairs, combining, separating, recombining, always avoiding the horrible stain on the sidewalk, never stepping over it, never stirring the air above it, never dissolving the palpable emptiness that lay just above it. That was DuForché, wasn't it, he thought, the space his body had been in, the space no one would violate. At first dark and shiny, the pool of DuForché's blood had begun to turn gritty as it dried and soaked into the stone. Everyone moved slowly, slowly and far away. How considerate, Adams thought, that they should do that. He sat on the stone wall and tried to breathe evenly.

He overheard an officer mutter something to his partner: "The fool was alone." Adams wanted to contest this, to explain to him what DuForché had done, why he was there, how it had come to be. DuForché deserved better than to be thought a fool. He almost rose to speak, but stopped himself: he couldn't. They were all too, too far away, too poignantly far away. The world must proceed without him. He didn't want to risk trying to get back to it for fear that in the trial he would discover he couldn't. And then where would he be? Here, watching, was fine.

Adams had knelt at DuForché's side until the ambulance wagon had come, offering what comfort he could. He thought DuForché had still been alive when he was loaded onto the wagon, but he hadn't been sure. Sometimes the body's breath is so subtle you can't find it. Especially after a shock: the spark inside grows quiet and small because it retreats from danger, from the inhospitable place the flesh has become; by this subtlety it hides from Death, succeeds if it can in being too insignificant to be seen; it wants to trick Death into overlooking its presumption, its want, its greed for life—its hopeless, pathetic desire to animate, cause, feel, know. It was a natural thing, this defense. Yes. DuForché would be all right.

Mostly he knew this wasn't true.

He was standing in Madame LeBlanc's parlor and he had no idea how he had gotten there. Someone had asked him to wait for an interview, and there he was. There was an openness to the house that disturbed him, a flow of air through its halls and a bustle of people who meant nothing to him, like a moving day, like those early autumn days when the Quincy household was packed and moved to Boston, men coming and going, doors left open to breezes that came to him from fields and marshes, came filled with their airs, reminding him of the loss contained in that departure. He smelled nothing now. He still felt DuForché's head on his thigh, and when he shut his eyes, he saw the pool of blood spreading underneath him, growing larger and larger, bigger than the pool of potassium cyanide beneath Clover, blue-black and shiny on the cold stone of the sidewalk, spread wide on the slate with no odor, none at all. Her fixative had had an acrid almondy smell that flowered into his sinuses, penetrated there and expanded, leaving no room for anything else, no room even for doubt, as it burrowed into his head. It wasn't so much a headache as a solid block of pain that took a definite size and shape within his head. It had been the last thing he remembered smelling for a year—until in Japan, with La Farge, on the trip they'd made him take, in a garden of chrysanthemums, when his sense of smell had returned. Her head, too, had rested on his thigh. He hadn't just stroked her face but had kissed it, had bent himself double to reach her cheek, had pulled her to him in longing and panic until he could feel her face on his, its heat declining too too quickly, and he could feel how completely final had been this, her solution to the sibilant whisper that beset her, that seductive murmuring that had never retreated far, not ever in her life. And knowing it was too late, he had nevertheless applied himself to her lips, blue but not yet cold, kissing her gently at first but then losing himself, thinking, *This hasn't happened don't let it happen*, as if the sheer force of his wanting, pressed through mouth and tongue, might undo this thing she had done to herself. All he wanted was more time. How could he not have something that simple? How could she not think of him? He actually had thought to make her remember, make her come back from this escape as if for a thing forgotten: Don't leave me! Yes, she would stir, waken, and reach for him.

But she didn't. And in that kiss he found the taste of her death: bitter, toxic, almonds made of biting metal. His mouth had rejected it, had immediately tried to wash it away on a flood of spit, and he had swallowed, again and again, kneeling on the floor with her head in his lap. His stomach hurt from the memory of it, and the wateriness in his mouth made him think he might gag. He could not swallow.

With his eyes open he breathed through his nose, feeling his mouth fill again.

He had to find a sink and rinse out his mouth. There was a policeman in the foyer, standing next to Madame LeBlanc. Behind the stairs: there must be a kitchen back there somewhere. The policeman called to him, but he paid no attention. His mouth was too full.

He found the kitchen and the sink and spat into it with great relief. Bending over it, he panted for a moment before turning on the tap. He wanted to wipe the inside of his mouth. He had forgotten that taste, forgotten that moment on the floor next to Clover's body. God, had he really done that?

He rinsed his mouth until the taste was gone, putting his head down into the porcelain bowl, below the faucet, turning his cheek to let the water fall clean and smooth into it.

Calmer now, he washed his face. It felt different under his hands: cold and smooth—like DuForché's, he thought, and he had an instant of anxiety before he remembered that he had shaved his beard. He didn't see a towel anywhere. He wiped his face with his hands, shook them, then wiped again. They weren't dry enough. He thought to wipe them on his pants, but no, he couldn't, his pants were wet with blood. He put his hands inside his coat, up to his armpits, and wiped down on his shirt. It wouldn't show. And the warmth of his armpits felt good. He left his hands there, hugging himself, leaning against the wall with his eyes closed until he felt better.

He needed to talk to Bertillon.

In the foyer he asked where he could find him.

"In there," said the policeman, jerking his head toward a door opposite the parlor. "But you can't go in there. He's interviewing someone."

Adams ignored him and made his way into the room. Bertillon was leaning against Madame LeBlanc's desk, talking to a woman who sat on one of the overstuffed couches. "I'm sorry," Adams said. "About DuForché. Your nephew. He was a good boy."

Bertillon narrowed his eyes. "You are?" he asked, in a voice that was cold, disjointed, flat. He doesn't believe me, Adams thought. What does he think I am, some kind of heartless wretch? "Yes, I am. Go to hell."

At this Bertillon looked puzzled. Suddenly his face relaxed. "Monsieur Adams! I didn't recognize you. You have shaved recently." His eyes were tired and drawn.

Adams was in no mood to be condescended to. "Oh. Of course. That explains it. You only insult strangers, I suppose."

Bertillon looked confused. "I was asking you who you were. Not expressing doubt." Adams heard this but could not make sense of the words. They seemed irrelevant. "I'm sorry for the misunderstanding," Bertillon said gently. "Forgive me." This made Adams feel better, but still he was wary. Even so he had to tell. "This is horrible. I'm sure that whoever shot your nephew intended to shoot me. I asked him to come here. I should have known. It's my fault."

"You mustn't think that," Bertillon said. "It is the fault of the man who shot him. You had no part." This seemed to Adams a wise thing, but he wasn't sure he could believe it. Bertillon reached a hand out to Adams's shoulder. "Let me finish with this woman. I'm almost done. I'll talk to you next." He steered Adams to the door.

When Bertillon called him in, Adams took a seat where he had seen the woman sit, and told him everything, every detail he could recall: the wall he had loitered near, the color of the team of the four-in-hand, his eagerness to test his disguise, the expression on Bertillon's nephew's face, the report of the gun. He spoke as if in a trance, seeing details he hadn't realized he had seen. He wanted to get it right, to explain how it was. A complete testament was his duty. And it was his only hope of not feeling so alone: he would make language carry his burden of witness, that others might know it.

As he spoke Bertillon nodded. "Thank you," he said when Adams was done. "Monsieur Adams, under no circumstances are you to blame yourself. This is one of the risks of police work. We all know it, and we accept the risk willingly. Understand?"

"He was doing me a favor, walking where I was expected."

"That's as may be. He was also on assignment from me. I expected trouble. He would have been there, even if you hadn't asked him." Bertillon's voice was firm. The two men looked at each other in silence. Adams wanted something with which to wipe his nose. He'd forgotten his handkerchief or left it somewhere.

Bertillon handed him his. "Keep it," he said. He watched Adams blow his nose. When Adams had folded the cloth and tucked it into a pocket, Bertillon went on. "I have found out something about the warrant for your arrest," he said simply.

"What?"

"Apparently the warrant is based on fingerprints found in your rooms. Prints from the dead woman—Miriam Talbott—were found on several surfaces."

"But that's—I never saw her until I saw her dead. You have to believe me. At the morgue. It's impossible."

"I've seen the prints," Bertillon said quietly. "They match."

"But . . ." This was impossible, Adams thought. "But you yourself are skeptical of fingerprints, aren't you? Didn't you say so?"

Bertillon shook his head. "No, Monsieur Adams. I may have decided to hold an investigation open based on a doubt that you and I collude in, but let us not delude ourselves that we delude ourselves. The match is exact. All the fingers. All ten. Whether or not each print is unique, it would be most unusual for two people to have ten fingerprints in common."

Adams felt a leaden weight in his stomach. "No. It couldn't have been she. Someone with the same prints . . ."

Bertillon was regretful. "At this point it is simple mathematics, Monsieur Adams, as I believe I explained to you. Do you need to hear it again?"

"You're going to arrest me, aren't you?" Adams suddenly pictured a trial. First Clover, now DuForché; how could he ever think he would escape a reckoning?

Bertillon shook his head. "No." He waited for Adams to look at him. "There are a number of irregularities here. First, the prefect made use of my department without my knowledge. I was shown the prints but did not participate in their collection, nor have I been allowed access to your rooms. This is not usual procedure and it troubles me; there must be some reason for it. Second, in my limited experience, it is highly unusual to collect ten perfect prints in the field. At the Prefecture when you arrest someone, yes, but from tables, glassware, surfaces out in the world, no."

"What are you saying?" Adams asked.

Bertillon shook his head. "I offer no conclusions. But here is a hypothesis. No. Let me couch this as an observation. This woman's fingertips were separated from her body. They have been places her body hasn't."

It took a moment for Adams to realize what he meant. "You think someone took her fingertips into my rooms and—and—" He couldn't finish the idea; the image of it was too grisly.

Bertillon shrugged. "Unheard of. Yes. Unpleasant. But not impossible, perhaps."

"But what about the, ah, isn't there oil from the skin that—that they would need . . . ?"

Silently Bertillon placed a finger next to his nostril, wiped, and showed his finger to Adams, shrugging.

"Who would do that?"

He smiled wanly. "You're asking me?" He turned his head sharply to the side for an instant, as if to free his neck from his collar. "Someone who wants to see you arrested, even if the arrest is temporary. Someone who does not want you to rendezvous with this young woman, perhaps. Or perhaps they've misjudged and truly believe that the techniques of science can be misled by manufactured evidence."

Adams remembered who had called on the prefect that morning. It seemed a lifetime ago that DuForché had come downstairs with the information. "Could Loubet have done this?"

"I don't know. That is an interesting inference. But perhaps we can establish this matter through direct testimony rather than inference." Bertillon stared levelly at Adams and must have seen the confusion on his face. "I think perhaps more investigation at your hotel might clear the matter up," he explained. "Who visited your rooms? It would have been sometime Tuesday—after the corpse was mutilated but before the fingertips were found in the pneumatique Wednesday morning."

Outside Madame LeBlanc's, as Bertillon escorted him to a police carriage, Adams wondered if the spectators who lingered at the scene of the shooting would think he was being arrested. He didn't care. When he turned and sat in the carriage, he was surprised to see Bertillon still standing on the curb. He had squeezed over to make room for him, but Bertillon wasn't following. He felt a panicked moment of abandonment. "Aren't you coming?"

"I can't. I have an investigation here. Don't worry. You'll

do fine. Just find out if they let anyone into your rooms. That shouldn't be too hard." He spoke soothingly and was nodding his head slightly.

"Yes. No. I mean, of course." He tried to convince himself that he would be all right.

"Oh, one other thing," said Bertillon. "I found out something that might interest you. About your friend Madame Dingler."

"What?"

"She was arrested on a warrant sworn by the director of the National Library." Adams frowned; this didn't make sense. "They've been after her for quite a while, it seems," Bertillon continued. "Destruction of state property. Theft of library materials. I think it is, mmm, justified, I believe you would say." Bertillon shook his head. "Apparently she went around slicing out and stealing anything she could that had any mention of her son. Some sort of obsession. A disturbed woman."

She was the one slicing out information about her son, Adams repeated to himself. He made himself understand the words. But if there was no conspiracy to suppress information about the scandal, why had DuForché been shot? "Do you have any idea who did it?" Adams asked. "Your nephew, I mean. Any idea who killed him?"

Bertillon looked off in the distance, toward the Chapel of Expiation. "The papers will probably say that this is the work of anarchists," he said slowly. "I think that as a provisional hypothesis, this is not too far off the mark." He leaned into the carriage and patted Adams on the knee. "Don't think of what could have been, Monsieur Adams. There is no benefit to be had from that."

As he jounced along in the cab, Adams gazed blankly at the streets as he passed through them, their swirling afternoon traffic mimicking the motion and transit of his thoughts. The life of the city went on, and he felt the lonelier for it.

"He was a good man," he said out loud to no one. "You should know that. He was a good man."

3:02 P.M.

HE WAITED OUTSIDE his hotel for fifteen minutes. If the prefect had officers watching for him, Adams couldn't find them. Inside, the lobby was deserted.

At the bell desk Adams questioned the clerk, whose cool gaze took in his bruises, his stained clothing, his beardless face. Had he been on duty Tuesday? Yes. Had he allowed anyone access to his rooms any time Tuesday? No. Had anyone been allowed upstairs, any unregistered visitors? No. And, the clerk wanted Monsieur Adams to know, when the manager found out about the burned photograph, which Monsieur Cameron had made known to him, he had implemented special security measures to make sure that his rooms and effects weren't disturbed. Ordinary cleaning activities had been suspended, so the maids no longer entered the rooms, and their keys had been collected. Of the two dozen visitors since that day, he, the clerk, could personally vouch that none had strayed from their appointed destinations. He'd had a bellhop follow each one. There was no mistake.

Adams digested this information. No one could have put the fingerprints there, yet there they had been. There must be some way in from the window, down from the roof perhaps . . . No. Someone had gotten into his rooms sometime Tuesday, to burn the picture; Tuesday was when the fingerprints had been left. God. To think he had been there, in the

same room, all that day, with things that those fingers had
touched . . .

"Monsieur Adams?"

"Mmm?"

"Is there some trouble, with the police, perhaps?"

Had the police been here? Had this clerk been deputized
to keep an eye out for him? "No. Why do you ask?"

"They were here to examine your rooms. Wednesday
morning."

"I know." The clerk obviously wanted information but
Adams was in no mood to divulge anything. If the hotel
knew that there was a warrant out for his arrest he would
have no place to go. "We assumed that it had something to
do with this photograph."

Adams didn't answer.

"They had a warrant, and we could not deny them."

"No. Of course not. An investigation. Of course they're
looking into it."

The clerk nodded. "Yes. Well. The manager went up with
them, and stayed to make sure that nothing was disturbed.
He said they did some very strange things. Powders, brushes,
looking at everything."

He didn't feel up to explaining it. "Yes. New police techniques. Very scientific."

"Everything is fine, then, I trust?"

"I don't know. I've hardly been in my rooms since then."

The clerk nodded, not in sympathy but wisely, and pointedly looked down to Adams's bloodstained clothing. What
was he thinking? Adams was too tired to ponder the possibilities. "A separate matter. An accident I witnessed. I've
reported it to the police. Very disturbing." He shook his
head, finishing with a little shiver to indicate his degree of
distress, then turned to go upstairs.

"Monsieur Adams?"

Had his answer not been satisfactory? He turned slowly.

"You have forgotten your mail." He hadn't seen the clerk
place a pair of envelopes on the desk, and realized with a
pang that he hadn't gotten his answer from Louise. Was her
reply still with DuForché? Had the boy put it in his pocket?
He went over the scene in his mind's eye but couldn't recall

seeing the envelope at all, once it passed from Madame LeBlanc to DuForché. How had he forgotten it? He began to admonish himself but stopped: of course he had forgotten it. He would have gladly traded the envelope with its reply from Louise for the chance to go back, stop DuForché, quit this whole thing.

The clerk called his name again. He had been standing, frozen, at the bell desk. Adams excused himself. He ought to retrieve his reply from Louise. A touchy business, doing that with a warrant out for his arrest. Well, he would do it. He would go back to Madame LeBlanc's, find Bertillon, and get his help. First he needed to change.

On the stairs he glanced at the envelopes. There were two: one from Elizabeth, the other from the Prefecture. He thought he knew what the former might contain. On the whole the summons would be easier to face. Wearily he climbed the stairs, one foot after the other. His damp trousers pulled at his legs with each step.

The air in his rooms smelled of containment, a cheesy, warm-sour smell of gaslight and old plaster. He laid the two unopened envelopes on his writing desk and sat down. A little powder on the desk was the only evidence of the fingerprinting he could find anywhere; no wonder he hadn't seen it before. He was careful not to touch anything, feeling as if he were trespassing in his own rooms, not wanting to leave any record of his presence. Gingerly he sat at his desk and opened the window. The cool air carried sounds of the afternoon street, the jangle of harnesses and the clattering of wheels, and far off, from the North Station, the whistle of a train clearing the yards.

The feel of DuForché's blood in his trousers was suddenly intolerable. He had to change his clothes. He stood and stripped, peeling off his vest, shirt, collar and cuffs, trousers, stockings and garters, underclothes, everything, until he stood nude at his desk. He carried his wadded-up clothing to the kitchen, where he threw it, all of it, into the wastebasket. With a washrag from the sink he washed his thighs.

When he had dressed he returned to his desk. Absently he tore open the envelope from the Prefecture.

It wasn't a summons. It was from the Bureau of Missing

Persons. He gave a short, sardonic snort after unfolding it: he knew where Miriam Talbott was, all right. She was in Père-Lachaise, dead and buried. Idly he scanned the report. Miriam Talbott, aged 23, American citizen. Born June 23, 1869, New York. Lately a resident of the Latin Quarter. A student at L'Ecole des Beaux Arts, she had no visible means of support and was presumed to be living on parental stipends, though the report noted that her rent had been paid by check drawn on a Crédit Lyonnais account established for the American Embassy in the name of John Hay.

3:48 P.M.

ADAMS PULLED ON his bloodstained overcoat and jammed the report into a pocket. If Hay had paid for the woman's apartment he must have known who she was all along. He must have known that Miriam Talbott was involved with Reinach. He must have known that the woman Adams met in Pontorson was someone else. *He must have known this all along.* He made himself take the stairs safely, every other step, methodically. Why had Hay hidden his connection to her? Like the thin edge of a crescent moon slicing up from the horizon, a cold, impossible idea began to force itself out of the pit of his stomach and move upward, illuminative, into his consciousness. What was it that Hay had said about the scandal?—that the more corruption the Panama affair revealed, the more obvious it was that France was finished in Panama. Was Hay working to reveal the scandal? Or could he have done what he could to instigate it—to encourage blackmail, bribery, extortion? Or worse: Hay's interest was in seeing the *chéquards* revealed, a revelation that Miriam Talbott had threatened to make but one which, if her blackmail had been successful, she ultimately didn't want; what if Hay had betrayed her somehow? Could Hay have been involved in her death? Could he have made it happen?

Adams felt sick at the thought. Whatever person or power had killed Miriam Talbott was just as hostile to Louise Martin. And if Hay knew who this woman was, and had paid her rent, how would he not know her roommate?

He had to talk to Bertillon. And he had to get Louise's reply.

He caught a cab to Madame LeBlanc's.

From the end of the street he could see that the investigation had wound down—there were just two police wagons left, and the crowd of curious onlookers had disbanded. He alighted from the cab, wanting not to know where DuForché's bloodstain was but powerless to stop himself from looking, from orienting himself by it: there, a dozen yards away.

Inside, he learned from an officer that Bertillon had gone. "Do you know where?"

"No. Back to the Prefecture, most likely."

The ambulance wagon was long gone with DuForché's body—and with his reply from Louise. To the morgue, the officer said.

Morgue, Prefecture—at least they were close to each other. But maybe—yes. First he had a question for Madame LeBlanc.

He found her in the parlor, perched on a divan, her hands folded together on its arm and one smooth feline cheek resting on her forearm. She didn't stir when he entered. "I must talk to Louise Martin. Where is she?"

"You've had your reply." She scarcely looked at him.

No, he explained, he hadn't. "You know where she is. Tell me."

"I don't know where she is."

"How did you get my message to her?"

"My arrangements are none of your business."

He had been abrupt, he realized. Patiently he explained. Madame LeBlanc eyed him skeptically until he finished, then turned away. "I still can't help you. Avril's the one who knows, and she went downtown with the police."

In the cab in a state of high agitation he tried to decide: morgue? or Prefecture? Find this woman Avril? Report to Bertillon about Hay? Get his reply from Louise? Which? Finally he decided on the morgue, thinking that if Bertillon had gone there with the body, he would see him all the sooner.

But Bertillon wasn't there. Luckily the morgue attendant thought nothing of letting Adams see the body. Still on the canvas stretcher on which it had been carried in, it lay to one side of the familiar room, against a wall: no one had touched it yet. Adams stood quietly at the head of the sheeted form, trying not to appear impatient. He was relieved that the boy's body was still fully clothed—not just because the combination of nudity and death was powerfully unsettling, more so than either could be separately, but because it simplified his search for the letter. The attendant, a trowel-chinned policeman, treated him solicitously, and Adams didn't want to misplay the role by seeming too brusque. But DuForché would have understood—he had to find Bertillon, Avril, Louise. He nodded grimly at the boy's sallow face. Handsome. Improving with age. He reached a hand out to touch the top of his head, those tight curls. "He—" He had to start over. "At the time of death he had a letter on his person. Addressed to me. He was picking it up. I must see it."

"I don't know . . ." The attendant let his voice trail off and looked around the room, avoiding Adams's eyes. I'm not going to get what I want, Adams thought. He tried again.

"Look. It was addressed to me. I just want to see it. I don't need to take it. I must see it. You can have it back. Is it still with him?" Without waiting permission Adams reached a hand inside DuForché's coat and found the envelope in its inside pocket.

It was on cheap notepaper, unsealed. He unfolded it and read:

I was painting a portrait of the archangel in peril: stone, lots of riparian stone, with the object of attention deceived and trapped, far from triumphant. You remember—the key, the absolute key, was the small wood snake. I think now I was too optimistic about the blue. You know what it means to me! I think if I were to repaint it this week, all of my blue would be gone by Friday. This will have to do. A reunion would be wonderful, though as you know it is not mine to say when. Somehow, soon, I hope. The sooner the better.

Bless her, he thought. She had managed to tell him enough, even with her captor watching. He hoped he had enough time.

4:21 P.M.

ADAMS HURRIED PAST Notre Dame and turned right, looking down the broad avenue toward the pont au Change and the Right Bank. A cab, a cab, he needed a cab. It was a mile downstream; he couldn't run that far.

By the time he got to the bridge, he still hadn't found a cab. He looked around, growing increasingly frantic. Maybe he should try to run. It was only a mile. No, that would be foolish. From the bridge he heard the steady chuffing of a taxi launch at the quai. It was reversing, angling, preparing to depart as a hand discharged the lines.

He just might make it.

He ran down the stone stairs, forcing his feet to keep up as he hurtled along. The boat was pulling away, heading downstream. Running on the quai he gathered himself for the leap and threw himself into the air.

He landed on the deck with a thud and crumpled, falling against the legs of the passengers sitting along the gunwale. Slowly he pulled himself up to sit cross-legged, checking to see if he had hurt anything. He seemed to be in one piece, though his stomach was newly sore. He nodded an apology to the faces above him, a solemn array that bore wordless witness.

The ticket taker was unruffled. With no trace of concern, as if passengers regularly threw themselves onto his boat across open water, he presented himself to Adams for the

fare. Adams fumbled in his coat pocket and dug out his billfold.

He was too anxious to sit. His arrival had drawn attention,
but the other passengers glanced away quickly whenever he
met their eyes. He paced to the rear of the boat and took a
few deep breaths, recovering, calming himself. This cleared
his head enough to allow him to feel fear, anticipating what
he would find when he found Louise. He couldn't bear to
stand still and walked to the front of the cockpit, where the
pilot stood in the wheelhouse.

"You must sit. No movement. Off you go," the money
taker said, shooing him back to a seat.

He took a seat on the starboard gunwale, thinking to be
the first out when the boat landed; the other passengers gave
him a wide berth. On either side the banks of the Seine un-
wound like slow ribbons. A trio of gulls loitered above the
launch, matching the boat's speed, their wings locking on
glide into wide, splayed M's. He scanned the quai off the
starboard side, checking every pedestrian, looking for a familiar face, anxious that the one face he most expected to
see he didn't want to see, not here. Some few people strolled
by the river, ordinary Parisians enjoying a late-afternoon
walk. Like smudges on a blank page they didn't signify; the
whole scene seemed flat, slow, empty, the more so because
the light coming down through the bare trees was spectral,
direct and clear but robbed by the season and the hour of its
capacity to warm. He had no idea what he would do, how
he could help Louise.

The next taxi-launch stop was beyond the swimming concession. As the concession slid past, he saw that the bottom
half of the Dutch door yawned open between the two espaliered trees. It couldn't have been more than fifteen yards
away; it might as well have been a hundred. Was that just
the leg of the table he saw, or was there something else
visible there, in the back? He stood to keep the scene in view
as it passed to the stern, watching intently until the boat
landed, making sure no one entered or left.

As soon as he was sure he could make it, he jumped ashore
and ran, ignoring the boatman's shouts.

Outside the door he paused to listen: nothing. Slowly he

crouched down to look under it. The room inside contained the concessionaire's table, chairs, things, but no people. He squatted under the door. Something in his overcoat pocket was bumping his thigh. He fished it out: that infernal mug. Also, he remembered, a razor; which pocket? He stood and patted himself quickly until he found it. With the open razor in one hand he took a cautious step. He felt a slight breeze blowing in his face: air, coming from somewhere.

In this room all was as it had been before. Slowly, with the razor in front of him, he moved toward the curtain at the back that billowed slightly on the breeze.

When he pulled it aside there was nothing behind it. To his right was the passageway through which he had retreated the night before; to his left, another passageway. Both were dark. He paused to listen, then realized that it might not be wise to stand in the middle of the doorway; quickly he flattened himself against the wall. He listened again but heard nothing. The passage on his right had no windows, just the one grating that the concessionaire had insisted he look through, which let a small patch of diffuse light fall upon the floor. Adams couldn't see beyond it, but he knew the passage dead-ended at another doorway. Louise wouldn't be down there. Riparian stones, the quai, she had to be here somewhere.

Careful to step as quietly as he could, he made his way to the other side of the doorway. Here he felt a breeze in his face again. The passageway went straight for ten feet, then turned. Pressing his back against the wall, holding tight to his razor, he listened.

Nothing.

Still, of the two directions, this was the more promising. He made his way down it, feeling the grit of the stone floor beneath his shoes, holding the open razor out ahead. The corridor turned—right, then left after a dozen small paces, then right again—and became so dark he couldn't see his own hand.

After a dozen more steps, his razor, with a quiet chink, ran into something unyielding: a stone wall, directly in front of him. The corridor had turned again. Groping, he felt along the wall, found an edge: again the hall turned left. Either that

or it opened into some kind of chamber. Yes. A very faint
light was filtering in from somewhere, or his eyes were getting used to the darkness. He could make out a vague, trap-
ezoidal shape below and in front of him. Was it a table? A
peculiar, close smell infested this place, a smell mixed of
dank stone and something else, something blunt and acrid
and musky. He patted his pockets, looking for a box of
matches, and when he found it, tried to set his razor down
to light one. He missed the table, but the razor didn't clatter
to the floor; there was a soft muffled plop, then the sound of
metal on stone.

Adams wanted to retrieve his weapon but didn't want to
put his hand down into the darkness, into whatever had broken its fall. Not without some light. He struck his match and
for a moment couldn't see beyond its sphere of brightness.

Directly beneath him lay the body of the concessionaire,
face up. He looked fat-eyed, grotesquely unconcerned at the
awkward angle his neck made with his body. Some foreign
object protruded from his mouth. Just before the match went
out, Adams noticed that he had been bound, hands and feet.

He lit another match. There, on the floor near the man's
neck, lay his razor. In the man's mouth was some sort of tin
of powder, which spilled out to form a yellow crust on his
lips and tongue.

Orpiment.

Adams shivered. Slowly he straightened and looked
around. This, apparently, was the concessionaire's bedroom.
There were no signs of struggle. When the match flared out,
he lit another and held it high. An iron bedstead, its head-
and footboards shaped like lyres, hugged the stone wall to
the left. A dark blanket covered the mattress and was
stretched taut, army-style; on the table was a glass lamp.
Adams struck a fresh match and lit the lamp, stepping carefully alongside the body. When he trimmed the wick, the
room took shape around him. In the corner there was a cheap
bureau, and on the wall above it were pictures—images of
the Virgin Mary from postcards and Mass programs. In the
center, with the others arranged around it, was a photograph
of a woman lying on her back on a white bedsheet. An aerial
view: a young woman, nude, early twenties maybe, her body

looking pale and forlorn as she lay there, her long dark hair pooling around her head like an inverse dark-on-light aura against the sheet. She was splayed across the bed, one knee bent, the other leg stretched straight, revealing all that modesty in life dictated a woman keep most hidden. Except for her eyes, which stared unnaturally at some point behind the camera, she might have been asleep: he realized with a dull twinge in his stomach that the woman in the photograph was dead. He could see, at her feet and on either side, the legs of the tripod that had been used to hold the camera above her.

There were photographs on the other walls as well, sometimes mixed in among clipped images of the Virgin. Adams brought the lamp close to examine them. All of them showed dead women in various stages of undress. One of them was poor Miriam Talbott, fresh from the water of the Seine, photographed against the cold, hard stone of the quai. Her dress and bodice were torn open to reveal long white thighs, round white breasts. Adams stared at the body on the floor in disgust. He could imagine the uses to which these photographs had been put. How had this man gotten them?

"Monsieur Adams. What a surprise to find you here."

He turned. There, in the entryway to the room—who was that? Adams hadn't heard him approach.

4:37 _{P.M.}

"OH DEAR, MONSIEUR Adams. This doesn't look good. Not good at all." Adams brought the lamp up and saw Pettibois shake his head slowly, the shadow of his nose lengthening and shortening on the round fullness of his face. "Alone with a dead body. *Again.* Your appetite for mayhem appears insatiable. You're going to have to come with me." Pettibois took a step toward him. "What made you do it? Why? Why this senseless taking of life?"

"I didn't. I didn't do this."

"Monsieur Adams." Pettibois sighed. "It will go more easily with you if you just tell the truth." He advanced a step.

Adams held the lamp in front of him, backing away. There was no other escape from the room.

"I'm not going to hurt you," Pettibois said in a gentle voice. "But, Monsieur Adams, you must be called to account for your crimes. This"—he gestured at the body on the ground—"this simply won't do. We can't have you running about, harming our citizenry, however disgusting and pathetic they happen to be." He was speaking in a low monotone, hypnotically, and Adams found this attempt to soothe even more threatening. As Pettibois spoke he took another slow step forward; again, instinctively, Adams backed away. He felt the edge of the table against his buttocks. He had no more room for retreat. "I didn't do this, I'm telling you. I

just got here. I—I—I got a message. From Miss Martin,
Louise Martin . . .''

Pettibois nodded. "Your famously absent friend. And how
is she?''

"I—I don't know. She didn't say.''

"No, she didn't. Quite the clever one, though, wouldn't
you say?''

Small wood, Adams realized. *Petit bois.* Louise had tried
to tell him and he hadn't stopped to puzzle it out.

It was absolutely necessary to keep distance between Pettibois and himself.

"To the rescue, eh, Monsieur Adams?'' Pettibois moved
a step closer. "Very heroic of you. Very noble. And, I ought
to tell you, predictable. What if I told you she has been
found, Monsieur Adams? She's been found and taken care
of. There's nothing to worry about. It's all over.'' Pettibois
sounded as if he were talking to a child. Of course, of course;
Adams saw it now in an instant. Who had found the bolt
cutters, ruining the fingerprints? Pettibois. Who had seen the
prefect the morning the prefect issued a warrant for Adams's
arrest? Pettibois. The fingertips in the pneumatic tube? Pettibois. At every turn, Pettibois. It seemed so obvious. Herz's
pony.

Out of the corner of his eye Adams saw his razor on the
floor. He could reach it before Pettibois was on him; he had
to reach it. "But I think you already know that, don't you,
Monsieur Adams. In fact, I suspect you are the one who took
care of her. Another victim, a beautiful woman this time,
struck down in the prime of life. Senseless, Monsieur Adams.
Why? Why this murderous rampage?'' Pettibois was shaking
his head solemnly. "Is it to feed some dark habit? Some
puerile and disgusting drive? We're seeing more and more
of this, you know, as Paris grows, but from a man of your
stature—well, I'm surprised, very surprised.''

Quickly Adams squatted and picked up the razor. He
opened it with a flick of his wrist. It felt awkward in his left
hand, but he couldn't do anything about that, not without
fumbling with the lamp. He didn't want to take his eyes off
Pettibois. He must have seen Dingler's picture when he came
to take Adams to the morgue, and realized right away it

disproved Herz's alibi; so he came back and burned it. Maybe he hadn't even needed Adams to identify the body of Miriam Talbott. Maybe he had been looking for someone to take the blame for her death and Adams had wandered in at just that moment, getting tangled up in events he had no way of understanding. And then, when he had so emphatically said that Miriam Talbott wasn't Miriam Talbott, that must have opened up new possibilities for him . . .

"Oh, now, Monsieur Adams, you won't need that. That won't be necessary." Adams, pressed against the table, could only shake his head. Had Pettibois come closer? He seemed to fill the room, to press on him, blocking all hope of escape. What had he meant when he said Louise had been taken care of?

"You'll find I'm a reasonable man, Monsieur Adams. Really. I can be very understanding." Pettibois took a step closer to him and nodded. "Keep the razor. Think of how you might use it. Think of the mess you're in. There's no denying it, is there? I'm sure that when Bertillon checks, he'll discover your fingerprints on that little tin of paint there. Again." Pettibois grinned at him, nodding toward the body. "You just might save yourself a great deal of embarrassment. Save your friend Monsieur Hay a big, messy international incident. Do Monsieurs Hay and Cameron get the railroad they want? Not if their friend Adams has a notorious trial. Do an honorable thing, Monsieur Adams. Another murder-suicide. A *double* murder-suicide, if we count the girl. It's not as if such a thing were unheard of, no?" He smiled graciously. "Nice, clean, no loose ends left. No, truly, I *like* the idea," he said, as if in response to a demurral from Adams. He took another step forward. "People would wonder what drove you to it. You'd have a certain kind of fame. It would elevate you above the ordinary. Jack the Ripper, Bluebeard, that woman, that Englishwoman, what's her name?" Pettibois thought, then shrugged and took a step.

"No. Stop. No closer." Adams held the razor up. "You're evil." The words had come out without thought, a reflex.

"Oh, name calling. Very productive." Pettibois advanced a step closer. "Yes," he said, returning to his soothing voice. "Well, of course. You're upset."

"You killed him," Adams said, nodding at the concessionaire. "And Miriam Talbott. And the coroner."

"Careful, Monsieur Adams. You're being extremely incautious. Are you sure you aren't speaking nonsense?"

"You must have known who Miriam Talbott was all along. You and Hay. You were hiding her identity to confuse the inquiry into her murder. You chopped her fingers off and sent them to me, after you used them to—to—to leave fingerprints all over my room. Then you got a warrant sworn out on me."

"Very interesting. And why did I do all this? For what possible reason?"

"You're in league with Herz and you're trying to protect the—the—the—the—the . . ." Adams couldn't think of the word. Damnit! He was stammering like a fool. "The *chéquards*."

Pettibois sighed. "Ah, Monsieur Herz. A fitting scapegoat, don't you think? Yes, let us blame him. I am in league with Herz, and Herz is in league with the devil." Pettibois smiled and shook his head. "And why should either he or I care one little bit about *chéquards*? Do you have a reason for that? What is the story, Monsieur Adams? You're a historian; tell me a story." When he spoke again, his voice was harder, colder. "Enough. This is no longer amusing. Give me the razor, Monsieur Adams. I'm placing you under arrest."

For a moment Adams entertained the possibility of submitting. There was, after all, a warrant out for his arrest; this man was an officer of the law. Maybe it would be best to untangle everything at the Prefecture. But looking at Pettibois he was certain that the man had no intention of letting it get that far.

"No."

He'd have to do something if Pettibois took another step. He had no plan in mind, but knew he had to keep Pettibois away. He forced himself to think. He could throw the lamp at Pettibois's feet, hard, hard enough for it to break, and then lunge at him with the razor. In the confusion he'd get past him and out the door. "Don't move," Adams said. "I'm warning you." He brandished both the lamp and the razor, trying to give some sense of the harm they were capable of.

The gesture felt awkward, and some annoying part of his mind registered the thought that brandishment worked best with a solitary object—divided attention diminished the effect.

"Give me the razor." Pettibois extended a hand to Adams and took another step forward.

Adams lifted the lamp high and brought it down, throwing it as hard as he could at the other man's feet. The lamp crashed and broke, sending its kerosene out in a low fireball, smaller than Adams expected. He crouched, ready to lunge, quickly switching the razor to his right hand. But Pettibois had seen him raise the lamp, had guessed what he was doing, and had jumped back. Across the room his face was lit by the declining fingers of flame that rose from the floor. "Oh now, Monsieur Adams. That wasn't very smart. Resisting arrest. I'm afraid I'm going to have to subdue you." A small pool of kerosene from the lamp spread on the floor, running down to the concessionaire's body, and on its surface there danced a weird geography of light. Slowly the inspector reached inside his jacket and produced a gun. "I employ this with some regret." He levelled the gun at Adams and smiled, a quick smile that pushed at his cheeks once, unconvincingly, and was gone. "All right. A change in plans. Lie down. No, first: grasp that tin in Marcel's mouth, there."

Adams, who had instinctively put his hands out from his body at the sight of the gun, didn't move.

"Now, damnit." Pettibois waved the gun barrel, jerking it toward him, trying to get him to move. "Just grasp it enough to leave your fingerprints."

Adams moved slowly, doing as he was told, trying to think. Maybe when it came to that, he could roll on the kerosene, put the flames out. A black, sooty smoke was rising from the fire on the floor.

"Now lie down. Right next to him, there." Pettibois pointed the gun at the pool of kerosene, which even as Adams watched was covered over with small, saw-toothed ranges of flame. No: he'd get his clothing soaked, and he'd be worse off than if he didn't roll around.

Pettibois waved the gun barrel at him. "Quickly, Monsieur Adams."

Adams reached for the floor as slowly as he dared. His only hope, he thought, was some distraction, a moment of inattention in which he could make a grab for the gun. Stopping in mid-crouch, with his eyes on Pettibois, he said as sincerely as he could, "Watch out! At your feet! The fire—it's getting closer."

Pettibois shook his head. "Really, Monsieur Adams." He gestured with a gloved hand out over the fire. "Move. *Now.*"

"No. You'll have to shoot me."

Pettibois cocked his pistol and sighed. He shot once, at the floor, close enough that Adams felt the spray of rock splinters against his trousers. The sound was unbearably loud. "I am serious, Monsieur Adams. Do not test me." Pettibois raised the gun and centered it on Adams's chest. "Lie down. Next to Marcel. It is only marginally more convenient to have you die by fire than by gunshot. I could explain either." Acrid smoke had gathered at the ceiling, and Pettibois crouched slightly to keep his head out of it.

"You could arrest me. Your plan has been very clever. I don't think I could wriggle out of this. It's your word against mine, and I'm a foreigner. I'm sure the courts—" Adams broke off, coughing, and thought, If I can talk long enough, we'll be asphyxiated. Him first—he's taller.

Pettibois answered him with another gunshot into the floor.

Adams looked down at the burning kerosene. Tentatively he stomped his foot, hoping to clear a space, but this just splashed the fire about, splashed kerosene onto the body of the concessionaire. He must do something. He heard the pistol cock again. He bent quickly, to show his eagerness to comply, but stopped to cough. He tried holding a hand to his face to filter the smoke. No good. In his bent-over position, though, the air was clearer. He tried not to breathe. He'd crouch, then hurl himself sideways at Pettibois. He had no clear idea of what this would accomplish; at best there'd be a struggle, he'd have to get the gun, Pettibois was bigger, but at least this offered some hope, something better than just lying down and burning to death.

He bent to the floor, not putting his hands in the burning fluid, and tensed himself for his sideways hurtle.

"Put it down, Inspector."

Who was that? Adams couldn't see past Pettibois. He raised his head as Pettibois turned and saw that behind him was Bertillon, lantern in hand, standing in the doorway, stooping below the worst of the smoke. "That's enough."

"Ah, Chief Bertillon. I'm glad of your help. I was just about to arrest this man." Pettibois, also hunched over, stepped back, positioning himself where he could keep both Adams and Bertillon in view, and swung his gun to point at Bertillon. "He's being very obstinate." Some trick of air current kept the room clear at waist level. Above shoulder height the smoke was too thick to tolerate; it pressed down on the three of them and they crouched, Bertillon with his hands on his knees, to escape it.

"Yes." Bertillon took note of the gun pointing at him before looking to Adams across the room. Adams could read nothing in his glance. "Hadn't you better put out that fire first?" Bertillon said to Pettibois, nodding toward the body, where flames licked at the concessionaire's clothing. He coughed, putting a leather-gloved fist in front of his mouth. "You don't want to allow evidence to be destroyed, do you?" His voice was a croak. For an instant Adams was struck by the absurdity of their half-heighted parley.

Pettibois hesitated, and began to cough.

"I can call my colleagues outside, if you think we need their help," Bertillon added. He held a hand over his mouth and nose and ducked lower.

Pettibois shook his head, lifted his gun. "No. No, I think we can manage," he said between coughs. Slowly he holstered the weapon beneath his jacket. "Hand me the blanket from that bed, will you?" he said to Adams. Adams backed over to the bed and tugged the blanket off it without looking, keeping low, keeping a wary eye on Pettibois.

When Adams tossed the blanket to him, Pettibois caught it and set about smothering the fire. The three of them were coughing, Adams and Bertillon sucking air filtered through their fingers. Neither took his eyes off Pettibois as he smothered the lantern fragments and wrapped the blanket around the body. The room was filled with the heavy smell of kerosene fumes and the awful, sulphurous smell of burned hair and flesh.

"What cause do you have for arresting this man?" Bertillon asked when the fire was out.

"There's a warrant on him." Pettibois coughed. He had brought his gun out again; the barrel pointed near Adams's feet. Nervously Adams shifted, and was disturbed to see the barrel follow him.

"It's been voided. Just this afternoon. By order of the prefect."

For an instant Pettibois looked surprised, then coughed again. "He was here, alone, with the body."

"He was at the morgue not half an hour ago," Bertillon said. His voice was a whisper: he was trying not to use precious breath. "We'll find out how long this man has been dead."

"We should leave," Adams judged. "The smoke will kill us."

It was as if he hadn't spoken; neither Pettibois nor Bertillon looked away from each other. "I think," Pettibois said, gesturing with his gun, "you'll find his prints on the tin of poison that's lodged in the man's mouth, there."

"He forced me to touch it!" Adams couldn't help the plaintive note that crept into his voice. The smoke was forcing tears from his eyes—he feared they'd think he was crying.

"Oh, now! The temerity!" Pettibois said. "Don't be ridiculous. Alphonse, look. The man has—"

"Quiet!" Bertillon commanded. He looked at Adams, at Pettibois, then at the blanket-wrapped body before speaking slowly and clearly. "We'll check for fingerprints. In the meantime, there is something else you could do for me, Inspector Pettibois." He held out his hand. "Could I have your service revolver?"

"Why?"

Adams sensed that Bertillon was weighing his answer carefully. "I'm relieving you of your position. Temporarily. I think it best."

"This is highly irregular, Alphonse. I can't recall ever hearing of this happening. I think not."

"As you say," Bertillon said quietly, "it is unusual. But necessary." Bertillon was moving toward Pettibois, slowly, awkwardly: he straightened from the knees but kept his head low by bending at the waist. "I could call my associates in. Perhaps you'd accept their participation. They are right outside."

For a moment Pettibois thought this over. "I don't know," he said offhandedly. "It's so hard to know whom to trust, don't you think, Monsieur Adams? What do you think?"

Adams was amazed, and could not speak.

"You can trust me," Bertillon said. He moved forward with another deliberate step. "Temporary. Until this matter is settled."

His answer seemed to satisfy Pettibois, who reached the gun toward him.

"Hold it by the barrel, if you would, please," Bertillon said. "You can't be too careful."

"Of course." Slowly Pettibois turned the gun around and handed it over.

"Now," said Bertillon when he held the gun. "Where is the girl?"

"Who?" Pettibois asked in innocence.

"You know. Mademoiselle Martin. Louise Martin."

"She's around here somewhere, I think," Pettibois said. He glanced about, as if visual survey would reveal her, then shrugged. The look that Bertillon gave him encouraged him to be more forthright. "She's in another chamber. Down the hallway. Shall I take you there?"

"Alive?" Adams asked.

Pettibois smiled at Adams. "Why don't we just go and find out?"

4:57 P.M.

"NO. NOT A good idea." Bertillon held the gun at the ready, not actually trained on Pettibois, but not actually pointed away from him, either. "But I will ask you to lead us out. It's too smoky in here." Bertillon stepped aside for Pettibois to leave the room, then followed. When Adams fell in step behind him, Bertillon whispered over his shoulder. "My apologies for not coming sooner. I had some difficult negotiations with the prefect about your warrant."

Outside, ducking under the Dutch door into the twilight, Adams discovered that a small crowd had gathered. He felt foolish, as though he were onstage for a performance he had no competence to give. He looked nervously to Bertillon, who clutched Pettibois with a more-than-casual hand on his arm. Bertillon leaned over to speak again to Adams. "Monsieur Pettibois and I are going to return to the Prefecture for a talk with the prefect. I would like you to stand guard here. Don't go in, don't touch anything. Make sure no one else touches anything until my men get here. Can you do that?"

"What about your men?" He wanted to look for Louise.

"I will send them. Just until they get here, Monsieur Adams." When he saw the expression on Adams's face he added, "A strategic misrepresentation. Forgive me."

"What about Miss Martin?"

Bertillon shook his head. "It would be best if my men were to—" He stopped, looked from Adams to Pettibois and back to Adams. "We need secure evidence. The most important thing you can do is stand guard."

"All right." Adams needed to swallow, but his larynx was a sharp-cornered cube in his throat. He thought maybe he wouldn't breathe for a while.

"I'm sorry to have to abandon you," Bertillon said. "I don't see any other way."

"Awkward, isn't it?" Pettibois smirked as Bertillon pulled his arm to start him up the quai.

Adams looked around. The loose crowd of curious citizens stared back in blank expectation. Finally, by working at it, he managed to swallow. He wanted these people to leave. He waited, but no one moved. "Shoo!" he croaked once, raising his arms. The only motion this caused was an indentation of the row of people directly in front of him. There was shifting in the back, where people apparently wanted a better view.

The attention was unnerving. He felt a momentary impulse command his legs, turning them toward the launch landing and the stairs, but stopped himself. He had to stay. Bertillon had asked him to. He looked again at the semicircle of people staring at him and took a half step backward.

He'd wait in the concessionaire's apartment. That would be easier.

In the stone-walled apartment smoke floated on the air and dipped near the door where, caught in the draft, it swelled down and out. None of them, he realized, had thought to unbolt the top half of the door. They had all ducked beneath it, wanting to disturb things as little as possible. He stood for a moment, conscious of his distance from any surface or object that he might affect, knowing that he shouldn't touch anything.

He waited, his eye roaming from the table with its bowl of strange artifacts to the rude shelves above the sink to the cupboard to the cast-iron stove that stood to the right of the doorway. Finally he couldn't stand not knowing. He was going to find Louise.

He took a candle from the concessionaire's table and dug in his pocket for a match. Cupping it with one hand, he walked down the corridor toward the room where he had found the body, sliding his feet carefully on the stone, crouching to keep his head out of the thickest smoke. The air was heavy with a rank odor, and the thought that part of its origin was burnt flesh nearly gagged him. It seemed not only unhealthy but immoral to breathe it. At the entrance to the concessionaire's bedroom there was another corridor off to the right. He held the candle high and looked into the bedroom: there, at the edge of visibility, was the blanket-wrapped body of the concessionaire. He edged away from it, not wanting to turn his back on it until he was well down the corridor.

Within ten feet he came to a door, bolted on the outside. He unbolted it and swung it open, not sure what he would find.

In the light from the candle he saw what he first took to be a large pile of clothing in the corner of the bare stone chamber. Women's clothing—a dress, a blouse . . .

The pile moved, drawing itself farther into the corner, and the relief he felt was immediate. "Louise? Louise! It's me, Henry Adams." The pile stirred and seemed to unfold. He could barely make out her face, smudged and dirty in the darkness. She didn't answer: he saw she had a gag in her mouth. He set the candle down, almost dropping it in his hurry to free her, but realized that if he let it drop, it would go out. Impatiently he searched the floor for a flat spot or a crack to wedge it into. "Everything's all right," he said soothingly. "Just let me get this, yes, there." Quickly he knelt next to her and untied the gag. Her hair, gathered into a loose bun, was matted and dirty and caught in the knot.

"Oh," she said when he took the gag out. "Oh my God. Thank you." She wriggled forward to let him untie her hands. "Thank God, thank God, thank God." Adams knelt behind her and worked on her bindings, but it was dark and he couldn't see at all: unless he moved the candle or got her to turn around, he'd have to work by feel. "Can you get it?" she asked.

"Yes, just a minute." She wasn't making it easier. "Just relax, put your wrists together." She had been tied with cloth and it was hard to distinguish the individual loops of the knot one from another. Her wrists were thin; her arm there seemed all cord and bone. He pulled the binding up to get a better angle on the knot and inadvertently caused her limp hands to graze the inside of his thigh, up to his crotch, an intimate and surprising contact whose charge he noted dully. For a moment he thought of getting the candle, of burning the cloth. No. The razor—that would do it. He fished in his pocket and brought it out. "There," he said when he had sliced through the knot. She bent immediately to untie her feet. "Here. Use this." He handed her the razor.

"I am very glad to see you, Mr. Adams," she said, sawing away at the cloth. "You got my note."

"Yes." He sat back, kneeling, hands on his thighs. He didn't want to admit that he hadn't understood part of it. As she worked the razor back and forth, he watched her profile, seeing the concentration in her face, the dimpled chin, those dark eyebrows almost disappearing into darkness in the dim light of the candle. Her mouth was open and he could see candlelight on her teeth. She is alive, he thought. Completely alive. The bulk of her long straw-blond hair sagged in its loose bun, grazing her shoulder, bouncing slightly as she sawed away at her binding. He could see the wisp of tiny, soft hair in front of her ears, where in the space of an inch the head's long covering gave way to soft mammalian down. She was perfectly herself, whole, in motion, alive. He had to bite his lip to stifle a laugh.

"Have you been to Madame Dingler's? You know who she is?"

"Yes, yes," he told her. She cut the cloth through and began unwinding it from her ankles.

"Oh good. So you have the photograph." He marvelled at the sheer brusque efficiency of her. Her white blouse, soiled from contact with the grit and grime of the stone floor, clung to her form, then flexed, clung, and then flexed as she bobbed forward, rhythmically removing the circlets of cloth from her feet. When she was done she stretched her legs and then reached down to massage her ankles and calves. Discreetly, Adams looked away.

The photograph that he had borrowed from Clemenceau? She couldn't know about that, but he asked anyway. When he saw she didn't understand, he described it. "A dozen men on the stairs of the canal company offices. The two Lesseps, Clemenceau, Dingler, Reinach—''

''I don't know what you're talking about. I'm talking about a photograph I got from Miriam, a photograph of a set of check stubs. From the account the *chéquards* were paid out of. Reinach burned the originals, but before he did, Miriam had this photograph made. Some idea she had—she was going to help him. It's too complicated to explain right now. It's the *chéquards*, the list. *Evidence*,'' she emphasized.

Adams understood. But before he could answer she was asking another question: ''What time is it?''

Adams felt for his watch, fished it out by the chain, and clicked it open. ''No,'' he told her. ''I never saw it.'' He couldn't read his watch: too dark. He brought it down to the candle, leaning close to her. ''Five o'clock. Five after, actually.''

''We haven't much time.'' She stood unsteadily and put a hand out to the wall. She gave her long skirt a few swipes with a hand. ''The evidence is sealed this afternoon, isn't it? I swore to God I'd help Miriam do this. God, I must be a sight,'' she muttered. ''Let's go.''

''Where? Where are we going?''

''To Madame Dingler's. We've got to get that photograph.''

''Louise,'' he said softly, shaking his head. ''No.''

5:06 P.M.

"SO THERE'S NOTHING at Madame Dingler's? None of her things? Her papers?" Louise asked.

That she was alive seemed to him so momentous a circumstance that he was having difficulty moving on to face the problem at hand. "No. I have no idea where they are. Her apartment is cleaned out, completely. Everything."

They stood in silence for a moment. "The police wouldn't have thrown all of that away," Louise reasoned. "Wouldn't they go through it and see what needs to be returned?"

"You'd think so." Now that he was with her, it was hard to reconcile the reality of her with his memory of her. She wasn't as tall as he remembered, and her features were more severe. Maybe the difference was that she was besmudged and grimy. Or had she not been fed? Could she have lost weight? Or was it just the strain of the week that was showing in her face? Maybe he hadn't remembered her well at all.

He hadn't misremembered her eyes: clear, cerulean blue. They looked at him now, questioning, and in his stomach, inside the residual ache from the punch he had taken the night before, he felt that wonderful clutching-together feeling, the one he still could feel whenever he thought of Clover, happy. The asterisk feeling, Clover had called it. He brought the candle higher to light her face better.

"So it's got to be in storage somewhere. We could ask at

the Prefecture.'' She looked back and forth, from one of his eyes to the other, trying to read his thoughts.

It took him a moment to remember what she was talking about. ''Yes. Yes, we could.'' She was turning then and stepping past him, and he had an urge to stop her, to reach out and hold her there, face to face with him. The Prefecture and Madame Dingler's archives and the whole Panama affair could go hang. But instead she moved on. He felt a panicked regret at the passage of this moment whose importance he couldn't quite articulate. She was leaving, taking her part of the instant with her.

He spurred himself to follow her down the hallway toward the concessionaire's office. Where were they going? To the Prefecture? That made sense: ''Bertillon will want to talk to you anyway.'' His legs were weak and rubbery and would hardly move. He was exhausted. ''You need to give a statement. Against Pettibois.''

She shook her head, the loose bun of hair swaying back and forth. She was striding away from him, just like that day at the Mount, and again he had to press himself to keep up. ''No time. Not now,'' she said. In the concessionaire's office she didn't hesitate but ducked quickly under the door without looking back. He was held in place for an instant by his duty to Bertillon, by the need to protect the crime scene. But he couldn't let her go alone. Besides, there were things he had to know, questions only she could answer.

On the quai the crowd still hung about, keeping a careful distance from the doorway. Louise was upriver a dozen yards already. He'd have to trot to catch up. He tried to deputize a man from the crowd, but they all shrank from him. He wasn't sure he had been understood.

He caught up with Louise and fell in step a few paces behind her, not quite able to make himself walk next to her. He watched her move and felt a kind of proprietary pride: she was making a wake through the world again, and he was in that wake, behind her, feeling the flow of her through space, having found her and set her free.

For a minute this was enough. To apprehend from a distance, though, is not permanently satisfying; he wanted to hear her voice, to see her face. He fell in step next to her, smiling at her glance. He wanted to hear what she had to say, to know the whys and wherefores of what she had done. Why had she lied about her name? What did she know about Reinach's death—was it a suicide or a murder? Was Pettibois the man the concessionaire had seen that night on the quai? Why? Why had Pettibois done these things? Did she know? And Hay—how in the world was Hay involved?

Suddenly each of the questions he had thought to ask seemed too large to wield smoothly in the small space between them. Walking next to her, he realized that for the past week she had been the central, animating cause of his life, and he had ignored everything else in pursuit of her. But of course she had never known that. To her, he was a nice old man she had met, her savior, yes, but no one she had ever expected anything from, certainly not someone she had expected would dedicate his life to finding her . . .

"What's the matter?" she asked, glancing over her shoulder.

"I'm fine, fine."

"You slowed down."

"It's nothing."

She eyed him carefully as he caught up with her again. "You look different."

Maybe he had been wrong. She knew him well enough to see what the week had done to him. Of course he looked different. It was only right that she should notice. "Mmm," he said.

"Your beard. You shaved it. And that bruise—that's new."

He had forgotten.

In profile her face was impossible to read. Her body moved fluidly, each leg pushing its long stride against the limp dirty cloth of her skirt. She walked with her eyes set on the horizon. He looked there, too, up the Seine toward the Ile de la Cité, and for no reason he could understand was reminded of Elizabeth. He had ignored her, here in Paris and back in Pontorson. She would forgive him, but he wondered at what he had done. What had moved him? What, exactly, had he gained? There were reasons, very credible reasons, for what he had done, but yes, Elizabeth was right: his search for Louise Martin had been as much an escape as it had been a thing worth undertaking in itself. From what? From Clover, from the empty house on Lafayette Square, from Elizabeth? He had thought himself motivated by respect, by duty, by care. But when all was said and done, what duty had compelled him? What did he owe her? Nothing, really. Nothing at all. He looked at her again, at that profile he once thought to memorize. How could he care for someone he didn't really know?

Louise had noticed his gaze. "What? What is it? What do you want?"

"Nothing." Part of him didn't want to know anything more from her. He ought to be satisfied simply with having found her, with having solved the puzzle. And there she was next to him, in all her physical reality, walking. He would talk to Elizabeth, apologize. He turned from Louise to gaze at the river and saw a taxi launch steaming by. Elizabeth and Amanda might be among its passengers; there was no reason to think they were, but it was possible. They had to be somewhere. They could be anywhere. He scanned the faces visible at the rail. Too far away.

No. He had to know. "Why did you lie to me about your name?" This came out more sharply than he intended.

When she answered, her voice was tired. "It's a long story. I don't want to talk about it."

Adams held up a hand, an ambiguous gesture: he might have been soothing her, might have been warding her off. "Certainly. I respect your discretion." When these words occurred to him, they had seemed solicitous, but as he spoke he heard a sarcastic edge. "I'm sorry," he said. "You don't owe me a thing. Really."

"But I do. You saved me. It's just—I don't want to go on about it. Not now."

They walked in silence for a few minutes. "I took my roommate's name because she asked me to," she said without looking at him. "It was supposed to help her somehow. I didn't ask for details."

"So you masqueraded as her around Paris."

"No. Just the once, in Pontorson. She bought a train ticket for me in her name, made reservations, and I went in her clothes.'' She turned to look at him without slowing. ''Satisfied?''

He had a dozen other questions. ''Yes.'' But his resolve wore thin: they hadn't gone far before he asked, ''Do you know why she did this?''

''It had something to do with helping Reinach, something she was doing. She said it wouldn't work if anyone knew she was in Paris. People had to think she was miles away.''

This didn't make a great deal of sense, but who could say what stories the dead woman had told? Everyone had a plan, a path through the scandal, their own scheme, their own vision. ''Miriam tried to get Clemenceau to talk to Herz,'' he told her. ''Herz was blackmailing Reinach, and she tried to get Clemenceau to get him to stop.'' Adams didn't know if she knew this.

''Clemenceau? She told me Loubet.''

He thought for a moment. ''Maybe she tried both. Maybe Delahaye, too.'' Delahaye had said in the Chamber that he'd seen the list, and there he was, at Madame LeBlanc's that night. Yes: that had been a meeting to decide how and when the list would come out, because all three of them knew about it, because she had shown it to all of them, separately, shopping for—extorting—help for Reinach. And that was why Clemenceau and Delahaye had wanted to see Adams— they were interested in finding Louise, the only one who knew where the list was. ''When did Pettibois take you captive? He wanted to make you tell where the list was, didn't he? Did Madame LeBlanc have anything to do with that? She told me you were being protected . . .''

Louise snorted. ''Protected. No. Who is Madame LeBlanc?''

Briefly he described her, explained her place.

''Never met her.''

''Avril worked for her.''

''Oh.''

That seemed all she was going to say. ''What about Pettibois? Why did he tie you up?''

''He didn't.'' Adams waited for her to continue, and when she didn't, he looked at her, watching her face. If Pettibois hadn't tied her up, it must have been that strange man, the concessionaire. Given the religious pictures and the horrible photographs he kept on the walls, God only knows what his intentions were. He wanted to speak to Louise sympathetically but didn't want to presume; she hadn't told him anything. "It must have been terrible," he said finally. "I'm sorry."

"Yes. Well." She walked, eyes on the horizon, without elaborating.

"If there's anything I can do . . ." He held out a hand, wanting to take her hers, to reassure her, tell her she was safe.

"Don't *touch* me." She drew back and kept her eyes on the quai in front of her as she walked. Adams watched, looking for some clue to her feeling in her face, but she seemed determined not to reveal anything. She is so brave, Adams thought. Finally the cumulative effect of his attention must have gotten through, for she turned to look at him. "Mr. Adams, I really do appreciate your finding me. I can't thank you enough. You saved me. But I just don't . . . I . . ." She turned away, looking up to the bare branches of a tree they walked under. He didn't follow her gaze, but kept his eyes on hers, thinking that with her wide eyes open, looking up, she was childlike. "You don't know me. I was pretending to be someone else in Pontorson. I'm sorry. If I led you on, I really am sorry. It wasn't what I meant."

Led him on? What was she talking about? "No. Oh God, no. Did you think . . . ? No. Not what I meant. Either." He just wanted her to know that she could feel safe now, that he would take care of her—if that's what she wanted. That's all he was interested in. "I'm sorry. I'm just trying to sort out this Panama affair. I want nothing from you."

"All right. As long as we understand each other."

They walked together up the quai toward the Ile de la Cité. A man wearing thick-rimmed glasses led a springer spaniel on a leash toward them, and as they neared, he pulled the leash up short to give them a wide berth. Louise took no notice; she was imperturbable. Adams turned back to look at the man after they had passed and saw him standing in place, holding his dog tight and looking after them. As if, Adams thought, he was securing himself in their wake.

"I just want a few answers," he said to Louise. "If it's

not too much trouble. To know how you got involved, I mean.''

She took a big breath. ''I guess I owe you that much.'' She spoke without slowing. ''I knew Mims wasn't a suicide. She had been very afraid. So afraid she gave me that photograph of the check stubs. She was very explicit: If anything should happen to her, I should send the photograph to Madame Dingler and not tell a soul. So when she died and this friend of hers, this Avril, came around asking about it and seemed to know all about it, I couldn't tell her I didn't have it. She said she knew someone I could be safe with. She put me there''—she waved a hand off behind her, indicating the concessionaire's place—''with that, that—'' Louise shuddered. ''It was all right at first, but one night he came in and grabbed me . . .'' She didn't finish.

Adams, sensing a fork in the path of the story, stuck to the scandal. ''He wanted the list of *chéquards* from you.''

''No,'' she said. ''But Pettibois did. But I didn't have it. Finally I told him where it was. Pettibois, I mean. He said he'd kill me anyway, but first he had to wait. A week, maybe two. Too many deaths at the same time would look suspicious.'' Adams heard her swallow.

''How did Pettibois come into the picture?''

''I don't know.''

''Was Miriam going to help the Socialists or the Boulangists?''

Louise snorted. ''She didn't care a fig for that. She just hated the company. All those men. All those bad men.''

Those bad men. He had another question for her. ''Why was the rent on your apartment paid by John Hay?''

''Was it? I didn't know.''

Could she be telling the truth? She seemed a bit too cavalier. ''Are you certain?''

''Of course I'm certain.'' He had made her angry. ''Really, Mr. Adams. If you are going to doubt my word—''

''I just found it . . . unlikely. Sorry.''

She glared at him for a moment before deciding to go on. ''We shared the rent, but I was moving out. Going back home. Mims had money troubles. They weren't any concern of mine, and I have no idea what she did about them. Who is John Hay?''

''You've never heard the name?'' Adams watched her carefully.

''No. Why?''

He believed her. ''It's not important. Not important at all.''

Monday,
NOVEMBER 28,
1892

2:00 P.M.

"LIZZIE, I OWE you an apology. Once again. I behaved abominably." He whispered to her across the sleeping form of Donald Cameron, whose left leg was elevated in traction. She was wearing a blue cloak over an afternoon tea dress, and atop her dark curls sat a new Parisian hat—a jaunty Madrid—in the same shade, with pale-blue rosettes on one side of the crown and a half-veil depending from the brim.

"Yes, you did." She spoke softly, a whisper, though her husband's sleep had already proven undisturbable by normal conversation. Behind her, out the window, Adams could see the Prefecture; to his left, out the other window, was the place du Parvis, where Cameron, when awake, would have an inspiring view of the equestrian statue of Charlemagne. A ground-floor corner room in the Hôtel-Dieu, the newest, most modern hospital in Paris: the senator could command the best.

"I know, and I'm apologizing. I'm sorry that I"—he couldn't quite bring himself to say "forgot you completely" and so temporized—"was so neglectful of you. I don't know what I was doing."

"I know what you were doing."

He raised an eyebrow. She could still surprise him.

Elizabeth looked down at the blanket on the bed, tented over her husband's leg. She touched it, poked it softly, idly testing its tautness. She let her finger run down its slope.

"You seized upon this woman as a way of avoiding me. Not just that. You wanted to save someone other than yourself. You wanted to save someone you *could* save. Someone who needed you as much as Clover."

He began to contradict her, but she shook her head and held up a gloved hand to stop him. She had more to say. "You don't think I need saving. Not that dramatically."

"Elizabeth, I—" He looked to Cameron's face as if expecting help. The senator dozed on, flat on his back, his head lolling awkwardly in profile on the pillow and his soft breaths stirring his mustache. Awake, Cameron affected a slight frown, a characteristic set of the face that he believed, correctly, contributed to a sense of nobility and intelligence in his features. Asleep, with his eyebrows at rest, his mouth agape and a spot of drool darkening the pillowcase, he was difficult to mistake for a dynamic force in the United States Senate.

"It's true. I'm fine with Donald. But we, you and I—we might have improved upon the merely acceptable. Or so I thought."

Adams wasn't sure how much to admit to, whether he should argue. "Mmmm." Was he agreeing? He wasn't sure he understood. He needed to say something for himself. "I'm old, Elizabeth. I *am* already. What I am is settled."

She pursed her lips and frowned at him, as if to say, Don't be silly. "If you believe that, there's a very great danger that it will in fact be true."

"True? True," Cameron mumbled without stirring; he closed his mouth, opened it again. Adams looked at Elizabeth in alarm.

"It's easier to pine for someone who isn't around, isn't it?" She wouldn't be distracted. Adams studied Cameron; he looked to be asleep again, but how deeply? "Very comfortable, and a practice that is no doubt familiar to you. Well, let me tell you, Henry Adams, life with a real woman, a flesh-and-blood person, is more difficult. It would change you, make no mistake. Think you wouldn't have changed if Clover had lived?" She spoke with force despite her near-whisper; her tone was measured and regular but didn't hide her anger. "It's no wonder you choose away from it, any chance you get."

"Lizzie, I—" This was impossible. Cameron could wake at any moment. How could she even imagine this conversation in the same room with him? He wanted the two of them to leave, to go somewhere, out in the hall, outside . . .

She saw his concern, let him writhe in it for a moment. "Morphine," she finally told him. "For the pain. You don't have to worry. Even if he hears us." She shrugged. "They say the effect is stronger in drinkers."

Adams felt like a man who has been bluffed at cards. He thought to protest, but stopped himself; this was interesting, this hard edge she had. And although he couldn't quite feel his way through what she had said, he suspected that about the larger matter she was right. He had never had reason to doubt her judgment. She was sharp in her assessments of people and their motives. He looked past her, out the window, to the traffic that coursed between the Hôtel-Dieu and the Prefecture in the cool November air. Winter coming, and traffic. So much traffic! It was a continual stream, its sound deadened by the glass of the window but still audible. Carriages and cabs, whispery-wheeled phaetons and slower-moving omnibuses, carts and wagons and buggies and diligences, people going this way and that, trucking and carrying, all of them passing him by.

When he looked at Elizabeth again, this is what he saw: she stood before the window, her cape a flowing splash of color from which emerged her two delicate hands, gloved, clasped in front; those clear blue eyes, fierce but open to him, looking to read his will, surmounted by those two long sweeps of eyebrow just visible beneath her hat; this hat, wide-brimmed, tipped to the side, the perfect shape for her face, its touch of a veil hinting at discovery, disguise, distance. He could imagine her this way, just as she was except smiling, standing by the mantel in the sitting room at Lafayette Square, this blue cloak draped about her. No, the hat and the cloak would be gone, out of sight, stowed in a closet. She would be warming herself by the fire, would be pleased to see him. He remembered her softness pressing against him, remembered everything he had felt with his arm, even to the whalebone stay secreted in some pocket or recess of her clothing.

"Lizzie, marry me."

"Are you insane? Don't be crazy." Her eyes flashed at him and then down to her husband.

"Are you worried about Donald? He'll be fine."

"It's not just Don."

"What then?" He wondered if he should go to her, around the bed, but couldn't resolve to move, because to move at all would be to move, first, farther away from her. When a man proposes, he should be close. He hadn't done this well at all. Perhaps he should reach across the hospital bed, reach across and touch her? No. This sleeping husband between them made it seem a bad idea. "Why? Amanda?"

"Partially her, yes, but not entirely." She had turned away to the window, and he read as carefully as he could the nuance of her voice, her posture. He thought it best to stay where he was. "Oh," she said, with a deep exhale. "I suppose I should—" Was she crying? Adams couldn't tell. He waited for her to continue. "I let myself imagine something," she said. "I shouldn't have. There is nothing that can come of it. It's just too impractical."

"If you mean by impractical 'not in practice,' well, of course. As a husband I am out of practice. You and I, as lovers, are very unpracticed. We're all theory." He smiled, wanting her to smile, wondering if she had.

She looked over her shoulder and he saw that he had succeeded, a little. "You're very sweet, Henry," she said. "This is a conversation we should have had before. I wish! I really do wish we could have talked this way." She turned back to the window, as if to find in the city's traffic some record of possibility, of a path forgone.

"Before—when? Before Pontorson? Before I went looking for Louise?" Elizabeth didn't answer. He waited. He had to know. "Would it have been any different?"

She thought for a long minute before answering. "No," she said softly, turning to face him. "Probably not."

Could she be right? In one view their lives seemed to have been aiming toward this congruence, toward his proposal, toward a life together: she enduring the indignities of her marriage to Cameron; he being tempered in the hard lessons of his widowerhood; and the two of them thus prepared to become mutually appreciative, mutually engaged. But to a colder, clearer eye they would appear quite different. In that view they had little more in common than wit and charm and flirtatious posture. His had been the role of the ersatz suitor, the declawed cat; she had been the pedestalled and perfect hostess, the recipient of attentions only slightly more effusive than those that were formally required and which, at any rate, in his life, had nowhere else to go. Had theirs been a mannered congruence, shaped more by the circumstances that had been dealt to them than by any inner life of its own? Perhaps. He was gazing down at the blanket on Cameron's bed, losing his focus in its blue wool nap. And what if they had? There was no shame in their having lived this; for a time it had suited them, and they had both found it quite enjoyable. But it was a limited, protected world, sharply circumscribed in what it offered and allowed. Had either of them seen its limits clearly enough to begin negotiating its transformation? Perhaps in Pontorson and Paris they could have tried.

They might have, he realized, if he hadn't turned up absent.

"I think you're right," he said, finally.

Elizabeth came around the bed to stand next to him, took up one of his hands in her gloved hands. She nodded. "Amanda is meeting me here to take me to tea. Stay till then. Don"—she nodded at his supine form—"would like to see you, I'm sure. He won't be under all afternoon."

He smiled, pleased to be petitioned. But he had to shake his head. "I'd love to. But I can't." He had other fences to mend.

3:00 P.M.

"DID YOU EVER figure why Loubet wasn't arrested?" Hay asked.

"I have a guess," Adams allowed quietly. The two of them stood, heads tilted back, in the nave of Notre Dame, admiring the huge expanse of the north rose window, where the Virgin and Child were centered in concentric rings of vibrant blue and violet and red: sixteen wedges in the first rank, thirty-two in the second, each terminating at the widest end in a circlet portrait of an Old Testament priest, judge, or prophet. "Either the prefect is totally corrupt or Loubet disguised his involvement so well that they can't get him. I don't think the prefect is totally corrupt—he wouldn't have quashed my warrant if he was. So I guess there just isn't enough evidence to go after him. Bertillon told me it was mostly circumstantial. I should have suspected him from the start."

"Why?"

"Of the three deputies who wanted to get the list from Louise Martin, the three that met at Madame LeBlanc's, he's the only one who hadn't tried to reach me."

"Meaning?"

"Meaning he wasn't looking for Miss Martin because he didn't have to. He knew where she was all along."

"And Pettibois was his agent." Hay did not make this a question.

"His pony." Hay looked at him, and Adams shrugged. "French slang. Agent, more or less. If Loubet isn't behind this, then it's Herz. Or Pettibois was acting on his own, which is in some ways a more frightening thought. Hard to see what moved him, even if you figure he was helping Loubet. Pride in France? A desire to see the canal company back on its feet and dredging? These are hardly things worth killing for."

A passing tourist shushed Adams, who nodded graciously in response. He turned and looked again at the rose window high above them. He took a sidelong glance at Hay, trying to judge his audience. Now, he thought, or never. "This cathedral is so different from the church at Mont-Saint-Michel," he began. "Here the Virgin is salve to a wound, a bridging of a gap between man and God, the avenue to uniting the many and the one." Was Hay interested? He wasn't sure. "It's a gap you don't even suspect could exist at the Mount. The bonds of warfare are very tight there, so tight they bind even across metaphysical chasms. And anyway, the culture that built the church at the Mount had a very low regard for the individual; God was all, and man a poor, pathetic, corrupt, sinful, insignificant thing. Here there's a different perception entirely. Of man, of the nature of sin. The Church *has* to be different; the whole world has changed. And part of the change is, the Church discovered that consolation of sorrow and guilt, not banishment of evil, is its biggest, most enduring function."

"Mmm-hmmm." Hay craned his neck to look at the vaulting. "What do you figure—a hundred, a hundred and ten feet?"

"Yes, yes. More or less." Couldn't Hay see what he was getting at? "Some say that people are by nature either Platonist or Aristotelian. I think there are other pairings as well. I think men are by nature either Mont-Saint-Michelians or, if you will, Virginians." Perhaps he was being too oblique; Hay was still idly inspecting the ceiling. "Either they see the protection of the collectivity as absolutely crucial or they see the collectivity as being justified only because it serves the development of individual moral excellence. So you have the basic question: What is one's social duty? The survival of the group or individual moral integrity? Reason of state or personal honor?''

He feared he had been too blunt. But no: Hay frowned at him quizzically. No. He hadn't. Adams exhaled and chose his words carefully. ''Of course people disagree about this. I understand. Even good friends can disagree.''

''Adams, what are you saying?''

He wasn't sure but that he should just get right to it. Yes. ''The rent. You paid the rent on Miriam Talbott's apartment.''

''And this is upsetting you?''

Stupid question. Adams glowered at him. ''You were involved in the Panama affair. Up to your neck in it. And you lied to me.''

''Adams, I—''

''I'm not done,'' Adams warned. ''All that time, I was looking for Miriam Talbott. You knew who she was, where she was, what she had done. Why didn't you tell me? You must think I'm a fool.'' He stood, facing Hay squarely, leaning toward him.

''No—not a fool. Never. Look, it's not that I didn't want to tell you,'' Hay said, dropping his voice. He glanced around, ensuring that he couldn't be overheard, before meeting Adams's eyes. ''You know as well as I that official business imposes a burden of discretion on a man. I had no choice.''

''*I* would have had a choice. Friendship is always a choice.''

''Yes. Well. That's the difference between us, isn't it? And what office do *you* hold?'' For a second the two men stared at each other, Adams trying to gauge the degree of intention in the insult he felt. He hadn't *wanted* public office; Hay knew that. After a moment Hay's dark eyes softened. ''This isn't good. I just wish you'd—'' Hay stopped himself and Adams saw the tip of his tongue lick his lips, wiping the underside of the white bristle that was his mustache. ''Look,'' Hay began again. ''It's relatively easy, isn't it, to second-guess the exercise of power. God knows, power needs to be judged. I'm not saying it doesn't. Just—try to have a little more empathy, could you? That's what I'm saying."

Adams thought this over. Perhaps his friend had a point.

"I simply couldn't jeopardize my purpose here in Paris. Not even for a friend. I did as much as I could, telling you the little I did." Hay was shaking his head, slowly. "I'm sorry. I'm sorry I couldn't tell you more."

"Why did you pay her rent?"

Hay let out a breath. "Perhaps that was a mistake." He waited for a pair of tourists, a man and a woman, to move out of earshot. "I did what I thought was right," he said in a low, rapid voice. "She came to me with a manner of business proposal, and I made a choice. I believed I was making the right choice."

"And in exchange—?"

Hay shook his head. "I can't. I wish I could but I can't."

His discretion was no surprise. But still Adams wondered: what *had* he gotten in return? It must have been the list of *chéquards*: Miriam Talbott must have shown it to him. In which case, Hay alone knew who was innocent, who was guilty. No: Hay was one of two. Delahaye had said he'd seen the list. Delahaye and Hay, completely different but united. The Frenchman and the American, the Boulangist and the bureaucrat, both of them knowers among the unknowing.

Adams frowned, then took a deep breath and looked up to the vaulting, as if some thought had called him from its reaches. "I understand," he murmured, because Hay seemed to be waiting for a response. Slowly Adams turned, shuffling his feet, rotating his body to survey the entire cavern of the church from his vantage point at the intersection of the nave. "See this, Hay. Here, right here. If you want to understand what is happening around us today, you have to go back to the twelfth century. The entire cosmology of the Church shifted then, and this building is evidence of it. 'It' being this new emphasis on the individual, the lessening of emphasis on the collective. In the face of omniscient judgment, a sinner left on his own, a sinner no longer making common cause with his God against a heathen other, must be given some sense of his God's potential for grace. Thus, the prominence of the Virgin. Empathy, if you will. The Church learned empathy.'' He looked at Hay; good, he was listening. ''But there was a cost. Make no mistake, there was a cost. There is always a cost.''

Hay waited, then raised an eyebrow. ''And it was . . . ?''

Adams shook his head. ''No. It would take a book to answer properly. You'll have to wait for the book.''

Hay nodded. He turned to face the north rose, the Virgin surrounded by circlets. ''I understand,'' he said. Without seeing his face Adams couldn't tell whether the irony was intended.

When they walked out of the cathedral into the late November afternoon, they turned away from the morgue and headed toward the quais. Above them the trees were leafless and the sky dull and heavy with the coming December. Adams drew the thick, cool air through his nose. Seven years, he thought. Six Decembers. The year was sliding toward it. But this year it might go more easily; perhaps, he thought, there was some magic in the number seven. A sabbatical. A sabbath.

Hay stopped in front of the cart of a chestnut vendor. Wisps of smoke escaped the fire, an incorporeal plume too thin to obscure anything. ''Two bags, please,'' Hay told him. When Hay stretched to pay the man, Adams noticed how gray his friend's hair was becoming. The warmth from the chestnuts in the bag that Hay handed him felt good.

They walked along the quai, each man removing a glove to work at a nut. Hay had tucked his bag under his arm; Adams tried to hold his in one hand while peeling away the shell.

''Your face is looking better,'' Hay allowed.

''Yes. It doesn't hurt as much anymore.''

They walked in silence for a bit, peeling chestnuts and eating them. ''Paris goes on, Adams. Isn't that extraordinary? You could feel something in the streets last week. A nervousness, a nervous excitement. But it's gone now. Everybody's used to it. There's a scandal, the government falls. Life goes on. What's changed? Nothing.''

Adams shook his head. ''Everything's changed. Look. The company is bankrupt, Crédit Lyonnais inherits the railroad, you and Cameron are out of the picture, the Socialists and

Boulangists are going to gain in the next election, almost half of the sitting deputies are going to be thrown out. I think it all left a bad taste in everyone's mouth. The anti-Semitic press is screaming for blood. The French are ready to declare war on somebody, just to make themselves feel better.''

''You may be right,'' Hay said. ''Guess what I read in the paper today.''

''Can't.''

''Come on, try.''

Adams stared at him.

Hay held up a hand. ''All right. Bernice Dingler. She confessed to library theft. That's no surprise. *But* she's claiming credit for starting the rumor of Lesseps's death.''

''No!''

''Yes!'' Hay laughed. ''She hated the company. She found a way to do them in.''

''How'd she do it?''

Hay shook his head. ''Paper didn't say. A bribe to the right key operator, a telegram to the newspaper, who knows? A regular Archimedes: find the right place, stick your lever in, and heave. One madwoman can bring down an entire million-dollar company.'' He looked into his bag of chestnuts, then held it out. ''Want these? It's not what I wanted.''

Was she that mad? How *had* she done it? ''I wonder,'' Adams said, half aloud. He took the bag from Hay and poured them in with his own, then crumpled the empty bag and jammed it in his pocket. ''You could ask her, but she might not tell you.''

''How is Miss Martin?'' Hay asked.

Adams glanced at him. ''As well as can be expected.'' He had a piece of chestnut stuck in a molar and discreetly inserted a fingernail to pry it out. ''She said she'd write.''

''She's gone home to New York?''

''Yes.''

''She didn't have to stay to testify?''

''No. They took statements from her. Consideration of her circumstances, that sort of thing, said she could go. They won't have any trouble convicting Pettibois.''

''How about you? Are you going to have to testify?''

''I don't think so.'' His last meeting with Bertillon had

demonstrated how little he actually knew. He could say the concessionaire had told him this, Lesseps had told him that, some unknown person had punched him in the stomach, a rifleman in a four-in-hand had shot DuForché. "I gave a long statement."

Hay nodded. "I bet Elizabeth is glad this is over."

Adams stared a warning.

"All right, all right, I won't. I won't even ask."

"You may ask. I won't answer."

Hay took this in stride. He pulled on his collar, bringing it up tighter around his neck, then stuck his hands back into his coat pockets. "Smells like snow."

"Mmmmm." Adams finished a chestnut and crumpled the bag around the rest. The nuts had cooled off, and much of the pleasure of eating them was gone. He jammed the bag into his pocket with the other and kept his hand there. "I can't help thinking," he said quietly, "how things would have been different if we had found the list of *chéquards* in time."

"There's no benefit in that. Besides, I'm betting it will turn up. The police will find it."

Perhaps they would. The investigation in the Chamber had been cut off, but there was talk of courts, of civil suits against the directors of the company, of extraditing this man Herz from England, where his doctors said he was too sick to travel. Adams and Hay stopped to stare into the river, both of them standing side by side on the edge of the quai, hands in their overcoat pockets, contemplating the moving water. "What are the prospects for your treaty? The canal concession?"

Hay looked away, downriver, down toward where the Chamber of Deputies presented its colonnaded façade to the banks of the Seine. "Not good. Not for a while. The new ministry has been talking about having another go at Panama. Who knows? Maybe the French will manage it this time. They've got another four years to try."

"A lot can happen in four years."

"Yes." Hay kicked a stone that landed in the water with a plop. Its ripples were swept away on the current. "We can wait that long. I don't think they have the heart or the finances to do what they need to do. If I'm wrong, then they'll be the ones to make us a two-ocean power. In which case we'll have to say, Hurray for them.''

''Yes. Hurray for them.''

Hay turned to look at Adams. ''I'm cold. Time to go back. Coming?''

Adams thought he would walk a little farther.

''All right. Until dinner.''

Adams walked for a time, then sat on a bench to watch the river, that sinuous thread, circling back on itself, sometimes no farther on, always downhill. But from the quai, close up, it was clearly force, massive force: all-encompassing, relentless, subtle. Implacable, even, in its continual descent.

He thought it an admirable companion.

He was pleased to have been able to tell Hay about his idea for a book. What he wanted was to find that point, somewhere in the twelfth century, when life had been most whole; when Church and culture had been one, when there hadn't been a cacophony of voices and visions in the world, when it had been possible to pursue both an individual moral life and the life of the community without feeling skewered by paradox. If he could find such a point, back seven centuries, he would have a base from which to measure change, the broad curving arc of time down to the present. And the twelfth century itself was an arc of change, between Mont-Saint-Michel and the later churches; somewhere on the arc was the point he sought. In the modern world he would have a more difficult time discovering where to set his benchmark. It seemed the only certainties, limited and conditional though they might be, were the certainties of individual experience. From theology, then, to psychology—the curve of change ran down from twelfth-century architecture to pass right through nineteenth-century biography.

He patted his pockets, searching for his pen. What to write on? He looked about, remembered the paper bags in his pocket, retrieved the empty one and smoothed it on a knee. Slowly, with chilled hands, he began to make some notes:

Descartes and the decline of the Church: ''I think therefore I am.'' Two senses of I think: I am engaged

*in mental process, etc., I am unsure. Since Descartes
the two are the same.*

He liked this.

And there was another thought, one he had been mulling
over since standing by Hay's side in the church. He bent to
get it down.

*God, at His worktable, willing mankind just exactly as
it is, while knowing that hardly one in a million will
escape damnation—at best, a vision of Supreme Indif-
ference. Not the best background for a Church. Thus,
the Virgin and the Saviour in the foreground. Man put
them there. Mankind hates the idea of an indifferent,
anarchical, multiple, even a dual universe. The world,
in its chaos, stares man in face; he insists on its unity
in self defense.*

He had written as quickly as his hand would let him, but
the cold was having an effect. He blew on his fingers to
warm them. "Two solutions," he jotted. "(1) man a machine—no free will. (2) nature = chaos; no order. For neither," he added, "is the world ready."

He put the piece of paper away. From there, he thought,
he'd work toward a discussion of Aquinas.

He wriggled his writing hand under his overcoat, placing
it in his armpit to warm it. He would have to go soon; it was
too cold.

With his eyes shut he breathed deeply. The work he was
projecting could take years, and he found this thought comforting. The first step would be to look at cathedrals. Chartres, Amiens, Tours—all of them. Perhaps Elizabeth and
Amanda would join him. He would like that.

He sat on his bench in the chill November air, breathing
deeply, taking in the pungent, fishy, slightly septic smell of
the Seine. He found the scent good; it seemed warm—even
human, somehow.

Epilogue

JOHN HAY BECAME United States Secretary of State in 1898, in which position he skillfully guided his country's diplomacy in the era of its emergence as a world and imperial power. Best known for his formulation of the Open Door Policy toward China, in 1899 and 1901 he negotiated with Great Britain the two Hay–Pauncefote Treaties (the first failed of ratification in the Senate), which freed the United States from a commitment to accept international control of any canal it might build in Central America. In 1903 he negotiated the Hay–Bunau–Varilla Treaty with the infant republic of Panama, gaining for the United States rights in perpetuity to a strip ten miles wide across the isthmus for canal construction.

Lizzie Cameron and Henry Adams remained lifelong friends, confidantes, and correspondents, until Adams's death in 1918.

Clemenceau failed of re-election in 1893, despite the general victory of Socialists at the polls. He spent the next nine years out of public life, returning eventually to the Chamber and becoming premier in 1906 for three years. He went on to earn the title of *le Père de la Victoire* during World War I when, recalled to the premiership in 1917, he replaced the cautious General Pétain with the attack-minded General Foch and succeeded in having Foch named commander in chief of the Allies.

Charles de Lesseps endured two separate trials for his role in the affair. The first sentenced him and his father to five-year prison terms and fines of 3,000 francs, a verdict over-turned later on a technicality. The second sentenced him to one year in prison and made him financially responsible should Charles Baïhaut (a deputy sentenced in the same trial to five years in prison) be unable to pay the fines and penalties assessed against him: 750,000 francs and the repay-ment of his original bribe of 375,000 francs.

Baïhaut was the sole elected official to be convicted of wrongdoing in the affair. He was convicted because there was nothing else the court could do: Baïhaut had intemper-ately confessed in open court. ("Even now I cannot under-stand how I could have sinned," he said, holding his face in his hands.) Other, more stalwart deputies succeeded in frus-trating their prosecution, despite the evidence of their initials on check stubs, despite the testimony of Charles de Lesseps and others about who, exactly, had accepted the bribes they were convicted of tendering.

Gustave Eiffel was convicted of misusing funds entrusted to him and was sentenced to two years in prison and fined 20,000 francs; his career as a builder of engineering marvels was over.

Cornelius Herz was never extradited from England; he died in seclusion at a seaside hotel in Bournemouth in 1898. He was too sick, his doctors said, to travel to France for trial (a verdict confirmed by Scotland Yard, by the Queen's own physician, and by doctors sent by the French government at the invitation of the Foreign Office). In the one interview he ever gave, Herz spoke of Reinach's involvement in a vast European intrigue designed to reshape the Continent's alli-ances and to reward a syndicate of politicians working under Reinach's direction.

Ferdinand de Lesseps died December 7, 1894, at the age of eighty-nine, a reclusive and perhaps addled old man who (it seems) never fully understood how and why the company he had founded spun apart, taking with it a government of France, a sense of national honor, and the confidence in pub-lic institutions of an entire generation of French citizens. In his eulogies no one spoke of Panama.

In the wake of the scandal the French reorganized their canal efforts, and in 1894 a Compagnie Nouvelle du Canal de Panama was formally incorporated. It persevered for eight years, though never on the scale of the original company. The maximum number of workers never exceeded 3,600; the company's main purpose seems to have been to retain rights to the concession (to have ceased work would have caused the concession to expire) and to keep the machinery in working, salable order.

The company's assets were bought by the United States in 1902 for $40 million; an American commission of investigation had suggested that at any higher price, a Nicaraguan route became more attractive. In November 1903 a revolution created the Republic of Panama with a government more amenable to American interests than Colombia's. The United States recognized the new government by return telegraph, before parts of Panama had even heard of the uprising.

American work in Panama began in 1904, the year that Henry Adams's volume on medieval culture and architecture, his *Mont-Saint-Michel and Chartres*, was printed privately, "for the amusement of a few friends." The first boat to travel from one ocean to the other through the canal (a tugboat, the *Gatun*) made the journey in 1913—thirty-eight long years, many lives, and many millions of dollars and francs after *Le Grand Français* first put his finger on a map and said, to a conference of specialists called to consult on the best route, "Build it there."